Pages

from the

Past

Pages from the Past

JoAnn Arnold

Horizon Publishers
Springville, Utah

ISBN: 0-88290-794-8
v.1
Order Number: C3001

Published by Horizon Publishers,
an imprint of Cedar Fort, Inc.
925 N. Main, Springville, Utah, 84663
www.cedarfort.com

Distributed by:

Cover design by Nicole Williams
Cover design © 2005 by Lyle Mortimer

Printed in the United States of America
10 9 8 7 6 5 4 3 2 1

Printed on acid-free paper.

acknowledgments

I want to express my appreciation to my son Cory, an electrical engineer who designs computer chips, for his patience in helping me understand how it all works.

I want to thank Nikki for her insight and talent in creating a cover for my book that brings the story to life even before the book is opened. And I thank my husband for his patience and input.

o n e

REBIRTH

Still wet from the shower and wrapped in a towel that ended just above her knees, Betsy caught a glance of her image in the floor-length mirror. She hesitated, turned, and stood directly in front of the likeness, viewing and reviewing the reflection that professed to be hers. Finally, she moaned, reached for the phone, and dialed.

"Mother," she sighed into the mouthpiece when she heard her mother's soft hello. "Why didn't you tell me my knees would begin to wrinkle the week after my fiftieth birthday?"

"You've got too much time on your hands, Babe," Betsy heard the laughter in her mother's voice as she spoke. "You need to get a life. It's a beautiful morning. Why not get one today?"

Every morning was a beautiful morning for Elmira Redding. At age eighty-one, she still climbed out of bed at precisely 6:00 AM, exercised with one of her yoga tapes, checked her Palm Pilot for her day's schedule and then ate a breakfast full of fiber. She had probably never taken the time to check her knees.

"Look in the mirror, Mom. Look at your knees. Are there a lot of wrinkles?"

"Of course there are, dear. In fact, there's not a spot on me that isn't wrinkled. God intended it that way. I can't quote scripture and verse, but he basically said that where there is wisdom and learning, there are wrinkles in which to store them."

"I love you, Mother," Betsy mused. "Can you slip lunch with your daughter into your schedule today?" She listened to the familiar tune her mother always hummed as she scrolled through her day on her Pal.

"Ah, yes, I think I can fit you in shortly after noon," Elmira chuckled. "Shall we meet in my kitchen? On Thursdays I serve a mean ham and cheese on rye. Oh . . . and bring your wrinkled knees. They'll make for interesting conversation."

Betsy wondered why God hadn't given her more of the genes of her mother instead of her father. Benjamin Franklin Redding had been a serious-minded professor of physics at the university, always in the left-brain mode, analyzing, studying, mulling over or working through, and always with a serious expression on his face. Even when he laughed at his wife's jokes, you could see he was analyzing, studying, and working through the punch line. The creases in his forehead were indelible.

Benjamin was a descendent of the patriot John Hancock, and he took his heritage very seriously. It was important to him that his family protect and respect the freedoms they enjoyed. "Even in the earliest days of this nation," he explained to his daughters, "the critics and the media twisted and tied the truth with hearsay and rumors, causing contention within the realm of society as these brave men fought to bring the Constitution to life."

Betsy learned from her father to believe only half of what she saw and nothing of what she heard until she researched and studied it out for herself.

"Then," he had said, the creases in his brow deepening, "and only then will you know the truth."

Her father understood the importance of protecting the

truth better than anyone she knew, and though her mother fully agreed with him, she added a few thoughts of her own. "When it comes to disastrous events and irrational political rhetoric where no research can give you an answer," she explained, "let the power and perfection of prayer be your guide, for that is where you will find your answers."

The balance was perfect in her parents' marriage. Elmira respected the left brain of her husband, while Benjamin rejoiced in the right brain of his wife.

Four years ago, Benjamin Redding had died at in the age of eighty-two. His wife of fifty-five years kissed his lips one last time and whispered how much she loved him and how she looked forward to the time they would be together again. She accepted his death with the sweetness of her soul and the knowledge that he was once again free to think, analyze, mull over, and inhale truth. She also knew if she ever needed his input, he would be close by to give it.

While Betsy's mother had accepted the death of her husband with faith and quiet dignity, Betsy refused to accept the death of her own husband with anything but anger. John had been her life. He was her right brain, and he was dead at the age of fifty-two.

Early every morning he would climb out of bed and quietly pull on his sweats and his running shoes. After kissing his sleeping wife on the forehead, he would silently open the glass door leading from their bedroom to the woods and begin his morning run on a path he had carved through the trees.

The morning he died, he did one thing differently. He woke her and told her how much he loved her. Forty-five minutes later, he lay in her arms, blood covering his face, mouthing to her something about taking something somewhere, his eyes pleading with her to understand. In her shock, however, she couldn't concentrate on his words, only his condition. He was dying.

An investigation uncovered blood on a large stump next to the path where he apparently fell, hitting his head. The police found no evidence of foul play. The only prints on the ground anywhere near the path were John's.

The pathologist's report revealed the blow to the head was such that it caused hemorrhaging to the brain. "The question," the doctor explained to Betsy, "is at what momentum did John's head hit the stump? Without any conclusive evidence, we can only determine that he was on a full run when he tripped, causing him to fall forward with enough force to do this kind of damage. It's a miracle he was able to get back to the house before he died."

During the first six months after his death, Betsy analyzed that day and those precious words, *I love you,* that he spoke to her before he walked out the door, almost as if he knew he was saying them for the last time.

In her mind she mulled over all the if only's. If only she had understood the message within those words, maybe she would have insisted he not run that morning. If only she had paid closer attention to the feeling that disrupted her sleep after he left. If only she had called 911 quicker when he fell, bleeding, into her arms. If only she had done even one of the three, perhaps he would be alive today.

Then she began analyzing another train of thought. If only she had appreciated his sense of humor more. If only she had laughed with him more over the small stuff. If only she had said *I love you* more. If only she had complained less about the clutter of his creativity.

She couldn't seem to bring herself out of the if-only mode. Then one day her mother sat her down, looked deep into her eyes, and said firmly, "It's time, Babe."

"Time for what?" she asked, not quite understanding.

"Time to end the pity party. Time to open your heart and let God back in. Time to live again. Time to let go."

"I can't." Tears filled Betsy's eyes.

"Certainly not until you allow yourself to." With intended drama, Elmira raised her eyes toward heaven. "John has to be up there wondering who this stranger is, living in his lovely wife's body. He's been rather patient through this whole thing, but right now I have a feeling he's getting tired of waiting for you."

"Tired of waiting? What are you talking about?"

Her mother took her by the hand and led her to a picture on her wall. "Look at what God has given you, Betsy," she said gently, wrapping her arm around her daughter's shoulder and bringing her close.

Smiling at them from a picture that had been taken three months before John's death were eleven happy faces. John sat next to her on a white bench with their children and grandchildren surrounding them.

Looking at the face of her husband, his deep-blue eyes smiling back at her, she replied harshly, "I can only think of what God has taken from me. I can only see what I've lost." She turned to her mother, "How did you do it, Mom? Where did you find the strength?"

"The strength comes from God when you seek him in prayer for relief of the pain you bear in your heart. The strength comes from the knowledge the Gospel brings of life here and life hereafter. The strength comes from knowing that God has taken nothing from you."

Elmira removed her arm from around her daughter and then took her by both arms, facing her. "You're like a ghost, walking without leaving footprints, touching without feeling emotion, looking through hollowed eyes seeing nothing, while John's been waiting for you to give his life meaning. Until you can let go of the pain, you can't do that for him. I'm asking you . . . no . . . I'm telling you, if you truly love your husband, give his life meaning by living yours once again."

The serious expression on Elmira's face softened. "You haven't lost John," she said gently. "He just graduated from this earthly school sooner than either of you expected. He moved on to gain a higher degree, while you moved on to a new semester on this planet. The class you are enrolled in at this time is called 'Trials and Blessings of Widowhood 101.'"

Elmira sighed and shook her head. "So far I fear you're failing the class."

As always, Elmira Redding's observation was correct. The strength of her words cracked the barrier Betsy had successfully crafted against the pain and guilt that constantly nagged at her. Having no foundation, the barrier crumbled, allowing the light to filter back into her world, leaving her vulnerable to its promise of contentment once again. Now she had to take the responsibility to find joy in a life that seemed empty to her.

Feeling the discomfort of rebirth, she made it a point to call her son Todd in Dallas and her daughter, Amy, in Vermont to give them the details of how she had been agonizingly revived by Grandma Redding. Strangely enough, they praised their grandmother's wisdom.

Trying not to let her children's attitude offend her, she focused her attention on her four grandchildren, the two little boys in Texas and the twin girls in Vermont. Their tender voices were like Band-Aids covering the emotional cuts that caused her heart to hurt so terribly. She found herself saying things to them that she was just beginning to realize herself, that their grandfather was close by, watching over them.

Her next call was to her youngest son Lincoln, a junior, majoring in electrical engineering at the same university where her father had taught as a member of an elite staff until the day he died. Lincoln was proud of his grandfather's legacy and seemed to be a modern replica of the man he so admired, except he had developed his right brain to match the left. His repertoire of talents included computer wizardry, which made life easier for his mother, who called him on a regular basis for advice on how to make her computer work the way it was designed to work.

When she knew he was out of class, she dialed his cell phone. "Hi, Mom," he said, his voice cheerful as always. "Computer problems, or is this a social call?"

"Let's just say it's far greater than any problem my computer could conceive to plot against me. It's your grandmother."

There was only a slight pause before Lincoln responded. "I gather from your tone she's well, so I'll assume she gave you some timely advice."

"And how would you know?"

"Because it's time."

"If I didn't know better," Betsy sighed, "I would think you and your grandmother have conspired in my behalf."

Lincoln chuckled. "So, tell me how it went."

Betsy admitted to her son that she had seen the light and was working through her emotions to get a grip on her world again.

The next day she went to the pet store and bought a golden retriever. Not that going to a pet store was her intention. She simply happened to be walking by when she glanced in the window and saw a beautiful gold puppy looking out at her with big, dark, liquid eyes; his not-so-little body jumping up and down with excitement; his tail wagging in rapid succession. Unable to help herself, she walked in the store and bought him.

Buying a dog certainly had not been the logical thing to do. For the duration of the next two weeks as she mopped the floor behind him, she began to question her irrational behavior. Her mother, on the other hand, was impressed and delighted, though she never offered to help with doggy clean-up.

At the pet store, Betsy was told the pup seemed exceptionally bright and intuitive. As she analyzed that statement, she wondered at her own intellect. The young woman behind the counter probably told every potential buyer the same story. It was what she didn't say about the five-month-old bundle of trouble that Betsy soon discovered.

At the end of the two weeks, she knew this whole pet owner thing was a mistake and returned to the store with full intentions of asking for a refund.

The man feeding three little puppies in one of the kennels looked up and smiled. "Ah, the lucky owner of my finest pup," he said, reaching out to pet the dog before she could say anything. "I expected you last week for your first training class."

"First training class?" Betsy frowned.

"Didn't Erika tell you? With your purchase of this fine specimen of a dog, you receive four free classes filled with hands-on training techniques from one of the finest dog trainers in the business." He grinned and handed her a pamphlet. On the cover was a picture of him working out with a German shepherd.

"As it says on the pamphlet, my name is Dayne." He reached out and shook her hand. "I also own this pet store, a dream come true."

Betsy took the pamphlet and was about to tell him she had made a mistake in buying the dog when he lifted the fluff of gold from her arms.

"I've missed you, golden boy," he cooed to the pup. Then he turned his attention back to Betsy. "To tell you the truth, I had decided not to sell him. He is one of the most intuitive and intelligent dogs I've ever worked with, and believe me, I've worked with a lot of intelligent dogs. You wouldn't consider selling him back to me, would you?" he said hopefully.

At that moment, Betsy made a quick and rational decision. "I'm sorry," she said lightly. "I just need some answers concerning the training process."

Dayne's eyes filled with disappointment, though he nodded that he understood. Betsy couldn't help but feel compassion for him, but her decision was final. She would keep this troublemaker.

"Well," he conceded, "if I can't have him back, Mrs. Braden, I'm glad you're the one who is giving him a home. Follow me and we'll get started on the first lesson."

By the end of that month, Betsy understood the rules of training, had forgiven her growing pup all his transgressions, and had begun to rethink their relationship.

She sat on the veranda watching the rays of the sun bounce off his silky coat as he chased a butterfly and, without warning, she began to feel his energy. Because of him, the joy of life once again opened its gate to her.

At that moment, Betsy named the dog: Dorado, Spanish for golden. It seemed very appropriate considering the color of his coat and the simple fact that he had the golden touch of a true missionary. She was his convert.

With that renewed commitment, she picked up the phone and called the newspaper to tell them she was ready to come back to work.

"Glad to hear it, Betsy," Frank, the owner and editor of the morning paper, replied, using his gruff editor's voice in an attempt to mask the fact that he was overjoyed to hear hers. "And it's about time. Your readers have been clamoring for your return."

Right after John's funeral, Frank had given her a leave of absence, telling her in his no-nonsense way, "You are of no use to me as a columnist as long as you feel no passion to write. When the passion returns, give me a call. Until then I don't want to see you in this office." Then he gave her an unexpected hug and sent her home. Time seemed to have a way of leaving its mark. Fourteen months ago, John lay dying in Betsy's arms. Today was the six-month anniversary of the day her mother brought her back to life. Five months had elapsed since she began to write again.

She surmised that time, in its way, had been both her enemy and her friend. Today, however, time seemed to be in a neutral corner, sending mixed signals to her brain. Lunch with her mother would set things back in order.

She checked herself once again in the mirror. Much better, she theorized. Being fully dressed, meaning the knees were covered, gave her more confidence, and she was thankful the wrinkles of wisdom still evaded her face. Her eyesight was a solid 20/20. Her soft brown hair had just enough natural curl and was cut the right length to simply wash and wear with style. She might want to drop a pound or two, she suspected, but all in all, she wasn't in too bad of shape, knees included.

She turned from the mirror and called to the one who had taken over her life. "Today," she said as a huge streak of gold landed on her bed, "I'm going to visit my mother. Do you want to come?"

The dog's eyes were large and filled with mischief. The fact that he was lying on her bed, his dusty paws planted on her white bedspread when he knew it was off limits, was proof of what was reflected.

Dorado's ears immediately shot up when he heard the word *Mother,* undeniable evidence that he understood the words coming from her mouth. What part of *do not get on the bed* didn't he understand?

"Let's go through this one more time," she explained as she carefully lifted the ever-growing dog from the bed, hoping there were no threads attached to his paw nails. "You do not get on the bed." She pointed to the bed and said again, "You do not get on the bed."

The beautiful dog gave a soft bark before reaching out with his velvety tongue and licking her cheek.

Her heart melted, and she wrapped her arms around his neck. "I love you too, you silly dog. Now let's go find breakfast."

Dorado obviously understood the meaning of breakfast because he led her right to the dog food. He sat patiently while she poured his breakfast into his bowl and her breakfast into her bowl.

"And to think," she shuddered, "I almost gave you back."

The retriever sat next to his bowl and continued to wait. She filled his water dish, sat it next to him, poured milk over her cereal and then sat down, folded her arms, and blessed the food.

When the word *amen* was said, Dorado barked, hit the water bowl with his paw in his haste to fill his mouth with food, and sprayed the floor with water.

Betsy couldn't get upset over something so trivial, when this exceptional dog understood the meaning of prayer. She smiled as she watched him, knowing John would have been pleased with her choice.

"If you behave yourself in the woods on the way to Mother's house," she said between bites of cereal, "you won't have to wear the leash coming home. Sound good to you?"

Dorado lifted his face out of his dish only for a second to bark his reply of approval. No leash meant freedom.

"I thought you'd like that," she replied.

She could feel his eyes following her as she put her breakfast dishes in the dishwasher and mopped up the water around his water bowl. She knew he loved the wooded area that separated her mother's home from her own. It was over five acres of foliage-covered land filled with trees and small critters, and had been in the family for four generations.

At first it was hard for her to step into the place where her husband had been fatally injured. But as time went on, and Dorado became eager for longer walks, she made herself take the one path John had cut for her, a direct quarter-mile walk to the home of her parents. Amazingly enough, she began to find a peace she had forgotten existed.

"Okay, big boy, let's go see what you need to do outside." She opened the door and stepped into the warmth of the morning sun. The gold of Dorado's coat shimmered in the brightness of the morning as he sped past her. He was off in search of whatever life had to offer.

While watching her dog annoy a squirrel, Betsy checked the items on her to-do list. Unlike her mother, she didn't need a Palm Pilot to remind her; she carried the list in her head.

She brought the laptop out to the veranda so she could finish the work she needed to do on her weekly article while Dorado frolicked and enjoyed the fresh air. This afternoon, after having lunch with her mother, she would drop the article off at the newspaper office and pick up the clothes from the cleaners.

Her column, "Pages from the Past," took her readers on a historical tour each week. She loved her work as she researched old books, papers, pictures, personal histories, and biographies.

This week she would introduce her readers to a five-part series on "The Birth of a Nation," a subject she felt strongly about. Coached by her father, she understood the true meaning of freedom and the price that had been paid to achieve it.

"Never take freedom for granted," he told her and her sister, Dawn. "It is not free. It comes at a great price, and as my children you will actively do your part to preserve the freedoms you enjoy. It is your responsibility. It is your privilege."

Betsy felt it was time to share with her readers the words her father had shared with her. She opened the laptop and scrolled through the article to make sure spell check had done its job. Then she read the final draft.

After quoting her father's words, she gave the topics of discussion.

1. *The greatest hero of the Constitution.* The heroes of the Constitution had lived in her heart as long as she could remember; they were her bedtime stories. But there was one who, in her father's words, stood above them all.

2. *The meaning and purpose of the flag.* She and her father had this discussion when she was six.

3. *The national anthem.* Although memorizing all four verses took awhile, Betsy had been introduced to Mr. Key as soon as she understood the meaning of the flag.

4. *The true meaning of liberty and freedom.* She couldn't remember when she didn't know their true meaning.

5. *Thoughts and theories of you, the readers.*

For those of you who know all the answers, you can move on to the sports section. For the rest of you, meet me here every Wednesday morning for the next five weeks and we'll explore "The Birth of a Nation."

It was just before noon when she finished. She glanced at Dorado lying next to her. His eyes were closed, and a look of contentment graced his face.

She left him there while she went into her office, plugged

her laptop into her printer, and made a copy for her mother to read before dropping it off at the newspaper office.

"Okay, Dorado," she called to her dog, "let's be on our way through the woods to Mother's house."

Elmira greeted her daughter at the door with a kiss on the cheek. "You are looking particularly lovely today," she commented. "And you, you gorgeous dog, are looking particularly lively, but I'll let you in my house anyway."

"What on earth have you got on your face?" Betsy scowled at her mother in shock while Dorado backed away cautiously from the hand that reached out to pat his head.

"Oh, my! I almost forgot. What time is it?" Elmira touched her face with her fingers.

"It's a quarter past twelve. Why?"

"Then it's been on long enough. I can peel it off now."

"And what is it you're peeling off?"

"Why, it's a deep-cleaning facial peel, Babe." Elmira blinked innocently at her daughter. "It cleans the pores, softens the lines, revitalizes aging skin, and leaves it softer, smoother, and younger-looking. You know all the propaganda they feed you to get you to buy this stuff."

"If you think it's propaganda, why are you using it?"

"Because."

"Because?"

"Yes, because." Elmira smiled and began pulling the peel away from her face with the tips of her fingers

"And when did you start worrying about having a more youthful look?" Betsy could hardly keep from laughing as she watched her mother work the peel from her face.

"Well, if you must know, I'm doing it as a favor for my beautician. The saleslady highly recommended it. But before Beatrice recommends it to any of her customers, she wants me to test it."

"And why you?"

"Because I'm her one customer with the perfect face to try it on: old and wrinkled."

"Oh, Mother, really."

"No, it's true." Elmira turned to Betsy after splashing her face with water. "It came off rather nicely, don't you think?"

Betsy had to admit her mother's face had a certain glow to it and told her so.

"Thank you, Babe. Now come and have lunch."

"I thought you said wrinkles were signs of wisdom," Betsy gleefully chided her mother on their way to the kitchen.

"Oh, they are, dear, but we don't need to strut them in public. It's best to keep a low profile."

"Right! Let me see your knees," Betsy demanded.

Elmira lifted her skirt.

"Thank heaven."

"What did you expect?" Elmira blinked. "Botox?"

Dorado was waiting in the kitchen for them. He seemed relieved to see Elmira looking normal again and gave a bark of approval.

"Just for that you get an extra dog biscuit for dessert," Elmira said.

While they ate, Betsy had her mother read her article and then asked for any suggestions, to which Elmira had none. "The article speaks for itself," she said, handing it back to her daughter. "I, along with everyone else, will be looking forward to each Wednesday morning for the next five weeks. As always, I look forward to the e-mails that light up the computer screen each Wednesday afternoon. Now, let's see the wrinkles in your knees."

Betsy lifted her skirt to reveal the two knees that had been her concern of the morning.

"Would you like to try some of my facial peel, dear?"

Betsy couldn't help but be amused over her mother's comment. She got the message.

"I think I was just feeling a little depressed this morning," she admitted. "Time seemed to be neither here nor there, leaving me in between emotions. But having lunch with you has changed that."

"I'm glad. And I'm glad you wanted to have lunch with me. Mothers need to know their children like to be with them."

It was after one o'clock when Betsy finally said goodbye to her mother and started her walk back through the woods, allowing Dorado to be free of his leash. He pranced back and forth, running in and out of the trees, barking at squirrels and rabbits and doing whatever dogs love to do.

Betsy thought about the articles she would be writing over the next several weeks as she watched her dog. The feeling of freedom to a dog was no different than the feeling of freedom to a human. Freedom meant coming and going without restrictions, barking at life without being censored, and doing whatever one loved to do.

While her thoughts occupied her mind, Dorado managed to find his way out of her eyesight.

"Dorado," she called, promising herself to reconnect his collar to the end of her leash as soon as she found him. There was no returning bark, however, only the echo of her voice bouncing off the trees and then silence.

He couldn't have gone beyond the sound of her voice so quickly, or could he? How long had she been daydreaming? Finally she spotted him, his nose to the ground, dust filling the air as his paws clawed at the earth, his full attention on his task.

By the time she reached him, ready to scold, she could see he had something trapped between his teeth. More curious than angry now, she knelt down to see what treasures he'd found. Dorado took a step toward her, dropped his head, and opened his mouth. A watch fell to the ground. It looked exactly like John's watch, except the band was broken and the glass covering the face was shattered. Then, suddenly her heart felt as if it had stopped. It didn't only look like John's watch, it was John's watch. She could see his name engraved on the inside of the band.

She looked at Dorado. "How could you know?" she asked in disbelief. "How could you know John's watch was there?"

What she had just witnessed slowly brought to mind something Dayne explained in one of the training sessions. "You have no idea the potential of this dog's ability," he said. "One day he'll give you a sample of his gift. That day you'll know what you have and what I let go."

"John's scent still lingers in the house, is that it? After all this time, the watch still carries his scent, and you could smell it?"

Then something else struck her like a sharp pain. Why was John's watch buried in the ground in the first place? It made no sense, unless . . . unless what? Unless there was something more to his death than what was concluded fourteen months ago?

She stood, her mind spinning, her body in shock from the discovery that perhaps John's death was not an accident. Slowly she began to back away from the watch and what it implied.

When tears finally began to flow, she allowed them to fall unchecked as she searched the area for anything that would give her a clue as to what might have happened. But what was she looking for, she wondered. She had no idea.

Dorado stood by the watch and waited. When Betsy regained control of her emotions, she realized he was waiting for her to pick it up. She took a hanky from her sweater pocket and, without touching it with her fingers, folded the watch into the cloth.

Kneeling down, she stroked her remarkable animal. "Good dog," she said, letting him lick her tears. "Good dog. Let's go home now."

The retriever stayed by her side as they followed the path to home. He watched her place the watch on the kitchen table to inspect it a little closer and seemed moved to a new level of protective awareness.

Betsy was careful not to touch the watch as she examined it. The links of the gold band had been pulled apart, she could only conclude, by force. Two links were missing. Questions kept creeping into her mind, where there were no answers.

Sometimes John wore his watch when he ran, and sometimes he didn't, so she wasn't suspicious when it wasn't on his wrist the morning he lay dying in her arms. She only assumed it was in the small jewelry box where he set it each night, next to his cuff links.

She had to know, beyond any doubt, that this watch belonged to her husband. Forcing herself to walk into the bedroom, she slowly removed the jewelry box from the top drawer of John's dresser. She wrapped her trembling hands around the box and held it close for a few seconds before removing the lid. Inside, several pairs of cuff links were clustered together, but there was no watch. She hadn't really expected to see one. The engraving on the watchband lying on her table was proof enough. With a deep sigh, she closed the jewelry box and carefully put it back into the drawer.

Anger and bewilderment gripped her as she stood over the table, once again staring at what lay in the hanky. Her mind tried to analyze and explore the circumstances surrounding the mystery it held.

"Father in Heaven," she whispered, "what have I found here?" In her mind she was trying to comprehend the idea that John's death was not from natural causes. But why would anyone want him dead? What was it that he knew or did that made it necessary for someone to take his life?

In her heart she listened . . . waiting for an answer, when she remembered John was trying to tell her something just before he died. Was it something to do with the circumstances of his death?

The air was hushed around her, and the gravity of the circumstances she didn't know existed, until now, was made known to her. Her Heavenly Father was at the helm, and she needed to listen.

She wrapped the hanky carefully around the watch then made a call to her older sister, Dawn, a forensic pathologist.

"Dawn," she said when she heard her sister's voice on the other end, "what's the rest of your day like?"

"It's interesting that you should call and ask me that," Dawn replied. "I was sitting here feeling sorry for myself because Dr. Paul Arington, busy head pathologist, who was supposed to take me to dinner and the theatre for our thirtieth wedding anniversary—which, by the way, was last week—has been called out on an emergency. He probably won't be finished until late, and I'm sitting here with two tickets to the most wonderful musical of the year, thinking I would call and ask you out for a date. Want to go?"

"Where are we eating?" Betsy was only too aware of Paul's taste for exotic food.

Dawn laughed. "Don't worry. I've cancelled the reservations at Hiatt's. You get to choose the restaurant."

"Bernards?"

"Bernards it is. Six o'clock sharp. See you then. I've got to go now. I'm in the middle of an autopsy, and, Betsy, thanks for saving my day."

If Dawn only knew what Betsy was going to ask of her in return for the opportunity to see the most wonderful musical of the year. Her husband had been murdered. Whatever it took, she would find out the *who* and the *why*. The whole experience seemed strange and imaginary, as if she was in the middle of a television drama.

Betsy felt Dorado's breath against her hand. She looked at him. His thick coat was covered with dirt and leaves and whatever else may have attached itself while he was digging. His mood was restless.

Relieved to occupy her mind with something other than what was now flooding it, she took him outside, reached for the grooming brush in the basket on the porch, and began the ritual Dorado usually took great pleasure in.

Flipping a leaf from behind his ear, she brushed his coat until it shone, pampering and soothing him, yet she was unable to ease his unpredicted melancholy. His eyes, sad and bemused, seemed focused on the wooded area.

She remembered during one of Dorado's training sessions, Dayne had explained that the retriever had the instinct of a dog trained for search and rescue. "When a dog becomes specialized in this kind of work," he said, "they experience stress and depression when they are unsuccessful in a rescue attempt. Physical and playful games are used to release that stress."

Though his training hadn't been that intense, the instinct was strong in him. In his mind, she could see, he was looking for something more than just a watch. How could she explain to him that there was nothing more to find?

It was almost two o'clock. Her column had to be on the editor's desk in an hour. She needed to shower and change into the appropriate attire but was wise enough to know that Dorado needed her attention at this moment. Grabbing his toy clown, she began a game of throw-and-seek. She threw the clown, shouting for him to go after it. He barked and sped away, seemingly happy for the game. After he returned the clown to her the third time, he was free of his burden.

"I hope you understand," she said softly, desperately wishing she didn't have to leave him. "But I need to run some errands. After that, Dawn is taking me to the theatre, a place where dogs aren't allowed. That means I have to leave you home."

Dorado managed a soft whimper.

"Would you like to spend the night with Mother?" she asked, knowing he loved to go to there. But when she mentioned it now, he simply gave another whimper and climbed into his favorite spot, the porch swing.

"I'll leave you outside so you can do what you need to do when you need to do it." She placed his toy next to him and brought him water, food, and a treat. He licked her hand, making her feel even guiltier.

"I wish I didn't have to go, but I need to talk to Dawn. I'll tell her how proud I am of you." She kissed his face. "She'll be proud of you too." She stroked his coat one more time before rushing into the house to get ready.

t w o

THE NOTEBOOKS

Breaking the speed limit, Betsy reached the newspaper office just as its editor was making final preparations for the printing of the next day's paper.

The smile on Frank's face told her he was happy to see her. "Just in the nick of time, as always," he said in his usual gruff voice. "What've we got today?"

"The first article of the five-part series we talked about."

"No controversy, I hope." Frank's remark was in jest, knowing controversy was what made Betsy's articles so enticing to her readers.

"No more than usual," she replied.

"Six more newspapers picked up your column this week. You now reach readers from coast to coast. Not many columnists can claim such fame."

Frank reached for the envelope in Betsy's hand. "I'm going to tell you something." His gruff voice was uncharacteristically soft. "It's the experiences that shape our lives which provide the passion necessary to touch others. You have that passion now." He paused and looked directly into her eyes. "I'm proud of you. I'm proud of the strength I see coming from your articles. I'm proud of the fires you start and the way you extinguish them. I'm just sorry it had to be at such a personal loss"

Betsy was moved by his remarks. "Thank you, Frank, and thank you for giving me time to discover myself again. Not many bosses would be so kind."

"Me, kind? Maybe. Clever? Yes," he gloated, his eyes revealing a mischievous glint. "Do you think I want any other editor to have you?" He stopped talking and tilted his head toward her, assessing her beneath heavy brows. "Something troubling you?" he asked.

"Hard to say, Frank." She didn't elaborate, and he let it go at that.

"See you next week," she said, stepping into the elevator and giving him a wave as the doors closed. Five minutes later, she walked into the cleaners.

"Hi, Mrs. Braden," the young woman at the counter said with a smile.

"Hello, Terri," Betsy replied. "It looks like your father isn't wasting your summer vacation."

"Right, especially since it just started yesterday."

Betsy laughed, "The last time I saw you, you and your father were negotiating a new car. Tell me, how did the negotiations go?"

"I think my mother actually came out the winner on that one," she replied solemnly. "I got the car and inherited my brother."

"I understand," Betsy nodded. "The day my sister got her driver's license, Dad gave her the old Ford and a list of the places I had to be during the week. I believe the day I got my driver's license was the happiest day of her life."

Terri giggled, showing deep dimples on each side of her face. Betsy couldn't help but notice how much she had changed. Yesterday she had been a plump child. Overnight she turned into a lovely young woman, tall and slim with dark, intelligent eyes.

"I'll get your cleaning." Terri disappeared into the back room. A minute later she returned with three plastic-covered items and hung them on the metal rod by the counter.

Singling out one of the items, she began to explain. "Dad tried to call you this morning about the jacket Mr. Braden dropped off the day before . . ." A sudden look of panic appeared on her face, and she fell silent.

"Before he died?" Betsy asked gently.

"I'm so sorry, I didn't mean . . ."

"It's okay, Terri. There's no other way to say it."

The relief on Terri's face was evident. "Dad said he found this in one of the pockets." She handed Betsy a small notebook.

Before Betsy had time to inspect it, Terri's father, Ned, walked through the front door. "Good afternoon, Betsy," he smiled. "I'm glad you're here. I tried to call you this morning about the jacket. John brought it in the day before . . ." Soberness replaced his smile, and he found he couldn't say the words.

"It's okay," Betsy said softly. She could see the pain in his eyes as his memory recalled that day. John had been his friend.

Ned nodded, took a deep breath, and cleared his throat before continuing, hoping to keep the emotion locked inside. He reached for the jacket and removed the protective plastic.

"I remember him telling me there was no hurry," he began to explain. "I was to just set it in the back until I had time to mend the right pocket. At the time I thought his request rather strange because he always wanted his jackets back the next day, but I had other customers waiting, and he seemed in a hurry."

Ned took the jacket from the hanger and laid it on the counter in front of Betsy. "For some reason I can't explain," he continued, "I did as he asked. Then with everything that happened after that, it was forgotten until yesterday morning. I was sitting at the table eating breakfast when, out of the blue, the thought came to me that I needed to mend John's jacket. I hurried to the shop and searched until I found it. It lay almost hidden on an old machine that hasn't been in use for several years. I have no idea how it got there. I apologize for the oversight."

"There's no need to apologize." Betsy's voice was barely audible.

Ned had been focused on the story of the jacket, and it wasn't until he heard her voice that he raised his eyes to see the tears forming in Betsy's. "I'm so sorry," he apologized once again. "I've been insensitive in my eagerness to tell you about the jacket."

"Oh, no, not at all, please go on." Betsy brushed her tears aside and smiled, prompting him to continue.

He nodded sympathetically and then placed his hand in the right pocket. "There was nothing to mend, Betsy. Instead, there was something stitched inside the lining of the pocket." He pulled the pocket inside out to show her. "When I removed the stitching, I found the notebook you have in your hand."

Betsy glanced down at the small notebook as if seeing it for the first time. It was just one of many in which John kept notes. Only this one wasn't tattered and worn from being carried around in his pocket like all the others. Looking at it was painful for her, and she quickly slipped it into her purse.

Terri, who had been silently listening, now entered the conversation. "I think I put it there," she admitted, hesitantly, "the jacket, I mean."

Ned looked at his daughter in surprise.

"I think that was the morning I had to stop at the shop to get a school book I left the night before. By the time I finally found it underneath the jacket, I realized I was going to be late for class, so I just tossed the jacket out of the way. I'm sorry, Dad." She gave him an apologetic look.

"It's okay, Terri. I should've never left it lying there in the first place."

"Thanks, Dad," she replied, a look of relief evident in her face. Then a frown appeared. "You said Mr. Braden was in a hurry, but I saw him talking to another man when I crossed the street outside the shop. They were standing next to Mr. Braden's car, and the other man was doing all the talking. The reason I remember is because the man kept poking Mr. Braden's chest with his finger, kind of like the football players do to the regular kids at school when they want to put the point across that they are tougher and meaner and you'd-better-be-afraid-of-me stuff."

"Had you ever seen the other man before?" Betsy asked.

Terri thought for a moment before answering. "No, but I've seen him, once, since. About a month ago, I was downtown, and I saw him come out of the courthouse. I recognized him because he had on that same silly hat he wore the day he was talking to Mr. Braden."

"What kind of hat?"

"Like this one." She reached for the picture of her great-grandfather hanging on the wall behind the counter and pointed to the hat on his head.

Ned took the picture from his daughter, studied it for a second, and handed it to Betsy. "Did the hat look worn?"

"No, it looked new and expensive. It was the style that caught my eye. I think because we clean so many hats I've become aware of what people put on their heads."

Both Ned and Betsy's eyes focused on Terri, neither of them saying a word.

"What?" she exclaimed.

"Did you get a look at the face under the hat?" They both asked simultaneously.

"Not really. I only saw him from the side both times. He wore the hat low over his face, and his clothes were expensive. He was about the same height as Mr. Braden and slim built. I remember that." She paused, the look on her face revealing the fact that she was walking her mind through the scene. "I think that's the best I can . . . no . . . wait a minute. I did see Mr. Braden's face. He was smiling. I remember because I thought what a contrast they represented and decided I had probably misread the meaning of the finger jabbing. I guess that's why I didn't think anymore of it until now."

"I'm amazed you could even recall the incident," Betsy said. "It's been over a year."

Ned hung the jacket back on its hanger and carefully covered it with the plastic as he listened to his daughter. "John always wore a smile," he said sadly. "Even when he was mad, he had a smile on his face. It used to irritate me when we were in college. I never knew what he was thinking."

He reached for the rest of Betsy's dry cleaning hanging on the rod. "The stain on your coat came out without a hitch," he said, attempting to hide the feelings that began to surface each time he thought about his friend.

Ned's mention of the stain reminded Betsy of a certain golden retriever who put it there. "Dorado has come a long way since that day," she exclaimed. "He's actually grown into a very lovable dog."

"You've got a dog?" Terri asked. "What kind?"

"A golden retriever who understands everything I say except 'don't get on the bed.' He has an unquenchable curiosity for adventure, the retention of a puppy, which he is, and the awkwardness of growing into his body."

"Sounds cool."

"Maybe I could call on you to doggy sit sometime."

"I'd like that," Terri replied with enthusiasm.

Betsy thanked her two friends standing behind the counter, paid for her dry cleaning, and hurried to her car.

Once inside, she took a deep breath and removed the notebook from her purse. Moisture touched the corners of her eyes as she glanced through the pages filled with John's shorthand, something he developed several years ago when he became an investigative reporter that only the two of them could decipher. She didn't attempt to read any of it; she would need to refresh her memory first. Right now she couldn't even focus her mind, let alone decode the meaning of the numbers, lines, and dots on the pages.

When she closed the notebook, she noticed something red

in the upper right-hand corner. She stared at the red mark for several seconds until she was finally able to recognize the word *Confidential* written in John's shorthand. She had never seen that mark on any of the notebooks she had helped him transcribe for his reports.

First there was the watch, now the notebook with its red mark. Her heart began to pound with the possibilities of their meanings. Questions were sparked, and she jotted them down mentally as they began to form. Why had John given his jacket to Ned, asking him to mend a pocket that didn't need mending? Why was the notebook concealed inside for Ned to find? Who was the man wearing the Elliott Ness hat? Finally, could the notebook hold the answers?

Knowing she would probably need the reference page, or cheat sheet as John called it, to help her decipher the shorthand, she checked her watch for time. If she broke the speed limit just one more time, she could stop at her home long enough to see if the cheat sheet was still in the safe before meeting her sister with whom she had much to discuss when they met.

Praying no police officers were lingering behind blind spots, Betsy pressed the gas peddle hard and felt her prayer was answered when she pulled into her driveway.

Dorado was wagging his tail at her when she ran up the stairs to the front door. She unhooked his leash and let him follow her into the house, explaining she was going to be leaving again in only a few minutes.

Quickly she made her way to John's office and the small safe beside his desk. She dialed the sequence, opened the door, and looked inside. The retriever nuzzled between her and the opened door to get a better view of what she was doing. She found herself chattering to him as a means of focusing her mind. She hadn't realized how difficult it would be to look inside the safe.

Searching for the cheat sheet, she found it beneath six notebooks carrying the same red mark as the one she had in her purse. They were tucked behind the stack of at least thirty well-used, tattered ones she was so familiar with. One glance at the smooth covers when she removed them from the safe told her these were notebooks she'd never seen. Maybe it was time she took a look.

She opened the first notebook to the first page. It was filled with the lines, dots, and numbers she had been so familiar with. Memories of sitting at the desk listening to her husband tell the story behind the story, after she had transcribed his latest investigative adventure, prevented her from going any further. She let the cover fall silently back in place.

The thought of her sister waiting in the restaurant at this moment, wondering where she was, gave Betsy a logical excuse to wait until tomorrow to do any further investigating. Quickly, she set her purse on the bottom shelf of the safe and slipped the notebooks into its opening. Closing the safe door, she gave the dial a spin and hurried to the door.

"I'm sorry, Dorado," she said, carefully slipping the leash back onto his collar. "I've got to go again. Be a good watch dog for me."

<hr />

While Betsy was driving to the restaurant, Ned was sitting in the back of his dry cleaners, his reading glasses on his nose, studying the note that was with the notebook, addressed to him.

Ned,

If you're reading this, it means I won't be back for my jacket. There are some things I've found in one of my investigations that were meant to remain hidden. I'm not sure I can find a way out of this. My only concern is to protect Betsy. If my death will do that, I'm consoled. Please give the notebook to her when it's time.

Remember when we were in college and debating the hereafter? Well, I may be in a position to prove to you that the veil is very thin.

I'm sorry to have to do this to you, but you're to only one I can trust.

See you on the other side,
John

Ned folded the paper in his hands, thinking back to the day he first met John. He was a freshman, lost and trying to find his way to the institute building. John, who was a junior, could see the bewildered look on his face and asked if he could help. That was the beginning of a long and valued friendship.

The debate on the hereafter and the thickness of the veil was still unsettled when John died. It wasn't really a debate per se but rather a friendly discussion of the spirit world and the influence of those beyond the veil.

John made a believer of him yesterday morning when the prompting came that he should go to the shop and mend the jacket. Ned could almost swear he heard John's voice. There was no longer any doubt in his mind; the veil was very thin, and the influence of those who have gone before is real and powerful. He had felt his friend's presence, if only for a second, and today was the day he was to give Betsy the notebook.

He didn't know if John meant for him to look inside the cover of the notebook, but his curiosity led him to do it anyway. He had to laugh when he did. The dots, lines, letters, and numbers were hen scratching to him. His curiosity had taken him nowhere.

Dawn was waiting for Betsy when she arrived at the restaurant. The smile that greeted her as she approached the table told her she was forgiven for being late.

"I hope you don't mind, I've already ordered. You look awful," Dawn observed as Betsy gave her a hug and took the seat facing her.

"Thanks, I needed that," Betsy replied,

"No, I mean it. You look terrible. You should have told me you weren't feeling well."

"It's not that. Something very strange has happened, and

we need to talk." Betsy glanced around her. The restaurant was full. "But not here."

Dawn looked deep into her sister's eyes, her brows furrowed. "What's up, Betsy?"

"Something I'm trying to piece together, and I can't do it without your help."

"Let's get our food to go." Dawn grabbed her purse with one hand and Betsy's arm with the other. "Whatever it is, I can see it can't wait." Leading her sister away from the table, Dawn stopped the waitress, gave her instructions, and paid at the register while they waited for their boxes.

Betsy led the way to her car. "Let's drive to the park near the lake," she suggested. Dawn agreed. Neither spoke again until Betsy turned off the key and their dinners were spread before them on a picnic table.

"Okay, sister," Dawn demanded, "start talking, and don't leave out a single detail."

The only detail Betsy left out as she told Dawn her story was finding the six notebooks in the safe, for no other reason except she forgot. When she finished, she felt nauseated. She put her head in her hands, closing her eyes. "Can you help me, Dawn?"

She felt her sister's arms go around her, giving her the comfort she so desperately needed.

"I'm here for you, Babe."

Betsy raised her eyes to meet those of her confidant. "I haven't said anything to Mother about this."

"I think that's wise. You, Paul, and me, that's as wide as the circle gets for now, okay?"

Betsy nodded, placing the watch on the table between them.

"Maybe there's something here and maybe not." Dawn touched the plastic bag that protected its contents. "But the one important lesson I've learned in the field of pathology is that until you discover the story within the evidence, it's best to keep the circle small."

"I agree. When can you start?"

"Paul should be home before midnight. Between the two of us, we'll work out a way to do this work when we have the lab to ourselves. What I don't have access to, he does. It may take a little time, but if there is anything to find, I promise you we'll find it."

Tears welled up in Betsy's eyes. "I'm sorry," she apologized. "This is not like me, but I can't seem to get a grip.

"Cry then, baby sister. You've just had a shock few of us experience. You're entitled to a tear or two. Do you want me to go home with you tonight?"

Betsy assured her sister that she would be fine and probably the best thing Dawn could do for her was to take her to see the best musical of the year. Dawn agreed that it might be a welcomed distraction while they waited for tomorrow to come.

Betsy could hear Dorado barking frantically the minute she pulled into the driveway. The intensity of the bark was new to her. He was at her side the minute the car door opened, prancing back and forth, his bark loud and continuous, dragging the broken leash with him.

"What is it, Dorado?" She reached out to him, but he wouldn't come to her. Instead he backed away, turned, and ran a short distance before turning to her again. She understood. He was trying to get her to follow him.

"Stay," she commanded, bewildered as to what would cause him to pull at the leash until he tore it loose. She had never seen him so agitated.

He obeyed, though he was obviously eager to lead her somewhere. She walked to him and was about to remove the leash from his collar when she noticed something caked on his coat just below his ear. She cooed to him softly to calm him while she examined what appeared to be dried, matted blood. He whimpered as she touched the spot and pulled away. Somehow her dog had been injured. The injury, she knew, could not have been caused from the leash. It was too high and too centralized.

She could taste the fear rising in her throat as she looked around, wishing she hadn't forgotten to turn on the outside lights.

"Come, Dorado," she commanded, hoping he would obey her without making her get any further from the car. He seemed to understand.

She opened the car door. "Get into the car, Dorado," she said with firmness.

The dog hesitated for a moment then did as he was told. As soon as they were on the road, Betsy called her sister on her cell phone and told her she was spending the night with her and Paul.

three

PRIVACY INVADED

Elmira, unaware of the events in her daughter's life the day before, opened the morning paper to Betsy's column. She eagerly read each word, savoring the content. Then she read it a second time and a third. She liked the way it made her feel to see her daughter's words in print. It was more than just ordinary pride a mother feels when she witnesses the success of her child. It was a feeling of extraordinary gratitude because, for some time after John's death, she wondered if her daughter would ever write again. Now, today, she was reading a thought-provoking, well-written column. She could hardly wait until next week and hoped every reader out there felt the same way.

Betsy was so much like her father in every aspect. Their emotions were deeply rooted, their discussions filled with the passion of their understanding. They preferred to be in control of their lives. They relished a challenge but needed order to facilitate their thinking. When something disrupted that order, they seemed to collapse for a time, desensitizing the analytical part that motivated them and gave them meaning. Another word for it could be depression, but Elmira preferred the more complicated version because it seemed to match their persona.

While Elmira was reading Betsy's column, Betsy was pulling back into the driveway she had driven away from the night before. Dorado was sitting in the seat next to her. Dawn followed in the car behind, Paul at the steering wheel. Once the cars were parked, Betsy let the retriever out of the car and gave him the lead.

In examining Dorado the night before, Paul determined he had been shot with a tranquilizer gun. Apparently whoever stepped onto her property was prepared for the dog. It was unsettling to the three of them that someone was so aware of her. Now they wanted to know why.

They followed Dorado to the veranda. He stopped at the door that opened into the bedroom and barked, turned and went back to Betsy, barked again, and walked back to the door.

"He's telling us someone's been here," Betsy said, reaching for the doorknob as she moved forward.

"Don't touch anything," Paul quickly cautioned her. "Let me get the equipment from the car, and we'll check for fingerprints." When he returned with the necessary tools, he slipped his hands into clear synthetic gloves and began brushing the door with a powder.

Dorado watched with curiosity and, though his stance said he was impatient to get inside, his training kept him at bay.

"When was the last time you washed your door?" Paul asked as he worked.

"Less than a week ago, right after the storm," Betsy replied. "I had to spray down the entire side of the house because of the debris the rain plastered against the brick."

"I've pulled off one set of fingerprints and two partials. Anyone else used this door?"

"The only other person that ever used this door is dead."

Paul looked up at his sister-in-law apologetically. "I'm sorry, Betsy. I wasn't implying anything. I guess I'm just used to asking the regular questions."

"Nor was I offended by your question. It was just a reminder that I'm the only one who walks through this door now. At this moment, however, it's a good thing, if you've found something."

Pulling the prints off with special tape, Paul placed them, side by side, inside a small case and closed the lid. "Okay, Dorado," he said, "let's go inside."

The door was locked, as it should have been, but once it was open, Dorado was the first to enter. He began sniffing and moving about the room without interruption. He stopped at the closet. Paul and Dawn waited until he gave the signal with his bark; then they made their way to the closet and began combing for physical evidence.

While all this was going on, Betsy stood by the door and looked about the room. Nothing seemed disturbed. There was nothing out of place.

"Betsy, we need you to look in the closet," Dawn called to her. "Check for missing clothing or anything out of order."

Betsy studied the inside of the closet. John's sweaters and Levis were neatly stacked on the shelves, his shoes arranged just as they should be on the floor. His jackets hung next to each other, his caps on the shelf above. Everything looked just as it did the day he died.

"Could it be that Dorado's simply sniffing out John's scent?" she asked. "That's what led him to the watch."

"It's possible," Dawn surmised. "But something set him off last night, and it didn't have anything to do with John. Let's give him some space again."

"Wait a minute," Paul called out. "There's an imprint of a shoe here, just inside the closet, and it's not John's size." He was holding one of John's shoes over what appeared to be a slight disturbance in the carpet.

Dawn took a measurement, spraying the shoe print with a solidifying mist to make the markings stand out. Then, using a small camera, she took a picture.

"Notice how smooth the carpet is everywhere else in the room, except where we've walked," she said, surveying the entire area. "Where there should be some disturbance in the carpet from your own prints, Betsy, there is none. This carpet has been swept."

Betsy sat on her bed listening and watching the three who knew what they were doing as if she was watching a television show. They were in one world, she was in another, and each of them focused on his or her role. In the script, someone had illegally entered a home for a reason yet undetermined. A small piece of evidence was picked out of the carpet as proof, and the actors were moving on, looking for more. She waited for the commercial, but there was no commercial. That's how she determined this show was real. How she wished she could simply reach up and push the *off* button to stop it from continuing.

"Betsy." Dawn was calling her name. That was her cue, only she didn't know her lines.

"Betsy!" Dawn repeated, sitting next to her. "Are you up to this?"

"I don't know my line."

"Your what?"

Betsy looked at Dawn, and their worlds merged once again. "I'm sorry. It's just that nothing seems real, and I'm trying to give it some order, some content, so I can examine what is not obvious." She paused for a second and looked around her. "I'm furious that someone dare infringe on my right of privacy. I'm angry that my personal freedom has been jeopardized. No one has that right. Am I up to this, you ask? With every part of my being, I am."

"Now you're beginning to sound like your father's daughter. Good! Dorado led Paul into John's office, but only you will know if there is anything missing or out of place."

Paul continued pulling fingerprints from John's desk as Dorado stood as sentinel as the women walked into the room. "The suspect was wearing protective gloves, obviously unaware that there was a tear in the index finger of the right hand," he said, turning to the two women standing in the doorway, watching him. "Walk the room while I finish pulling prints that may or may not belong to John and Betsy. The carpet's been swept in here also, I've already checked."

He watched them as they walked around the room. Except for the delicate lines that etched Dawn's face, showing the difference in their ages, and the fact that her hair was somewhat longer with touches of gray beginning to creep into the light brown, the two sisters were the same, same in likeness but not in personality.

Both had brilliant minds, but where Betsy seemed concentrated on logic, Dawn was blessed with a sense of humor. He smiled as he thought about that subtle difference and was thankful for his wife's gift of wit.

"I almost put John's watch in here yesterday," Betsy said after she found nothing amiss in the room and opened the middle drawer of his desk. "But something stopped me. Now I know why." She looked down into the drawer, and a frown suddenly crossed her face. "There's something different here."

"What's different?" Paul asked, leaning over her.

"Yesterday, when I opened the drawer, the blue pen was in front of the red pen. Now the red pen is in front of the blue." Where there was no sense of humor, there was a photographic memory, and at this moment, Paul was thankful for Betsy's gift.

Dawn snapped a picture and then lifted the two pens from the drawer with gloved hands and placed them in small plastic bags. Taking the time to check the chair, just in case the suspect may have sat there while looking through the drawers, she used the infrared and ultra light to search for whatever might be available. There were a few strands of hair, which may or may not be of importance but were worthy of further investigation. She pulled them from the chair with the tape and dropped them into a small plastic container. Other than a small daub of mud stuck to the upholstery, there was nothing else.

"And that was not there," Betsy retorted, pointing to the mud smudge. Dawn didn't hesitate in placing the piece of mud in a bag, although they already knew where it came from.

Paul took Dorado back to the veranda. "See what's out there, boy," he said, patting the dog on the backside. Dorado's ears went up, and he was gone, the three of them following. He paused only two times to sniff out the scent, leading them past a clump of rocks and grass just to the left of the wooded area. He stopped next to a set of tire tracks just behind the rocks.

Paul knelt beside one of the tracks, pulled a measuring tape from his pocket and measured the width. Moving his hand over the ground, touching around the fresh tracks, he could feel and see earlier impressions. He stood and walked several feet, following them, before kneeling again. At that point, he brushed the fresh dirt away to find the grass growing around dried tire tracks. The ground was hard enough for him to cast imprints showing the different layers of tracks.

It had been five years since Paul had seen any field work. Once he took the reins as leader of the lab, as he jokingly called himself, he was confined to the lab. He had forgotten how much he enjoyed gathering the evidence. Not that he didn't enjoy lab work, but it felt good to be doing what he was doing right now. He only hoped, for Betsy's sake, he hadn't lost his touch.

"I've finished making a cast of the fresh tire tracks," Dawn called to him. "Do you want casts of what you found further down?"

He nodded in the affirmative. "I don't think yesterday was the first time this area has been used for a road," he said, brushing the dirt from his pant leg. "I'll bring a probe out later today and do some testing and hopefully come up with a timetable as to when and how often a vehicle parked here."

Putting his arm around Betsy and leading her away from the tracks and back to her house, he suggested she come and stay with them until they could find some answers. Dawn was right in step with them, insisting on it.

"Thanks, but I don't think so," Betsy said. "I believe I'll stay right here and help Dorado protect my home from any more intrusions." She stopped and looked appreciatively at the two people who loved her and wanted to protect her. Then she allowed logic, once again, to rule her thoughts.

"It's obvious," she said, methodically, "that whoever's behind this went to a great deal of trouble to erase any evidence that would arouse suspicion on my part. The question is why? Could it be they have no desire to harm me, only find whatever it is they're looking for? And what were they looking for? Did they find it this time, because I don't think this was the first time they've been inside my house."

"You're saying that you've seen evidence of entry in the past and never mentioned it to either one of us?" Dawn was shocked.

"Until now I had no reason to think of it as anything but something I may have done myself, without thinking."

"What kind of evidence?" Paul asked.

"Remember John's three pair of shoes in the closet?"

They both nodded.

"He always lined them up—brown pair, black pair, boots—in that order, from left to right. About a month after his funeral, I was sitting on the bed trying to make myself pack his clothes and store them away. The closet door was open, and I was looking at his shoes, remembering how much he loved those silly boots when I noticed they weren't in the right order. The black pair and the brown pair were reversed. I let it pass, thinking maybe I had reversed them when I was cleaning and still in shock over his death. Now I know differently.

"That same day I was sitting at his desk. It brought me comfort just to sit in his office; it was as if a part of him still existed there. I happened to glance at the world globe on the bookshelf and noticed the United States was not facing the desk. When John looked up from his reading, he liked to see America looking back. When either of us dusted, we always made sure the globe was lined up that way. Even after he died, I kept doing that, but that day, the United States was turned away from the desk. Again, I thought it was something I had overlooked."

Paul and Dawn stood there, looking at Betsy for several seconds. Finally Dawn broke the silence. "Can you tell us where you'd been when you came home to find this evidence?"

"I was at the cemetery putting fresh flowers on John's grave. I'd say I was gone less than two hours."

Paul turned and ran to his car, returning with yet another box. "I have an idea. Mind if I check it out?"

"Of course not, but what is it?"

"This gadget you see before you seeks out hidden listening devices or cameras. We'll take one room at a time."

The two women followed him through the front room to John's office. He specifically pointed the instrument toward the world globe. A red light appeared on the tiny screen stationed on the handle of the detector.

"Ah ha, just as I thought. Dawn, check the globe."

Dawn pulled on the protective gloves, picked up the globe and studied it, using the ultra light. "You're right," she cried, tipping it upside down. "The bug is gone but there are traces of its residue tucked beneath the base."

Paul went back through the living room, where residue was found beneath the base of the floor lamp.

"Next stop, the bedroom," he said, directing the women to follow.

The detector, when placed high above the shoes, began to glow. Once again the light picked up traces left from a microphone hidden on the shelf, directly above the shoes. Apparently, in order to place the bug, the shoes had to be set aside. When they were put back in place they were done so, unknowingly, out of order.

"Whoever was here yesterday," Paul concluded, "came to retrieve not to search."

"Take that detector and search every room," Dawn

insisted, "then we'll go outside and search the yard." She turned to Betsy. "I refuse to leave you alone until we know everything is bug free." She shook her head. "I can't believe this is happening."

Paul's search resulted in uncovering residue from three more bugs: one inside the telephone base on the kitchen counter, one on the veranda, and one on the front porch.

"The sound equipment used here was state of the art," Paul explained. "That tells us they, whoever *they* are, have money and means."

"You're sure everything's clean?" Betsy needed to know.

Paul nodded in the affirmative. "Everything's clean."

"Then let's talk in the house." She led the way to John's office and asked Paul to dust the safe. There he found the same partial print in three different places. He pulled one from the top, one from the dial, and one from the side of the door. Just like the others, these prints were fresh.

"Tell me you've got a clue as to what's going on here?" Paul asked, his brows scrunched into a frown.

First, Betsy invited her sister and brother-in-law to sit on the small settee. Then she hurried to the bedroom and returned with her purse. Sitting at the desk, she removed one of the notebooks.

"I don't think they were here only to remove their equipment," she began. "I think they still hadn't found what they're looking for. I think they were hoping I would lead them to it. That's why they installed the listening device and, for over a year, waited for me to say something, read something, or find something. When I didn't, they were satisfied that I knew nothing.

"Today, we'll assume their purpose was to remove the equipment and to make one final, thorough search of John's office. I don't doubt for a second that the safe was searched in the beginning. But perhaps this time they had a better idea of what they were looking for. The first time, the innocent little notebooks filled with unreadable hen scratching meant nothing to them. They were looking for something more sophisticated. If my theory is correct, yesterday they were looking for notebooks."

She walked over to the safe, dialed the sequence, and opened the door. The notebooks were gone. "But what they still don't know is that yesterday I took from the safe what they think they have today."

The two facing her shook their heads in bewilderment. "You're telling us there's more to this than a broken watch and one notebook?" Dawn said quietly. "What was John involved in, Betsy?"

Betsy handed Paul and Dawn each a notebook. "Look at the red mark on the front. It says *Confidential.*"

She explained that when John first became an investigating reporter, he devised a form of shorthand that only he could read to help him in getting all the information down quickly. While on a case, he filled a notebook with his findings and comments.

"After we were married, John gave me what he called a cheat sheet so I could learn the shorthand and read back to him what he had written. It was a complicated concoction of letters, lines, dots, and numbers, and it took me several hours to learn the shorthand."

"Yes, I can only imagine," Dawn all but interrupted. The thought of her sister struggling to learn anything was actually beyond her imagination.

Fascinated with the story, Paul gave his wife a quick nudge which meant *shhh.* In return, she gave him a stop-being-pushy glance. He looked back at her with loving patience, soothing her ruffled feelings, and the two settled down like two children listening to a fairy tale.

Betsy proceeded with her story. "From that time on, I read each page of every notebook and helped John type the final drafts of his investigations." She focused on the notebook in her hand. "But until yesterday, I had never seen these. There are seven in all—the one Ned gave me and the six I found when I was looking in the safe for my reference page, which I prefer to call it, so I could refresh my memory. I thought I was anxious to find out what was in the book that John stitched inside his jacket. I found the paper tucked beneath the six books, but now I hesitate to read what is written for fear of what I might find."

"You didn't tell me about the other six notebooks yesterday," Dawn looked at her sister with intent. "Why?"

Betsy only shook her head, not knowing why.

"You say Ned gave you the notebook yesterday?" Paul's question was fair but disturbing.

"I know what you're thinking, Paul. I couldn't help thinking it myself. Yesterday Ned gives me a notebook. Today someone comes into my house, opens the safe, and takes every notebook sitting on the shelf that, a year ago, meant nothing to them. But I find it hard to believe that Ned would be involved in anything that would hurt John. There has to be another explanation."

"Who else could have known about the book?"

"Only Terri, his daughter, but I believe the information came from me while I was searching the safe before the microphone was apparently removed."

"Was Dorado with you when you opened the safe?"

"Of course," Betsy cuddled the dog who sat at her side.

"Then you're probably right. You're always talking to him as if he were human," Dawn said, raising her eyebrow.

"That's only because he's a good listener," Betsy responded with a chuckle. Then she became serious again. "He was squeezing in front of me to get a better view of the inside of the safe, and I told him to slide over because he was standing on a very important notebook. That may have been enough to arouse their interest."

"Tell me you removed the six without making an announcement," Paul moaned.

"I promise I was speechless when I found them," Betsy assured him.

Paul smiled, but his eyes showed concern. He looked at his watch. "I hate to leave you alone, but we need to be on our way. We're already late for work. Will you be all right?"

"I'm not alone. I have Dorado constantly at my side, as you can see. Besides, Lincoln will be home for the summer in a few days."

"That's my one consolation," Dawn sighed.

"It's my consolation and also my worry," Betsy noted. "I don't want my son dragged into something that could possibly bring him harm. I almost wish he could stay at school until this is over, whatever it is."

"And I can hardly wait until he gets home." Dawn linked her arm through her sister's. "I see Dorado's devotion, and I have no doubt that he would give his life for you. I am comforted by that. But when Lincoln gets home, I'll feel more than comforted—I'll feel relieved."

Before he left, Paul suggested he send out a man he personally knew to change the locks on all the doors. Betsy nodded her approval, and Paul made the call.

"The guy who'll be coming is named Rich," Paul said. "He's about fifty years old, around five feet, nine inches tall, and slight of build. He has light brown hair, blue eyes, and drives a late-model tan van with his insignia on the side, *Rich's Locks and Keys*. He'll be here this afternoon about 4:00—just so you know who to expect."

"Thank you both for everything," Betsy said, closing the car door after Dawn got in the front seat.

"What are families for if they can't do a little forensics work for each other now and then?" Dawn responded jokingly, trying to smile. But a smile would contradict the apprehension she felt inside and couldn't quite materialize. She looked back and waved as they drove away.

four

DISCOVERIES & FACTS

"You know something, Dorado?" Betsy said to the retriever by her side as they walked back to the house. "I think we've got time to read a couple of those notebooks before lunch. Shall we give it a try?"

Dorado didn't seem to care one way or the other, so instead, they sat on the porch, nestled against each other, until the sun reached its highest peak.

"I'll tell you what," Betsy said, as she stood and motioned to her dog. "Let's eat lunch, and then we'll go into John's office and find out what the story is behind all of our trouble."

Lunch didn't take long enough. Betsy wasn't ready to start the task. Instead she decided to work on her article for the next week. After that, she thought, she would open the notebook Ned found in John's jacket.

Just as she sat at her computer, the doorbell rang. Her heart started pulsating, and her mouth felt dry. She wasn't expecting anyone. Why hadn't she locked the door? The bell rang again, and the door opened. She froze, unable to move her limbs, unable to hide from the intruder.

"Babe, are you here?"

It was her mother's voice. Tears started falling, and she

began to shake as the fear drained from her body.

"Babe, what's wrong?" Her mother was at her side. "Are you ill?"

Betsy wiped the tears from her cheeks and reached out, taking her mother's arms and wrapping them around her shaking body. For several minutes, Elmira held her daughter close, soothing her, thankful she had listened to a prompting to stop here on her way home.

"Tell me what's made you so upset," she pleaded.

"I didn't want to burden you with this," Betsy muttered through her tears.

"Pamper me, Babe," her mother replied. "Hand me the burden."

Betsy looked at her mother. "Sit with me on the sofa. It's a long story."

When the story ended, they sat silent, Elmira's hands folded over her daughter's protectively.

"Why is it that while I want to know what John has written in those notebooks, they've been in my purse for a day now, and I have yet to read one line?"

"Are you afraid of what you'll find?"

Moved by the question, Betsy's mind began to examine its implication. She looked at her mother. "Why are you here right at this time?" she asked.

"Because you needed me," her mother replied.

Betsy nodded. "To help me see that, subconsciously, I've allowed myself to believe what I didn't know would give me shelter. Once I open one of the notebooks, I become knowledgeable, therefore accountable."

She stood and walked to the window, viewing the world from a new perspective. "I think I've been rather cowardly, Mother, when I should have been brave."

"Oh, but I think you're even more than brave, my dear. The fact that you are sitting here when you could have run away tells me that."

"But I let fear override any courage I might have felt the

minute you rang the doorbell."

"Oh, that. Don't be concerned about feeling frightened. Fear itself is an important part of courage. It's the part that keeps us alert and triggers the courage to surface. Never feel badly about being afraid, only feel badly when you don't act in its presence. Now I'm going to go and let you get back to your computer—which reminds me. I read your article three times: the first time to make sure your editor didn't change your words; the second time to feel the pride I have in you; and the third time for your father. Wait, I actually read it four times; the last time was just for fun." Elmira kissed Betsy's cheek. "You'll know when to sit down with the notebooks, Babe. God will instruct you."

Betsy smiled. "I'm just thankful He knows when to send you to me." She walked her mother to the car and watched her drive away. What she didn't see were the tears in her mother's eyes and the deep concern that shadowed her face.

Believing that God would instruct her, Betsy decided to write her next column while she waited, relieved she didn't feel any promptings at this time. Or perhaps this was a prompting. It was possible that God had already given the instructions. Maybe she had to prove to herself that, no matter what, no one or nothing would keep her from living her life. Maybe she had to prove to herself that fear could not control her thoughts; then she could take the next step. Maybe these were His instructions to her.

With that notion in mind, Betsy checked her e-mail for responses. Her readers seemed to like being informed about the percentages of the opinion poll. One or two messages were obviously deletable, as was always the case. But for the most part, the day's greetings were enjoyable to read. For Betsy, it didn't matter if those who wrote the e-mails were for or against, what mattered is that they each had a voice.

Writing her column was something Betsy could always lose herself in as the world around her simply disappeared from view. She felt soothed in the freedom writing brought to her mind, and when she finished typing, she sat back, took a deep breath, and read what she had written.

As I promised you a week ago, we are going to discuss the birth of America. I realize it will be a one-sided discussion until you get your e-mails on their way . . . which reminds me, this week's e-mail responses were 89 percent for and 11 percent against spending five weeks on this topic. Some of the 11 percent already know everything and some, through their response let me know that they couldn't care less. This is called freedom of speech.

Who were the heroes of our Constitution? They were men who, in support of the Declaration, with a firm reliance on the protection of divine providence, mutually pledged to each other their lives, their fortunes, and their sacred honor. I might add here that the wives of many of those men stood alongside their husbands, making sacrifices equally as noble.

These were men and women of righteous natures who, without exception, accepted the composition of the Constitution as the handiwork of God.

Betsy studied the quotes she had selected by Benjamin Franklin, Thomas Jefferson, James Madison, and John Adams demonstrating their conviction that belief in God is essential to the moral order of the world and to the happiness of man.

There were fifty-six men who placed their signatures beneath the Declaration of Independence. They were an elite group of men, each bringing with him a gift that, when intertwined by divine intervention, was used to create an inspired document.

I will include one more name in this list of patriots: Patrick Henry, a man whose name does not appear as a signer of the Declaration but whose courage is undeniable in pursuing liberty and who delivered a most powerful and historical speech on March 23, 1775.

The British had the upper hand. The king refused to hear American petitions. Patrick Henry stood before a large crowd in St. John's Church in Richmond, Virginia. In one section of his speech, he

spoke these words: *"Besides, sir, we shall not fight our battles alone. There is a just God who presides over the destinies of nations, and who will raise up friends to fight our battles for us. The battle, sir, is not to the strong alone, it is to the vigilant, the active, the brave."*

Some of you may say my theme refers more to God than the true heroes of the Constitution. Let me explain. The men involved in the writing and preparing the way for the writing of the Constitution knew what they were doing was well beyond their own capabilities. They knew there was a greater hero, One who instructed, guided, and protected them as they did His work. Not once did they question that God was in charge. If they did not, how can we?

May those who prefer to leave God out of government soon learn that without God, we would have no government. Let them understand that God and country are one and inseparable, for there cannot be one without the other. Within the walls of the construction, God is our greatest hero.

It was William Penn who wrote: "Those people who will not be governed by God will be ruled by Tyrants."

I look forward to your e-mails, but I must remind you that my mother will be reading them, so those of you who feel inclined to be a little colorful in your remarks, remember to keep them pastel.

Betsy looked at the clock. It had taken less than an hour to put this column together. For the next four weeks, she knew her columns would all but write themselves. No research required. That gave her an idea. Why not write the next column right now? So she did. Then she wrote the next and the next. For two more hours, she sat at her computer writing columns that would appear in future editions of the newspaper. It was easier to write about something of which she had full knowledge and understanding than to open a notebook and study something she wasn't sure she wanted to know.

Was she afraid her husband had been involved in something illegal, something that would damage his character in the eyes of those he loved or worked with, or both?

Given time to write and ponder about courage, she recognized the message and knew it was time for her to show some. She printed the pages she had typed and organized them according to the week they were to appear in the paper. Once that was done, she reluctantly reached for her purse.

"Well, Dorado," she said, taking a notebook in her hand, "I can no longer give an excuse that would keep me from the inevitable. It's time to read what's written on these pages." Betsy removed the rest of the books and laid them on her desk, staring at them for a minute before returning to the one that was stitched in the pocket of her husband's jacket. With her heart in her throat, she began to read and transcribe the first page while she waited for Rich to come and change the locks.

In a park directly across the street from a large office building, two men sat on a bench, deep in quiet conversation.

"Tell me about the notebooks," demanded the man in an expensive, Italian cut, pinstripe suit. A felt hat concealed his face.

"There's thirty-six in all. They may or may not give you what you want," answered the younger man, who was wearing a leather jacket, a ball cap, and dark glasses. "They're written in some kind of code. My partner's working on them now."

"The equipment has been removed then?" The voice beneath the felt hat had a slight accent. "I want no evidence left behind."

The leather jacket straightened. "The area's been swept clean. My partner is good at what he does, and Mrs. Braden will never know she's been under surveillance."

"And the dog? I didn't want the dog harmed." The man in the pinstripe reached into his pocket and wrapped his fingers around a Cuban cigar. Removing the cellophane, he moistened the butt of the cigar with his tongue and then put it between his lips.

The younger man took a lighter from the pocket of his

leather jacket and, directing its flame, lit the cigar, hoping to get a better look at the face beneath the hat. His attempt was in vain. Dark glasses and a recently grown beard covered the face all too well.

"The dog sniffed us out immediately," he replied, "just as we knew he would. We had to tranquilize him. He was just coming around when we left."

The face beneath the disguise nodded an approval. "Tell me about the woman. You're positive she's oblivious?" Whiffs of smoke escaped his mouth as he spoke.

"There's nothing on any of the tapes that would indicate she knows anything. We've gone over them several times, finding nothing suspicious: no phone calls, conversations, or visitors that would raise a flag. We monitored her movements for the past year with no deviation in her routine. She seems to be a religious woman with strong family ties. Hardly fits the criteria for intrigue."

"Yet she's the one who led you to the notebooks." The man inhaled the smoke of his cigar and slowly released it in the form of a ring before continuing. "You still believe she knows nothing while I find myself concerned that we may have removed the equipment too soon."

"Do you want us to go back?"

"Not yet. First, I want to hear the tape."

A small piece of equipment was retrieved from the pocket of the leather jacket and handed to the man. While he listened, the younger man waited quietly.

It wasn't that he was afraid of the person sitting next to him, but he thought it important to show respect for him as an employer. Respect without trust, however. In his profession, he trusted no one who needed his expertise. Though this man showed compassion for a dog, he doubted that same compassion would be extended to the woman if he found that she knew something.

He often found it ironic that he endangered himself as much as those he spied on virtually each time he took an assignment of this kind. It's what he knew when the equipment was pulled that put him in danger. After two encounters with bullets aimed at his body once a job was done, his partner devised a resourceful means of self-protection. Mac had the mind of a genius and the mentality for stratagem, gifts that made the two of them more than just good at what they did.

The older man snuffed out his cigar, removed the earphone and nodded. "Just as you said, the notebooks apparently were not her purpose for opening the safe, nor does there seem to be any indication that she was interested in them after the initial comment."

"We opened the safe one more time simply because, in the year we had her under surveillance, she had never opened it herself until now. A year ago, none of the items on your list were inside. We wanted to verify that nothing had changed. It was a mere precaution turned to our advantage.

"Out of curiosity, I decided to flip through one of the notebooks. Whether the information inside is coded and will lead you to what you're searching for or is simply a form of shorthand Mr. Braden used to take notes as a reporter, we'll find out soon enough."

"I'll want full details as soon as they're decoded." Each man studied the other behind dark glasses as the man in the pinstripe spoke. "After that, we'll decide the next step."

The man in the leather jacket nodded and returned the device to his pocket. He accepted an envelope the older man handed to him. Then he turned and walked to a black Fiat parked on the other side of the park. The man in the pinstripe made a call on his cell phone before turning the opposite direction to a waiting limo.

Once inside the Fiat, the leather jacket was removed, the dark glasses adjusted, and the question asked, "Is the transmitter in place?"

"Tricky but solid, Chandler," came a reply from somewhere inside the glasses that he wore.

"Well done, Mac. Check in when you have something."

Mac sat in his telephone maintenance van and watched the man in the fancy suit climb into the limo. He pushed a button on a small screen to the side of him as the driver pulled out. A tiny light began to flash. The transmitter attached to the underside of the car seemed to be working perfectly.

"Okay, my man," he whispered, a grin spreading across his face. "We've just become one and inseparable. I just hope it's not for long." The light blinked its way along the map on the computer screen. Mac watched it and touched certain keys, giving it instructions to catalog the course. He wasn't in any hurry to follow. His new invention transmitted further than any known piece of equipment of its kind. Besides, he had to wait until a second car carrying two men looking sinister enough to be bodyguards pulled away from the curb. He counted two minutes after the limo made its departure before the car started its engine. Apparently they wanted to make sure their boss wasn't being followed. Little did they know.

While Mac sat watching the screen, he let his mind go back to the first day his company had been contacted to do this surveillance work. His partner, Chandler, was given a time and a place where he would meet the mystery man, who preferred to keep his private information just that, private—no address, no phone number. The meeting was held in a limo with darkened windows. The man wore a hat low over his face. Apparently he felt that what he was after was so secret, he could trust no one but himself to be the contact. That was their first clue as to the danger involved in taking the assignment.

After several months of research and some trial and error, Mac had invented an implant transmitter/receiver. It was an invention of necessity for self-protection, and Mac was proud of its abilities. It was the color of flesh, completely undetectable once attached. Chandler wore his just on the inside of his upper arm, in the shadow of the muscle. When activated, it allowed Mac not only to keep in touch with his partner but also listen to any conversation he had.

There was only one problem the day he wore it to his

appointment inside the limo. There was a transmitter detector somewhere in the interior, setting off a signal the minute Chandler was inside. But luck had been with him, as it always was, and he removed a transmitter he carried in his jacket for communication convenience with his partner and explained as much to his new employer, saying he would turn it off. Mac counted to three and did just that. It had been a close call, but it gave Mac a new challenge. He would have to invent a transmitter that wouldn't transmit to a transmitter detector. That new invention was now affixed to the bottom of the limo.

Its placement hadn't been his first choice because its microphone would pick up the sounds of the engine and whatever else was running before any conversation inside the limo itself. However, with the two bodybuilders watching from a short distance, he had to be inventive to even get close enough to attach the device.

In the movies, there's always a manhole beneath the car of attention. In this case, there was no manhole to use as a prop. He had to create a diversion. He made a quick phone call and then opened the door of the van, pulled out some tools, and walked into one of the office buildings. Five minutes later, as he was walking back to his van, an old Chrysler came chugging down the street and died just as its front bumper was level with the limo's back bumper. A man and a very attractive woman got out of the car. The man opened the hood of the car while the woman adjusted her short skirt before leaning over the fender to watch. Mac's attractive distraction knew how to do her job.

The limo driver, who was leaning against his door, reading a newspaper, did a double take as she flashed him a smile.

We men are so predictable, Mac thought to himself as he asked if he could be of assistance.

"Thank you, yes," replied the man.

Together they checked beneath the hood, and while the woman kept two pair of male eyes on her, Mac slipped beneath the limo. It took all of thirty seconds to plant the device.

"Think I found the problem," he said as he stood and brushed the dirt from his clothes. Then he climbed into the car and turned the key. The car started without a cough.

"Thanks for your help," the owner of the Chrysler said, tipping his cap.

"Anytime," Mac replied in return.

Everything was as good as it was going to get, for now He knew if he was able to catch any conversation inside the limo, it would be fragmented. But when he had something to report, it would be every stop the limo made, as well as the home address of the man of mystery and, with any luck, bits and pieces of conversation.

Betsy sat with the notebook John had sewn into his jacket in her hand. She began studying the shorthand and transcribing in her mind, without the aid of her reference page, the words her husband had written to her before he died.

My lovely Betsy,

What I have written will take you into the past, much like your weekly article, because when you finally read this, the pages will be from the past.

John wrote of his love for her and an explanation that if she was reading this, she needed to know his death was necessary to protect her life. He explained his love for his country and his willingness to pay the ultimate price to protect it.

As she turned the pages, she read about the man she knew so well with a secret life in an organization she knew nothing about. It was an incredible story.

Then, in the last sentence, he made a request. *When the time comes, I need you to do the one thing I was unable to do.* There was no explanation of what that one thing was, only the request. It was as if he had been interrupted before he could finish.

She thought back to that morning when he struggled to tell her something before dying in her arms. Was he trying to tell her what she needed to do for him? Another thought made her shudder. Could this be why someone had invaded her home and her privacy? To find out what she knew or might do in connection with John's other life? Only she didn't know anything, therefore, she could do nothing. A wasted year of listening to everything she said.

Serves them right, she thought to herself. *I hope they were bored out of their skulls, and I hope there was a huge price tag attached.*

Betsy began to pray silently—a little paranoid of hidden listening devices—that the words John had whispered to her the morning he died would be made known to her. She was just now beginning to understand the miracle in his determination to get back to her. She only hoped she hadn't already failed him in her unwillingness to accept his death.

She sat quietly, trying to listen, trying to be receptive, but nothing came. Kneeling, she set the notebook beside her on the floor and once again pleaded with God to bring the words to her mind, determined to stay on her knees until she received an answer.

The answer didn't come easily. It was as if she had to prove that she was strong enough to accept what was ahead of her if she was given the answer. When it came, it was her husband's whispered voice she heard. *"Tell Lincoln what they're after will be with me, wherever I am."* She repeated the words in her mind. At first they didn't seem to make sense. Who was after what? And what did Lincoln have to do with any of this?

Why Lincoln? But even as she asked the question in her mind, she knew the answer in her heart. Lincoln, the boy who idolized his father, was a part of that life her husband spoke of in his notebook. Lincoln believed what his father and his grandfather taught, that to protect our liberty each man has a responsibility. Had her father been a member of this organization as well, the one John wrote about in his notebook? The one that dated back to the signing of the Declaration of

Independence?

Now she knew why she had to be prepared to receive the answer. The revelation was stunning, the truth of it powerful and frightening. She felt the strength of the revelation soar through her as well as the weakness of guilt, wondering if she would have known this much sooner had she been stronger. But even as the thought crossed her mind, the words *"the timetable is as it should be"* cut through the guilt and gave her a new understanding. Time had to pass so those who had murdered her husband would believe she knew nothing of his other life.

She reread the part John wrote, explaining that the men who brought the Constitution to life knew it had to be protected against those who would defile it, therefore, a society was organized to protect its purpose. It would be a society of patriots who worked independently of the government yet in protection of the government. Their duty was, and still is, to search out and defeat any plan to destroy what God had intended for this country.

John wrote that the society was alive and well, its strength greater than ever before in the history of the country. Yet, opposition continued to gain ground through the very means that made America strong—*freedom.*

Betsy closed the book and let her thoughts go back to the years she had with this incredible man. In his work, he traveled to several foreign countries. When he returned home, he shared his adventures as they transcribed his notes. How many times, when he traveled abroad, or even within the United States, did he write information in one of these six notebooks he couldn't share with her? By the time she finished transcribing the notes in the last book, would she know all the answers that plagued her mind at this moment?

She decided it was time to talk to her mother again. She put the seven notebooks in her purse because, for now, wherever she went they would go with her.

Dorado, who had been lounging in his chair after chasing

everything smaller than himself, lifted his head when she walked out the door. "Want to go on your favorite walk to Mother's?" she asked him.

He bounded off the chair and, with a bark, led the way.

Betsy found her mother sitting on her veranda, reading. Dorado found some doggy treats in a dish next to her.

"Your message came through loud and clear," she said to Dorado. "But your master seems a little quiet." She turned to face Betsy. "Your face tells me you've read the notebook."

"Tell me, Mother, how much do you know?"

"Sit down, Babe, and we'll talk." Elmira patted the empty seat next to her in the porch swing.

Betsy sat down, her eyes focused on her mother's face. "Was my father a member of this . . . this organization?"

Elmira nodded. "It's not an organization, as you would think of an organization, but a union of defenders and protectors of the Constitution, Babe. The answer to your question is yes, as was his father before him and his father before him, and so on."

"Did he recruit John and Lincoln?" She knew her mother would understand that she needed to know the answer.

Elmira reached out and took her daughter's hand. "John's father raised his own son to be a patriot, Betsy," she said softly. "Matthew Braden was one of the most successful loyalists this country has ever conceived, yet this generation will never know his name or that he gave his life for the sake of their freedom, just as they will never know of John's bravery."

The world grew quiet around them. Even the swaying sound of the porch swing seemed hushed as the minutes passed and Betsy struggled to comprehend it all.

"Why didn't John tell me?" Her question seemed logical.

"What would you have done if you had known?"

She opened her mouth to reply, but there was no answer within her. In reality, she didn't know. She had been taught patriotism from childhood yet had never understood the cost until now.

"John never told you about this part of his life because it was the only way to protect you; the fact that you knew nothing has been your protection. But now, I suppose, it's time for you to do more than just write about the things you truly believe. It's time for you to be the shadow in the spotlight."

Betsy lifted her eyes to meet her mother's. "I sat at my computer and wrote four articles about America, and the flag, and liberty, and patriotism. It's one thing to write with commitment, yet I wonder, Mother, have I the courage to do more than just write?"

"I can't quote scripture or verse," Elmira told her daughter, "but the content goes something like this: The Constitution is more fragile today than ever before because of those who take its truths and interweave them with lies. They have battered and scarred its very purpose, through their twisted interpretation, to change its meaning. The Constitution can only be as strong as those who stand by it. Who will stand by it?

"We demand much of our government," Elmira continued, "yet we are the ones who decide if we will have freedom, not the government. Unless we begin to demand much of ourselves and step up to protect our Constitution, then our Constitution cannot protect us.

"The American patriots committed themselves to a long and bloody struggle for liberty and independence. That battle still wages. Who will carry the burden? Who will be the protector?"

Betsy listened to the words of her mother and was reminded of the words of her father as he instilled in her the meaning of the Constitution. In a way, he had opened the door for her; now her mother was charting the path. She couldn't help but feel the passion of her responsibility. It was frightening and exulting at the same time.

With a mixture of pride and uncertainty, Betsy straightened her shoulders, lifted herself from the swing, and walked to the edge of the veranda. She leaned against the gable and let her eyes focus on the beauty of the safe little world she thought she lived in. The past few days, however, had been an awakening, and she was no longer naïve.

It would certainly have been easier had she never lifted the cover of that notebook, yet Betsy could sense an extraordinary feeling of gratitude and peace within her, knowing John had not left her, just as her mother said. Within that feeling of peace, she became aware of the warmth of his spirit. She could not disappoint him. She would do as her mother suggested that day when Elmira demanded she return to the living. She would give his life meaning.

"You told me to get a life, Mother," she said. "Well, it seems I finally have one. I only hope I know what to do with it." She turned and smiled. "The wrinkles in my knees are now the least of my worries. Tell me, what is it that I must do?"

Elmira stood beside her daughter. Without saying a word, she expressed her love and concern through an embrace. "Do nothing until Lincoln gets home," she said quietly. "Share with him everything that has happened and what you've found. Then together you will know what you must do."

five

COURAGE OF HEROES

Betsy looked at the clock by her bedside. The digital numbers 4:30 gave a hint of light in the darkness of the room. She couldn't sleep. When she tried, her memories produced dreams of John sitting at his desk reciting one of his latest adventures. She couldn't understand what he was saying because he was talking in shorthand. The numbers, dots, lines, and letters flowed from his mouth in comic strip form.

She sat up and turned on the lamp, thankful today was Saturday. Lincoln would be home around noon, and she could tell him everything. She prayed that sharing this burden with her son would take some of the sadness from her.

She could feel the terrible loneliness that had consumed her after John's death begin to envelope her once again. She couldn't allow that to happen. She didn't have time to be hindered by its dread. Quickly she climbed out of bed and punched the key on the computer that opened her office e-mail. Wrapping herself in her robe, she sat down in front of the screen. There were more than three hundred e-mails waiting for her from the Midwest to the West Coast. She gave a sigh and brought the first one up on the screen. It read:

"I'm sorry, Betsy, but we've come a long way from believing in a

supreme being, who doesn't really exist, to blame all our problems on,
expect divine council from, or rely on for blessings to make us happy.
We've finally grown up and learned to use common sense, along with
our own initiative, to create a life for ourselves. Those who believe in a
higher intelligence do so because they lack intelligence of their own.

"The men who wrote the Constitution were all well-educated men
with ingenious minds. They needed no help except that which they
gleaned from each other. The greatest heroes of the Constitution are
those who gave everything for its conception.

I pose this question: If there is a God, whose side was He on
during the Civil War?

The mind-set of that e-mail was all Betsy needed. She
threw off the robe, jumped into the shower, grabbed some
comfortable clothes, and with enlightened energy began
clicking through each message. There were seventeen messages
that could be deleted without reading past the first line. She
refused to waste her time on any correspondence that started
with vulgarity or innuendos.

By 9:00 AM, all 302 e-mails had been opened. She didn't
fail to notice that all colorful comments had been respectively
whitewashed to pastel, and she was pleased. But what pleased
her most of all was that only 3 percent of her readers felt that
God was a myth. Interestingly, 21 percent wondered why,
if God actually wrote the Constitution, there were so many
amendments; 67 percent thought her column hit the nail on
the head; and to her surprise, 9 percent went even deeper into
God's role in the history of the country. One e-mail let her
know there were people out there who thought as she did.

"Not only did God influence the writers of the Constitution," it
read, *"but He personally selected each man who would be involved in*
its creation. Not one of the signers was there by chance, but all were
foreordained in premortality to be in the right place at the right time.
Thank you for having the courage to write the truth."

Betsy sat back in her chair and dialed her mother's
number. Elmira carried the e-mail address for the East Coast,
which worked very well. That way Betsy didn't have to load

her computer down, and it gave her mother something to do—or so Betsy thought. Now she suspected her mother had something more important to do than read her e-mail. She just wasn't sure what it was.

"Good morning, Babe," her mother said into the phone. "I've been reading some exciting e-mails, 379 altogether. Most people out there believe in God. Some don't. Some express themselves in various colors, and others are worthy of deletion even before they get to express themselves at all. Approximately 89.5 percent agree with you. What's the West Coast like?"

"Comparable," Betsy replied. "Interesting that while we think the people in the West and people in the East are so different in their thinking and philosophies, we find they are all very much the same."

"If you were to poll the world, I think you would find the same percentages," Elmira interjected. "People aren't that much different in their hearts, just their environments. Now, tell me how you are doing."

"I'm still trying to digest all that I've learned in the first notebook. It makes my mind spin in the knowledge, my heart falter in the responsibility, and my spirit sour in the understanding. I'm curious to know more yet fearful of what I might learn . . ."

"In other words," her mother interrupted, "you're confused and enlightened at the same time?"

"Simply put. However, I suppose that would be the consensus."

"You are your father's daughter," Elmira nodded. "And, because you are, I have no doubt that sometime short of tomorrow you will have everything arranged in your mind. At that point, there will be nothing that can get in your way. What time does Lincoln arrive?"

"You move from one subject to another smoother than anyone I know," Betsy chuckled.

"You haven't answered my question," Elmira reminded her.

"Hopefully around noon," Betsy replied, looking at the clock. She found herself missing Lincoln more now than she did the two years he served his mission. But it was different then. John was alive. Now she found herself watching and waiting, almost impatiently, until she could see his car pull into the driveway.

"You've missed him more than you thought you would, haven't you, Babe?"

"And I wish you would refrain from reading my mind," Betsy scolded. "I'd ask how you're doing this morning, but I think I already know. I'd say you had a good yoga session."

"Indeed I did, my dear. Perhaps you should make it a part of yours."

"Perhaps I should." Betsy surprised herself in the seriousness of her reply. "I may need it in the coming weeks."

"I'll be delighted to pick out a tape for you," her mother said jubilantly.

Lincoln felt the emptiness in the loss of his father each time he drove through the streets of Boston, winding his way south to the outskirts and the acres of trees surrounding the property that had been in his mother's family for generations. In about thirty minutes, he would be pulling into the driveway of his childhood home, where she would be waiting at the door to greet him. He was looking forward to being home for the summer.

He glanced into his rearview mirror and noticed a light colored van in the distance. He couldn't be sure, but he thought he had seen the same one, or maybe one just like it, behind him about an hour ago just before he pulled off for gas.

He let the feeling of concern pass and turned his attention back to the little white dotted lines leading him home. His mind drifted back to the day he loaded his car with suitcases while his mother stood close by, watching, fighting back tears that refused to be contained. His father was making sure he had enough air in the tires, plenty of gas in the tank, and enough ready cash in his wallet, along with his credit card, to see him through the first semester of college.

It wasn't easy to leave them that day nor had it been any easier when he walked away from them a year later to board a plane for Ukraine to serve his mission.

It was during those two years in the mission field that he came to view his home land with deeper perception and appreciation. Sovereignty became more than just a word to him—it became a commitment. He loved the Ukrainian people, but his love of America became more precious to him, and he longed for its warmth.

When he returned home, he talked with his father about his feelings. Through their conversations, his commitment became even more defined. It was one that would test his bravery as it had his forefathers.

Lincoln found himself studying the road behind him once again, unable to shake a feeling of uneasiness that plagued him. To his relief, the van was no longer in sight, and he scolded himself for being suspicious.

His relationship with his parents had always been close, but since the death of his father seven months after he returned home from his mission, he had grown even closer to his mother. He felt responsible for her despite being the youngest. Amy and Todd had their own families and lived too far away. He was within a few hours drive, and besides, he rather liked looking after her when she gave him the chance.

During the time she was struggling to pull herself out of her grief, he sought the help of his grandmother, who was more than willing to do the dirty work. The matriarch of the family with her silver-gray hair and delicate features defied her age with strength that couldn't be ignored. He was glad she was on his side. He could hardly wait to sit at her table and tell her of his latest adventure.

He had encountered a dissident yesterday on campus, who

had invited him to a flag-burning ceremony.

"I thought that went out with the '60s," he said to the tattooed teenager, who sported pierced earrings of all sizes protruding from his lips, ears, nose, eyebrows, and, most painfully, his tongue.

"No way, dude," the response was raspy. "Gotta let 'em know how we feel about things. Gotta make a statement, man!"

Lincoln couldn't help but smile. The guy's appearance alone made a statement. He took a deep breath. "My grandmother made a statement once. I liked what she said. Do you mind if I repeat it to you?"

"Go, Bro!"

"She said 'When someone burns the flag, he's setting his own soul on fire as well. When he rips its beauty into shreds, he's ripping out his own heart.'"

As he spoke the words, he could almost hear his grandmother's gentle voice saying, *I can't quote scripture or verse but* . . . which was her way of telling them they would never read the words that came after that little introduction in any book in any library. They were words that were penned from her own thoughts.

The dissenter looked at him, a low whistle escaping his lips. "That's heavy, man!" He locked hands with Lincoln. "That's real heavy."

Lincoln swore there was a tear in the corner of the young man's eye as he turned and disappeared behind a light colored van . . . then it struck! That's where he had seen the van.

He glanced into his rearview mirror. The van was back. The thought came to him to pull off the road. He took his cell phone from his pocket and placed it against his ear, as if he was talking to someone. Then he signaled, braked, and parked the car on a turn-out, keeping the van in view, praying it would simply drive by without incident.

The van actually increased its speed as it passed him, making it impossible to get a clear look inside the slightly darkened windows. The fleeting glance, however, told him there was one person inside; the outline revealed a man's profile.

His heart was pounding as he made a quick study of the license plate number before the van slipped from view. He didn't need to write it down; it was burned into his memory.

Betsy's phone rang five minutes before noon. She didn't reach for it, nor did it ring again. It was simply Lincoln's signal, telling her he had just turned onto the lane that led to their home. She opened the front door and walked to the end of the porch, leaned against the pillar, and, with a tearful smile, waited. Dorado stood beside her, watching the lane, his tail wagging and his tongue dripping.

This little ritual had become their tradition. She wasn't sure whose idea it was in the beginning, but it proved to be a very satisfying one. Her heart felt light as she saw his Jeep pull into the circular driveway. She wiped away the tears, knowing she was in no hurry for this young man to marry.

As soon as the Jeep stopped, the door opened and Betsy watched her handsome, dark-haired, blue-eyed son emerge. He was a replica of her father in height and build, but his facial features and mannerisms were his father's. His laughing eyes and innocent face would always be her reminder of the man who gave her so much in this life.

His smile brought more tears as she walked to him, put her arms around him, and held him to her. "I'm so glad you're home," she said emotionally, letting her tears absorb into his shirt.

"That makes two of us," he laughed, wrapping his arms around his mother. It felt so good to be home that tears welled up in his eyes. He didn't mind. His grandmother informed him one day, years ago, that tears were good for the soul, and he never doubted his grandmother's words.

Dorado waited his turn, and when mother and son

separated, he was immediately between them, barking his welcome home to the one person who would wrestle with him. Lincoln knelt down and tugged gently at the dog's ears. "I missed you too, you big pup. Come and help me unpack the Jeep."

Once the unpacking was done and Lincoln's room cluttered with his possessions, Betsy prepared lunch. She listened while her son talked about college life and his concern over finals. She chuckled inwardly, knowing the ability of this young man. His grades were the least of her concerns.

When he finished what he had to say, he looked at her for a moment with furrowed brows, "There's something wrong, Mom," he said gently, reaching out to touch her hand. "I felt it the minute I stepped out of the Jeep, and I can see it in your eyes. Now it's your turn to talk."

Betsy hadn't realized her son knew her so well, but she was relieved he had given her an opening. She stood and, taking his hand, led him to the sofa.

"There's much I have to tell you," she said, motioning for him to sit beside her. "Some of which is very disturbing. I wish there was an easier way, but there isn't, and the things I must tell you are things you must know."

Hearing herself tell the story of the past week made her feel as if she had taken the script from a mystery novel. It sounded too fictional to be true. As she talked, she studied her son's face, wondering what he might be thinking, but found that he, like his father, was able to hide his thoughts beneath a natural expression. His only reaction was to cradle her hand in his as he listened.

When she finished talking, his eyes met hers and she could see into their depth. It was then she recognized the anger and concern hidden behind a façade of calm. She could feel the hands that held hers turn cold, but he said nothing, only stood and walked to the window.

Subconsciously, he was looking out the window for any signs of a van, even though he knew if it was out there, it would be hidden from view. In his mind, he couldn't help but feel it was a continuation of his mother's story. For now, he would say nothing about the incident.

Betsy waited until Lincoln turned to face her and then asked, "Tell me how you became a part of this?" She needed to hear his answer as much as she needed to know what was in the six notebooks.

He tucked his fingers in the pockets of his Levis and leaned against the window frame. "While I was serving my mission, I saw and heard things that brought with them an unexpected awareness of true liberty. People would talk to me in confidence because I was a servant of God, and they trusted me. When I came home, I talked with Dad about what I had learned. He gave me more to think about. He told me of things that would be happening in my generation and in the one following unless we could stop it. That's when I found out about his second life, as he lightheartedly called it."

Betsy's body suddenly began to tremble. Without saying more, Lincoln was beside her, wrapping his arms around her and holding her until the trembling ceased.

"I'm sorry. I seem to be rather emotional today." She sniffled. "Your grandmother promised to have a yoga tape waiting for me when we go to her house for dinner this evening." She took a deep breath and released it as a demonstration, attempting a smile as Lincoln released her.

"Now I need you to continue. I have to know why all of this is happening, and I'm afraid you're the only one who can tell me."

"Where are the notebooks?"

"In here." Betsy reached for her purse sitting on the table beside them. Removing the six notebooks, she handed them to him.

He opened the first one, flipped the cover to the back, and studied the first page before laying it on the glass table in front of them. He did the same with the next one, and the next, until he had them in order. Betsy watched his eyes as they scanned the first few lines of each book. He could read John's shorthand. Why didn't it surprise her?

Lincoln glanced up at her. "Dad taught it to me before I went to college. He felt I could take better notes if I used it."

"And did you?"

"There were times I relied completely on the shorthand."

As Betsy observed her son in his task, she began to feel his quiet strength. It was as if the heavy burden had been lifted from her, making her feel almost light-headed. The knowledge that he could read the shorthand as well as she could and would be by her side was all she needed to make her feel equal to the task. She was ready to find the reason for her husband's death.

Lincoln wondered again if the van he had seen had something to do with all of this. The thought of it sent a shiver down his spine. Could whoever killed his father and had his mother's house tapped now be focusing on him?

He thought about Todd and Amy and wondered if they were under the microscope as well. Neither of them knew anything about their father's other life. He hoped that would be their protection, as it had been his mother's. Many times he had wanted to tell Todd because he thought his brother should know, but he'd never had the chance. Now he was thankful he hadn't.

They, whoever *they* were, apparently hadn't found what they were looking for but thought he, Lincoln, knew where to look and wanted to be there when he went looking. Then, again, maybe it was just his imagination working overtime. Right! The only problem was at this moment there was no imagination. Everything was real, up close, and very personal.

After they had pulled the equipment from Lincoln's dorm the day before, they had studied the tapes, which were clean of any evidence that he was involved in, or knew anything about, his father's work. However, the mystery man still wanted Lincoln tailed during summer break for the sake of knowing what he was up to, so Mac had spent the morning attached to the late-model Jeep.

"The boy pulled off the road, like a good driver, to talk on his cell phone about a mile before his street but he's almost home, safe and sound," he said into the headset as he turned onto the freeway. "I'll be in to give you the latest on the mystery-man saga,"

"Good," came the reply over the air. "Bring lunch."

Chandler sat at his desk staring at the computer screen, his eyes burning for lack of moisture. He leaned back and closed them for a second; then he began rapid blinking. His back hurt, his head hurt worse, and he was hungry. He looked at his watch. In about forty-five minutes, Mac would be walking through the door with food in his arms.

He turned his attention back to the screen. A page from John Braden's notebook lit up the right side of the screen; a page showing shorthand symbols filled the left. Both he and Mac had experience in breaking codes, and both had decided this was not a code but an original form of shorthand.

He needed a break from the doodles on the screen, so turned his attention to a case they were trying to wrap up for the people in Los Angeles. He dialed a number on his cell phone and waited.

"Martin Cab," a woman's voice said through the receiver.

"Yes," Chandler replied in a slightly nasal voice, "I'm looking for some information. Cab eight picked up a guy yesterday afternoon at about 3:00 PM in front of the City Bank on Sixth Avenue. The problem is, the guy dropped a money clip from his pocket. I saw it happen, but he got into the cab before I could get his attention."

There was a pause on the other end before the voice asked, "Why did you wait until today to call?"

Think fast, Chandler. "I guess because of the temptation to keep the six hundred bucks in the clip. You might say my conscience got the best of me, so here I am talking to you."

There was another pause before the voice relented and told Chandler to wait while she looked in the log book. "It looks like the cab driver took that fare to the Hyatt Regency Hotel."

"Thank you very much." Chandler hung up the phone just as Mac walked into the office, food in hand.

"Need you to do some hotel hacking," he said, explaining why.

"Just let me limber up my fingers." Mac cracked a smile and then his knuckles before planting himself in front of his computer. "Name of hotel?"

"Hyatt Regency."

While Chandler ate his deli sandwich, Mac hummed away at the keys until he had the hotel records for a three-day span.

"Recognize any names?" Chandler moved in to get a good look at the screen.

"Room number 603," Mac answered, spinning his chair around to face his co-worker. "Want to check it out?"

Twenty minutes later, they pulled in front of the hotel. Mac stayed in the van with the equipment while Chandler walked through the door of the hotel wearing his dark glasses. He started toward the elevator when the man he was looking for passed him in the lobby, his travel bag over his shoulder.

"He's on his way out," Chandler whispered. "Stay with him. I'll search the room."

Room 603 was two doors down from the elevator. The hall was empty with no housekeeping cart in sight. If Mac's latest invention worked, all Chandler needed to do was to slip the card he was holding in his hand through the slot and the door would open. It was that simple, and he was inside.

His eyes scanned the room for anything that would help identify their tag. On the sink was a used glass. That would work. Grabbing a towel from the floor, he wrapped it around the glass, hoping he had a bonus of a few strands of hair as well.

When he turned to leave, he came face-to-face with a woman in a blue dress and a white half apron.

"Going somewhere with the towel?" she asked, her face puckered in an all-knowing expression.

"I need this towel. How much will it cost me?" he pleaded, thinking bribery may be the best approach.

"I'd say fifty dollars ought to do it."

"Excuse me!"

The woman reached out her hand. "You heard right."

Chandler quickly deduced that it would be worth the price if it had what they needed. He reached into his pocket with his free hand and pulled out a handful of bills. Shoving them into her hand, he walked by her and into the hallway.

"Mac, where are you?"

"Our tag is heading to the airport. Find anything?"

"Maybe! See you at the office."

Once inside the office, Chandler unrolled the towel, carefully removed the glass, and dusted for prints. Seeing the results, he decided the bribe was fair. The glass produced uncontaminated fingerprints, and by the time Mac walked through the door, Chandler had identified the tag, alias Monte Larsen, as Michael Layne from Toronto, Canada.

"Now we have a real name, where's our guy headed?"

"Let me take a look." Mac scooted Chandler off the chair, clicked away at the computer and then, placing his hands behind his head and looking rather cocky, commented, "Michael Layne is on flight 1102, Delta, LA Airport, 4:30 PM, Gate 6."

Chandler smiled. "I'll make the call. He's now LA's responsibility."

Five minutes later both men sat at their desks, the feeling of elation having peaked, leaving them restless.

"Back to work," Chandler recommended, motioning Mac to the screen displaying the symbols. "John Braden actually uses several shorthand symbols in his notes. Maybe if we transcribe them, we can begin to make some sense of his original stuff."

"Good idea. Let me scan in the first three pages." Mac opened one of the notebooks and placed it on the scanner. "Before we get started, however, you might be interested in a few new facts concerning our man of mystery."

Chandler turned his chair to face his partner, leaned back into its leather, and waited for the story.

"The limo pulls into a driveway of an expensive house on the west side of the city," Mac began. "The limo driver opens the door for our mystery man and pushes a button to open the garage door. Inside is a dark blue Jaguar, license plate conveniently covered with mud. The mystery man says a few words to the driver and then climbs in the Jaguar and drives off. The driver parks the limo in the garage, closes the door, and walks two blocks to a white Stingray parked in a parking lot, leaving my equipment under the limo and almost useless. The license plate turns out to be a fake."

"And the good news is?"

Mac looked across at Chandler and grinned mischievously. "That is the good news. Want the bad?"

Chandler glared. "Just tell me you didn't do anything illegal."

"Only if you consider it illegal to remove my equipment from a vehicle that's parked in a garage of a house belonging to someone other than the owner of the vehicle?" Mac paused and gave Chandler an innocent look. "Want to know who owns the house?"

"If you don't mind." Chandler began tapping his finger on the desk, a habit he exhibited when Mac tested his endurance with little mysteries.

"The house belongs to an Andrew Hoffman. Have you ever heard of him?"

Chandler shook his head.

"Mr. Hoffman is sixty-nine years old and lives in a posh convalescent home in Quincy. He suffers from Parkinson's disease. The name on the admittance form as next of kin is a son, Leonard Hoffman."

"That's the bad news?"

"You haven't heard the rest of the story."

Chandler twisted in his chair. "Please continue."

Mac pulled a newspaper clipping from his pocket and spread it out on his desk. "A box just happened to get knocked over when I was getting out from under the limo. Its contents landed all over the place." He winked. "Couldn't leave any tell-tale signs, so I cleaned it up. In doing so, I came across this article."

Chandler was breathing over Mac's shoulder now. He could see the date in the top right-hand corner. September 2, 1971. He frowned slightly at a photo of two men, one older, one younger, and an attractive young woman standing between them as they posed for the photographer.

Below the picture, the article read: *Mr. Harriman Hoffman, well known for his achievements in the field of aeronautics, and his daughter, Clarisa, attended the annual "Hope for the Future" fund-raising event sponsored by the Hope Research Foundation. His son, Andrew, pictured at his right, is the founder and CEO of Hope.*

The event was attended by many top celebrities in the field of science even as this year's focus of fund-raising is one of controversy among the great minds of chemistry.

Mr. Hoffman's donation of well over $1,000,000.00, according to internal sources, will be used for brain cell research. The hope of Hope Research Laboratories is to better understand the brain so that, in the future, there can be hope for those who are born with, or develop after birth, abnormalities within the brain itself. . . .

"When can we talk to Mr. Andrew Hoffman?" Chandler asked, glancing at his partner. "We need to know why our mystery man uses Mr. Hoffman's garage for storage."

"I've already made an appointment," Mac grinned. "We can see him Thursday morning, 10:00 AM"

"Could this Leonard be our mystery man?"

"I don't think so." Mac reached into his pocket, removed a small black leather box, and handed it to Chandler. "I also found this with a letter of commendation."

Chandler lifted the lid and looked inside. The Purple Heart was tucked in between red velvet. The name Lieutenant Leonard Hoffman was imprinted on a gold bar beneath the medal.

"You found these things in a box in the garage?"

"In a box? Yes. In the garage? No."

"Tell me, Mac, where did you find them?"

"In the attic."

"And you were in the attic for . . . ?"

"I don't know," Mac replied, shaking his head. "You might call it instinct." He looked at Chandler, his expression somber. "Or you might call it inspiration. All I know is that one minute I was in the garage, and the next minute, I was in the attic looking at this box."

He touched it as he spoke. "It was sitting on an old dresser. It was like a voice in my head telling me where to go and what to do." His face softened. "I can't explain it in simple words because there are none."

Chandler could hear the emotion in Mac's voice. What had happened to his friend was remarkable. Maybe it was more than instinct, more than inspiration. Maybe it was more like a miracle. Chandler wasn't immune to such miracles. They had appeared in his life more than once.

"The medal tells me Leonard is a brave man," Mac was saying. "The letter tells me he is a man of honor. Leonard Hoffman's not our mystery man, but I think he knows who is.

"The house looks like it's been closed up for at least a year, sheets over the furniture, etc. I've got feelers out now trying to locate the whereabouts of our war hero."

When Chandler didn't respond, Mac glanced at him. "Are you with me, man?"

"Do you believe in miracles, Mac?"

"If you mean do I think what happened to me in that house could have been a miracle, I would have to say I believe it could have been." Mac leaned back in his chair, taking a deep breath. "Where do you want to go from here?"

"First the meeting with Mr. Andrew Hoffman. That will tell us where we go from here."

FORENSICS & SCENARIOS

Paul stood over a table where plastic bags, containers, saucers, and cups held everything he had found when he returned to Betsy's property Wednesday afternoon. He had taken with him equipment more suitable for what he needed to do, but had he gathered enough to piece together a story?

He had meticulously covered the ground from the first impressions of tire tracks to the spot they found the blood on the tree limb. He measured distances between the deepest impressions of tire tracks, implying a parking spot, to get the approximate length of each vehicle. He gathered evidence to give him approximate weight.

Using another tool of the future, which he called *the sniffer* because it was almost as sensitive as Dorado's nose but without the bark, he had begun his search for anything laying around inside the wooded area that might be considered out of the ordinary.

A feeling of excitement surged through him as he surveyed the contents of the table, and he felt like a kid at Christmas with many presents to unwrap.

He unfolded a piece of paper and laid it on the table. It

was a makeshift map of the area he searched. Small numbers indicated where each piece of evidence was found. He cross-referenced the numbers with the labels attached to the evidence, making sure everything matched up.

Logging it all came next. He sat at the computer and began typing.

Two cigarette butts (2 & 5)

One comb (8)

One lighter (3)

One Cuban cigar wrapper (1)

One half-smoked Cuban cigar (6)

Two gun cartridges (10)

Three gum wrappers (4, 7, 9)

Casts had been made of three different shoe prints and a boot print. Those were logged and labeled. When that was done, Paul added the following information:

Limo (14–16 months ago)

Van (12–14 months ago)

Van (3 days to 1 week ago)

Paul was still waiting for the lab results to finalize his suspicions on the time lapse, but he had done extensive legwork as far as identifying the types of vehicles. These two matched the length and weight measurements, as well as the track impressions.

He scrolled up to the previous page and read over the lab results on the strand of hair, two pens, and partial print that had already gone through testing. The hair belonged to Betsy, and the only fingerprints on the two pens were John's.

The partial print was a camouflage. It wasn't the first time he'd seen something like this and should have been more suspicious considering where he found it. When working with sensitive equipment where touch is a necessary tool, the person wearing gloves coats the finger to be exposed with clear polish then makes a tear, allowing them a more sensitive grip. This creates a fingerprint camouflage.

Making sure everything was safely logged, Paul typed the

necessary keys to save the information to a disk only. When he was satisfied everything was in order, he exited the program, removed the disk, tucked it in his shirt pocket, and deleted the information from the hard drive.

"I brought you something from the deli," Dawn said as she walked through the door and set a take-out sack on his desk. She reached up and gave him a kiss. "Sit down and eat, Paul. The evidence isn't going anywhere, and you need a break."

"It's all there," he sighed as he slumped into his chair, twisting a pencil between his fingers. "We just have to put it together." He glanced up at her. "Anything on the watch?"

"The markings show that someone removed the two links with a small knife blade. There are scrapings on the face of the watch, indicating that a rock of some kind was used to break the glass. The only prints are John's."

"Interesting," Paul mused, his right brow arched and his eyes glassed over, indicating he was in deep concentration.

She couldn't help but admire the man with the glassy eyes. His blond, unruly hair contradicted the precision of his genius. He lived because she made sure there was food in front of him; his appearance was neat because she laid out his clothes each morning. He was honest, forthright, forgetful, good looking in an intellectual way, and assertive. He knew no fear, was at his best when challenged, and could hold his own in any debate. She couldn't ask for a better husband.

It was Saturday, their one day off. They had been in the lab since 6:00 AM It was now going on 2:00 PM Neither of them had eaten since early evening the night before.

"Eat," she scowled.

"Excuse me?" Paul's brow dropped back into place.

"Eat!"

Paul looked down at the chicken salad and bread sticks, his brain registering them for the first time. In turn, the brain sent a reminder to his stomach of how important food was to his existence.

Dawn handed him a fork then sat across from him, chewing

on her salad for a minute before proposing a scenario. "John knows someone is after him," she said, pointing her fork in Paul's direction. "He takes off his watch, quickly removes two links, smashes the glass of the face with a rock and then buries it."

"Why would John remove his watch when someone was about to kill him?" Paul questioned, wiping his mouth with his napkin. "Why take the time to remove two links?"

"First, we have to assume there was something hidden inside the links." Dawn stood and started pacing. "Say they knew that John had whatever it was they wanted hidden somewhere, something small enough to fit inside the link of a watch. If they'd found the watch on him, they would have torn it apart, looking for whatever it was they were looking for." She stopped pacing and turned her attention to the watch sitting on the counter. Picking it up, she took a small pointed screwdriver and pried open one of the links. There was nothing there but dirt and signs of wear.

"I doubt you'll find anything," Paul warned her as he watched her separate the links.

"Why?" Dawn stopped and asked him. "What's your theory?"

"Let's say they knew where to look and that's why the missing links. Maybe they got what they were looking for, after all."

"Why spy on Betsy then? Why not just take what they found and disappear? No, I think they're still looking."

"Okay, let's start over again. John has what they want in the watch. He knows they're going to kill him anyway. He hides long enough to remove the watch and take out the links that contain whatever it is. Maybe he smashes the face to stop the date and the time for some reason."

"Because he wants someone in the future to know when he was killed?"

"Good thought!" Paul's eyebrow shot back up, and he squinted his eyes to envision the crime.

"Why does he bury the watch then?"

"And where are the two missing links?"

They look at each other. "That part of the mystery is yet to be uncovered, my dear Watson," groaned Dawn.

Paul looked at his wife. "Maybe he didn't bury the watch. Maybe one of those little rodents living in the forest of trees buried the watch."

"Possible but not probable," Dawn felt weary and impatient. This was all so personal. "Tell me that we're making some progress here," she begged, her face revealing the apprehension she felt inside.

Paul walked over to her and placed his hand on her back. Pulling her close to him, he kissed her forehead. "We've only just begun to fight," he soothed her. "There are clues and there are answers sitting in front of us. They'll show themselves soon, I promise."

She looked up at him and smiled. "Thank you. I needed that."

As quick as the smile appeared, it was gone, a frown in its place. "Wait a minute," she said, her voice filled with intensity. "Let me give you another scenario." She stepped back and tapped his chest with her finger. "In his hurry to remove the links, John hits the watch against a rock and doesn't have time to get it back together, so he hurries and buries it. That way they know nothing about the watch or the links. They kill him and check his body, and when they find nothing, they tag Betsy for information."

"Okay, that sounds more plausible than the rodent wearing a Timex," Paul admitted. "However, one question still remains. Where are the missing links?"

"Would he give them the links, hoping that would save his life?" Dawn shook her head and answered her own question. "We know he wouldn't do that. Whatever he was hiding was worth more than his life."

"There's still the chance they took the links with them, thinking they had what they wanted only to find out, after they killed him, he had tricked them." Paul ran his fingers through his hair and rolled his head from side to side in an attempt to relieve the stiffness caused from extensive lab work. "Maybe that's why they turned their attention to Betsy. When she could give them nothing, they pulled the equipment and are now focusing their concentration elsewhere. I can't help but wonder where."

Dawn leaned against the desk, her arms folded, her eyes focused on the table of evidence. "The *sniffer* was unable to locate the links anywhere in the area around the crime scene, correct?"

"Correct."

Paul sat on the desk, next to her. Neither one said a word, each in a world of their own, theorizing, analyzing, and guessing.

After several minutes, Dawn closed her eyes to visualize internally. That was when a theory they hadn't thought of came to her. "Unless . . ." she said, almost to herself, letting the word fade into silence before it reached Paul's ears.

⁂

Elmira looked at her watch. Everything should be ready right on schedule if everyone arrived on schedule. She was looking forward to seeing her grandson. He reminded her of Benjamin in the way he stood tall and confident. He reminded her of John in his solid good looks and his unpretentious temperament. He had the best of both men in him. He would prove to be their strength through this ordeal, she had no doubt.

She thought of Benjamin and how badly he wanted a son to take his place when the time came. Though he loved his two daughters and spoiled them as any loving father would, his disappointment was apparent when they found they couldn't have more children. When Lincoln was born, Benjamin all but adopted the boy, teaching him everything he knew to inspire him in carrying on the cause of freedom. Little did Benjamin know it would be his daughter who would step into his shoes.

The doorbell gave two quick rings, telling her that her grandson was at the door. She didn't need to go to the door; it was already open.

"Hello, Grandmother," Lincoln called out as he walked toward her. Though there was only five inches difference in their heights, he seemed to tower over her with his broad shoulders. She was tall and thin. He was tall and covered in muscle, which he wrapped around her shoulders, gently hugging her as if she was made of glass.

"Well, hello to you, Lincoln," she grinned, wrapping her arms around him and hugging him back as if he were made of muscle. "I see you brought your mother with you. Now I'll have to set another place at the table."

Betsy scoffed at her mother's remark and held the door open to her sister and brother-in-law. Dorado came bounding in behind them. "I just hope you have a place set for the golden boy."

Dawn walked in the house and over to Lincoln without breaking her stride. She reached up, kissed his cheek, and placed her hands on each side of his face. Looking directly into his eyes, she sighed dramatically. "You don't know how glad I am that you're home. Your mother is not easy to look after."

Lincoln laughed and gave her an affectionate hug. "I'm so happy to see you, too, Aunt Dawn."

Lincoln clasped his uncle in an embrace and whispered, "I need to talk to you."

"Dinner is ready," Elmira's caterer announced, interrupting any further conversation.

"It looks and smells wonderful, Gloria," Lincoln said, giving her a kiss on the cheek.

"Thank you, Linc," she replied, touching his arm. "It's so good to see you. How's college life?"

"Barbaric."

"I can see that." Gloria lifted her glasses from around her neck and put them to her eyes for a closer look. Shaking her head, she gave a sigh and looked at Betsy. "He's a handsome child, Betsy. Enjoy him while you can before some smart young woman snatches him away." She patted his shoulder and excused herself from the room, saying, "There will be two of my assistants here in an hour to do kitchen duty. Have a nice evening."

The first hour passed quickly with good food and good conversation, everyone avoiding the subject that haunted their minds, saving it until later. During the second hour, while the caterers finished their cleanup work, the family moved their conversation to the veranda that spread itself the length of Elmira's house. The view beyond was magnetic and soothing, a dramatic contrast to what they had to discuss.

As they watched the sun begin its descent, Lincoln told his family about the colorful, bejeweled dissenter he met on campus the day before. "I counted twelve rings," he scoffed. "I didn't even attempt to number the tattoos; they covered his upper arms and neck. What was interesting is that the rings, the tattoos, and his invitation to a flag burning sent a message that wasn't entirely correct. I think he's just trying to find a place to fit in. He seemed moved when I shared Grandmother's wisdom with him. I swear I saw a tear as he turned and walked away, and I have to admit it left an impression on me."

"Reminds me of something Benjamin told me one day after we had given a homeless man a ride," Elmira responded. "I was fearful, but Benjamin was bold. He said that truth is in the eyes. Until you look into another man's eyes and see his truth, he reminded me, you should not judge him. After that I felt at peace with his decision."

Paul agreed. "I hope the young man finds his way."

Dorado, who had been lying on the soft rug in front of the screen door, stood and began the ritual of making everyone aware he needed to go out.

"Come, nephew," Paul said, opening the door for the

waiting dog. "Let's take this fellow out for a walk."

Once they were out of ear shot, Paul turned to Lincoln and said, "Tell me what's on your mind, dear boy."

"Mom told me all that's happened and what you're doing for her. I can't tell you how much I appreciate that."

"It's simply all part of what families do for each other."

Lincoln took a deep breath and then released it before continuing. "How far are you prepared to go for family?"

"As far as we need to, without doubt."

"That's all I need to know because someone's following me."

Paul's face was grim as he studied Lincoln's face. "You sure?" he asked.

"Have you ever had a feeling that directed you to look in a certain direction or do a certain thing and you don't know why until you've done it?" Lincoln scrunched his face. "Have I explained that in the way that gives it some credibility?"

"Oh, I think so, and yes, I have. Let's sit over here and talk." Paul pointed to a thick old tree trunk. Resting his back against the gnarled bark, he listened as Lincoln told him about the van and the impressions that came over him.

"I don't know if I should leave in order to protect Mom because I'm the target of surveillance, or if I'm being followed because of Dad, which now involves Mom, and I should stay here to protect her." Lincoln sat down on the grass, brought his knees to his chest, rested his arms on them, and looked at his uncle. "Am I even making any sense?"

"More than you think. May I suggest, for now, that you stay here? Our numbers may be small, but our ability to outwit the enemy, I think, is far greater than they will anticipate."

"But who is the enemy?"

"Good question," Paul admitted. "Let me fill you in on what we've found so far that may lead us to an answer." Paul began to describe the evidence he had discovered while Lincoln listened with interest.

"We're running tests on the cigarette butts and cigar,

hoping to lift some prints and DNA off them. Any prints on the lighter were all but washed away by the rains we had a few weeks ago, but we know it's an expensive lighter, the kind you buy at one of those one-of-a-kind, exclusive, untraceable, and out-of-the-way establishments which retains no receipts, better known as the black market."

Paul barely took time to breath. "The gum wrappers were soaked, but who knows, we could still find something there. The partials we picked up at the house were camouflaged which, in itself, tells us something.

"I know it doesn't sound like much, but the clues are there. We just need to reach deep enough to find them. Sooner or later, we'll have our story."

Even in the dim light of the sunset, Lincoln could see the excitement in his uncle's eyes. "You're actually enjoying this, aren't you?"

"This is what I do. This is my expertise. How can I not be enthralled when I'm personally involved in this one? Look at our strength, Lincoln. Look at what's available to us in searching for the truth."

Lincoln had to admit his uncle was right. If they worked together they just might find answers.

"Let's find that smart dog of your mother's and return to the veranda. We need to get a plan in place." Paul watched as Lincoln called to Dorado, knowing whoever murdered John was now focusing in on his son.

"There you are," Elmira said as the two men opened the screen, letting the golden boy enter first. "Have you had enough of the night air, Dorado?" She motioned to him. "Come, sit by me."

Dorado didn't have to be coaxed. He had been all but ignored the whole evening and was ready for some attention.

"I was explaining to Dawn," Betsy said, once the men were seated, "that I spent a lot of time praying I would recall the words John said to me that morning he died. It took some time, but when I was ready and my knees were sore with determination, the words came to me. '*Tell Lincoln, what they're after will be with me, wherever I am.*' That's when I knew Lincoln was part of John's other world. It frightened me at first then excited me and gave me comfort, knowing I wasn't alone in all of this."

"Tell Lincoln what they're after will be with me, wherever I am," Paul repeated, his brow raised in concentration. "Will be with me, where . . ." He stopped in mid-sentence, the second eyebrow shot up, and he turned to Dawn, their eyes locking. "I believe you had it figured out before we left the lab," he said to her.

"It was the only possible conclusion," she nodded.

"I'm right with you, darlin'," he replied.

"What?" Lincoln demanded, looking from Dawn to Paul and then back again.

"We were discussing scenarios in the lab today," Dawn explained. "None of which could answer the question of the missing links. It wasn't until we were ready to leave that an idea surfaced. What your mother just said confirms my suspicion." Dawn walked over to her sister and knelt beside her, putting her hand on Betsy's.

"Betsy," she said gently, "we think that John may have swallowed the two links before he died so those who were about to kill him would not find them. Whatever is inside the links must be what they were looking for."

Betsy frowned at her sister but what Dawn said was true. There was no other answer.

"It only makes sense," Paul said. "And if we figured it out, the enemy cannot be far behind."

"What you're telling me is that we need to exhume John's body?"

"Yes."

"And those who are after whatever is most likely inside the links will come to the same conclusion even if they didn't know John was wearing a watch? Isn't that why he buried the watch: so they wouldn't know he was wearing one?

"Perhaps he knew there was a possibility the watch would eventually be found, and he couldn't take the chance." Betsy looked at her mother. "I don't want to have his body exhumed, Mother. Tell me if you think whoever's behind this may someday figure it out."

Elmira felt the chill of Betsy's hands when she wrapped them in her own. "I can't say they will or they won't. You have to think this one out for yourself, Babe. It is your decision."

Betsy thought for a minute. "No," she finally said, turning to her son. "It is your decision, Lincoln. The message he left was for you."

"Before we make a final decision on opening Dad's casket, I have another question." Lincoln stood. "Why did Dad wear the watch in the first place, if he thought he was walking into an ambush?"

There was a veil of silence in the room. No one had considered that question.

"Was it possible John hadn't expected to be killed?" Paul questioned, his face revealing his shock.

"Or perhaps he was going to meet someone to give them what was inside the watch." Elmira exchanged looks with her son-in-law.

"Okay." Dawn picked up the pace. "Let's say he was going to meet someone and that someone turned traitor, sending the enemy instead."

"Or failed to show because he was no longer alive himself," Betsy interceded.

"I think the answers are in the notebooks and the links. We need to know what they contain." Lincoln was adamant. "Maybe then we'll have some answers."

"Exhuming the body might bring about one more problem, however," Paul said, thinking of the knowledge he shared with Lincoln. "If they—and I wish I knew who in the heck they are—are still watching and we exhume the body, we're telling them we know something."

"We'll find a way," Dawn assured him.

❧❧❧❧

Betsy set the books on the kitchen table. Lincoln filled two glasses with lemonade, pulled two candy bars from the cupboard, and sat down next to her.

"Are you sure you want to start this tonight?" he asked. "It's after 9:00."

"I'm sure," Betsy replied, opening the first notebook. "I've waited long enough."

The date on the first page dated back three years. John was on an overseas assignment covering an election. His shorthand detailed interviews with dignitaries as well as people on the street. His appointment schedule listed when and who he talked with each day. At the end of the book, he jotted down his thoughts and opinions, some of which were better left untouched with translation.

Book two dated back two and a half years while he was in Germany. It was filled with much of the same bits and pieces as the first book.

In book three, dated six months later, John was covering a big company takeover. After reading through the pages, Lincoln and Betsy decided they should transcribe everything they thought might help them find answers. Betsy placed a check mark at the beginning of each idiom as Lincoln dictated.

There's something sinister going on here, something I can feel more than see. I'll talk it over with 'G' tomorrow.

Talked with 'G.' He agreed.

Suspect they're researching ideas beyond something man shouldn't even attempt.

Discovered the lab, quite by accident. Lucky no one saw me.

Mr. Bane's secretary doesn't work midnights. Lucky for me. I was able to search the files without interruption. Found some interesting documents.

I've decided that what they think to be a good thing could be dangerous stuff.

Lincoln reached for book one and flipped through the

pages until he found what he was looking for and transcribed it. When he finished, he handed it to his mother to read.

Interesting new technology is being discussed by the government. They claim it will change the prisons of the future.

"Book two, page eight, I believe," Betsy said, handing book two to her son. He turned to page eight. It read:

Research has been moved up a notch. Much talk about a new idea to bring crime to an end. They claim to be making great progress.

He quickly transcribed the words on paper before they moved on. The last pages of notebook four were written a month later.

Research, I believe, is meant for the good and betterment of man, but what happens when someone turns what is good to bad?

I have no proof yet, I only suspect. What I suspect is frightening, but I can't do anything to stop the research until I find what I'm looking for.

How many companies in how many countries, I wonder, or is it, in fact, just one company in several countries doing this research? (scary thought)

'G' has found some information that will help in our investigation. Meet with him tonight.

Need proof!!!

"I can only guess that 'G' was the contact man or the partner," Betsy concluded. "If he was, where is he now?"

Lincoln rubbed his eyes and looked at the clock. It was almost midnight, and they still had two books to transcribe. Knowing his mother wouldn't quit until she had read the last book, he unwrapped his candy bar and took a big bite.

Betsy hardly seemed to notice Lincoln's fatigue, or hers, for that matter. She took the candy bar he unwrapped for her and opened the next book, where 'G' became a real name.

Garrett will fly back today with the documents he has obtained. There are some pretty convincing arguments now that we've found the proof we need. I'll give him what I have when we meet, and he'll take it on to those who can stop this crazy research. Garret didn't come to the place where we were to meet today. I'll watch for him tomorrow.

Lincoln was now wide awake. He looked over at his mother whose eyes were clouded with tears. He touched her hand. "It's going to be okay, Mom," he promised her, in the attempt to convince himself as well. "Do you want to save the rest until tomorrow?"

Betsy shook her head. Holding tight to the pencil in her hand, she waited for him to read. Lincoln continued.

They killed Dr. Patero, but not before he gave me the disk.

What I have is dangerous.

I'll bury what I found in the trees until I find someone I can trust to take it.

They'll search until they find out I'm the one who has what they want, but the box is safe. There are too many trees for them.

I contacted Mr. Lear this morning.

Someone is following me.

Is Lear the mole?

The map.

The last date in the notebook was just one week before John's death. There was a span of two and a half years from book one through the book they had just finished. One more book and then maybe they could begin to piece together the clues.

Betsy closed her eyes for a moment and released a sigh from deep within her. Letting her shoulders relax, she fluttered her eyelids, hoping to bring moisture to the dryness of her eyes. "Tomorrow's Sunday," she muttered. "Do you think God will mind if we work on the last book during the Sabbath?"

"It's already the Sabbath," Lincoln said softly, "but I think He'll understand." He slipped his arm around her shoulders and lifted her from the chair. "It's going to take a little time, we both know that, but we have Grandmother, Dawn, and Paul to help. I can't think of a brighter team."

"You forget Dorado," Betsy said in all seriousness, as she gathered the notebooks together and slipped them into a cloth shoulder bag, along with the pages of transcript. "I think he'll prove to be a vital member of this team." She smiled at her son

and kissed him on the cheek. "I'm sorry I've kept you up so
late. You look as if you need some serious sleep."

"I always look like this at two o'clock in the morning.
What time's church?"

"Not until eleven. Sleep tight."

"You too."

Lincoln watched as his mother disappeared into her room
and prayed they could get through this bizarre mystery without
anyone else losing their life. Betsy's strong will would insist
that nothing stop her from seeing it through to the end, he
knew that. But he felt the same way. Nothing would stop him
from finding his father's murderer.

It was after nine Sunday morning when Lincoln walked
into the kitchen to find his mother sitting at the table, her eyes
transfixed on the small book in front of her.

"I picked up the wrong notebook last night," she said,
acknowledging him without looking up. "This is actually the
fifth book. Listen."

*I know Dr. Patero thinks what he's doing is good for mankind, but
I can't help but feel there's something wrong here, something sinister.
My investigation uncovered the purpose of his research, and I have to
ask myself if he fully understands the consequences of his genius, or is
he so focused on the project that he's blinded to its potential?*

*If his research is successful, he will have discovered a formula that
will alter the criminal mind, eliminating the need for prisons, or so it
states in his contract. What the contract fails to mention, however,
is that if he is successful he will have created a monster: chemical
mind control. Why is it that a man with that much genius fails to
comprehend the danger of his creation? Does he also strive for power
in the acknowledgement of such a discovery, or is he totally naïve?
Perhaps it's a little of both.*

Betsy stopped reading and looked at her son. "There's more,
but I'll let you read it for yourself while I fix breakfast."

Lincoln could see the circles under his mother's eyes had
darkened since he'd left her at two in the morning. "How long
have you been up?" he asked.

Betsy placed a glass of orange juice in front of him. "I didn't check the clock," she muttered, suppressing a yawn. "Would you like hot cakes or waffles?"

"A bowl of cold cereal will be fine."

Betsy nodded, and Lincoln flipped to the next page, picked up the pencil, and began writing in longhand what he was reading in shorthand. The more he read, however, the less he wrote.

"This is incredible," he said at last, running his fingers across his forehead. "Listen!"

It's been two days since I talked with Dr. Patero. Today I heard rumors that there's more to this operation. I borrowed an executive pass from one of the security guards while he was busy talking on the phone to someone who obviously had the wrong number. I like it when things go as scheduled.

Pretending to know a lot more than I do, I asked the head engineer to show me the layout of the latest chip in their design lab. I asked the right questions, and he gave the correct answers. Answers that, when discussing a simple chip, were innocent, but when combined with the potential of Dr Patero's work left me with a hollow sensation in the pit of my stomach.

I found what I came here to find. It's time to leave before anyone becomes suspicious.

Lincoln looked up at his mother. She was moving toward him, a bowl of his favorite cereal in her hand.

"It's your turn to pray," she said, reaching down and taking the book from him. "We'll finish this after breakfast."

Prayer was the one thing that had always been constant in his life. He learned at an early age that prayer brought strength to endure as well as strength to confront. His mother was simply reminding him that prayer would be their ally.

In his prayer, Lincoln asked for help as they began to piece together the puzzle laid out before them. He prayed that they would be guided and protected as they sought to find the truth.

After their church meetings, Elmira suggested that she

bring the leftovers over from the night before and invite Dawn and Paul to spend the day with them.

"Perhaps we need to share our concerns with God as a family. We each must be guided in our own field of expertise to bring about the results needed to solve this strange and infuriating mystery," she observed. "Its web has wrapped itself around each of our lives because it attached itself to the life of one of us. If we include Him in our work, we'll not fail in our search."

Once again Elmira Redding was right. By the end of the day, the family had put together the beginning of a remarkable story.

seven

THE BREAKTHROUGH

Three men sat in the darkest corner of an exclusive nightclub with only a hint of light from the stage to silhouette them in the shadows. Three empty glasses cluttered the small table that separated them.

"We're missing something here," one of the men said. His voice, carrying a slight accent, was barely audible. "Walk me through that morning and tell me why you had to kill the guy before you got what we needed."

"Look," the man sitting directly across the table replied, agitation apparent in his voice. "I watched him through the field glasses; he was suspicious the minute he walked out of his house. He didn't start his run immediately like every other morning that week, he just stood there looking around him and checking his watch. When he finally started down the path, he was all too cautious."

"Yeah," the man sitting next to him interrupted. "I waited where you told me to wait, and when I saw him, he'd already seen me. It didn't take him long to make out I wasn't the guy he was supposed to meet, and he took off. Mitch and me, we closed in on him. We knew the only way to get anything out of him was to put the pressure on. We found him crouched behind a bush. He came at us swingin' a tree branch. Caught me in the chest, knockin' me to the ground, but Mitch grabbed him before he could get me again."

Mitch took over the conversation. "Hal pulled his gun while I subdued the guy. Once we had him under control, we asked the questions, but he wasn't giving any answers. When Hal told him we'd just go get his wife and bring her there, he about tore my arm off to get to Hal. I fell backwards, and by the time I was on my feet again, they were fighting over the gun, shooting bullets into the air. Luckily it had a silencer."

"He was a fightin' man," Hal broke in. "Mean and tough and mad, but killing him was an accident. Mitch only hit him hard enough to dull his senses. Can't figure out why he died."

"Did you ever stop to think that maybe he assisted in his own death to prevent you from ever finding what he seems to have so successfully hidden?"

"What do you mean?" Mitch asked, straightening himself in his chair.

"What I mean is, could he have had a suicide pill between his teeth?"

There was silence for several seconds while the two men considered what had been implied; then the man continued. "You revealed something in your conversation a minute ago, Mitch. Something you failed to mention before."

"Yeah, what's that?"

"You said he kept looking at his watch."

"That's right, so?"

"So, where's the watch?"

Hal and Mitch looked at each other and then at the man on the other side of the table. "We searched him good. There wasn't any watch on him," Hal stammered.

"Something tells me we need that watch." He stood. "Find the watch. Don't come back without it." He turned and walked away.

The two still sitting at the table looked at each other.

"Why didn't we think of that?" Mitch said finally.

"'Cause at the time we had other things to worry about, like the guy dying before we got the stuff." Hal motioned to the waitress for two more drinks, and they began to plot their next visit to the Braden property.

"Okay, let's say he buried it." Mitch touched the rim of his glass with his finger. "That's why he was hiding in the brush." Finishing off the last of his drink, he grabbed his jacket from the back of the chair. "Come on, Hal, we've got work to do."

"I've been thinkin'," Hal said as they drove away from the nightclub. "That guy would have killed both of us with his bare hands before he'd kill himself. If you hadn't got him hard with that piece of wood, it woulda been us lyin' there that day, blood runnin' outta us instead of him."

"What are you saying?"

"I saw his eyes. They weren't the eyes of a man ready to chew up a suicide pill. He had the hold on me, Mitch. He had the gun. He had the muscle. That's what I'm sayin'."

"And what I'm saying," Mitch growled, "is that no one but you and me will ever know how hard I hit him, you understand?"

"Who do you think I'm gonna tell?" Hal looked at his partner, anger apparent in his voice.

"I'm talking for both of us Hal, not just you, okay?"

Hal nodded. "He was still breathin' when we left."

"I know," Mitch replied.

"Do you think we could've gotten something outta him if we'd forced him?"

"He was unconscious, Hal. He was bleeding heavily. I bet he was dead before we even got to the car."

It was close to midnight when Mitch switched off the headlights and turned onto the little patch of road they were familiar with. Parking next to the grove of trees, they grabbed their flashlights but relied on the light of the half-moon to direct them to the path that would lead them to the watch. However, the moon's rays were quickly lost in the shadows of the trees. They turned on their flashlights to direct them, confident their movements would go undetected.

In a house not far away, a dog suddenly became alert. A low growl escaped his throat as he moved toward the veranda door, waking Betsy with his noise.

"What is it, boy?" she whispered to him.

Dorado pranced and then pressed his nose against the door. He turned to her, giving a soft warning bark, and turned back to the door.

Lincoln, hearing the dog, was immediately standing in the doorway of his mother's bedroom, his eyes fixed on Dorado.

"Someone's out there," he whispered. He walked to the dog and knelt beside him. "Wait a minute, golden boy. Let me get dressed; then we'll go hunting."

Dorado acknowledged Lincoln's comment with a quiet growl. Putting his back legs beneath him, he sat protectively against the veranda door, his front legs prancing in anticipation of the adventure.

He didn't have to wait long. Lincoln was back in less than three minutes. In his hand, he carried a rifle.

Betsy wasn't about to let her son go outside alone. She was ready and waiting for him when he returned, a small handgun by her side. "You'll not go without me," she told him when he attempted to persuade her to stay in the house, and he knew she meant it.

Lincoln opened the door. "You stay behind me then, close behind, okay?"

She nodded giving the dog his lead. "Let's see what's out there, Dorado," she said, her voice no more than a whisper.

The dog was out and on the move even before she could finish her request, following his nose. He led the way until they saw the glow from what appeared to be two flashlights flickering through the trees.

Lincoln placed his hand on Dorado's nose, ordering him to be silent as the three of them inched their way closer. When they were within twenty-five yards of the lights, they could see two figures. Their heads were down, their flashlights searching the ground in front of them. He turned to his mother silently begging her to stay back while he continued on.

Knowing it would be safer for her son, Betsy positioned herself behind a small tree, keeping Dorado by her side, and watched him move toward the two figures.

Lincoln knew the path well and moved quickly. He was less than twenty feet away from the two men when he heard their voices echo softly against the trees. Hiding in the darkness, listening to them talk about the morning they killed his father, Lincoln could do nothing but remain concealed.

"It's gotta be somewhere around here, Mitch." Hal's voice was quiet and harsh. "This is where he jumped me."

"Looks like someone's already been here," Mitch groaned. "There's footprints and paw prints all over." He followed the beam of his flashlight. "And a hole in the ground." He cursed, raising his flashlight to reveal Hal's face in its beam. "That woman and her dog already found it."

"Get that light outta my face, man, and let's get outta here. We got some thinkin' to do before we talk to the boss." Hal turned and headed back the way they came. Mitch followed, still cursing beneath his breath.

Lincoln almost cursed himself, thinking of the mistake he made by not covering the hole and the prints. Any amateur detective would have thought of it. Why hadn't he?

His one consolation was that he had seen the face of one of the men who killed his father and knew the first name of the other.

Quickly he made his way back to where his mother and Dorado were waiting. "They were looking for the watch," he explained, "but found your prints instead. I'm sorry; I should have made sure everything was cleaned up."

"Don't blame yourself, Lincoln. How could you know that someone would come searching?"

Lincoln looked at his mother. She didn't seem frightened by the fact her life was in danger. He could almost see the fire in her eyes by the determination in her voice.

Taking his mother's arm, Lincoln walked Betsy back to the house, keeping an eye out for headlights along the main road. Once she was safely inside the house, he turned to Dorado. "Come on, golden boy," he said, motioning for the smartest member of the team to follow him. "Let's you and I keep watch for awhile."

Lincoln found his mother in his father's office working on her article for the newspaper. "I thought you'd sleep in this morning," he said, surprised how much more rested she looked than he felt. The night of vigilance had left him emotionally and physically exhausted. "Can you explain why you look like an angel while the devil dances inside my head?"

Betsy looked up from her work, and her eyes filled with sympathy. "Because I had two brave warriors defending my home while I slept. I suppose the rest of the night was uneventful."

"Fortunately, yes," Lincoln muttered. "But I don't think we've seen the last of them."

"Neither do I." Betsy stood and touched her son's cheek. "But for now, let me prepare your breakfast, give you something for the pain in your head and then send you to bed. You look awful."

"Thanks." He tried to smile, but it only made the pounding in his head more acute. "I didn't realize a smile took so many muscles," he sighed and carefully lowered himself onto the soft cushions of the sofa.

Within five minutes, Betsy was back with a cup of herbal tea, buttered toast, and Elmira's famous headache-relief potion, all on a tray. "Lincoln," she said, gently shaking the young man with ruffled hair and wrinkled clothes, who was already asleep. "You need to drink this." She handed him a small glass of dark liquid.

"Do I have to?" He almost gagged in his response.

"Once your headache is introduced to your grandmother's remedy, the pain will subside. It will be worth it, I promise."

Lincoln nodded, took a bite of toast, chewing it slowly, and sipped the tea in preparation for the inevitable. Reluctantly, he lifted the small glass to his mouth and, while holding his nose, poured the smelly liquid down his throat. "Ugh!" he shuddered, as the taste reached his nostrils with its unpleasant aroma. "Why is it that the things that are so good for you taste so bad?"

"As your grandmother would say, 'It wouldn't taste so bad if you hadn't tasted anything good.' Now eat the rest of your toast to get rid of its flavor."

As the headache subsided, Lincoln's eyes closed in relief. When he awoke three hours later, he found himself wrapped in a blanket, his headache completely gone. The aftertaste of Elmira's potion still lingered, however, and he exchanged his comfortable makeshift bed for his toothbrush and a shower.

Once he made himself presentable, he went in search of his mother. Walking by her bedroom, he spotted her on the veranda leaning against a pillar. "Good morning," he yawned as he walked out and stood by her side.

"Evidently you haven't looked at your watch yet," she sighed and looked into his bloodshot eyes. "Is the headache a thing of the past?"

"It is, but when the pain left, it forgot to take the nasty taste in my mouth with it." Lincoln glanced at his watch and was surprised to see it was after one in the afternoon.

Betsy chuckled at her son. How she loved him. How safe she felt with him beside her. "I was standing here thinking about last night," she said quietly, "and I tried to imagine myself in a position where I would have to shoot another human being in order to save my own life or the life of someone I loved." She turned her face up to look into Lincoln's face. "I found, in my soul searching, I wouldn't hesitate to use my gun in the defense of my family. Is that wrong of me?"

"No! Actually I'm thankful you feel that way." Lincoln rested his cheek against the top of his mother's head. "Last night I realized that instead of recoiling under all of this, you've become defiant and bold. I am in awe."

"As I am of you." Betsy allowed the tension of her body to be absorbed by the warmth of her son's arm, and together they watched Dorado chase a butterfly, each thankful for the other and for the golden retriever busy at play, and neither was ready to disrupt their afternoon by discussing the events of the previous night. There was plenty of time for that later.

"Did you get your article finished?" Lincoln asked.

"I only had to fine tune it," Betsy replied. "I think I'll have you take it to your grandmother for any editing later this afternoon. She needs some quality time with you. Are you hungry?"

The growling in Lincoln's stomach answered for him. Betsy took his hand and led him to the kitchen, where sandwiches and salads were waiting. While they ate, their conversation turned to the inevitable. Their concern was not only the invasion of their private lives but possibly that of Elmira's as well.

The information they were able to pull together had to be examined and researched. They had to know what it was they were looking for and what they were up against. For now that was Dawn and Paul's department. The rest of them had to go on as if their lives were normal, knowing their lives would never be normal again.

The phone rang, and Betsy lifted the receiver to her ear.

"I was just wondering," Elmira's cheerful voice came through, "if Lincoln would like some lemon meringue pie? I have a fresh one on my counter this very minute."

"I was just getting ready to send him to you." Betsy smiled at her son as she spoke to her mother. "I need you to read my column before I take it to the office."

"That would be lovely, Babe. Send it over with my grandson."

"Lemon pie is waiting for you." Betsy watched Lincoln's eyes light up as she relayed the message from his grandmother.

"Then I won't dally." He rose dramatically from the chair, reached for the folder containing the column, bid his mother farewell, and walked toward the door.

"Dorado," he called to the dog, "want to go for a walk?"

Usually eager for the opportunity, Dorado held back, unwilling to leave Betsy alone. He took his place beside her, standing as sentinel, and barked his refusal to leave her side.

"He's an incredible dog," Lincoln marveled.

"I know," replied Betsy.

The walk through the woods to Grandmother's house had always been refreshing until today. The memory of the night before was too poignant in Lincoln's mind, and he found himself in the area where the two men stood the night before. There was not much to see. A few generic shoe prints dotting the scene and their voices echoing in his head. It chilled him that they knew exactly where to return to after all this time.

Elmira watched as her grandson walked out of the trees and onto her veranda. She greeted him with a kiss on the cheek. He returned her affection with a gentle hug.

"The lemon pie is waiting," she said with a smile.

"And Mother's column is ready for your inspection," he chuckled.

Lincoln ate lemon pie and watched Elmira as she read the column. She would nod and give a sound of approval every now and again, but other than that she was silent in her reading. When she finished, she set the pages on the table and tapped her fingers against the paper. "She did it again. It's perfect." She glanced at Lincoln. "Have you read it yet?"

"No," he replied between bites. "You're the only one who gets to peruse."

Elmira slid the typed pages in front of him, picked up her fork, and cut into her pie. "Read it." She said.

Lincoln set his fork down and, skipping the percentages of the e-mail poll, began to read.

Today, dear readers, we are going to discuss the flag, Francis Scott Key, and the national anthem. We'll travel back to the year 1812. Major George Armistead, the Commander of Fort McHenry (the fort that guarded the entrance to Baltimore harbor), was preparing for the British warships heading his way. His desire was to have a flag that would identify his position, one that would be visible to the enemy from a distance. Perhaps the thoughts of intimidation even entered his mind as he fathomed a flag measuring 30 feet by 40 feet.

For several weeks, Mary Young Pickersgill and her thirteen-year-old daughter, Caroline, cut, measured, and sewed together a flag of that dimension. The rooms of the Pickersgill house were not large enough to spread the material out for sewing so the floor of Claggett's brewery was used instead.

The article went on to describe the making of the flag and its imposing beauty. The pride it brought to those who served under it. The influence it commanded as it waved, infinite and powerful, above the walls of the fort. The article continued by recording how, on September 13, 1814, a thirty-five-year-old lawyer and poet felt inspired by the scene he witnessed from the deck of a British warship during its attack of Fort McHenry.

All night and into the early morning hours, there had been a bombardment of fire by the warship with only sporadic return from the guns behind the fort. At dawn, Francis Scott Key was standing on the deck of the ship, fearful that perhaps the fort had been captured. He placed a telescope to his eye, training it on the flagpole inside the fort. There he saw the huge proud flag waving defiantly in the morning breeze.

You might interrupt our conversation with the question, "What was the man doing on a British warship if he was on the side of the Americans?

The article quickly summarized Key's purpose, explaining to the reader that the whole story would make for good reading if they would like to visit their public library.

Lincoln had to smile at her suggestion. It had always been his mother's contention that a public library was the one place a person could go to receive an education beyond his or her wildest dreams for free, yet so few took advantage of the opportunity.

The article explained the emotions Mr. Key experienced as he caught sight of the flag waving defiantly against the British attack. It told how he penned the words storming his mind on the only piece of paper he could find, the back of a letter he had in his pocket.

At the end of the column, Betsy had written all four verses of the national anthem with the closing statement.

We are familiar with the first verse, but in the years that have passed, the song in its entirety has been misplaced. It is, however, in is entirety that its meaning is complete.

There are those who have lobbied to change the national anthem to a more gentle song like "God Bless America" or "My Country 'Tis of Thee." They claim "The Star Spangled Banner" is too violent in its prose. I ask each of you to study and consider the words. Consider their meaning in our lives as they remind us of the blood that was shed and sacrifices that were made to make this land free. Consider the words that speak of the flag, its purpose, its triumph, its glory, its humility, and its pride. Consider the fact that this flag will fly only as long as it flies o'er the land of the free and the home of the brave.

Consider the fact that perhaps we need to hear these words often so we will never forget.

I will look forward to your e-mails.

Lincoln looked at his grandmother. "She's good, isn't she?"

"I love her spunk," Elmira shouted, startling Lincoln.

"I love her strength," he shouted back, making Elmira laugh. Then his voice became sober. "There's something I have to tell you," he said, proceeding to give Elmira the details of the previous night and their concern for her welfare.

When he finished, Elmira looked deep into Lincoln's eyes. "Don't worry about me, Lincoln." She reached out and placed her hand on his. "The Lord takes care of me and will continue to do so until He calls me home. Pending that time, I will continue to do His will. Today His will instructs me to help those who place themselves in harm's way so the liberty of our descendants will not be jeopardized. I fear no man, Lincoln, only God."

Elmira cut another piece of pie and placed it on her grandson's plate. "Did you wonder, as you read this article, how your mother could even concentrate on her column after last night? When you woke this morning, were you surprised to see her column finished and ready for delivery?"

Lincoln nodded. His mouth filled with lemon meringue made it impossible to give a verbal response.

"It's because she will no longer allow herself to be controlled by fear. For a few days, she let fear of what would be revealed in the notebooks keep her from the knowledge they contained. She learned from that experience and won't let it happen again. No one or nothing will dictate through trepidation how she will live or think or feel. Watch your mother, Lincoln, and learn from her. The experience she went through after John's death was, in its way, an education. Once she gleaned what was needed from that experience and introduced it into her life, she was ready to take on whatever was waiting for her in the wings.

"I can't quote scripture or verse, but the point I'm trying to make goes something like this, 'If we can't learn from ourselves, who can we learn from? We live, and through living, we experience love and hate; pain and well-being; anger and calm; agony and joy; both physical and emotional. If we cannot teach ourselves something with each experience then that experience is wasted, and we are pitiful in our learning, for we are the teachers of our own destiny.'"

Lincoln's eyes never left his grandmother's face as she talked. He had never thought of life in that way before. Well, maybe he had to a certain extent but not to this degree.

"Tell me, Grandmother," he said, leaning over the table, his hands under his chin, "did I choose to be your grandson in the pre-existence because you were such an amazing teacher?"

Elmira laughed at the young man whose eyes were filled with admiration. "Actually," she grinned, "I chose you because you were so teachable. Now I need to talk to my daughter about something very important. Let's take a walk through the woods."

"Thank you for the pie." Betsy smiled at her mother. "It was delicious as always. I'm surprised there was a piece left."

Lincoln's eyebrows shot up in defense. "It's not my fault," he scoffed. "Grandmother slapped my hand when I reached for it."

"Thank you for watching out for me, Mother."

"You're welcome, Babe." Elmira hesitated, looking intently at her daughter. "I have to admit, however, that the pie is simply a bribe."

Betsy couldn't help but frown. "What do you mean?"

"I've been asked to give you an assignment of sorts."

"An assignment of what kind of sorts?" Lincoln's mouth dropped.

"I'm wondering, is that proper use of English?" Elmira chided, patting Lincoln on the knee, "Of what kind of sorts?" She sat there as if mulling it over in her mind for a moment while two pair of eyes glared at her. "Oh, well," she sighed. "I suppose when questioning the statement made, one could excuse the wording."

"M-o-t-h-e-r!" Betsy voice pierced the room

"Sorry, dear. As I was saying, I've been asked to offer you an assignment, one that would be very helpful to the society without placing any suspicion on you." She reached into her pocket and removed a piece of paper, which she unfolded and handed to Betsy.

Looking down at the paper now in her hand, Betsy read

the short sentence written in black ink. *The journey may require a passport.*

"What does this mean?" she asked, raising her eyes to meet her mother's.

"It's meaning," Elmira retrieved the paper and quickly tore it into shreds before saying, "will never be known to you. It will just be read somewhere in the content of your article tomorrow."

Betsy opened her mouth to speak then shut it abruptly, her mind connecting with her mother's. Taking the shredded paper from Elmira's hand, she handed it to Lincoln. "Burn this," she said.

Lincoln understood and left the room.

"Each week," Elmira continued, "there will be a message."

"And it will be in my column," Betsy assured her.

"Thank you, Betsy. Thank you for being so brave."

"I never knew that you . . ." Betsy sputtered, the words refusing to surface. "How long?"

Elmira looked at her daughter and smiled, her eyes glistening. "I was sixteen when I had my first assignment." Her voice was soft as she spoke. "It was simple, of course, but nonetheless filled with intrigue for a sixteen-year-old. My life took on new meaning after that, and I became obsessed with the work."

"I met your father on one of my assignments when I was twenty. It was love at first sight for me. He, of course, had to ponder it in his mind, mull it over, and think it through logically." She laughed. The memory, strong in her mind, caused tears to moisten her cheeks.

Immediately Betsy was beside her mother, wrapping her arms around her. There was nothing she could say, nor did she have any desire to speak; the feeling spoke for itself.

Lincoln stood in the doorway watching the two most important women in his life, awakening to the fact that he came from an extraordinary family.

Betsy released her mother and hurried to the computer, bringing up the column. She knew the spot where she would add the needed words: *Today, dear readers, our journey may require a passport. . . .*

"Perfect," Elmira muttered, watching the screen as her daughter typed. "You always have a little sarcasm in your articles. This would be expected."

"Thank you for those kind words, Mother."

"Well, Babe, it's true. It wouldn't be the same without your wit, and you know it."

"She's right, Mom." Lincoln agreed. "That's what draws people to your column. Sometimes you insult their intelligence, but you always leave them with something to think about and they like that."

"I suppose you're both right," she admitted, acknowledging some of the e-mails she received hinted as much.

Lincoln nodded. "People love you for simply calling it as you see it."

"There's one thing I don't understand." Betsy changed the subject, a look of confusion on her face. "With all the high tech in this world, why do they need my newspaper column to send messages?"

"It's because of all the high tech in this world that we need your column to send messages," Lincoln said. "I can break into and find anything I want to break into and find. Who we are and what we represent has to be completely unidentifiable as well as untraceable. To stay that way, you continually hide the trail, change the address, use the high tech to help you find what you need but avoid it to carry out the assignment.

"Even using the Internet to find something or to do research, you open yourself to being unveiled. Everything has to be done in fragments, from different points on the map, on different computers, leaving no trail to follow. Those first involved in this work had a simple yet effective plan. We can't be found because we're not there. It's still the best plan."

"I understand," Betsy nodded. "Agents across the nation

will read the same message, and its meaning will be the same to all of them." A sensation of excitement raced through her, and suddenly she felt energized and, to her surprise, almost giddy.

Her mother smiled. "The meaning of the message is not in the full message itself but in bits and pieces to different agents, as you wish to call them. It's rather complicated to explain. To know that what you are doing is of great value."

Betsy eyed her mother for a moment, trying to make sense of her words. Then she thought better of it and turned back to the computer, hitting Save, then Print, and relishing the feeling of being in control again.

"Here you go, Lincoln," she said, handing him her column secured in an envelope. "Frank will be waiting for this."

Lincoln took the envelope from his mother and turned to the dog sitting next to her. "Want to take a ride in my Jeep, golden boy?"

Dorado looked up at Betsy and then Lincoln. He could see the dog was torn between going and staying. "Come on, boy. Mom's got Grandmother to protect her. I'll even take the roof off, and your ears can flip in the breeze."

Dorado's bark and his dash for the front door was answer enough. Lincoln hurried to keep up. One happy dog, his gangly ears flapping in the wind, his tail beating rhythmically against the leathered seat, filled the passenger side of the Jeep. Lincoln could almost swear he saw a hint of a smile on the dog's face as he greeted each passing car with a bark.

Lincoln delivered the envelope to the editor's office and nearly collided with a young woman when he stepped out onto the sidewalk.

"Excuse me," he apologized. "I wasn't watching where I was going."

The young woman accepted his apology with a beautiful smile that he recognized.

"Terri?" he exclaimed.

"Hi, Lincoln."

"When did you grow up?" he frowned as he studied her from head to toe.

"It took me eighteen years, but I finally made it," she giggled. "And you?"

"I'm still working on it." He felt himself blush. "So . . . how are you doing?"

"Fine, now that I got my scholarship."

He noted that under long lashes her eyes were a beautiful blue green. "Great! Where to?"

"Boston U," she said excitedly. "I could hardly believe it when the letter came."

Lincoln couldn't help but notice the dimples that appeared and disappeared as she talked. Just a few short years ago, she was a chubby adolescent. Now she was quite the opposite.

"You're staring at me . . . is there something on my face?" She brushed her fingers across her mouth.

"Oh, no! I don't mean to stare, it's just that you look so nice . . . not that you didn't look nice before . . . it's just that you look a different kind of nice." He had never been cool around girls. He always made a fool of himself, just as he was doing now. Nice? What kind of word is that when you're describing a beautiful girl? Why couldn't he just shut his mouth?

"Thank you," she replied with a blush of her own. "No one has ever said that to me before with such eloquence."

They both laughed, and Lincoln found himself relaxing a little. A bark interrupted from the Jeep. "Meet Dorado," he motioned to the dog, thankful for the opportunity to change the subject.

"I've heard all about you," Terri said, reaching out to pet the beautiful golden retriever sniffing at her hand. "I'm glad to finally meet you." She leaned against the side of the Jeep and ruffled Dorado's coat, allowing him to lick her cheek.

Lincoln watched Terri become acquainted with Dorado and wondered if it was too soon to ask her out. He wouldn't know. He had never really asked a girl out on a date before. Girls usually asked him.

It wasn't as if they were strangers, though he couldn't place them in the friend category either. The first time the two families got together he hadn't particularly liked her. He was ten; she was six and a nuisance. The last time he had seen her, she was thirteen. He was seventeen and on his way to college. Today he was still four years older, but things had changed. Now he liked her instantly.

"How's Tad?" he asked, knowing it was a subject they could discuss that would keep her next to him for a minute or two longer. "He was still on his mission when I went back to school. Then he was at the Air Force Academy when I came home for break. I haven't seen him for over three years."

"My brother loves the Air Force. He's in Afghanistan right now, and believe it or not, I miss him terribly." Lincoln could hear the sadness in her voice.

"Would you get me his address?"

"I can do that." She reached in her wallet and pulled out a pen and a piece of paper. After writing the address, she handed the paper to Lincoln. "He'll be so happy to hear from you." She looked at her watch. "Now I had better get back to work,"

Why couldn't he say something intelligent like, "Would you like to go out to dinner?" Instead, he simply smiled and said, "See you later."

Real smart guy, he chastised himself as he climbed back into the jeep and fastened the seat belt. He started the engine but kept his eyes on Terri until she disappeared into the dry cleaner.

Paul had been up half the night going through his collection of analytical papers written by professors of science as well as research papers written by the finest chemical scientists in the world. He could find nothing that would prove to be of any help. It wasn't until Tuesday afternoon, while he was at the lab, that he and Dawn finally had a breakthrough.

In between everything else on their day's agenda, Paul surfed files of companies, inside and outside of the country, who were doing any kind of research in the field John had referred to. It had been tedious simply because the information he needed could be hidden in something as universal as cancer research or as complicated as cloning or stem cell research.

Another thing that kept him alert was the fact that what he was doing was considered illegal. He had to type in codes that would take him through the confidential walls of research, codes he was not supposed to have access to. If he got caught within the web net, it could mean his job.

There was something else running through his mind as he surfed. If *they* caught him nosing around, more than his job could be in danger.

Dawn guarded the door of the lab while he sat at the computer in case someone walked in. It had been a quiet day, and they were undisturbed except for an occasional question from a technician or a request to authorize an autopsy report with a deadline—nothing Dawn couldn't handle while Paul searched for clues.

Paul was just about ready to give up when some highly confidential material hinting about scientific studies actually being conducted to better understand the criminal mind turned up on the screen. His heart leaped with the discovery.

"Listen to this," he breathed with excitement, reaching out and grabbing Dawn's lab coat, pulling her close. "Research into the development of a chemical that could, in theory, alter brain cells that are contaminated." He raised his eyebrow and glanced up at his wife. "That's the word they've used— 'contaminated with criminal intent.' It's being considered as a way to eliminate horrific and senseless acts of violence."

Dawn stared at the computer screen. "I wonder," she contemplated, slipping her reading glasses over her nose. "Could a simple statement sandwiched between legitimate research phenomenon, sounding innocent in its intent, be overlooked in discussion? Could someone who acquired the go-ahead to mess around inside the brain with the intent of altering its ability to perform, have something sinister in mind instead?"

"Definitely," Paul theorized.

"Print it," she whispered in his ear.

"Consider it done." With a few taps of the keys, the printer began to hum and, within seconds, spit out in black and white information that would add another chapter to their journal of mystery.

Folding the single piece of paper several times, Paul slipped it into his wallet. "We need to call a family meeting," he said, urgency evident in his voice.

eight

SOURCES &
INTRODUCTIONS

Wednesday afternoon a family meeting was held. Time was of the essence, and they needed as much information as possible to help them determine their plan of action, not only how to proceed in their investigation but how to protect themselves while conducting the investigation.

Paul presented their findings, and a comparison was made to the information found in John's notebooks.

"John said in the notebook that the scientist working on the project was murdered, but not before he handed his research material over to John." Paul's face reflected the seriousness of his voice. "In the report I stumbled onto, a Dr. Patero was supposedly working on some highly confidential research when he was killed in a car accident just about the time of John's journal date."

"That's all we were able to find," Dawn continued. "There is nothing written about a chip matching one John describes. That may be, of course, because John was able to get hold of it before it was ready to leave the design lab."

"Maybe it was still under the microscope, and he swiped it right out from under their lenses." Paul chuckled lightly at his own humor. Then his face grew serious once again, his eyes resting on Lincoln. "We need to get those links."

"How do we do it without drawing attention?" Lincoln asked. "Obviously someone knows Dad took whatever is hidden in the links of his watch. Mom and I were a witness to that the other night. And now they think we have the watch. From now on, they'll be aware of every move we make."

"We've already discussed that, and we think we have an idea," Dawn explained, unfolding a piece of paper showing a layout of the cemetery. "I copied this from the memorial park record book." She pointed to a red dot next to one of the hundreds of small rectangles. "This is John's grave, and here is our proposal." She nodded to her husband to take over the conversation.

"It'll take a couple of days to get everything together," Paul explained. "I've been very discreet in my communications with the curator of the cemetery. He told me they will be doing some work in the area where John's grave is located, adding some fencing and rose bushes to give more seclusion to that area when patrons visit the grave sites of their loved ones. Tents will enclose each grave to protect them from equipment traffic. When all is in place and activity is at its fullest, we hopefully will be able to slip in and out undetected."

"You don't think someone might get suspicious when we walk into one of the tents and start digging?" asked Lincoln. "Which brings up another question. What will we be digging with?"

"John's grave is the most secluded of the eight or ten that will be tented." Dawn continued. "You'll dress to blend in with the workers. The crew will carry about fourteen men, assigned different working areas. You'll just be working in an area assigned to you, as far as they are concerned."

"It could work," agreed Lincoln. "How did you get the curator to go along with it?"

"He's an old family friend." Paul nodded thoughtfully. "One who can be trusted."

Wednesday afternoon Mitch and Hal were in a meeting of their own, once again facing their employer across a small table in the dark corner of a nightclub.

"At least we know the woman has some knowledge of her husband's business transactions away from his day job," Mitch reported, hoping that information would buffer their failed attempt to get the watch.

"I'm still tryin' to figure out how she knew where to find the watch, and why she waited so long to go lookin'." Hal surprised both men with his unexpected insight.

"Consider the fact that she may have known she was under surveillance all along and waited until she was no longer considered a player before she went after the watch. The question that concerns me now is one that should also concern the two of you. Who else knows?" The mystery man's voice was laced with menace as he spoke. "Do whatever you have to do to get the watch." He dismissed the two men and then made a phone call.

Chandler closed his cell phone and looked at his partner. "Things are heating up, Mac. I think the real work is just beginning."

"Your mystery friend?" Mac pointed to the cell phone.

Chandler nodded. "He's paying us top dollar to stick to the Bradens from here on in. Apparently Mrs. Braden found a watch that somehow links her husband to more than simple investigative reporting."

"Isn't this what we've been waiting for?" Mac's face lit with excitement.

"We'll find out just how good we are, won't we, Mac?"

"We're the best, Chandler."

"I pray we are. There's too much at stake here not to be."

Chandler could feel the weight of the responsibility now placed upon his shoulders.

"I feel it too, my friend," Mac said, seeing his own concerns reflected in the eyes of his partner. "I feel it too."

They had one appointment to keep before they could begin the Braden surveillance. At ten o'clock on Thursday morning, they pulled into the parking lot of the very posh Harmony Assisted Living Center where Andrew Hoffman resided.

The hour they spent with Mr. Hoffman was enjoyable yet basically uninformative. He graciously received the two men wearing journalist badges, welcoming them into his luxuriously decorated one-bedroom apartment. He answered their questions about his father's aeronautic brilliance and his own research successes at Hope Research Laboratory but refused to talk about the reported brain cell research. He stated that if that kind of research had been successful, his wife would still be alive, and he wouldn't be in a care center for the rich. Neither Mac nor Chandler could dispute that argument, and they were even more disappointed when he refused to talk about his son, Leonard.

Mac glanced around the room searching for a photo that would identify the son, but the room was free of photos. He asked if he might use the restroom. Andrew pointed in the direction he should go and continued talking with Chandler.

Mac took the opportunity to give the bedroom a quick go through on his way. A family photo showing a mother, a father, and a son in his late teens sat on a small table under the window. The photo, Mac determined, had to be at least ten years old. He slipped it from its frame and snapped his own copy with a mini camera he carried for an occasion such as this, put everything back in place, and hurried to the bathroom. He did the flushing and washing sounds and walked back to the front room.

They thanked Andrew for visiting with them and left with not much more than what they had come with. Back at the office, Mac plugged his camera into his computer, punched a few keys, and waited while the printer produced a picture. He saved the photo to a program and then studied it. He tapped a few keys and waited; then he tapped a few more and waited again. Finally he printed a copy of the finished product and handed it to Chandler. "Meet Leonard," he said triumphantly.

"How many years did you age him?"

"Ten."

Chandler pinned the photo to the board and leaned back in his chair, his brain trying to bring to the surface where he had seen the man before. "I think Mr. Hoffman knew we weren't journalists," he said finally.

"I have to agree." Mac put the camera back in his shirt pocket, picked up a pair of hand weights and began lifting. "I think he wanted me to find the picture," he grunted under the pressure of the weights. "It was as if his mouth was telling you one thing while his eyes were saying something entirely different."

Chandler stood and walked to the window, his face showing deep concentration. He stood, watching rain clouds forming in the distance. After several minutes, he turned and posed a question. "Could there be a connection between our mystery man and the fact that Hoffman's laboratory has the equipment to do highly sensitive research?"

Mac stared at his partner, lowering the weights slowly. "I think as soon as we get this surveillance set up we'd better start looking for Leonard Hoffman."

By midnight that night, extended surveillance was in place. The camouflaged van filled with equipment would be home away from home until they had what they hoped for or until they could prove it wasn't available. They would keep track of everyone entering and leaving the house, putting names to faces. Planting the listening devices again was unnecessary because they were stationed close enough with a receiver to do the job. It had the capacity to pick up voices within the calculated radius and relay them to the base inside the van.

Just after midnight, Mac lit the switchboard while Chandler made one last call. He waited until he heard a click on the other end of the receiver then uttered a few words, hung up, took a deep breath, and leaned back in his chair, swiveling it in Mac's direction. "We can check the young rally mongrel off our list. He's under the watchful eye of California's finest."

"That opens a spot for Leonard Hoffman," Mac said, biting into a piece of cold pizza. "I don't think we're going to get bored."

"Tomorrow we'll chart the Hoffman layout." Chandler yawned. He lay down on the sleeping bag stuffed into the corner of the van and fell asleep. Mac found his bedroll in the opposite corner. In the morning, he would adjust the wireless dish. By noon they would be recording everything said inside the Braden home, but tonight he would get some much-needed sleep.

It was Thursday morning before the e-mails were read. Those worthy of deletion were taken care of first; then Betsy prepared herself for some serious reading. Lincoln had her breakfast sitting at her desk by the time she finished reading the fifth e-mail. It was one of those e-mails that made the column worth the work.

Good morning, Betsy. I don't usually get caught up in reading columns, but yours is worth sitting down to. I read each column to my ten-year-old son, and he loves them.

Yesterday, after you hinted about the life of Francis Scott Key, my son, Darin, insisted we go to the library immediately. We did. It was a wonderful experience to see him so excited about something other than video games. Thank you for stirring our curiosity and leaving us wanting for more. We took the challenge and by doing so have enriched our lives.

Betsy took the time to print this one out and then went on. Most agreed with what she had written, although a few of them, well maybe a little more than a few, thought she had insulted their intelligence again. Some people, she decided, loved to find fault. She was glad she could accommodate them.

She continued reading through the e-mails until one appeared on the screen that caused her heart to tremble. "Lincoln!" she called, her voice piercing. "Come quick."

When he was at her side, she pointed to the e mail and read it aloud to him.

I need to talk with you about your husband. I will be in the student library at Boston University today from 2:00–4:00 PM So you can recognize me, I will be wearing a dark jacket and a Red Sox baseball cap, and I'll be sitting at the small round table in the east corner on the second floor. Please come. It is vital that I speak to you.

"Who would . . ." Lincoln started to ask.

"Know about John?" Betsy finished his sentence for him.

Together, they read the e-mail one more time.

"What do you want to do?" Lincoln asked, still staring at the screen.

"I think I'd like to meet this person in the library, but I'll meet whoever it is alone."

"I don't think so." Lincoln turned to see the determination in his mother's look as she stared back at him. He knew he couldn't change her mind.

"Listen to what I have to say. You will go early and wait until this person arrives. We'll assume he's a man. Once he sits down at the table, you call my cell phone. Let it ring twice and then hang up."

"I see where you're going," Lincoln nodded.

"I'll have Paul fit me with a microphone so you can hear everything that is said. You stay close but out of sight, unless needed."

Lincoln looked at his watch. "It's noon already. I'll call Paul, and see if he and Dawn will meet us for lunch while you get ready."

Fifteen minutes after they locked the door and drove away,

a switch was turned on inside a van, and the sounds inside Betsy's home were once again recorded on tape.

❧❧❧❧

Betsy walked up the steps of the library to the second floor, feeling strangely calm, though the small piece of equipment Paul attached beneath her collar made her wonder how well it worked. In Lincoln's ear, the receiver would pick up the full conversation as long as she didn't cover the microphone with anything. She was committed to keeping her hands on the table.

Scanning the east side of the library, she walked between bookshelves pretending to search for a book. Pulling two books from a shelf, she opened the cover of one while her eyes darted from table to table where students sat studying or taking a nap on their open books. Several of the young men were wearing Red Sox baseball caps.

Now what do I do? she asked herself. Her cell phone vibrated twice. There was no one on the other end when she put it to her ear. Lincoln had seen whoever it was she was to meet. She took a deep breath and began walking east.

It wasn't until she walked past three round tables scattered about in the large corner room that she noticed another one, off by itself. It was smaller than the others, and the only person sitting there was wearing a dark jacket, his back to her. A baseball cap perched on his head. Though she couldn't see the insignia, the color was correct.

Betsy's heart began to pound even more, and her palms became moist. With her nerves tingling, she walked to the table and asked. "May I sit here?"

The person simply nodded an affirmative without looking up. Betsy sat, opened one of the books, and pretended to read.

"May I ask your name?" a voice said softly.

"Betsy Braden," she replied while turning a page.

The face beneath the cap came into view as a young woman lifted her eyes to meet Betsy's, a few strands of blonde hair escaping from inside the lined cap.

"I'm the one who e-mailed you." The voice was hushed.

"You'll forgive me if I seem a little cautious."

"I understand and thank you for coming. I don't mean to be melodramatic, but I needed to know you were who I thought you were. I knew if you were the right Mrs. Braden, you would come."

"Tell me what this is all about," Betsy whispered, impatient to hear the story.

"My name is April Garrett. My father was your husband's partner. Your husband died because my father couldn't get to him. You need to understand why.

Betsy's body went limp. "Tell me," she cried softly.

April placed an envelope in Betsy's hand. "I've been waiting for over a year to give this to you. Last week I read your column, quite by accident, and knew I had to contact you." She directed Betsy's attention to the envelope with her eyes. "This will explain everything. Thank you for coming." With that, the young woman stood and walked away.

Betsy tried not to look around her as she carefully slid the envelope into her purse. Once again pretending to read the book opened in front of her, she remained at the table for several minutes. When she felt the timing was right, she picked up the books, put them on the book cart, and left the building.

Walking to her car, she hoped to see her son close by, but he was nowhere in sight. She whispered into the microphone and waited for her cell phone to ring. She felt relief when she heard his voice on the other end.

"Where are you?" she asked.

"Making sure Miss Garrett gets to her dorm safely."

"Good idea. I'll meet you at home." Betsy put the car in gear and pulled out of the parking lot.

This meeting hadn't been at all what she expected. She

didn't need a hidden microphone. She didn't need her son standing by in case of danger. She was never in any danger. She sat at a table with a lovely young woman who was far more nervous than she was. Had she overreacted? With all that was happening, she didn't think so. Common sense told her the precautions were warranted.

❦

Lincoln walked casually behind April at a safe distance, looking every bit a student, so she wouldn't become suspicious. When she reached her dorm, she removed the cap and let her long, blonde hair fall to her shoulders before disappearing through the door.

Walking past the dorm, he crossed the street, stepped into the foyer of another building, and stood there for several minutes, his eyes searching for anything out of the ordinary. When he was satisfied that all seemed quiet enough, he started to leave the building but made a quick retreat when a blonde emerged from the dorm wearing a business suit and carrying a brief case. It was the same person who had gone into the building ten minutes earlier wearing a baseball cap and dark jacket. If it hadn't been for the hair and the swing of the hips, he wouldn't have recognized her. She had changed from a college coed to a business executive in less than ten minutes.

He watched her climb into a dark gray, late-model Mercedes, with a New York license plate, #101 NYC.

An obvious question presented itself. Was this girl April Garrett, or was she someone posing as April Garrett, if there was an April Garrett? Why would she pretend to be a college student unless there was an April Garrett enrolled as a student here? But then, that could be easy to fix. A little intrusion into the student records and, like magic, the name April Garrett appears on the list.

He stood there watching the car drive down the street with no way to follow; his Jeep was parked two blocks away.

Smart move, Lincoln! He would have to be satisfied with the things he did know, for now, not the things he didn't. He had a description, a license plate number, and the make of car. It was a beginning.

He reached for his cell phone, pushed a button, and waited for his mother to answer as he walked back to his Jeep. "I'm on my way to the office to see if April Garrett is actually a student," he said, when she answered. "Then I'll be home."

"Stop at your grandmother's. I'll be there."

Lincoln put his phone in his pocket and entered the Administration Building, asking a student he met coming through the door for directions to the office.

"Take the second hallway to your left," the student replied. "You can't miss the sign."

Lincoln expressed his thanks and stepped into the large student lounge. There he saw several undergraduates lounging on couches, looking through the summer class schedules or browsing through brochures.

"Professor Hamilton is the best chemistry teacher," he heard one student advising another as he walked past them. That would work, he thought to himself.

When he opened the door to the office, the woman behind the desk gave him a less-than-friendly glare, telling him without having to speak the words, *can't you see I'm busy?* When he asked her for April Garrett's class schedule, she looked at him as if he were less than intelligent. "If you want that information, you'll have to talk to April Garrett."

"Could I just ask if she had chemistry from Professor Hamilton this year?" he inquired. "I need to find a book for the class, and a friend of mine told me he thought she had taken that class last semester. She may have gone home for the summer, and I just need to know if I should look elsewhere."

The woman sighed with annoyance but looked at her computer screen and clicked away at the keyboard for a minute. When he shifted his stance, she glanced up at him with a scowl, warning him not to even attempt a look at the screen.

He stepped away from the counter to keep in her good graces until she was finished.

"You're out of luck. April Garrett graduated in December."

"Graduated? My friend told me she was a junior."

"Well, I'm afraid your friend had the wrong information. Sorry."

He thanked the secretary for her help and walked back into the lounge. There was an April Garrett who had graduated in December. If she graduated in December, why was she here now? What he needed was a picture.

An hour later he was sitting in his grandmother's kitchen eating dinner. A letter to his father from Garrett lay on the table next to him; beside it, a note from April to his mother was at the moment the focus of his attention. His mother sat across from him waiting silently as he read.

Mrs. Braden,

I found this letter in my father's things. I did some research and found that Mr. Braden died two days after my father mysteriously disappeared. I thought you might like an explanation as to what happened.

I can only assume that my father is dead also. It took me a long time before I could go into his room, but when I did, I found his wallet, his shoes, all his clothes, everything laid out as if he was getting ready to put them on. In the pocket of his jacket, I found this letter.

I'm sorry for your loss.

Betsy had been very careful to keep the letters free of her fingerprints, and Lincoln did the same. Taking the end of a knife, he slid the letter to his father closer to him so he could read it without picking it up.

John,

Times and places change for there are men who value gold more than life. The great reward, for those who seek it, is well over a million, but silence has more value. Best to leave gold buried. It only takes two days to receive what it used to take weeks to deliver. Still nothing in life is guaranteed except perhaps peace to the soul.

*Trust is a valued friend, but a friend cannot always be trusted.
Don't be fooled. Take care, my friend.*

   R. Garrett

"Are you thinking what I'm thinking?" Betsy asked.

"That the letter is in code," Lincoln replied, "and the girl who gave you this letter may know its meaning? That her appearance today hardly seems just a coincidence in light of everything that has happened in the past week?"

Betsy nodded. "I'll take the letters to Dawn while you do what you can to find out more about this April Garrett."

Left to his assignment, Lincoln drove back to the house, sat at his computer, and typed his way into the university student records.

There was no picture for April Garrett, born November 2, 1973, but there was some information: five foot six, blonde hair, hazel eyes; Father, Roger Garrett, deceased; mother, Adella (no maiden name) deceased; next-of-kin—unknown; present address—unknown. The rest of the information was just as noninformative.

He pushed himself back from the computer and made a phone call, giving two license plate numbers to the person on the other end.

"Mac," Chandler said, resting the earphones on his shoulders. "The kid's checking your license plate number."

"You're kidding!" Mac turned from his computer, his eyes questioning.

"What will he find?"

"That I have a grandmother who's unrelated to me." Mac smiled jokingly.

"He's also running a check on another plate—101 NYC."

Mac's smile faded when his mouth dropped in disbelief. "You're kidding!"

"I wish I was. What's he going to find there?"

"Nothing, and that has me worried. He's a smart kid. He's not going to be fooled for a minute." Mac ran his fingers through his hair while Chandler bit at his fingernails. "We need to find out why, and we need to find out soon."

nine

UNANSWERED QUESTIONS

A second family meeting was called by Paul and Dawn. At 7:30 PM, everyone was seated in their study, which some would consider an in-home laboratory. A large whiteboard faced everyone.

"Let's bring together everything we have so far," Paul said, a green marker in his right hand and red and black markers entwined between the fingers in his left. Beneath his eyes, dark circles were taking shape. In contrast, however, his eyes were bright with the mystery that had woven itself into their lives.

"Our story," he said, making notations in green on the left side of the whiteboard as he spoke, "updated through today, reveals the following: There were at least five different people, other than family, combing the wooded area in the past year and a half. Two were smokers. We have DNA samples awaiting matches. We have the bullet casings to a 945, .45 ACP Caliber Smith & Wesson pistol. Our vehicles are more than likely a van and a limo."

He glanced at Betsy, his eyes filled with compassion. "I have everything we need lined up at the cemetery. Work begins at seven Saturday morning. If everything goes as it should, three hours will be ample time to get what we need and leave the site looking undisturbed."

Betsy smiled up at him, touched by his sensitivity in dealing with what had to be done. "Thank you," she said softly.

Paul cleared the emotional frog from his throat and adjusted his glasses, motioning for Lincoln to take the floor.

Lincoln handed each one of them a copy of the annotations taken from the seven notebooks, explaining their purpose as resource material. He talked about the two men who couldn't get past Dorado's nose and what they had said to each other about his father's death.

"We now know that they know we have the watch," he continued. "That means they'll be looking for an opportunity to go after it. I suggest we give them that opportunity as soon as possible. Let them find the watch once we've replaced the links. We, in turn, find out where they take it."

"Brilliant," Paul gestured, his right eyebrow raised. "My concern is how will they know where to find it?"

"I wonder how long it will be before someone's listening to the conversations inside the house again, now that the watch has become a priority." Lincoln crossed his arms and looked at his mother, who only shook her head in acknowledgement of the fact.

"Point well taken, my boy." Paul extended his hand and offered the red marker to his nephew, encouraging him to add that bit of information to what was already written on the board. Lincoln wrote: *Let the watch be found to find out the who and why.*

Shifting his attention, he leaned against the desk beside the white board. "April Garrett has become another concern." He paused and wrote her name in red. "The university records show an April Garrett graduated last December, but her records are evasive and could be plants within the computer. The license plate yields no match, which sends up a red flag. Tomorrow, I'll check at the library for university yearbooks that might cough up a picture.

"The letter from Garrett, we think, is in code. I want you to listen as much for the meaning as to the words as I read it.

"Times and places change for there are men who value gold more than life. The great reward, for those who seek it, is well over a million, but silence has more value. Best to leave gold buried.

It only takes two days to receive what it used to take weeks to deliver. Still nothing in life is guaranteed except perhaps peace to the soul.

Trust is a valued friend, but a friend cannot always be trusted. Don't be fooled. Take care, my friend."

He gave each person a copy of the letter. "Study it on your own and then we'll talk about it later. Maybe together we can decode it."

He made another notation. "The van's license plate matched with a ninety-year-old Magen Maden, which has to be a cover. Lots of questions . . . no answers," he shrugged and yielded the floor.

Elmira, having already acquired the black marker, stood. "I've made some contacts, and I found that Roger Garrett has been missing for as long as John's been dead. He's presumed dead as well. Mr. Oscar Lear was the man both Garrett and John reported to. Nevertheless, in all my inquiries, I can't seem to locate him. Neither could I find information as to what triggered this chain of events. The feelers are still out, however, and I should have more information within the next two days."

She turned to the board. "Here are some of the things we need to know." The black marker made a funny little squeaky sound as she wrote:

1. *What's in the casket?*
2. *What's hidden in the woods?*
3. *Who's watching us?*
4. *Who may be listening?*
5. *Who's driving the van?*
6. *What are they looking for inside the watch?*

7. *What are we looking for besides what's inside the links?*
8. *Is Garrett dead or alive?*
9. *Is Oscar Lear the mole, as John suspected?*
10. *Who is April Garrett?*
11. *Can we decode the letter?*

Everyone was silent as she wrote, paying close attention to each item written in black. When she finished, she turned back to her family. "I'm sure the things I've written are things you've already thought of. It's just that when they're written down, they become more visible in our minds."

They all nodded as they studied the board together.

"We need to put Dr. Patero, the scientist who was supposedly murdered, on our list," Paul added, checking the notations on the paper Lincoln handed out. "Plus the idea that the documents may contain the formula he was working on." He raised two fingers in the air. "Two more things: what's hidden in the box among the trees and where do we find the map? I believe the map he's talking about is the one that will lead us to the box in the trees."

Elmira turned and wrote:

12. *What kind of technology could alter the criminal mind?*
13. *Who is Dr. Patero?*
14. *What do his documents contain?*
15. *Where, among the trees, is the box?*
16. *Where is the map?*

"John writes that he found something sinister and dangerous, something that should be left alone," Dawn said, pointing to the paper in her hand. "I'm assuming he meant technology that would alter the criminal mind. In one place he says he has documentation. Then he says he needs proof. Yet, I think we'll find answers to many of our questions as we study the notes."

"You're right," Betsy responded. "I think number fourteen will answer number two and number seven. We're looking for a box containing something that Dr. Patero gave to John before Dr. Patero, himself, was murdered. That something has to be the documents containing the technology that will alter the criminal mind, therefore answering number twelve. We just need to find the map, which will tell us where to look."

"And we have to be very careful because someone, perhaps in a light colored van, has the sophisticated equipment to watch and listen," Dawn interceded. "By finding the answer to number five, we'll be able to answer number three and number four."

"Once the links are removed from the casket, taking care of number one," Paul surmised, "we'll attach them to the watch. We'll allow whoever is watching and listening to find the watch; then we answer numbers three, four, and possibly five by becoming the watcher and the listener. It's almost perfect."

"Now to get the other guys to play by our rules," Dawn said in all seriousness.

"That's the only flaw," her husband admitted. "And I think we need a break. Follow me to the kitchen for warm brownies and cold pop. The sugar hype will energize the brain stems that have been working profusely to put together an almost-flawless plan."

The voting was unanimous, and the meeting was in recess for fifteen minutes. When they reconvened, the group focused on Garrett's letter.

"I think the first part means that Garrett was changing the time and the place they were to meet because . . ." Paul glanced around the room. "Help me out, guys."

"Because someone was getting a lot of money to blow their covers?" Elmira ventured. "Maybe over a million dollars?"

Paul squinted his eyes and pursed his lips for only a second before announcing, "I believe you've got it nailed, Elmira. Does everyone agree?"

Everyone quietly skimmed through the paragraph once more and found themselves in perfect agreement.

"That has to be the meaning," Dawn surmised. "And I think we know enough to say that he's telling John to stay away and leave the box buried for now, agreed?"

"Agreed!" the voices around her were in unison.

"The next paragraph is more complicated." Betsy repeated the words aloud. *"It only takes two days to receive what it used to take weeks to deliver. Still nothing in life is guaranteed except perhaps peace to the soul."*

They were mouthing the words, but there seemed to be no explanation. "Let's leave that one for now and go to the next paragraph," Betsy suggested.

"He could be saying that someone they trusted betrayed them, or because he says 'take care, my friend,' he may be saying that John is not to trust anyone, not even him." Paul raised his brow as his eyes narrowed. "'Don't be fooled' could simply mean don't be fooled." He shrugged his shoulders in resignation.

"You're probably right," Elmira said with approval. "Does everyone agree?"

"I think you should take a crack at the paragraph we're struggling with while you're on a roll," chuckled Dawn, obviously proud of her husband's ability.

"Okay, darlin'. Read it to me again."

"It only takes two days to receive what it used to take weeks to deliver. Still, nothing in life is guaranteed except perhaps peace to the soul."

Paul was quiet, his face frozen in thought once again. Everyone waited until his brow fell back into place. "I think," he said, the fingers on his hands pressed together barely touching his lips, "Garrett's talking about their deaths. I think he's saying that it would only take a few days before their names and their findings would be handed to the highest bidder and they would be dead unless they could go into hiding."

"Brilliant," Betsy whispered.

"More than brilliant," Lincoln added.

"There's still one question to be answered," Paul muttered, almost to himself. "Why was the letter still in a jacket that seemingly wasn't to be worn, only made to look that way? I have to believe there's something else here. Something we're missing. Let's get some rest, let things set for a few days then come back to it Saturday afternoon after we get the links."

Chandler's cell phone rang, the caller ID alerting him that the person on the other end was their man of mystery. He listened and commented only once before closing the cover.

"What's up?" Mac inquired, looking lazily over his half-eaten candy bar.

"A watch!" Chandler replied. "One that our mystery man wants very badly and one that Mrs. Braden apparently found in the woods. We're to forget the notebooks and listen for anything that would lead him to the watch, but we're not to go after it."

"Think he's found what he's looking for?"

"Could be. We're on double alert from . . ." Chandler didn't finish his sentence. Mac's hand shot up, meaning he was getting sounds through the earphones. He motioned for Chandler to pick up.

Together they listened to a dog's friendly bark and the sound of a door opening and closing. The conversation was light with the discussion of delicious chocolate brownies and plans for a quiet weekend.

Mrs. Braden yawned and told her son she was going to bed. Her son, Lincoln, said he thought he would turn in also. The dog barked again and then there was silence.

"So M&M wants us to eliminate the notebooks as possible clues?" Mac inquired, lowering his earphones to his neck.

"M&M?"

"New name for our mystery man," Mac said, grinning.

Chandler had a hard time keeping a straight face. "M&M doesn't want us to focus on anything but the watch." He gave his partner a quirky look and stood. "I think I'll stretch my legs before crawling into the bedroll. M&M," he chuckled to himself as he closed the door to the back of the van.

Friday morning, Lincoln found a jacket in his closet that looked like it could use a cleaning. "I'm off to the cleaners," he called to his mother. "Want me to take anything for you?"

"No, dear," she replied from the office, "but tell Ned and Terri 'hello' for me."

Lincoln whistled for Dorado. "Want to go to town, boy?"

Dorado gave him that sad look of a dog who wants to go more than he wants to stay but knows he has to stay.

"I understand, golden boy. Take good care of her for me while I'm gone." He climbed into his Jeep and waved. Dorado's return bark was almost a whine.

Twenty minutes later, Lincoln stood outside Ned's Cleaners, rehearsing what he would say once he walked through the door. Although he was relieved when it was Terri behind the counter and not her father, he wished he had more girl/boy repertoire.

When Terri looked up at him and smiled, his mind went completely blank, leaving him feeling much like a fool. Terri, however, didn't seem to notice, calling out to him. "Good morning, Lincoln. It's good to see you again. How's your mom?"

Those were questions he could answer without his tongue getting all tangled, so he attempted it with confidence. "Good morning. She's fine, thank you." Then he added, "I'm glad it's you at the counter instead of your dad. He used to scare me."

"What's that?" a voice from the back room called out.

Oh, no! Lincoln could hardly believe his luck.

"Hello, Lincoln," shouted Ned, his face peeking around the door. "I'm happy to know that you had some respect for me." He laughed as he came through the door to embrace Lincoln in a way a father would. "It's good to see you again. Home for the summer?"

"I am, sir," Lincoln said, feeling the warmth of a blush and trying hard to stifle it.

Ned stepped back and looked into the young man's face. "It's amazing. You're a young reminder of your father. I miss him, you know."

Lincoln nodded.

Ned patted him on the shoulder and turned to Terri. "I've got some errands to run for your mother. I'll be back so you can go to lunch around one. And, Lincoln," he said cheerfully, facing him again, "tell your mother 'hi' for us."

"I will, sir."

"The next time we meet, you can call me Ned," he leaned close and whispered as he walked past Lincoln and out the door.

"What can I do for you?" Terri smiled.

"Uh, I need this jacket cleaned."

"When do you need it?"

"Uh . . . will the day after tomorrow be okay?"

"I think it will be fine." She smiled again.

He turned, not wanting to leave but not knowing what else to say in reference to asking for a date.

"Lincoln?" he heard her say.

"Yes?" he replied.

"Do you want to give me your jacket?"

Complete idiot. "Yes, of course." He felt awkward setting his jacket down in front of her, as if there was a correct and incorrect way to place a jacket on the counter of a dry cleaners and he was in complete incorrectness. *In complete incorrectness! Is that even a correct thought? Come on, Lincoln, why not just make a complete fool out of yourself and ask her to lunch?*

"I just had a thought," he said in complete honesty. "Why don't I come back at one and take you to lunch so I can apologize for all the things I said to you when you were a kid and I was a jerky teenager?"

"I think that would be a great idea," he heard her say.

"You do?"

"Yes, I've been waiting a long time for an apology."

"You have?"

"I have." She smiled, and the dimples deepened.

Lincoln had to admit that even when he hadn't liked her, he liked her dimples. "Great! I'll see you then." He walked out the front door without tripping over his feet, feeling very pleased with himself. He had done it! He had actually asked a girl out for a date. It may not have been a class act, but it went well, once his brain kicked in.

He looked at his watch. He had two hours to kill before returning to the dry cleaners. That gave him time to go to the library to see if he could find any yearbooks from the university. Once inside, the librarian directed him to the second floor, west side, where he found yearbooks dating from this year back to the early 1900s. He removed the books from the last four years and found a table, eager to see what he would find.

Searching the most recent one, which should have been April's senior year, he failed to find her name listed anywhere. The next one gave him nothing. But the book dated the year she would have been a sophomore gave him a name in the index. *April S. Garrett; pages 63, 89, 101, 160.* He could hardly contain his excitement as he shuffled the pages with his itching fingers.

Page 63, now open to view, gave him rows of smiling faces with names beneath them. His eyes darted from one name to the other until he spotted the one he was searching for. He made his eyes focus on the picture. Relief etched its way through his body when he saw the face of the girl who had given his mother the letters. He almost felt like shedding tears. The strain of this whole situation had been heavier than he realized.

He turned to page 89 and a picture of April with the Debate Club. The caption read: *This year's debate team received high honors in national competition . . .*

He turned to page 101 showing a picture of the stage production. The caption read:

West Side Story . . . April was in full costume.

Turning to page 160, he found that April also received honors in Science and was on the Dean's List.

Why had she been so active and then suddenly disappeared from the book for the next two years? He flipped open his cell phone and punched in a number that would reach his uncle at the lab.

"Hello," the familiar voice said.

"Uncle Paul, it's Lincoln. I wonder if you could do something for me."

"Name it, my boy."

"Who do you know at the university?"

"Almost everyone. Give me an assignment."

Lincoln found a sports magazine and a comfortable chair while he waited for his uncle to get back to him. One more hour, and he could meet Terri. With fifteen minutes to spare, his cell phone rang.

"It seems April Garrett finished her college studies as an off-campus student," Paul recited over the phone.

"Meaning?"

"Meaning she was unable to attend classes because of illness or other complications."

"That's a simple enough answer, I guess. Thanks, Uncle Paul, for your help. Now I need to find out what actually kept her from on-campus studies."

"Open heart surgery. Complications. Recovery."

"I see," Lincoln replied. "I think I misjudged her."

"But you solved the mystery. There is an April Garrett."

Terri was waiting when he walked into the cleaners. "Just let me tell Dad I'm leaving," she said, disappearing into another room.

When she reappeared, her father was at her side. "Just have her back by two thirty," he said with a grin.

"I promise, sir."

"Ned, please."

"Yes, sir." Lincoln gulped as he opened the door for Terri.

"Dad really likes you," she giggled as they walked into the restaurant just a block from the cleaners.

"And I feel just a little uncomfortable in his presence," Lincoln admitted.

After the waitress took their orders, Terri asked Lincoln if he was ready to make his request for forgiveness. The ice was broken, and Lincoln suddenly felt very comfortable sitting next to the young woman he had teased unmercifully years before.

"I really didn't mean all the things I said, especially one or two of which we won't go into."

"Is there a reason we won't go into them?" Terri blinked her eyes and placed her hands under her chin.

"There is, and I won't go into that either."

Terri laughed. "I think I know one, and you were right—I was a spoiled, fat little brat."

"I said that?" Lincoln looked shocked.

Terri nodded her head and grinned.

"For that one I beg forgiveness."

They laughed and slowly the conversation turned to the present and college and future hopes and dreams. The time slipped by far too quickly, and long before Lincoln was ready to say goodbye, it was time to return Terri to work.

As they walked back to the cleaners, Terri asked if Betsy had read the notebook her father found sewn inside his father's jacket pocket.

He replied that she had.

"Did your mother tell you what we talked about that day?"

"I don't recall that she did," he replied, his face lined in thought.

"I've wondered since then if it would have been best not to mention the man in the felt hat."

Lincoln knew, in all the things she had told him, his mother never mentioned a man wearing a felt hat, so he asked Terri to repeat the story.

"I saw him again," she said, after she finished telling the story. "He was coming out of the courthouse on Monday. It's the felt hat that draws my attention."

"What kind is it?"

"I'd call it an Indiana Jones hat. I tried hard to get a look at his face this time, but all I could see was a short beard beneath the brim. He wears the hat low." She looked at her watch. "Well, I guess I'd better get back to work before the boss fires me."

"Can I call you again?" The words were out of Lincoln's mouth before he realized it.

"I'd like that," she replied. She looked into his eyes. "I've always liked you, Lincoln, even when I didn't like you."

Before he could respond, she disappeared through the door, and he was left on the sidewalk to ponder her words. His heart felt light as he climbed into his Jeep and drove home.

ten

CEMETERIES &
REVELATIONS

Saturday morning at seven, Lincoln, Dawn, and Paul stood with seventeen contracted workers. Those in charge of beautification were circled around a map indicating where bushes and greenery were to be planted, discussing their approach. The contractors who were building and repairing the fence were circling the area to be fenced, going over their plan of attack.

Lincoln, dressed for construction, walked with the fence people while Paul and Dawn, in their conservative straw hats, seemed to be listening intently to the plant people. When everyone began separating into their individual responsibilities, the three made their way to the tent in the upper left-hand corner. A robotic digger was waiting for them inside the tent, and putting emotions aside, they began their task.

By eight thirty, they had the concrete lid connected to the wires that would lift it away from the tomb. A mechanical arm was turned to the on position, and a grinding sound was heard as the lid slowly ascended toward them revealing a beautiful crimson coffin lid. With soft brushes, they began to wipe the dust away to prevent it from falling into the casket when the lid was raised. As they worked, Dawn watched Lincoln's face lose its color and his eyes begin to water.

She motioned to Paul who, in turn, paused to look at his nephew. "Lincoln," he said, wiping the sweat from his face with his handkerchief, "if at any time you feel you need to leave, we'll understand."

"I'll be fine." Lincoln's voice was shaky, but he stood firm.

Dawn touched his arm. "We can't prepare you for what you'll see inside."

"I promise, I'll be fine," he repeated in an effort to convince himself as much as the two of them.

Dawn nodded to Paul, and he reached down to release the lid. Lincoln stepped back, feeling as if he was going to pass out. *Come on, Lincoln, you can do this.* But even as he attempted to convince himself, he knew he couldn't.

By the time he heard the click of the lock, he was outside the tent, his knees too weak to hold him up. His hands were shaking, his heart was pounding, beads of perspiration were forming on his forehead, and his stomach was begging to be rid of its contents.

The minutes passed as tears fell unchecked. The love he felt for his father seared his heart and, for the first time in his life, he could taste the bitterness of hate. He thought about the two men who stood on his mother's property discussing the murder of his father, and instantly he was in control again. He turned and entered the tent, knowing he could do what he had to do to finish what his father couldn't.

Paul was lowering the lid as he stepped inside. In Dawn's hand, he could see two small watch links.

"We've got them," she said softly. "They were there waiting for us, Lincoln." She reached and handed them to him. "We'll take them to the lab as soon as we finish here."

Lincoln took the links and studied them. The decision to exhume the body had been the right decision, and relief flooded his body.

Dawn put her arms around him. "I know it was a hunch that led us here, hoping we would find them. I know that it was one of the most difficult things you've ever done, but it was necessary."

"I know, and I'm sorry I couldn't stay," he muttered apologetically, letting her arms comfort him.

"Oh, Lincoln, don't be sorry." She stepped away from him, placing her hands on his arms. "I don't think John would have wanted you to have that memory."

Lincoln handed her the links. "What about you? I can see it wasn't easy for you, yet you stayed."

"It wasn't the first time I've had to do this, nor will it be the last. This time, however, it was personal and, I admit, disturbing, but he wasn't my father."

Dawn slipped the links into a plastic bag and then put the plastic bag into her pocket. "Even though we know he's not here, we know he carried what remains in the casket as part of his being here on earth. It's almost impossible for us to separate the two because of the love we carry inside for him. Don't feel badly because you had to leave, feel joy because you loved him so much that you couldn't stay." She reached up, wiped the tears from his face, and kissed his cheek.

"Thank you, Aunt Dawn." Lincoln felt his shame vanish in her comfort.

It took two more hours to make the grave site look almost untouched. The tamper worked well to make the ground even again, its noise blending with the racket echoing throughout the working area.

"A person would have to stand pretty close to see any disturbance here," Paul said proudly when they were finished. "What time is it?"

"Almost noon," Lincoln replied, eyeing his uncle. "Do I look as dirty as you do?" He grinned as Paul removed the protective glasses from his face, leaving him with an owlish look.

"You might wear it a little better, however," Paul chuckled.

"For some reason, youth tends to wear dirt well."

They studied each other for a second; then both burst out laughing. The tension of the task lifted with the magnitude of the find sinking in. Both observations were grounds for rejoicing.

"Lunch break," Dawn called as she peeked in. "I cased the area for anything that would be deemed suspicious. All seems as it should be."

"You don't consider three people digging up a grave somewhat suspicious?" joked Lincoln.

"Not if you're the ones doing the digging."

"Who's digging?" Paul asked. "I can see no one digging."

"You're not going to convince anyone with that face of yours," scoffed Dawn. "Now come on out and clean yourself up a little so you can have a nice sack lunch provided by the city."

Sitting in front of the tent eating their lunch, they watched the other workers in various parts of the cemetery either eating or lying on the grass resting. Most of them looked as dirty as Paul and Lincoln.

"When can we leave?" Lincoln asked, his head beginning to throb from the tension in his body. Tension was evident in the faces of Dawn and Paul as well. Despite their attempt to lighten the mood, the reality of their task weighed heavily on their minds.

"Whenever we're ready," Paul explained. "We'll just work our way back to our vehicles, looking officially busy, commenting to each other on this or that as we go. There will be someone by later this afternoon to pick up the equipment we used. There will be no signs that we were even here by quitting time. My friend has been very discreet, and I must thank him. I promised I'd let him know when we were finished, so you two go ahead. I'll meet you at the house.

They followed Paul's suggestion, and in forty-five minutes they were sitting in the Arington's well-equipped in-home laboratory. While Dawn worked the first link apart, the two men hovered over her shoulder, watching anxiously. The vibrating sound of the delicate tool in her hand seemed to fill the room with its clatter as little beads of perspiration kept getting in the way of her vision.

"Would you two mind giving me a little space?" she ventured.

"Sorry!" both men chimed together, backing away perhaps an inch.

There was a clicking sound, and the link was open. Inside lay a tiny chip. Carefully, Dawn removed it and placed it in a clear lab dish.

The second link proved to be as productive, revealing another tiny chip inside its chamber. It, likewise, was placed in a clear lab dish.

Paul picked up the phone and instructed it to dial Betsy's number. When Betsy answered, he invited her and Elmira to a barbecue in their back yard. "Bring Lincoln so he can make the ice cream," he added for good measure.

After Lincoln left to meet Paul and Dawn at the cemetery, Betsy had tried to write, but there was nothing she wanted to write. All she wanted to do was think about the grave site of her husband. Finally, she called Dorado, and together they went for a walk. As they walked, she talked and the golden boy listened.

"We met at a university ward social," she said, keeping her voice quiet in the silence of the trees. "He was entertaining the group with a slide show of his mission in the islands. He was hilarious as he told the stories behind the slides. That's what I fell in love with at first, Dorado. I fell in love with his sense of humor long before I fell in love with him."

She told her dog about John's smile, how gentle he was with each baby that entered their lives, and how he loved them. She explained how proud he was of each one of their children as they set out on their own path.

"He was so full of conversation, Dorado, so full of humor, so full of love, so full of life."

In the mist of the trees, Dorado gave a soft bark and moved closer to Betsy. "What is it, boy?" she asked, feeling the tingle that swept down her spine. It was so quiet she could hear herself breathing. Even the birds were silent. She stood still. The calm around her reflected a reverence she had never experienced before. Then she saw him, or felt his presence, she wasn't sure which. The only thing she knew was that he was here.

"John?" she whispered. She could feel his caressing hand on her cheek and the deepness of his voice in her ear. "I miss you too," she heard herself say. Then she listened.

When Paul called half an hour later, she already knew they had found the microchips. She knew there was still much ahead, but her greatest knowledge was that she was unafraid because John was not far from her.

❧❦❧❦❧

Elmira was waiting on her steps, a chocolate cake in one hand and a DVD in the other, when Betsy's car pulled into her driveway.

"I ask myself," Betsy said, eyeing the cake in her mother's arms, "where does that woman who calls herself my mother, get all her energy?"

Elmira smiled, closed the car door, and handed over the DVD. The label read *Yoga for Beginners*. "We'll start you out on the simple stuff for now. In a few months, if you follow the instructions, I think we can move you up to the intermediate. Any questions?"

"You're telling me, in your own way, that if I study yoga, I'll know the answer to my question, right?"

"Close, dear. Now from what you didn't tell me on the phone, I'm assuming the news from the grave diggers is good."

Betsy gave her mother a shocked look. "Don't you think you're being somewhat irreverent?"

"Sorry, Babe, can't be helped."

"And what does that mean?"

"Simply that."

"Sometimes you don't make sense," Betsy complained.

"Good!"

"Good?"

"Yes, good. Now what didn't Paul tell you on the phone."

Betsy rolled her eyes at her mother.

"No dramatics, dear, just facts." Elmira's eyes danced as she buckled her seat belt.

Betsy pulled out of the driveway while repeating Paul's message. "What he didn't say was that things went well and they found what they were looking for, and actually, I'm so thankful they did. I didn't want John's body disturbed for no reason."

Elmira reached over and patted her daughter's shoulder. "I'm thankful too."

Betsy glanced out of the corner of her eye and got a glimpse of a tear in the corner of her mother's. "I love you, Mother," she sighed.

"I love you too, Babe," her mother replied.

They drove for a short distance saying nothing, only listening to the music on the radio. Then, without warning, Elmira reached out and turned the radio off. "Tell me, Babe," she brushed her fingers through her daughter's hair.

Betsy turned and stared at her mother, registering disbelief.

"You might want to redirect your eyes and keep us from wrecking."

"How do you always know?" Betsy moaned, quickly regaining herself.

"Because you're my daughter."

There was silence for the next few miles and then Betsy confided in her mother. "I felt very unsettled about what was happening this morning," she said simply. "To ease my mind I took Dorado for a walk in the woods . . ."

Elmira waited.

"I felt John's presence, Mother. I felt his hand on my cheek. We talked."

"He has faith in you, now. He knows you've got the courage." Elmira adjusted the cake on her lap and smiled contently.

Betsy watched her out of the corner of her eye. "Is that all you have to say?"

"That's all that needs to be said. Besides, we're almost there. I hope Paul is barbecuing T-bones."

"I'm curious, Mother," Betsy said, as they pulled into the driveway, "as to why you insist on producing one-liners?"

"There are times when more words would be a waste of time, be misunderstood, or cause unnecessary confrontation. There are times when the less that is said, the more it is understood."

"For example?"

"Exactly!"

Betsy turned to her mother and once again rolled her eyes. Then together they climbed out of the car.

"See, dear, sometimes not even words are necessary to convey a message." Elmira took her daughter's arm and led her to the door. "I can't quote scripture or verse, but I know that words are powerful, Babe. They are used to influence others, to embellish, destroy, encourage, or discourage. We have to be careful how we use them. If one word will accomplish what a hundred won't, why waste the ninety-nine?"

Before Betsy could comment, Dawn opened the door and hurried them inside. As soon as the door was closed, she wrapped her arms around her sister. "It went well, Betsy," she said tenderly. "The links were right where we only had to reach in and take them. We didn't have to disturb anything. Come see what we found. Paul is connecting them to the watch right now."

"First, I have to ask," Betsy looked Dawn in the eye. "Was it painful for him to swallow the links?"

"I can't say. If they were to go down length-wise, I'd say they would slide down with very little discomfort."

Betsy nodded.

"You two go into the study and see what we found while I take this cake to the kitchen."

"Ah, there you are," Paul greeted Elmira at the door of the lab with a kiss on her cheek; then, putting his arm around Betsy's shoulders, he guided the women to the dishes that held the microchips.

"Let me tell you a little bit about these tiny marvels," Lincoln said, taking one of the chips and placing it in his mother's hand. He handed the second one to Elmira.

"Inside this chip there are tiny wire and transistors designed to do certain things. There may be more than one layer of wires and transistors, giving the chip the ability to accomplish more complicated tasks. Monday morning I'll take a trip to my college lab where I'll have the equipment to study their configurations. Once we know the configurations, we'll know what this one has been designed to do."

"Is this what electrical engineers do?" Elmira asked, turning the chip over in her hand, giving it a full inspection. "Design these tiny little chips?"

"Those who chose that field, yes." Lincoln smiled at her.

"Is this what you'll do?"

"That's the plan."

"The power to control a computer sits inside this tiny chip, is that right?" Elmira looked at her grandson for verification.

He smiled and nodded. "More or less."

"Remember what we were talking about in the car, Betsy?" she turned to her daughter. "Compare the power of this tiny chip to the power of a single word. It looks harmless, even vulnerable, but in reality, its power goes almost beyond the imagination."

"Yes, it does," Betsy admitted.

"Things are coming together, Babe. The way is opening for us to find the answers. We are not alone in this." Elmira set her chip back into the dish. Betsy did the same.

"Elmira's right, you know," Paul assured Betsy as he padded the dishes then placed a lid over them to protect the chips. "Things are coming together."

Betsy looked at her brother-in-law, the fatigue in his voice audible. It made her realize that exhuming John's body had been as difficult for them as it had been for her.

"Yes, Paul," she said, as she reached out, wrapping her arm around her mother and drawing her close. "Elmira's always right, and aren't we blessed to have her?"

"Pretty quiet at the Braden home," Mac said, when Chandler climbed into the van. "They're having a barbecue at the sister's house."

"The sister, the brother-in-law, and the kid had a busy morning though." Chandler's comment brought Mac straight up in his seat.

"Doing what?"

"They visited the husband's grave. Seems the city's doing some work there. Tent covers for the grave sites—the works."

"And?" Mac leaned forward in his chair.

"I think they did some digging," Chandler continued. "After they left, I took the opportunity to peek inside the tent. Good cover-up but not perfect."

"Why would they dig up the grave . . . unless it was to get something buried with John."

"Right! But why would they bury something only to dig it up over a year later . . . unless they didn't know it was there at the time of the burial?"

"How could they not know?" Mac asked, his face scrunched in a frown. "Unless . . ."

"My thoughts exactly."

"Okay, what do you do now?"

Chandler took a scrap of paper from the lining of his wallet, unfolded it carefully, and dialed the number written on the inside. He waited for the connection; then he greeted the person on the other end warmly. "It may be time," he said.

After a few minutes of conversation, he closed the cover of his cell phone and nodded to his partner. Mac nodded back, and they resumed the task at hand—waiting.

Three hours later, Chandler woke Mac from a deep sleep and signaled for him to begin recording. They listened while Betsy and Lincoln talked.

"I've got something I want to show you," they heard Betsy say.

"They're walking into the study," Mac observed. "Now she's turning the dial of the safe."

"Dorado dug this out of the ground near the walking path."

There was a pause and then Lincoln's voice came over the earphones mentioning a watch and claiming it looked like his father's, to which his mother replied that it was. They continued to discuss the watch while the machine picked up their conversation.

Their conversation revealed their concern about why John would bury his watch and their thoughts about the brilliance of Dorado. In the hours that followed, generic dialogue took fifteen minutes of tape time. Simple conversation commenting on the movie they were watching on TV wasted another two hours.

"Okay," Mac said behind a yawn, when the evening was finally over and the Bradens had gone to bed. "We know where the watch is."

When Chandler didn't respond, Mac looked over to see his partner's legs propped up on the desk, his eyes squinted in thought, and his pencil tapping rhythmically against his thigh.

"Do you think," Chandler said after a time, "that the

son went to the cemetery with the Arlington's without his mother's knowledge?"

"Could happen," Mac replied, his finger on the rewind button. "But you don't think it's likely, right?"

"Hard to say. The Bradens have spent a lot of time away from their house lately. We actually know very little of what's been said. Then a trip to the cemetery today, and tonight they discuss the watch. Could be a coincidence. Then, again, maybe not."

"What made you go to the cemetery?" Mac inquired.

"I'm not sure. Just a hunch, I suppose. Maybe it's because we weren't having any success with what we were collecting on tape. Maybe it's because the kid seems to always be going somewhere and, this time, I decided to follow. Maybe it's because of his interest in the license plates. Maybe it's a combination of all three."

"Well, it paid off. I'm not sure how yet, but I have a feeling we'll find out."

"Do you want M&M to know where the watch is?"

"Something tells me he's not going to find what he's looking for." He looked at Mac. "Yes, I think we can tell M&M where the watch is."

"They go to church at eleven tomorrow, and at two, they are going to the mother's house for dinner. The dog goes with them when they go there. I'd say we have a two-hour window in which his men could get in and out without being spotted."

"What if tomorrow they leave the dog home?" Mac asked.

"Then we'll take care of the dog," Chandler promised. He opened the cover of his cell phone once again and dialed a number he had memorized. He told the voice on the other end the watch had been found and they could go in, undisturbed, the next day between two fifteen and four o'clock. He gave the combination to the safe and explained where the study was located.

"We'll go in and clean up after they leave," he explained and closed the cover.

The next day everything went as planned. At two fifteen, the house was empty. The two men did their thing and left but not without being photographed by Mac. The clean up was minimal, and by three, Mac and Chandler were looking at the faces of Mitch and Hal on a computer screen.

"I'll go to the office and work on a match," Mac said, flexing his fingers, "while you work on your suspicions." He opened the door to the van, then turned back to Chandler. "I may have some information on the Hoffman saga when I get to the office." He waved, closed the door, and climbed into the Fiat.

Mac knew Chandler's concern over the letter was pressing. He wished he could get the web moving a little faster for his friend, but information on Leonard Hoffman seemed to be buried deep. He couldn't help but wonder why. Were the Hoffmans involved in this triangle of mystery, or were they victims caught in its web? He wanted to believe, after sitting with Andrew Hoffman for an hour, that they were victims. But, until he located Leonard Hoffman, he wouldn't know why.

eleven

EVIDENCE UNCOVERED, MYSTERIES UNVEILED

Mitch pulled away from the Braden property with understandable vigilance. He'd be a fool not to. The break-in seemed so easy, so perfect. The watch was where it was supposed to be. The place was quiet when they got there and quiet when they left.

The only other human being they saw was a biker who pulled alongside them at the stop sign and asked how long it would take him to get to I-95. Mitch might have been suspicious except that when the biker thanked them, he turned left and was out of sight without looking back in their direction. Just to make sure he didn't return, however, Mitch waited at the stop sign for a few minutes before making a right turn.

"Kinda like it when things go smooth," Hal quipped. "Might say it's like takin' candy from a baby, as the old saying goes."

"Well don't undo the wrapper yet." Mitch eyed his partner. "I don't like following orders from guys I don't know."

"They're workin' for us, man! We're givin' the orders," Hal argued, taking in the area as they drove. But he found himself suddenly feeling a little edgy. "Geez, you sure know how to take the fun out of doin' a job."

Mitch's fingers were wrapped tight around the steering wheel, his eyes darting from the road in front of him to the road behind. He wouldn't relax until they were back on the main highway. "Make the call and let him know we got the watch," he said.

Hal pulled a phone from his jacket pocket and reported in. "He'll meet us at the club," he muttered, replacing the phone. "How much longer do ya think this job's gonna last? I'm startin' to feel a little antsy."

"Let's just hope the watch delivers whatever it is the boss is looking for."

"That's part of what makes me antsy," Hal replied. "The boss is too secretive about everything."

Mitch let Hal's words work on him. Though his brains seemed to be in his muscles, it was a different kind of intellect that motivated Hal, one that had kept him alive. He was like an animal in the way he could read the people they worked with. Maybe it was because he understood their way of thinking.

"How long we been workin' for this guy?" Hal asked, interrupting his thoughts.

"Almost three years."

"Right! And what d'ya know about him? I mean, where does the guy live, for example?"

Mitch looked over at Hal, his face wrinkled with thought. "I don't know."

"What's our business with him?"

"I don't know that either," Mitch replied, conscious that Hal had a point.

"He never gives us any conversation, only orders. Every other guy we've worked for gives us an address. Maybe we see a wife, or a girlfriend. Maybe we see some kids. But we always know what our business is with him. We always know what he looks like. We always know his name."

Mitch nodded. Hal was right. They had never really seen the boss's face in the light. Their meetings were held in the dark corner of a club. Even then, the man wore that hat of his, like a mask.

"What's his name, Mitch?"

"I don't know, Hal. Maybe that's why he pays up front and pays well. He keeps us happy, and we don't ask questions."

"Don't keep them from poppin' up in my mind," Hal retorted. "I say we watch our backs from here on out."

Mitch's thoughts went back to the morning he killed John Braden. He had never killed before, and the flashbacks still haunted him. He had done some bad things in his life, but murder was not one of them. Now he had to live with what he had done. His desire for this line of work had waned after that. The money was the only thing that motivated him now. But even the money was beginning to lose its appeal.

He had rotted away his life to get back at his parents, who called him unworthy to be their son. In doing so, he only proved how unworthy he was.

He glanced over at his partner. "Hal," he said, "I'm getting out of the business. I'm tired."

"Yer kiddin'!" Hal's face registered bewilderment. "Why, man?"

"I think maybe I'll try going straight. Maybe go to college. I've always been fascinated with law. Had my mind set on being a lawyer once."

"C'mon, man, yer scarin' me," Hal stammered.

<hr />

Lincoln turned left, leaving the car at the stop sign, and pushed his bike speed to thirty miles per hour. Two miles up the road, he made a quick exit onto a side road and parked behind some trees next to his Jeep.

The bike had belonged to his father, who kept it parked in Grandmother's garage because Betsy was unhappy with him for buying the dangerous thing. Today it was being put to good use, he knew, with his mother's blessing.

As soon as he was off the bike, he pulled the helmet from his head and pressed his cell phone to his ear. "Is it working?" he shouted when Paul picked up.

"Like a charm, nephew."

The tracker beam Lincoln had attached to the car when he leaned over to ask directions was simply a clear patch, undetectable, but also untested outside the laboratory. Two unknown factors existed: How long would the patch remain stable, and how long could the beam send its signal?

This new invention belonged to a colleague of Paul's. Knowing it would be perfect for their needs if it lasted only a few hours, Paul had offered to test its ability on the road if the colleague would take him golfing the following Wednesday.

The deal was made, and Paul's plan was, in his words, almost without blemish. The blemish would materialize only if the patch disintegrated or failed to transfer the beam before the car reached it destination.

"Is there a back-up plan?" Dawn wanted to know.

"I'm banking on the tracker beam," Paul replied. "I've seen it tested in the lab. It's been through twenty-five tests without failing. We're basically testing endurance not performance."

"It's the endurance I'm worried about," his wife chided.

Despite the question of endurance, the family voted to go with Paul's plan, along with a back-up plan. The beam would guide them, but someone would always be within visual contact of the vehicle they were following, just in case the beam failed. There was too much at stake. Both plans, put together, would eliminate the possible blemish, according to Elmira.

Lincoln climbed in his Jeep and headed toward the freeway while Paul directed him to go to exit 2A on I-95.

"The car is moving toward Arlington on Highway 225," Paul told him. "Betsy's right behind it. Dawn is waiting on the outskirts of Arlington. She drove there earlier, thinking they would probably move in that direction. Elmira's with me, and together we've got this whole tracking thing down. However,

I'm not sure of the tracker's radius, so I'll stay relatively close.

And so it went. The car continued on through Arlington on the main road, with Betsy turning off and Dawn waiting to turn on just after the car passed by. Lincoln stayed on the freeway and headed to Lexington. The car made a turn after driving through Medford and took the entrance to I-93 to Lexington, not far behind him.

The tracker monitored each move the car made while Paul choreographed the moves of the cars that followed it.

An hour into their adventure, Paul glanced over at Elmira who was watching the monitor carefully. "It kind of reminds me of the swan dance," he chuckled, "each swan taking its place to fill in the gap." While outwardly he was jovial, inside he was praying the tracker would hold until the end.

He hadn't fooled Elmira. She could easily see beneath the façade, and she silently prayed that he would be blessed for his efforts.

When the car took the Summerville exit in Cambridge, the car behind it continued on while another one pulled off two cars behind.

"They're going into Cambridge," Elmira informed everyone. She gave directions to Lincoln as they followed the car to an alleyway behind a building. The car parked somewhere inside the alley, and the light on the monitor was still.

Paul parked on the street and waited. The light remained stationary. "I think we have a destination, but I don't know if it's the one we want," he said to Lincoln over the phone. "How far away are you?"

"About five minutes," Lincoln replied.

While they waited for Lincoln, Paul got out of the car and strolled by the building that would be directly in front of the tracker beam. He could hear music coming from inside. He crossed the street, making note of the sign revealing a name, and made his way back to the car.

"I'd say it's a chic night club," he told Elmira. "The

University Club." He used his hands to create the illusion of an impressive sign.

"You don't say?"

Before he could say anymore, Lincoln pulled in behind them. Paul's phone rang. "It's the third building on this side of the street. Is five thirty a good time to walk into a chic club for a drink?"

"I'll soon find out," Lincoln replied.

Paul closed his phone and, together, he and Elmira watched Lincoln run a comb through his hair, straighten his shirt, and walk toward the night club.

Soft music greeted him as he opened the door and walked into the dimness of a large, elegant room filled with tables, chairs, and greenery. Several people were sitting at a bar next to a well-lighted stage. Several more sat around the tables. He would be just one of the many customers stopping in for a drink. He would probably be the only customer, however, who didn't know how or what to order.

On the stage, a man was doing an imitation of Dean Martin. He was pretty good too. Lincoln walked to the bar, took a stool just as he had seen it done in the movies, and ordered a Scotch and water, knowing that's what they always order in the movies. When the bartender brought his drink, Lincoln handed him a five-dollar bill. No change was forthcoming. *Expensive little drink,* he thought to himself. No one watched to see if he drank it because no one cared. He was safe.

He let his eyes wander about the room, looking for the two faces he had seen in the car and decided they weren't in this part of the club. He stood and walked to a lone table in the corner, away from the main party. He sat there, eating pretzels from the bowl sitting in the middle of the table, and waited.

Time passed, faces changed, but none of them belonging to the two men. He lifted the cover of his cell phone. "Any movement out there?" he asked.

"None. The car is still behind the building, and I believe the tracker is beginning to fragment. The beam's starting to fade. Do what you can in there."

Lincoln decided it was time to do a little exploring. The audience seemed entranced with the entertainer, so he melted into the darkness and worked his way to the back of the club. To his right he could see the signs to the restrooms, to his left chef's hats greeted him behind swinging doors. In front of him, he could see a dim corridor.

He looked around him. He was alone. He followed the corridor, keeping close to the wall, until he could hear voices coming from somewhere to his left. He held his breath and listened but couldn't make out the words. He crept closer until a thin wall was the only thing that separated him from the two men on the other side.

A third man joined the party. He had a soft-spoken voice with a slight accent. He asked to see the watch. In the silence that followed, Lincoln imagined he was inspecting it.

"You've done well," the voice said.

The sound of what Lincoln imagined to be an envelope of money being tossed on the table came next. Then the man spoke again. "Did it go as we were informed it would?"

"Yes, sir," he heard another man's voice say. "There was no one home, the combination was correct, and the watch was in the safe, just as they said it would be."

"Good! You may leave now."

It was then that Lincoln could hear footsteps coming in his direction. He looked around him. He was at the end of the corridor with no place to hide. He eased his body into the corner and pressed himself against the wall. The footsteps were getting louder, or was it the thumping of his heart he could hear?

Knowing the gravity of his situation, he held his breath, closed his eyes, and prayed that, if it were at all possible, he would become invisible.

He could smell the cologne and feel the disturbance in the air as someone passed by him. The next thing he heard was a voice saying, "Your room is ready."

"Thank you," the voice with the accent replied.

Lincoln heard footsteps again, but this time they were moving away from him. With his heart pounding in his throat, constricting the breathing passages, he made himself inch along the wall until he could peek into the other room. Two men were ascending a flight of steps, their backs to him. Both of them were about the same height, a little over six feet. One was dark and wore a hotel jacket, the other one was slim and wore a hat that resembled the one Terri described to him. He would have given anything to get a glimpse at the man's face.

After they disappeared and the trembling in his body began to subside, Lincoln willed his feet to move, one in front of the other until they carried him to the restroom. Once inside, he splashed cold water over his face to wake up his senses. When he looked at himself in the mirror, he hardly recognized the ghostly face. *Take your time, Lincoln, breath in . . . out . . . in . . . out. Okay, now pull yourself together!*

He wiped his face, combed his hair, opened the door of the restroom, and managed to walk out of the club without calling attention to himself. By the time he reached his car, he was able to take deep breaths again. It was exhilarating. He nodded to Paul, who was pulling away from the curb.

Lincoln opened his car door just as his cell phone rang. He listened to the instructions while fastening his seat belt. He was anxious to be away from this place.

When he walked through the doors of Paul's favorite restaurant in Cambridge, the headwaiter led him to a small room where everyone was waiting for him.

"You look a little pale under the gills," Paul said, once Lincoln was seated next to his mother.

"You mean my brush with death shows?" he asked, with attempted humor. Then, breathing a heavy sigh, he admitted, "I've decided I'm claustrophobic."

Betsy put her arm through her son's and handed him a glass of water. "Drink this," she urged. "It will make you feel better."

He did so without questioning. The coolness of the water felt good against the heat of his insides. He couldn't help but wonder if he was more a coward than the brave soul he thought himself to be.

The waiter appeared at the door, took their orders then withdrew, leaving them alone to talk.

Dawn was the first to speak. "I think we should hear what Lincoln has to say first." Lincoln was anxious to tell them his story. He tried not to leave anything out but avoided the part about the frozen fear that engulfed him for that short period of time. Before he got to the part about the hat, however, Dawn interrupted.

"Let's get this straight," Dawn said. "There are at least two people who are listening to everything you say, but they are not the two men who took the watch. Instead, those who are listening are the ones who told the two who took the watch where to look. But none of them want the watch. Instead, it is the man with the accent who wants the watch. Is that correct, so far?"

"Thank you, dear," Elmira chuckled. "You make it so much easier to understand."

"Speaking of the two who took the watch," Lincoln said. "Where are they now?"

"The patch disintegrated before they came back out," Paul explained. "As soon as I realized what was happening, I called Dawn. She was waiting to follow them when they got in the car and drove away."

"I followed them to a tavern about six blocks away," Dawn intervened. They were still there when I left to come here. I don't think, however, they will be of any help to us."

"I agree," Betsy added. "It's the man with the accent and the men who are doing the listening we need to focus on now."

"There's one more thing I've got to tell you about the man with the accent," Lincoln said, looking at his mother. "He wears an expensive felt hat."

Betsy's body went rigid. "He's the one." Her voice was hardly a whisper.

Lincoln nodded. "He has to be the one, and we know where to find him." He smiled, took his mother's hand, and kissed the back of it and then turned to Paul. "We've accomplished what we set out to do, thanks to Paul's ingenuity." He raised his glass of water for a toast. "To Paul."

The glasses came together. "To Paul."

"I need to share something," Lincoln said, when the glasses were back on the table. "I was pretty scared when I heard footsteps coming down the corridor, and I had no place to hide except to squeeze myself against the wall. I closed my eyes so the whites were covered. Then I prayed that I would be invisible to whoever was coming toward me. I have to tell you, the man walked so close to me I could feel his breath and smell his aftershave, but he didn't see me. For that one moment, I was invisible. My prayer had been heard, and the answer was immediate. I know that we are where we're supposed to be at this time and at this moment."

"I hear you, grandson," Elmira whispered.

Chandler laid down the earphones, massaged his temples, and looked at his watch. It was almost midnight. Where was the family? It startled him that he should feel concern for these people. But in reality he was concerned. Mrs. Braden had become of part of his life over the past year. He knew more about her than he knew about his own mother. Her family had become his family, yet to them, he was a stranger.

He stepped outside the van and looked up at the stars. The sounds of the night filled the air, and the tension in his back began to recede. He rolled his head from side to side, trying to relieve the stiffness in his neck. Taking a deep breath, he walked in an attempt to clear his head.

The latest recorded conversations between Mrs. Braden

and her son had been generic. He couldn't help wondering why. She had to be aware that her husband's body had been exhumed, yet it was not discussed in the privacy of her home.

The word *privacy* made him wince. What privacy? She had none. He was listening to everything she said; he knew every move she made. And because he had been listening for a year, he knew something was different this time. The atmosphere of conversation had changed. It had become guarded.

He stopped walking and leaned against a tree. Breathing in the night air seemed to open the channels to his brain, and he found himself processing information with more logic.

As things came to his mind, he put them in prospective. There was the change in Mrs. Braden's routine, the cemetery, the watch, and the conversation between mother and son.

How long has she known? he asked himself when it became obvious. *And how did she find out?* Had they left something behind when they removed the equipment, or were they too articulate in their clean-up?

Something else became apparent in his mind. If the Bradens were aware their every word was being recorded, they meant whoever was listening to know about the watch, where it was found, and the fact that it was now in the safe.

If Mrs. Braden had opened the safe, she knew the notebooks were missing. He had to wonder if they actually carried any significance, at least the ones he had in his possession. There could possibly be other notebooks, however—notebooks filled with the kind of information he needed. Information concerning the watch.

He could hear the soft hum of the Fiat returning. He hurried back to the van to meet Mac. They had a lot to discuss.

"Out for a stroll?" Mac grinned, when he climbed out of the car. "Family must be asleep."

"The family's not even home," Chandler remarked.

"Are you worried?"

"You're the one I should be worried about," Chandler said, when he got a good look at Mac's disheveled appearance.

"Didn't the tiger like the way you tasted?"

Mac opened the door to the van and stepped inside, ignoring the comment. "I may or may not have found Leonard Hoffman. I may or may not have found out why Lincoln Braden was looking up the 101 NYC license plate. But I do know for a fact who our watch seekers are."

"Give me details."

"Okay. First, Hal O'Brian." He opened his briefcase and pulled out pictures and pages of manuscript. Setting them in front of Chandler, he continued. "O'Brian has a police record starting in the early '80s. He's from the wrong side of the tracks, raised by a grandmother who spent most of her time in gambling casinos. He learned at an early age how to survive on the streets. Never went to high school. He was too busy, as you can see by the rap sheet. His crimes include theft, fraud, assault with a deadly weapon, and so forth. He was a fighter for a few years. Then he went to work for some gentlemen who like to commit crime in high places, so to speak."

Chandler picked up O'Brian's rap sheet, studied it for a minute and then waited for Mac to continue.

"Mitchell Miller—perfect father, perfect mother, perfect home. The only problem was the imperfect son. His SAT scores were in the top 10 percent of the nation as a sophomore, but he didn't like school. He proved to be more trouble than his parents wanted to handle, so they kicked him out of the house when he was eighteen with no more than the shirt on his back and disinherited him. He got back at them by stealing over half a million bucks from their investment accounts and disappearing. He's a freelancer for the gentlemen of crime. He's been charged but never convicted of any crime because he's too clever for the law. The sad thing is, he has a brilliant mind but will never realize his potential.

"Mitch and Hal have been partners for over ten years. Right now they're working for a private investor whose name I can't seem to find."

Chandler looked at the picture of a man about thirty-five,

blond hair, steel-blue eyes, nice-looking face, yet a face filled with sadness. It surprised him.

"Noticed it, huh? It makes you wonder if he knows he could have done great things with his life."

Mac put the information back in his briefcase and pulled out another folder. The label read: *Leonard Hoffman.*

"This one has me a bit puzzled." Mac rubbed the back of his neck to release the tension caused from sitting in front of a computer and wearing a phone in your ear all day. He opened the folder and placed it in front of Chandler.

"Until approximately fifteen months ago, Leonard Hoffman was a happy, busy man. He was an inventor, a scientist, a musician, a war hero. He traveled all over the world promoting good will. He had a beautiful wife and three healthy children. He was well thought of. Hope Laboratory was making millions. He had everything. Then, suddenly, things began to change. His son becomes very ill. With Andrew's help, he begins researching and supposedly finds a cure. The boy is healed.

"What the child suffered from is a mystery, but by this time, Andrew is diagnosed with Parkinson's. Leonard begins to spend all of his time in the lab, researching an idea his father had many years ago. Guess what it is?"

"Brain cell research?"

"Got it."

"A year ago, Leonard tells his family he is going on a business trip to Europe and will be gone for a month. He writes home several times a week, telling his wife and children how much he loves them. He tells his children stories through his letters because he can't be there to tell them in person. But he never calls home, nor can his wife reach him by phone.

"At the end of the month, she becomes concerned. He doesn't return, and the letters have stopped. Another month passes; still no word from him. She closes the house, takes the children to her parents, and sets out to find him.

"By this time Andrew had moved into the posh convalescent

home where he can receive treatment for his Parkinson's. A few weeks later, the wife returns home with no clue as to what has happened to her husband. She goes to live with her parents. End of story."

"Do you think we could talk to the wife?"

Mac shrugged. "I should know in a couple of days. I keep wondering, do you think Andrew knows where his son is?"

"No, but I think M&M knows, and I think he's using the father."

Mac looked at Chandler for a minute, letting his words register. "Give me your logic."

Chandler leaned forward in his chair, planted his elbows on his knees, and clasped his hands together, the first finger of each hand pointing at Mac. "Everything seems to point in one direction, to one man—M&M.

"He has us plant listening devices in a house where the husband is dead after a strange accident to find out what the wife knows. What is she supposed to know?

"Then I ask myself, why did the family dig up the grave? Maybe to find something buried with John Braden? That night, after the visit to the cemetery while we're listening in on the Bradens' conversation, we hear about the dog digging up a watch. Was it the watch that took the family to the cemetery, and why does M&M want the watch?"

Mac interjected thoughtfully. "What you're saying is that M&M is parking his car in the garage of the Hoffman estate, so he has to know Leonard and Andrew Hoffman. You believe there's some connection between the Hoffmans and John Braden, right?"

Chandler nodded.

"You think there could be a connection between Braden and what was going on in the Hope Laboratory?"

"There's something else." Chandler fingered a notebook. "I don't think these notebooks will give us anything, but I believe somewhere there are notebooks that would have."

Mac picked up one of the notebooks and flipped through

its pages. "Mrs. Braden opened that safe before we did that day. She could have removed some of the notebooks. If the dog dug up her husband's watch, like she claims he did on the tape, she received her first clue that there was something more to his death. After that she probably became more alert to her environment. She's a smart woman with smart relatives, which may be why they are getting together more often lately."

Mac eyed Chandler and shook his head. "You're the best bloodhound I've ever come across. I'd be the last one to rebut your theory."

The van became quiet as the two of them sat analyzing the possibilities of what they had put together, each in his own way. Chandler with his back resting against the soft leather chair, his ankles crossed and propped on the desk, the pencil between his fingers tapping against his thigh. Mac with his twenty-pound hand weights, lifting them up and down to the rhythm of his thought patterns.

Ten minutes later, Mac set the weights in the corner and stretched. "This little net just keeps getting bigger and bigger," he concluded. "What's our next step?"

Chandler pulled himself upright in his chair and heaved a sigh. "We need to know more about M&M. We need to know why he hired us and how he knew something was hidden inside the watch. We also need to know why Leonard Hoffman is missing.

"As soon as M&M finds out the watch has already been relieved of its contents, he'll be calling for a meeting. That's when you plant a few bugs inside the two cars that just might lead us to some answers."

Knowing M&M would find nothing inside the watch, Chandler made sure it was placed in his hands. The man wanted what was no longer there, and Chandler hoped he wanted it badly enough to make a few mistakes. Mac was right. Everything pointed to M&M. Everything depended on his next move. They just had to wait.

"I think," Mac said, interrupted his thoughts, "that it

might be a good idea to let the Braden family lead us where they want us to go."

Chandler looked at him dubiously.

"What I'm saying," Mac's eyes narrowed in deliberation, "is that we listen to what they're not saying as much as what they are because what they're not saying, they're doing."

"As bizarre as that sounds, you're making a lot of sense." Chandler turned to the computer. "Okay, from now on one of us sticks with the family by physical means. Starting tomorrow, I'll follow whoever leaves the house first. You take the second. If people come to the house, you stay with the equipment, in case someone hints at another clue, which I'm sure they will."

"Unless they only needed to give one clue to find out what they wanted to know," Mac debated, as he began pacing back and forth in the small area he was afforded. "Think about it. They needed someone to come for the watch while they were watching. We're one step behind them on this one, buddy."

"Then we better catch up."

twelve

THE LAB

Lincoln checked his watch for the tenth time. His trip to the lab had been postponed until the next day in favor of a family meeting at four at his grandmother's. That gave him some free time, and he decided to use it wisely. An hour from now he would walk into Ned's Dry Cleaning and talk to Terri about the man with the felt hat. Actually, in his heart, he knew he would have wanted to see Terri even if there had been no man with a felt hat to discuss.

He pulled out a couple of dress shirts and a pair of nice slacks and shoved them into a plastic sack. As long as he took things to be dry cleaned, he would have an excuse to stop at the dry cleaners. Logical deduction!

He went in search of his mother to tell her where he was going and found her at her desk, editing her column for the week.

"I'm going to pick up my jacket at the cleaners. Do you want to ride with me?" he asked, leaning over her shoulder, the bag of prospective dry cleaning in his hand.

Betsy looked up at her son and smiled. "I see you've thought ahead."

Lincoln blushed. Was he that obvious? "Do you know," he

admitted, "that I've only asked one girl out on a date and that was just the other day when I took Terri to lunch?"

"May I ask why?"

"Because it's so hard to do, I suppose." He looked around. "Where's the golden boy?"

"He went out to take care of a few things. Perhaps you should check on him."

Their conversation had been safe, Betsy thought as she finished looking through her article. She hoped whoever was listening enjoyed that little bit of trivia concerning her son's dating habits.

The events of the past few weeks seemed to be affecting her rather dramatically. Privacy was now more precious to her. Freedom and liberty were words that, when spoken in her mind, brought tears to her eyes. Today she had a stronger conviction of the passion with which the Constitution was written and a deeper understanding of those willing to give their lives to protect its principles.

Frank, her editor, was right when he told her that life's experiences continually change people. She was a living example of that. She had gone from simply being to actually living, and she could never go back. She knew too much. She wondered who she would eventually become in this life or what she could eventually accomplish because of this experience.

The sound of Dorado's bark released her from her thoughts and let her know it was time for lunch.

"I'm on my way," Lincoln said, when he saw her walk into the kitchen. "Are you sure you don't want to come?"

"I think I'll get some work done around here." She brushed some lint from his shirt. "Tell Terri hello for me."

Lincoln asked Dorado if he would like to go to town, but the dog took his place beside Betsy, declining the invitation.

"I guess I'm on my own," he sighed, and with a smile that hinted he didn't mind, he headed for his Jeep.

By the time he parked in front of the cleaners, it was almost one. Taking a deep breath, he walked through the door, hoping to see Terri waiting behind the counter. Disappointment was apparent on his face when Ned greeted him instead.

"Sorry," Ned laughed, recognizing the look. "Somehow I get the feeling I'm not the one you came to see."

Lincoln had forgotten to do the math. *Story problem: Terri and her father both worked at the cleaners. If they each work five days a week, at what time of day would Terri most likely be behind the counter?* "Hello, sir, I just came to pick up my jacket and leave some more things to be cleaned."

"It would really make me happy if you'd call me Ned."

"Thank you, sir, I'll remember that." The bell chimed, and Lincoln turned to see Terri walk through the door. When their eyes met, she smiled. His knees went weak.

"Hi, Lincoln," she said. "I've got your jacket ready. Have you had lunch yet?"

He could hear himself mumble no.

"Good. On Mondays, I pack a lunch and eat down by the lake. Do you want to come?"

"Sure."

Ned watched the young man who was obviously interested in his daughter. Lincoln was so much like John, and that made him almost perfect in Ned's opinion. He would promote this relationship. He walked into the back room, returning a few seconds later with the jacket. Handing it to his daughter, he quickly disappeared again but not before giving Lincoln a wink of approval.

"Here, let me take the things you brought in to be cleaned." She reached for his bag. He handed it to her. She set it just inside the door to the back room, picked up a covered basket from behind the counter, handed a blanket to Lincoln, and motioned for him to take the lead.

Luckily, he had enough sense to offer to carry the basket to the lake as well. She graciously handed it to him, and they walked out the door.

"Why is it," Lincoln asked as they crossed the street, "that inside your father's cleaners, I lose my power of reason?"

Terri giggled. "Because he's still a giant of a man and you're still that little boy. That's your memory."

"I used to ask myself, 'How did he get so tall?'"

"You'd be surprised how many people ask him that question. When you're six foot six, you kind of stand out, I suppose."

Lincoln spread the blanket under a shade tree while Terri removed two paper plates, two sandwiches—two of everything.

"Do you always eat this much?" he asked in amazement.

She met his gaze, her beautiful eyes shadowed under long lashes. "I packed double hoping you would come into the store to pick up your jacket, so I could invite you to the lake for lunch."

He felt his heart leap, and he found himself falling in love for the first time in his life. "Terri," he said softly, "would you like to go to dinner and a movie with me tonight?"

"Yes, I would."

"Thank you."

"You're welcome."

Everything was so perfect at that moment in time. They shared the lunch Terri had so meticulously prepared. They talked about things they were both acquainted with, like the lake, the huge shade trees that clustered its shore, how peaceful it was to sit here listening to the geese prattle, education, the weather, and college.

It was difficult for Lincoln to bring up the subject he needed to discuss with her. Her lunch hour would be over soon, and time was getting short. He had no choice.

He gave her a look of apology and then made his request. "Would you mind describing what you saw that morning my father was talking to the man in the Indiana Jones hat?"

She looked at him for a second before replying. "It's odd you should bring that up. Ever since I told your mother what I saw, it keeps playing back in my mind, like moving frames of a photograph."

She leaned against the trunk of the shade tree and closed her eyes. "I was coming across the street toward the store when I saw them. The man was slim but well built, though he wasn't as muscular as your father. I remember thinking what an interesting photo it would make, and I was wishing I had my camera." She smiled without opening her eyes. "I'm rather fascinated with photography, in case you couldn't tell."

Her face became serious again, and her eyebrows came together in her attempt to focus on the image in her mind. "In the photo I would have taken, there would be a man wearing an expensive suit and a classy, if outdated, felt hat. He's holding a cigar in his right hand, its smoke circling in the air. His face is shadowed under the wide brim of the hat pulled low over his eyes. But the back of his head is visible, and the camera catches the sunlight in his blond hair.

"The other man stands almost in contrast. His handsome face wears a pleasant smile. His hair is dark. His clothes are casual. He stands there, undaunted by the finger that keeps stabbing at his chest."

She gave a sigh and opened her eyes. "I'm sorry, that's all that I could see."

"That's incredible. I could almost envision what you were describing."

"Does that mean you don't want to cancel our date even though I go around carrying imaginary photos in my head?"

"Can I describe to you the photo I see in my head right now?"

She smiled shyly and nodded.

Lincoln closed his eyes. "In my photo, I see a chubby little girl with long, dark hair sitting on a rock. Tears are running down her cheeks as she tries to wipe away the mud that covers her pretty white dress. Two really stupid boys are standing on the hill behind her with big ugly grins on their faces."

He heard Terri sigh. "Your description made me feel as if I was there." She scrunched her face for a moment and then made a gesture of surprise. "Oops, I was!"

"Are you sure you still want to go out with me?" he winced.

"Can you promise there will be no mud?"

"I can promise there'll be no mud."

"Then I'll still go out with you."

Their eyes connected, and their hands met. The past was forgiven. "And now I must go back to work," she moaned.

When they parted at the door of the cleaners, it was with the promise that Lincoln would be back for her at six that night.

Despite the fact he hadn't slept all night and it felt like someone had used his head for batting practice, Paul felt pretty good. They knew more today than they knew yesterday because things had gone almost without blemish, just as he had hoped.

He met with his colleague earlier in the day to discuss the experimental tracker beam at length. He explained that he had to stay within a ten-mile radius of the car in order to maintain contact and the life-span of the patch was two hours and twenty-three minutes. It was a successful experiment for both.

When the family meeting was called to order by Elmira at one minute after four, Paul gave them the same report. He was very pleased with the success of the tracker patch for two reasons: it actually worked, and they were able to find out some pretty high priority information that would help them in their quest.

They now had an idea who was after the microchips. They had faces to put with the names Mitch and Hal, the two who removed the watch from the safe. They were all but positive the third man was the same man seen talking to John the day before he was murdered. They knew where he was staying, for now at least.

"I think our plan was efficiently executed and was more successful than we anticipated," Paul reported. "We know what was in the casket, and I'm relieved, as I'm sure the rest of you are, that our theory was correct.

"Today, I hired a private investigator to tail the man we'll now concentrate on. We need more than just a face and an address. Until we have that, he'll not make a move without our knowledge.

"Tomorrow, Lincoln will take the chips to the college lab and, hopefully within the next few days, we should know what they were designed to do."

Lincoln nodded. "I've called and made arrangements. Luckily it's summer break. There's very few people interested in the lab."

Betsy watched her family as they discussed how each step they would take from this point on would depend on the outcome of the one before it. Suddenly, she felt overwhelmed with gratitude.

"Forgive me for getting off the subject for a moment," she said, looking into each of their faces, "but I've been sitting here thinking about the expertise each one of you brings with you as you so willingly put your lives in danger in my behalf. It humbles me when I consider how blessed I am to have you."

"That's what families do for each other," Elmira said, tenderly touching her daughter's hand. "That's where love comes in. I can't quote scripture or verse, but it goes something like this: 'He who shows love, shows courage. Love is constant, never changing. It's reliable and secure. It is the force that drives a person beyond his or her own physical abilities to protect. Love is the graciousness of gratitude and the element of commitment. Love is the true affection of family.' I think that about sums up our feelings at this time. We love you, Betsy. We love you more than life."

"I think the voting is in on that one," Dawn smiled. "It's unanimous in the affirmative." She reached out and touched her sister's cheek with a kiss.

"Speaking of love," she continued, turning to Lincoln with an impish twinkle in her eye. "I understand you have a date?"

"And how would you know that?" he laughed, giving his aunt a gentle nudge.

"I have my sources."

"Then may I suggest that if you want me to stay in the good graces of the young lady I've asked out, we adjourn this meeting in a timely manner."

Betsy smiled as she listened to Dawn ask what Lincoln considered to be a timely manner. She watched Paul and Elmira as they studied the whiteboard, jotting down notes and nodding their heads in unison. Her mother was right. Love is the true affection of family. She loved each one of them. She loved them more than life.

Lincoln was relieved when Terri answered the door at his knock. He had forgotten to do the math once again. The force, however, was with him.

"Please come in," she said sweetly. "Mom wants to say hi and Dad promises he'll stay seated." She giggled and then took his hand, pulling him through the doorway and into the living room.

"Hello, Lincoln," Mrs. Burton said, reaching up and giving him a quick embrace. "It's so good to see you again. Tad asks about you in his letters, and your mother keeps me informed. He'll be happy to know we've seen you and that Terri has forgiven the both of you." The sound of her laughter reminded him of another time. She was a lovely woman, full of life and laughter, who shared with her daughter those same qualities. He wanted to give her a big hug to show his gratitude but thought better of it. Instead, he smiled and apologized for being a brat when he was younger.

"A brat hardly describes you at the age of ten, but I loved

you just the same. Actually you helped to make wonderful memories." She grinned and begged him to sit down for a moment and visit, now that he was older and better behaved.

Lincoln couldn't help but laugh. Terri's mother had always made him feel welcome, and tonight was no exception. By the time they left to go to dinner, Lincoln had actually called Ned by his first name and felt comfortable in doing so. It seemed Terri's parents recognized him for the man he had become and were happy to have their daughter go out with him. The whole evening was a great success.

When he got home, his mother was watching the late news, Dorado by her side. As he told her about the evening, his eyes told her that he had fallen in love. She was pleased with his choice.

The next morning, Lincoln told his mother he would be gone for the day, for the benefit of those who were listening. What he didn't realize was that one of those listening was making plans to be with him all the way.

Two hours later, when he pulled into the university laboratory parking lot, a black Fiat parked three cars away.

He grabbed his backpack and made his way through the door and up the stairs. Once inside the lab, he put on a white jacket, pinned his name tag on the pocket, and seated himself beside the equipment he would be working with.

Looking around him, he spotted three other lab students. They were fully engrossed in their own research and had probably not even noticed him. Pulling two small containers from his pack, he set them on the counter and began the preparations.

The lab door opened, and he caught a glimpse of another man walking into the room. He let his eyes follow the new arrival, who acknowledged the other students and then made his way to Lincoln.

Quickly, Lincoln hid the containers from view until he saw the name tag that identified the man as *Lab Assistant*. Beneath the title was the name *Chandler*.

Lincoln relaxed a little and asked, "Are you the one I'm supposed to work with?"

"Are you Lincoln Braden?"

"I am."

"Then let's get started." Chandler felt lucky. In talking to the coordinator, he was able to find out the name of the lab assistant who had been assigned to Lincoln. Her name was Lois. He watched for her and when she arrived, he explained that they had both been assigned to the same student and asked if she would mind if he did the assisting. She gave him a big smile, thanked him, and disappeared.

The only thing he had to worry about now was Professor Jennings. If he happened to stop by, things could get a little difficult.

He knew the risk was worth it when Lincoln opened the two small containers and revealed the chips. Chandler studied them for a moment before commenting in an attempt to contain his excitement. "Why don't you explain what you are looking for here," he said at last, his voice noncommittal, his face showing no real interest.

"I need to know what this chip has been designed to do."

"Are you a good detective?"

"Excuse me?"

"Since a computer chip is essentially a black box, it will require some good detective work to figure it out."

"I guess that's why you're here to help me," Lincoln grinned.

"Okay," Chandler replied. "The first thing you want to do is look for part numbers or identifying markings on the outside. Most chips have part numbers that immediately identify the company where they are manufactured. Once we find the part number, we can look up the part on the manufacturer's web site to figure out its function."

"It's that easy?"

"Not necessarily," Chandler chuckled, "but it's a starting point." He could hardly believe his luck. He was standing next to the young man who had what M&M was looking for—two computer chips. Not only that, but by the time they were finished, he would hopefully know exactly what these chips were designed to do.

Together, the two men examined the first chip for markings that would identify it. "Is this an assignment?" Chandler inquired innocently.

"More like an experiment," Lincoln replied.

Chandler liked this kid. He wished he could ask him about his date last night. Instead, he could only explain that even a flash memory or an FPGA would have the part number. "So though we didn't know exactly what was programmed into the chips, we will know basic ways to electronically communicate with them," he said. "Once we can communicate, we can read out the contents of the memory if the chip is a flash memory. In the case of an FPGA, it will allow us to connect a computer interface to the chip and start analyzing its logical functions."

Lincoln listened while Chandler explained that analyzing the logical functions would entail figuring out which pins were configured as inputs and outputs. The two were able to identify the manufacturer but not the function. That made the procedure a little more difficult, thus the detective work. Several hours later, they were finally able to have the computer start entering sequences of bytes and do the analyzing.

Once they had that information, they attempted to reconstruct as much of the logical design as possible.

"Tell me," Chandler said, his brows furrowed in professional repose, "Is this supposed to be a malicious chip?"

"I don't know. My responsibility is to break it down and find out." Lincoln didn't lie in his response to the lab assistant. That was his responsibility.

By the end of the day, they concluded the chip was malicious, but it would take more time to break it down, and time was one thing Chandler had just run out of. He could hear Professor Jennings's deep voice call out to a lab student as he opened the door into the lab.

"Over here, professor," a voice answered back.

Without looking in their direction, the professor busied himself with a project three tables away. Chandler knew it was time to leave.

"The lab won't be closing for another hour," he said, checking his watch. His voice was low, and his face partially hidden by his clipboard, "but I have another appointment in five minutes. Do you think you can work without me?

Lincoln indicated that he thought he could. "With the layers of programs we found on these chips, giving them more complicated tasks, how much longer do you think it will take before I break it down?" he inquired.

"If you're lucky, three days."

"If I'm not?"

"Could take two to three weeks."

"I knew you'd say that." Lincoln's disappointment was apparent.

"I'll tell you what," Chandler said, after of a moment of supposed deliberation. "I'll meet you here at 8:00 in the morning, and we'll take it from there."

"You wouldn't mind?"

"I'll make the arrangements for this same spot on my way out." He gave Lincoln a wave and hurried out the door, grateful to escape unseen by the one man who knew he was no longer a lab assistant, the man who had personally barred him from the lab four years ago when he blew out several circuits while attempting his own experiment.

Once he was inside the Fiat, he called Mac to tell him the good news. "In a few days," he said, "we'll know why M&M wants the chips so badly."

"I wish I could be there to see the unveiling," Mac mumbled. "You get all the fun."

"The frustrating thing is Professor Jennings is still over the lab."

"Oops!" exclaimed Mac. "Your past is creeping back to haunt you, my friend. Be careful. That reminds me, you may want to have a talk with your sister."

Before Chandler could reply, his call waiting beeped. He signed off with Mac and on to the next caller. It was M&M. "The watch was of no help. Meet me Thursday at two." M&M barked out an address and hung up.

Chandler punched in the van number one more time. "We're on for Thursday," he said with a grin. He had forgotten Mac's comment about his sister, but then so had Mac. Something else had become much more important.

Lincoln watched Chandler leave; then, following the instructions the assistant had given him, he began to run more tests. Just before the lab closed at six, he listened to the computer as it hummed through the analysis then watched the printer as it printed out the results, limited though they were. At least he had scratched the surface.

By seven, he was sitting in a restaurant eating a steak and going over the pages of information when he glanced up and saw a young woman with flowing blonde hair walk through the door of the restaurant. She was wearing casual slacks, a red blouse, and looking ever so much like a model, but he recognized her immediately. He had to admit she was beautiful, if not dangerous.

As she came closer, he pretended to be studying the pages in front of him. She stopped at his table and asked if she might sit down. He looked up, surprise apparent on his face, and stammered, "Yes . . . of course!"

He stood and held the chair out for her. She sat down. He took the chair on the opposite side.

"I'm sorry to intrude, but I think someone is following me," she leaned over the table and whispered to him.

At first he thought he had misunderstood her until he looked into her face and recognized fear in her eyes. "What can I do to help you?" he asked, making his voice audible only to her.

"Could you reach over and take my hands as if we were dating?"

She placed her delicate, manicured hands on the table. Lincoln was shocked when he touched them and felt the chill of her fingers. He immediately wrapped both his hands around hers to warm them and comfort her. She reminded him of a frightened child as he studied her face in the dimness of the room. Her eyes were luminous, her skin pale.

She held his gaze. "You need to know that I know who you are, and please don't let go of my hands."

He hadn't realized he was letting go. It was just that he hadn't expected to hear her say what she said.

"I did some research before I e-mailed your mother," she continued. "I recognized your face the minute you walked into the library that day."

"And you are following me?" Lincoln's voice turned suspicious. "How did you know I was even in the city?"

"I didn't know, and I wasn't following you. In fact, I was surprised to see you when I walked through the door. Surprised and very relieved, to be more accurate."

He patted her hands then slid his away. Leaning back on his chair, he turned his face away from her in an effort to decide whether or not to believe her.

"I know how it must look to you." She was close to tears as she spoke. "But I'm telling you the truth. I eat here every Tuesday. Ask the waiter when he comes over to our table."

Just then a waiter appeared. "Good evening, Miss Garrett," he smiled. "The usual?"

"Yes, thank you, Walter." She turned to Lincoln. "Do you believe me now?"

"It could have all been staged," he replied swiftly.

"Yes, indeed it could, but it wasn't. I can assure you."

Something told him she was telling him the truth, and he softened. He watched her as she glanced around the room and found himself checking out the customers as well. He watched while Walter placed a Cobb salad in front of her, a roll on a small plate to the right of her, and a glass of water to the left. He watched as she thanked Walter with an appreciative smile.

"I believe you," he said after Walter left them. "Where do we go from here?"

"Thank you," she whispered, tears touching the corners of her eyes. "I know you have many questions. There are even more questions in my own mind. Perhaps we can help each other find the answers."

Lincoln nodded and suggested they eat so as to maintain an appearance. Their conversation was generic while April ate her salad and he finished his steak.

As soon as the check was paid, Lincoln took her arm and together they walked to his car, their eyes alert to any movement. They were both totally aware that someone could still be watching.

Once inside the car, April quickly locked her door and trembled.

"What makes you think you were being followed?" Lincoln inquired

"I could sense someone behind me, watching me. It gave me an eerie feeling." She trembled again and clasped her hands tightly on her lap. "I always eat at the Heritage Restaurant on Tuesdays because every Tuesday while I was growing up my father took me there. He called it our night out. After he disappeared, I continued to go, hoping that one night he would walk into the restaurant, and when he did, I would be there waiting." She was unable to say anymore because of the emotions that seemed determined to surface.

Seeing her like this and hearing her story made him realize that she had suffered as much as he had. He reached over and touched her shoulder. "I'm sorry," he said gently.

He pulled out of the parking lot, watching through his rear-view mirror for any headlights that might be following. There were none. "Is there someplace I can take you where you would feel safe?" he asked.

"I live two blocks away." She gave him the address. He

recognized it as the address of an exclusive, high-rise apartment building.

Her apartment was even classier than he expected when she opened the door and invited him in. It reeked of money. When he asked her how she could afford the rent, she explained that her grandfather owned the building.

"This was my parents' home," she explained. "Come, I want to show you something." She led him down a corridor decorated with expensive paintings and statues atop pedestals into a spacious bedroom. Its furnishings were rather plain in contrast to the elegance of the corridor. "This was my father's room." She gave no other explanation.

A pair of dress slacks, a light blue shirt, dark blue tie, and a jacket were neatly laid out of the bed. A pair of shoes, a pair of dark socks tucked inside one shoe, were on the floor beneath.

"It's as he left it," she explained. "I've tried to understand why he set out his clothes the morning he disappeared if he hadn't planned to put them on." She pointed to the jacket. "I found the letter he wrote to your father in the inside pocket."

The sadness in her eyes as she talked about her father tugged at Lincoln's heart. He thought of question number ten on the whiteboard: who was April Garrett? April Garrett was simply a frightened yet determined young woman trying to find out what happened to her father. That was all. Boy, had he misjudged her.

"I couldn't help but wonder why the letter was in his jacket," he heard her say. "It wasn't until I began to really think it through that I came up with a plausible answer."

April sat on the bed next to the jacket and ran her fingers along its sleeve. "The letter was dated two days before your father was murdered, the day my father disappeared. I can only assume he was planning to mail it that day, thinking they had more time, but he was wrong. Either whoever murdered your father murdered mine first, or my father couldn't warn yours because he was suddenly being pursued himself and had to get out in a hurry. Do you have an opinion?"

Lincoln sat on the bed next to her. "I agree with your scenario as to what could have happened that day. I wish I could say I think your father's alive, but if he hasn't tried to get in touch with you, it casts doubt on his survival."

"I know. I think that's why I e-mailed your mother. I need to find out who did this and why. Your mother was the only one who I could trust with the letter. I think I secretly hoped she would know something about my father. I'm sorry if I've made it more difficult for her."

"Believe me," Lincoln remarked, "you did the right thing." He looked around the room. "Do you mind if I look through his things?"

"I've already gone through the drawers and closet. I couldn't find anything that would be considered a clue, but you're welcome to look, if you like." She got up to leave.

"Please don't go," Lincoln begged. "I would like you to stay, if you would. Maybe between the two of us we could find something."

She agreed, and together they checked every drawer, the closet, behind all the furniture, even between the mattress and box springs. Finally, there was nowhere else to look. Lincoln reached out to turn off the light and close the door when a thought came to him.

"Wait!" he almost shouted. Hurrying to the night stand, he removed the shade from the small lamp and examined it, hoping to find even a slight bulge. When there was nothing, he felt drained of emotion. He sat on the bed staring at the shade for several seconds before slipping it back over the bulb. That was when he noticed the bulb looked different. He unscrewed it and held it in his hands. It was heavier than a regular bulb. He turned it around, trying to see inside, but the glass was far from transparent. He began to feel a rush of excitement as logic told him to remove the bulb from its base. He twisted, and the bulb gave way.

April was immediately by his side. Their heads came close together as they peered into the shell of the bulb. There they saw a small metallic object next to a piece of paper that was rolled and tied. Lincoln tipped the bulb so its contents fell into April's hands. In their examination of the small object, they found it to be a disk from a digital camera.

The paper appeared to be blank when it was unrolled, until April touched her finger to her tongue and ran it across the center. The moisture immediately brought to the surface the letters O.C.L, as well as a street address and a telephone number with no area code.

"We used to play the hidden-message game when I was little," she explained.

Lincoln gave her a look of admiration. He was becoming more conscious of the fact that her childhood had been very much like his own. He waited while she picked up the phone and dialed the number. It didn't surprise them to find it had been disconnected. They searched the area telephone book. There was no such address.

"Do you have the equipment we need to view this disk?" Lincoln asked, lifting his head from the book. In doing so, his cheek brushed against April's hair, startling him. He hadn't realized how close they were sitting. Feeling a little embarrassed, he jumped to his feet and moved away.

April, sensing his discomfort, stayed where she was, explaining there was a video camera in a closet halfway down the corridor and to the right. Once he left the room, she stood and followed him.

The moment was quickly forgotten when the camera was found, the disk inserted, and they began to view the contents on the small screen.

The camera's lens was focused on a building. The voice behind the camera was his father's. It was difficult for Lincoln to maintain his composure as he listened to his father's voice describe what the camera was seeing. The dates in the lower right-hand corner concurred with his entries in notebooks four and five.

At the end, there were close-ups of a microchip with

detailed information as to its function.

When the disk had exhausted its information, Lincoln asked if he could take it with him. "We have several notebooks my father kept notes in," he explained. "Many of his entries coincide with the information on the disk."

"I know it was painful for you to hear your father's voice," April observed. "I want you to know I share your feelings." The warmth of her hand as she touched his arm in a gesture of sympathy brought his emotions to the surface. For the first time in months, he let the tears fall unchecked. She put her arms around him, and he embraced her. In the strength of their tears, together they released the pain that had been locked inside them for so long.

thirteen

E-MAILS AND ANSWERS

Wednesday morning at seven, Lincoln was in front of the lab building waiting for the doors to open. He now knew what the chips were designed to do. They were definitely malicious. He looked at his watch. He had an hour before the lab assistant would be there. He hoped they would let him start running tests without him.

He didn't have to worry about waiting for Chandler to arrive, however, because Chandler was there waiting for him when he stepped inside the lab.

"Find anything after I left yesterday?" Chandler asked as they put their arms in the sleeves of the lab coats.

"I was just beginning to understand this stuff when the bell rang." The humor in Lincoln's voice caught Chandler off guard, and he found himself wishing they could have met under different circumstances.

"I'd like to try something," Lincoln suggested. "Will you go along with me for awhile?"

"Let's see what you have." Chandler folded his arms and leaned against the counter in anticipation of what Lincoln had in mind. He paid close attention while the young man walked him through the steps, explaining that he wanted the computer to start entering sequences of bytes and analyze what kind of output they produced.

"With this information, we could try to reconstruct as much of the logical design as possible," he said. "I realize that it's almost impossible to extract all of it, but I might be able to extract enough to get a basic idea of what's going on. Maybe then we can begin to communicate with the chip."

"Go for it," Chandler agreed. *Smart kid, smart mother, smart family is how Mac described them.*

Wednesday morning, Betsy's column carried not only a message to the readers but also a message to another group of people who would now rely on the column for information necessary to their cause.

Carrying the paper to her veranda, Elmira made herself comfortable then opened the paper to the column and read.

I was overwhelmed with e-mails this past week, for which I may say I am truly grateful. As the e-mails testify, 89 percent of you get emotional when you place your hand on your heart in reverence to the flag and 92 percent believe the national anthem should remain as is, for the very reason I cited last week.

The e-mails of a negative nature were down from last week. That could mean one of two things. Either those who do not agree have agreed not to read any more of my columns, or they have converted. Whatever the case may be, I thank all of you for taking the time to e-mail.

This week we'll discuss our flag with its glorious stars and stripes. When sewn together, it can only represent and stand for something in which we truly believe in. What is it, dear readers, that we believe in?

The following description is a quote from the Secretary of the Continental Congress. "The colors of the pales (the vertical stripes) are those used in the flag of the United States of America; White signifies purity and innocence; Red, hardiness and valor; and Blue, the color of the Chief (the broad band above the strips) signifies vigilance, perseverance, and justice." I ask, do we truly believe in these things?

Betsy devoted the next section of her column to talking about the folding of the flag, explaining what each of the thirteen folds represent, and noting the reverence that should exist during the ceremony. Then she spoke to parents.

Teach your children the meaning of the flag. Help them understand that freedom must be protected within our own consciousness. For just as our hearts beat within us and we breathe the air of life, so are we the heart and the breath of our nation. We decide her future.

I end this column with two facts that you may or may not be aware of.

1) The thirteen stars were placed in a circle to signify that the thirteen colonies were equal.

2) At military funerals, the twenty-one gun salute stands for the sum of the numbers in the year 1776.

I look forward to your e-mails

No one would know, unless they were watching for the specific wording, that a neatly disguised message was included in her column, *freedom must be protected within our own consciousness.*

"Well done, Babe," Elmira whispered. "Your father and I are very proud."

Picking up the phone, she dialed Betsy's number and waited. Before her daughter could even say hello, Elmira asked about Lincoln.

"He called last night as he was leaving the lab," Betsy told her mother. "It's going to take a few more days, but he thinks he has some pretty sophisticated help in the lab assistant they've assigned to him. I'll just be glad when he gets home. I realize he can't pass up this opportunity to work on an experiment of this magnitude, but I miss him all the same."

"I know, dear. Why don't you bring your wrinkled knees and your dog to my house for lunch?"

"Thank you, Mother, I'd like that."

"By the way, your column was classic. See you at noon."

Betsy listened to the click as her mother hung up her receiver. "Well, Dorado," she said to the dog lying at her feet, "we have a luncheon date with your favorite lady. All we have to do is take a walk through the woods."

Dorado looked up at her and raised himself on his front legs. His tongue came into full view, and his tail wagged with joy.

"I knew that would work for you." She reached out and stroked behind his ear. "Let's go find you a snack, pretty dog."

Dorado led Betsy into the kitchen and to the cupboard where his snacks were kept. She grabbed two doggy treats and coaxed Dorado onto the front porch. Leaning against the frame of the porch, she tossed one of the treats into the air. Immediately Dorado ran after it. It was all a game to him, and she was a willing participant.

She was watching the doggy treat fall back to earth and into Dorado's mouth when something in the tops of the trees far on the other side of the main road caught her eye. It seemed to glisten in the sunlight. She tossed the other treat to the dog and then hurried back in the house to get her field glasses.

She focused the glasses in on the target trying to pinpoint its location before the sun's rays moved on, knowing in a few short minutes whatever was among the trees would, once again, be hidden. When she lowered the glasses, she felt confident she knew the location of those who were listening.

"Come, Dorado," she called. "I think we'll go to Mother's house a little early." Dorado didn't argue. They walked slowly, venturing further into the woods than the dog had ever been. He took advantage of the opportunity by chasing rodents, sending them scattering for safety.

"Oh, you are scary," Betsy scoffed. "Look at you, prancing around like a king." He didn't seem to mind her mockery. He felt like a king.

By the time they got to Elmira's, it was close to noon. She watched their approach and welcomed their arrival with a glass of lemonade and a bowl of water.

"It's a beautiful day, isn't it?" Elmira exclaimed, handing Betsy a napkin.

"It is all of that, Mother," Betsy replied, "and I have something new to report."

"As have I," Elmira commented. "Let's have your report first."

Betsy told her mother how she found the location of the sonar station. "When Lincoln gets home, we may take a little hike. Now tell me what you have."

Elmira set her glass on the table and handed Betsy several sheets of paper filled with e-mail conversations. "All of my inquiries have finally paid off."

"You mean you've been able to locate Oscar Lear?"

"Only his reputation, Babe. He was, indeed, in the same contact post as John and Roger Garrett. It seems he was caught with his fingers in the pie and was asked to leave." She motioned to the pages in front of Betsy. "These pages tell of his escapades and traitor activities. He used what is sacred and turned it into the devil's lair.

"After his expulsion from the post, he went into business for himself, exchanging information and knowledge for millions of dollars. With all the skills the organization has, this man has been able to elude them, while using his terrorist tactics to get gain."

"Is there a description of him anywhere on these pages?" Betsy asked, as she searched through each one.

"Oh, yes! It's earmarked."

Betsy found it and began to read. "He sounds very much like the man Terri described to me the day I picked up John's jacket, only she didn't get a look at his face. This tells us he has blue, wide-set eyes, blond hair, and a small scar across the bridge of his nose." She looked at her mother, a smile spreading across her face. "And we know where he lives."

"I do believe we've answered number nine on the whiteboard," Elmira commented. "Oscar Lear is our mole."

Inside the laboratory, Lincoln and Chandler worked feverishly through the morning, taking one short break for food. They were getting to know each other on a personal basis, and Lincoln decided he had found a friend in his assistant, even though he knew little about him. What he did know was that Chandler graduated three years ago, was still single but had a girlfriend, drove a black Fiat, and enjoyed skiing. The one thing he didn't know about his new friend was what he did when he wasn't assisting undergraduates in the lab, nor was that information offered him.

Chandler, on the other hand, knew everything about Lincoln, or at least everything he needed to know.

The work they were doing seemed to bring them even closer. It was as if they were of one mind when it came to deciding which direction to take with the chips. Lincoln couldn't tell Chandler why he knew to run certain tests, and Chandler didn't ask. He just stood there, observing, commenting when needed, and waiting for the final results.

It was almost noon when they were actually able to communicate with the chips in order to bring forth the results they needed to draw a conclusion. Lincoln couldn't tell Chandler that he already knew what the results would be, and Chandler didn't seem at all surprised when the results came in.

"Did you suspect the chip was that malicious?" Chandler asked, as they cleaned up the area and Lincoln placed the chips back into their cases.

"I wasn't sure. Did you?"

"There was something about the layers that made me question their purpose. I was impressed that you seemed to know which direction to take them though."

"Was I good, or what!" Lincoln laughed.

"More like ingenious, I would say," Chandler admitted. "I've enjoyed working with you. Maybe someday we'll have the opportunity to work together again."

In the middle of their conversation, Professor Jennings walked into the room, muttering to himself just the way Chandler remembered. He found himself missing the association he had with the man before he all but blew up his laboratory.

Today, instead of having a stimulating conversation with him, Chandler had to hide his face from him. It hurt his pride to do so, but he had no choice in the matter. Before the professor could work his way around the lab and to their table, he had to be gone. He looked at his watch, explaining he was late for an appointment. He thanked Lincoln for letting him be a part of the experiment and said goodbye.

The professor watched him leave out of the corner of his eye and smiled. He liked Chandler, even though he could be dangerous in the lab. He decided to let the boy get away with coming into his lab without permission today.

He walked over to Lincoln. "Was your assistant helpful?" he asked.

"He's the best one I've ever worked with," Lincoln remarked. "He has a brilliant mind."

"Yes, I agree," Professor Jennings grunted. "I only hope he remembers to use it. Well, I assume you found what you were looking for in your experiment."

"I did, sir. Thank you."

"Good. Then I'll leave you to your cleanup. Good day."

"Good day, sir."

The professor nodded and left the room. It surprised him when Chandler was waiting when he stepped into the hall.

"May I talk to you for a minute, Professor Jennings?"

"To apologize for entering my lab when you have been barred for life?" The professor smirked.

"You saw me?"

"How can I not see you, you've been here two days in a row. But come into my office anyway and tell me what it is you need to talk about."

Lincoln walked out of the lab just as the professor's door closed. He pulled his cell phone from his pocket and dialed a number. Then he waited to hear his Uncle Paul's voice on the other end.

※ ※ ※

By two PM, Chandler was waiting for M&M at the appointed place. When the limousine pulled into the parking area, he sent the message to Mac, who was waiting a block from the Hoffman home.

When the coast was clear, Mac opened the back door into the Hoffman's garage, where a car was waiting to be bugged. Next he went in search of the second car. Ten minutes later, he was sitting in his vehicle listening to the conversation between his partner and the mystery man.

"I can't help but wonder if you already knew the watch no longer carried whatever it was inside the links," he heard M&M say sarcastically. His arrogance irritated Mac, and he had never even met the guy.

"You no longer have to wonder," Chandler said. "I found out yesterday that there were two microchips hidden in the links. I'm making arrangements to intercept one of them and will get it to you day after tomorrow."

"There was a pause before M&M's voice was heard again. "Why so long and why only one?"

"Because I'm going to have to steal it and because the chips are identical."

"Tell me, how do you know they are identical?" M&M's voice came across the wire controlled and suspicious, and Mac knew Chandler had to be careful how he answered the question.

"The sonar picked up Lincoln telling someone over the phone that he had taken the chips to the lab and found they were identical." Would Chandler's lie be convincing enough?

There was another pause before M&M responded. "I want

the chip no later than Saturday by five."

Mac was chewing his nails by this time. "Was there anything else you needed, or will this be the end of our contract?" he heard his partner ask.

"You have done well in the job I've given you, but I think there is one more thing I'll need before we dissolve the contract. You say the Bradens have the chips, am I correct?"

"You are."

"I'm going to assume then that their next step will be to search for some documents. I need you there, listening, gathering the information that will lead us to them first. Once I have the documents, our contract will be fulfilled."

Mac shuddered. *Right, and we'll have to be one step ahead of you to stay alive.*

He could hear M&M tell Chandler that he would call tomorrow and give him the address of their next meeting. He could hear the rustle of Chandler walking to his car and, finally, the door opening and closing.

"Did you get all that down?" Chandler's voice came over the wire.

"Every word," Mac replied.

"I'm going to the office to change vehicles. I'll get to you as soon as I can."

Mac waited twenty minutes before the limo came in view. He watched a replay of the garage door opening, M&M climbing into his car and driving off, and then the driver parking the limo in the garage and walking two blocks to his own car. By that time, Chandler was only three blocks away. "Do you have the driver on screen?" he asked.

"He's the yellow dot?"

"You got him. Now stay with him, and I'll follow M&M."

Mac focused his attention on the green light as it made a turn about a mile ahead of him and listened for any conversation that might transpire inside the car. The only thing he heard was classical music. He cared for classical music about as much as he cared for the man listening to it.

The blinking light took him to a hotel in downtown Boston. M&M apparently was parking in an underground garage because the small blinking light turned from green to red, telling him it was underground.

The next several minutes were going to be critical. He needed to know that the man actually parked the car, and he needed to know which room he was in. He did the only thing he could do once the blinking light stopped moving. He stopped right in front of the hotel, flipped the button that turned on the vehicle's emergency flashing lights, jumped out, and ran into the hotel lobby.

Once inside, his eyes searched for the elevators. There were four directly above the garage area. He calculated the time it would take M&M to park his car and walk to the elevator. If an elevator was available, he would probably be moving upward at this moment. He would have to bank on the assumption that there was an elevator vacant and waiting on the level M&M parked.

Two of the elevators were moving. One stopped at the lobby and a young couple got out on the main floor. Instinct prompted him to get into that same elevator before the doors closed. Knowing that M&M would stay in nothing but the best, he punched the button that would take him to the twenty-first floor and prayed he was right.

By the time the doors opened, he was suffering from claustrophobia to the point of near hysteria. He didn't like elevators, and they thought less of him. He would have fallen to the floor and kissed it had he had time, but just as he stepped onto solid wood, he heard the bell of elevator number three ring. He stepped back into the shadows and waited.

Three people exited the elevator. None of them answered the description of M&M. Had he miscalculated? Maybe the guy had stopped for a drink. He took a deep breath and settled in for the haul. Fifteen minutes passed before another elevator stopped. Mac watched the light go on and the doors open.

His theory had paid off. A man with a crazy hat in his hands stepped off the elevator and walked to the first door, pushing his key card in and disappearing inside the room.

Mac stood there for several minutes amazed at his luck. Not only did he have a hotel number, he knew what the guy looked like, at least from the side. He was blond, had a nice profile, and Mac thought he saw a slight elevation on the nose, indicating a possible scar.

He hurried back to the van and started punching computer keys until he was inside the hotel's registration book. He scrolled until he found room 2106. It was registered to an O. Lane—an obvious alias. He was registered for three more days.

Okay, that would give them some leeway. He just had to get some bugs in the guy's room, no problem.

"Mac, where are you?" Chandler's voice came over the air.

"I'm just outside a luxury hotel verifying our man's ID and thinking it might be nice to get a room for the night. It would certainly make it more convenient since I have to be here early in the morning anyway. I've got some implanting to do. Oh, and by the way, I got a good side view look at our man. Tell me about your evening."

"I'm outside a luxury motel," Chandler said, giving him the address.

"Well, you're just a couple blocks away, my man."

"The name on the registry is Con Law. Cute, huh? But there's something I don't understand. Why all this and the limo?"

"Maybe he prefers an office without an address. One big briefcase he can take with him everywhere he goes," Mac considered. "Except maybe he doesn't want to park it in a hotel parking lot. Safest place for it would be in the large garage of the Hoffman estate because there's nobody home."

"Maybe I'll run by the Hoffman mansion before I head back to our home away from home," Chandler scoffed, "while you're sipping lemon water and relaxing in the Jacuzzi."

Mac laughed. "Good idea, and tomorrow morning while you're still fast asleep in your warm sleeping bag, I'll climb out of the comfort of my luxury bed and put my life on the line."

"Fair trade," Chandler admitted. "Just be careful."

"Will do, partner. I'm hoping the bugs will provide us with information that will lead us to Leonard Hoffman. It would be nice to tell his wife that her husband is alive somewhere, when and if we get to talk with her."

"I pray that we can, Mac. Keep in touch."

"Over and out, big fella."

"Right."

A family meeting was called to order Friday evening at five thirty in the Arington study. Paul was conducting.

"There's much to report on tonight," he said enthusiastically. "We may be here for some time, so I hope you don't have a date, Lincoln."

Lincoln grinned and shook his head. "Family first," he sighed.

"Good." He gave his nephew a sympathetic look. "Also, we have brownies and soda on the desk to keep us alert, so let's get started." He pulled the whiteboard out where all could see it.

He tapped the board with his pen. "Numbers two through eight are still up for grabs, but Elmira has found that Oscar Lear is most likely our mole." He handed out copies of the e-mail messages and the description of the man they believed to be Lear. "Also, Betsy may have spotted the location of those who are listening."

As they discussed the issues, it was decided that Betsy, Dawn, and Paul would take a hike in the hills the next morning.

Paul motioned for Lincoln to take the floor and report on April Garrett and the lab results on the microchips.

Lincoln took them, step by step, through his Tuesday night adventure with April Garrett. He showed them the camera disk and the piece of paper with the initials, phone number, and address believed to be, at one time at least, personal information on Lear.

"I also found out something else," he said, taking a marker and running a line through question number ten. "I found out who April Garrett is. She's just like me. She's hurt and angry over what has happened to her father, only it's worse for her. She doesn't know if he is dead or alive. She sits in that restaurant every Tuesday night, just in case he might be alive. The rest of the time she hunts for clues to confirm his death."

He held up the disk. "The voice on this disk is my father's. He gives information and pictures of the building where the chips were designed. He tells what they're designed to do. There's footage of the lab, and he explains that it's the lab where Dr. Patero was doing his brain cell research under the watchful eye of a man named Andrew Hoffman."

He laid the disk on the table. "He tells the story of Dr. Patero, his work, and his death. He wants whoever was supposed to see this to know that the doctor was an innocent man drawn into an evil plan." He took the marker and drew a line through question number thirteen: *Who is Dr. Patero?*

Lincoln slid the dish that held one of the chips to the front of the desk. "A brilliant lab assistant and the video disk helped me uncover the reason this chip was designed." Lincoln sat on the desk and held the chip between his thumb and his index finger. "This tiny piece of electronics, if inserted into a video game, can do more damage than any bomb created." He handed the chip to Dawn who had reached out her hand. "This chip was on the buying list of toy companies, video game companies, television stations, drug companies, etc. Once inserted, it's programmed to cause a failure in the main chip then take control. It seems there is a plot to steal the minds of our children.

"It all started with brain cell research, which in itself, is a wonderful idea. Think of the millions of people who would benefit from its gift. But the idea twisted into a concept of controlling the brain cells of convicts in prison and the criminal on the street. From there, it lost its flavor completely. A whole generation could be swept up in one gulp, not to die but to live and serve those who wish to undermine this nation. I hadn't realized until I studied the chip how easily it could happen." Taking the marker, he drew a line through number twelve: *What kind of technology could alter the criminal mind?*

"We know, because of this disk, what Lear is looking for and what we are now looking for to go along with the microchips. We need to find the documents Dr. Patero gave my father before the doctor was murdered." He drew a line through questions number six and seven.

"What the documents are is a journal the doctor kept of his research. His research was amazingly successful, but he realized too late it wasn't going to be used for the good of mankind. His plan was to expose the company after he managed to get the journal in safe hands. I believe the journal is hidden in the woods. Whether the disk mentioned in the notebook is this disk, or if there's another disk with the documents, I don't know. Or it's possible the documents were saved to a disk. I only know we need to find what is buried soon." He drew a line through question number two, handed the marker back to Paul, and sat down.

Elmira proudly congratulated her grandson on his success, knowing how difficult it must have been for him to listen to his father's voice.

"The interesting thing was," Lincoln replied to his grandmother's concern, "having April there made it easier. Maybe because she understood what I was experiencing. The people of this country will never know that my father died to protect their children, that Dr. Patero died because he refused to create the monster, that Mr. Garrett is probably dead because he had the courage to fight back."

"Sitting here, listening to what has been said," Dawn

surmised, "it seems that the fight has now been placed in our hands. Am I right?"

There was silence in the room as everyone pondered her statement.

"Am I right?" she repeated as she walked to the front of the room.

"I think we have been given a responsibility," Elmira said, "that we dare not back away from."

"That's all I needed to know. Lincoln has given us the answers to six more questions. Tomorrow our little hike may give us answers to three more. What do we do with this information?"

"While we're searching for answers to questions number three, four, and five," Paul suggested. "Lincoln will concentrate on numbers fourteen and fifteen. In the meantime, our private eye is still on the job. So far, he has uncovered four important facts. Oscar Lear has no permanent address. He tends to change his hotel rooms, as well as his name, every two to three weeks, with intervals of being nowhere at all. But he never changes his initials. He is German by birth, fifty-four years old, and single."

"I think," Betsy commented, "we have a deadly spider out of his lair. All we have to do now is wrap him in his own web."

"And we do it all without anyone knowing we are doing it," Elmira added.

All eyes were on her. She had brought up a whole new proposal they hadn't given a second thought to—one of being invisible.

"No one must know of our involvement," Elmira declared. "It has to be made to look like he was caught by the authorities for doing something terribly illegal, like murder, which is only one of his crimes."

fourteen

A CHANGE OF VENUE

The stars were just beginning to make their appearance and the night breeze felt refreshing as Chandler walked the distance to the Hoffman mansion from his car, hidden among the trees a mile away. He unlocked the door with his tools and entered the blackness of the garage that housed the limo. In his backpack was the necessary equipment to disengage the security system to the car.

He spotted two cameras. He watched their rotation for several minutes, getting the timing down before he inched his way to the passenger side of the limo and began searching for the combination that would safely unlock the door. In his gloved hand, his palm-size, mini-miraculous machine, faithful in its performance, had the door unlocked in just a little over a minute. Opening the door just enough to squeeze his slim body through, he entered different sequences of numbers into the mechanism, enabling him to shut down any systems that would trigger weight alarms.

Once he finished the housecleaning, he began the real work. His investigation revealed rather elaborate, if limited, living quarters. A man could survive in this motor home disguised as a limousine for an indefinite period of time. The back of the luxurious passenger seat folded back into a bed. Beneath the front seat was a storage area for food. Beneath the seat in the middle section, he discovered pull-out drawers for clothing. In the back where the trunk extended beyond the tires, there was a fridge, a stove, and a sink. A foldaway door hid their existence. A small water closet had been installed on the right-hand side of the back area, arranged so the walls could be slid up and down according to the need, giving personal privacy when required and hiding the fact that it even existed. A small table pulled up from the floor of the middle section in front of M&M's seat, a computer was installed in a small wet bar behind the front seat, and a TV sat in full view. This was how Lear retained his anonymity. The whole thing was incredible. This was not only his office but his home as well.

Chandler's next thought was that with all these wonderful conveniences, there had to be a safe to store M&M's business portfolio. A logical place to start looking, he thought, would be the glove compartment. The drawer was locked, but its bulk extended to the floor, its width from the door to the console. He programmed his key and slid it into the slot. The door opened. When he shined the flashlight inside he could see it was indeed a safe but not the kind he'd hoped for. Instead this safe housed six pistols and three top-of-the-line, Marine-issue rifles, dismantled for storage. He wasn't disappointed to find such a stash. That knowledge might come in handy in the future.

Chandler had just climbed over into the cushy and elaborate passenger seating when he heard a sound. Someone was opening the back door. His flashlight went dark in an instant, and he slithered into the back, tucking himself under the bulge of the stuffed leather that spilled over. Just this once he would be thankful for M&M's extravagance. He struggled to silence his breathing and willed himself to freeze as footsteps came nearer and beeping sounds told him someone was planning to step inside.

He heard a voice. He listened. "It's Simeon, sir. I'm

checking the gun safe. Everything's secure." There was a pause, and Chandler could hear another door open. "The main safe is secure. I'll check for a short in the system." The door closed. The man was in the front seat again, apparently checking the system. Fifteen minutes later, he locked the car and walked out of the garage.

Chandler stayed still for several minutes before he felt it was safe to move. He had an idea where the main safe was hidden now that the man had all but shown him. He moved his limbs and was just about to climb over the seat when he heard the garage door open again. He held his position.

He could hear footsteps echoing against the concrete as the man moved about the garage. From the different sounds that filtered into the car, Chandler concluded the video cameras were being reset and new tapes inserted.

Taking a chance, he lifted his head just enough to get a glimpse of M&M's driver climbing down from the ladder. He estimated him to be around five-foot-ten, muscular and lean. His hair was dark, and he wore glasses. Chandler dropped his head again and listened as the sounds became limited to echoes of footsteps retreating, a door shutting, and then quiet again.

This time he waited five minutes and then five minutes more before attempting his climb into the middle section. When he was certain the coast was clear, he began to probe the door that had been opened several minutes before. The thick padding suddenly felt solid to his touch. He had the safe. Now he only had to find the way to open it without setting off another silent alarm.

His throat felt dry, and his eyes were burning from the beads of sweat running down his face. He could hardly breathe beneath the tension that stormed him. He could only rely on the technology of the equipment he carried with him to do the job he needed to do. As he worked, his eyes and ears became alert to any movement or sound.

He attached a probing device to the padded leather of the door and placed a tiny instrument in his ear. He touched keys on the probe that sent signals so he could find the location of the lock mechanism. It was inside the ashtray.

Opening the tray, he attached the probing device to the lock and touched more keys as he learned the combination. When that was complete, he programmed the frequency of his palm computer until a little green light came on. Was there something he had forgotten? He hoped not.

The inside of the safe revealed what he was looking for. Removing a small camera from his pocket, he proceeded to snap pictures until everything was recorded on disk. Then, just as cautiously as he opened the door to the safe, he closed it. He wiped the beads of sweat from his forehead and proceeded to cover his tracks.

He found himself drained as he slipped through the door and into the night air. The sounds of night soothed his nerves. The camera in his pocket soothed his conscious.

Saturday morning brought rain. The thunder woke Chandler from a deep sleep. He lay on his sleeping bag, wondering how Mac's bed at the hotel had been. In an effort to feel sorry for himself, he yawned a whimper then looked at his watch. It was almost eight. He had to meet Professor Jennings at noon, and he needed a shower. The rain gave him an idea. He stripped down, set a towel by the door, and stepped outside. His cell phone was ringing when he returned to the van, clean and awake. He opened the cover. Max's voice came over the wire.

"Can't bug the room," he said dejectedly. "M&M's got bug catchers all over the place. I have a sneaky suspicion he's paranoid."

"Come on back to the van," Chandler consoled him. "I've got something you might be interested in, and just so you'll know, it was me who put my life on the line last night."

"You had to shoot the limo?" Mac snickered.

"Right. I'll tell you all about it when you get here."

While Chandler waited for Mac to return, he put the headphones on and rewound the tape. The conversation was generic until he listened to a phone conversation between Betsy and her mother. Elmira had asked about Lincoln, and Betsy was telling her about his work at the lab. "He thinks he has some pretty sophisticated help in the lab assistant they've assigned to him."

Chandler stopped the tape and removed the headphones. He was grateful Lincoln had trusted him. He wondered how the boy would feel if he found out the lab assistant he trusted was also the man who was listening to everything that was said in his mother's home.

This had been a complicated assignment. He had never become emotionally involved in the lives of those he tracked before. He didn't know how to feel about it except continue to do the job he was hired to do.

Mac was a welcome sight when he stepped into the van. Chandler could change gears and tell Mac about the limo. He didn't have to think about the Bradens for a few hours.

When the story was told, Chandler handed Mac the camera. "Everything we need is on the disk. Print it out and read it while I'm gone. It'll make you feel better. When I get back, we'll decide what to do. "

"You have what you need for the meeting with our mystery man?"

"I will after I see Professor Jennings."

"Keep in touch and be careful."

"I'll do that."

"Oh, and did you get in touch with your sister?"

"Yes, I did."

Saturday was a good day to be at the laboratory. Everyone else was off enjoying the weekend. Chandler knocked on Professor Jennings's office door.

"Come in, Chandler," a voice called out.

Professor Jennings was a man of distinction and carried

the look well. There was no mustache to clutter his face. His hair was short and neatly combed, and he dressed casual with a touch of class. He refused to wear sweaters because he considered them type-cast attire. Instead he wore colored shirts with contrasting ties. He looked every bit his sixty-five years. His hair was white, his glasses rimmed, and he was brilliant. He also loved his country with a passion and was very vocal about his convictions.

Chandler knew he could trust him. "It's good to see you, Professor," he said as he entered the room.

"Come and sit down, my boy." The professor motioned him to a chair directly in front of his desk.

"Is it ready?" Chandler asked as he took his seat.

"It's ready."

Chandler felt a surge of relief, and he released the air he had been holding in his lungs all the way up the stairs in anticipation of the answer to that question.

"I've worked around the clock and just finished it this morning."

Chandler looked closely at the professor who didn't look as if he'd had any sleep for two nights. The professor laughed a hearty laugh and leaned back in his chair. "You're thinking to yourself that I look none the worse for wear, but I remind you that's because I've learned to sleep on the job. Now let me show you the chip." He opened the center drawer of his desk and removed a small metal box. "Let's take it into the lab," he said, rising from his chair.

Chandler followed the man he so admired into the laboratory and waited until he placed the chip under a microscope to view. "For your inspection," the professor nodded.

Chandler brought the chip into focus as he studied it through the lenses. After several minutes of careful examination, he raised his head and looked at the professor. "It's perfect."

"Thank you. But I must say that I can't take all the credit. Your blueprint was outstanding. I had forgotten how well your mind performs." The professor sat on a stool and watched Chandler as he put the chip back into the box. "It's designed to burn itself out after six hours. Is that long enough?"

"Six hours should do it." He looked into the professor's eyes. "I'll never be able to thank you enough. I can only pay you the price you ask."

"Don't insult me, Chandler." Professor Jennings scolded. Then his look softened, and he smiled. "I didn't do this for money. I did this for you because you needed it done for a reason we both understand. The satisfaction I received when you trusted me enough to ask for my help is payment enough." He put his hand on Chandler's shoulder. "You are the brightest student I ever had in my classroom, so I forgive you for blowing up my lab."

Chandler nodded and smiled. "Thank you, sir. That means a great deal to me."

The professor walked him to the door. "You need to know that I miss you, boy. I miss your brain. Come back anytime."

"Thank you, sir, and you need to know that you are the reason I stuck it out. You challenged me in a way that made me want to prove myself, not only to you but to myself as well. Your lessons have stayed with me, and I'm proud to know you."

Professor Jennings reached out and gave Chandler a quick embrace then opened the door for him to leave.

Chandler took his time walking down the stairs and to his car. He was in no hurry to leave the campus today. He almost felt melancholy as he drove away. The cell phone in his pocket brought him back to reality with its ring. He knew who it was, and he would be glad when this day was over.

Lincoln gathered the equipment he would need and piled it on the trailer bed hooked to the small tractor. He loved going among the trees and cleaning up after them. It was a full-time job, and he was getting a late start. He whistled for Dorado to jump up onto the bed, but the dog had to think about it for a moment. He paced back and forth, barking his concerns until Lincoln simply picked him up and set him on. Nevertheless, once Dorado got the hang of it, he seemed delighted to be there.

"Today," Lincoln told him when they reached their first destination, "you are king of the forest. You can go wherever you so desire."

It seemed Dorado struggled with the translation at first. He stayed on the trailer while Lincoln loaded the dead limbs and vacuumed dead leaves. But after a few hours of this monotonous routine and the sight of a large squirrel, he was off and running.

At one thirty, Betsy stopped by with food, pop, and good conversation. "Where's Dorado?" she asked.

"Enjoying his freedom," Lincoln replied, making his mother a place on the trailer to sit. "What time's the hike?"

"Paul and Dawn will pick me up around three. Isn't it just a little too soon after the rain to work out here?" She brushed dead leaves from her son's wet Levis and frowned at the mud clinging to his shoes.

"This is all part of the fun," he laughed. Then his face became serious, and his eyes darkened. "The time I spent with April I could sense the sorrow in her heart, and it opened the wound in my own. I feel angry, and I need to rid myself of the anger, or I will be of no use to you. I can do that here. I can work the anger out of me, but I still can't help April."

"I'm so proud of you, Lincoln. I don't think you realize the strength you have and the strength you share. I think you helped April more than you think just by being in that restaurant the other night when she needed someone."

Lincoln took a deep breath and reached for one of his grandmother's homemade cookies. "Where does she find all of her energy?" he asked.

"Yoga."

"Yoga?"

Betsy nodded. "It works."

"You've tried it?"

"I have." She smiled at her son. "Your grandmother thinks it will help me through this. I think she might be right. We've had quite a summer so far, haven't we, Lincoln?"

"And I'm afraid we're just getting a taste of it."

"Oh, Lincoln," she said, her voice tense and hushed. "I don't want anything to happen to anyone, and I'm so afraid that something will."

Lincoln put his arm around his mother and drew her close. "I'm sorry. I've been so concerned with my own feelings, I've failed to identify with yours." He turned so he could see into her eyes. "John Braden was not only a husband, he was a son-in-law, a brother-in-law, a father, and a friend. You can't carry all the responsibility for what has to be done. It has to be shared with those who carry the responsibility of family. I wish I could make the worry in you go away with words, yet I know you'll still worry despite my words. Just remember them, okay?"

Betsy held her son's gaze. "I'll never forget them," she promised.

"Hellooo," a voice called out from somewhere in the distance.

"Over here," Lincoln shouted.

"Oh, there you are." Paul and Dawn appeared, dressed for the hike. "We thought we'd go a little early, if you're ready, Betsy," Dawn said, looking her sister up and down. "You're ready. Let's go."

"Be careful," Lincoln warned them.

They waved goodbye and disappeared. A few minutes later Lincoln heard another voice calling through the trees. "Hellooo."

He recognized the voice immediately. "Over here, Terri," he called, trying unsuccessfully to brush himself clean.

"You look like you've been in the mud again," she noted.

"Is it safe to venture close?"

"I can't promise anything," he laughed, watching her as she approached. "By the way, you look beautiful surrounded by trees."

"Why, thank you." She sounded surprised at his compliment.

"I'm glad you could come."

"I'm glad you invited me."

"Well, I haven't seen you for three days." He reached for her hand. "I've missed you."

"I've missed you too."

He didn't mean to, but he found himself touching her lips with his own. She didn't seem to mind, so he decided he wouldn't blush. The blush, nonetheless, appeared.

"What can I help you with?" she asked, secretly pleased that he blushed.

"The forest," he shouted, spreading his arms and slowly turning in a circle.

"Then I better get started," she giggled.

Secretly, he loved the sound of her giggle.

Mac finished reading through the documents he had printed out earlier in the day and decided he needed a walk to clear his head. There was nothing going on at the Bradens the tape couldn't handle. In fact, Lincoln had gone off to clean the woods and Betsy was working in her garden. The only thing the tape was picking up was background music.

He shut the door to the van, locked it, stretched out his legs, and went in search of the path leading up the hill. Once he discovered it, he began his climb while his mind clicked away at the information stored there.

According to the papers he had just finished reading, their mystery man, Oscar Lear, had been a very busy man for the past five years. Most of his business seemed to be with individuals and companies overseas, but he had some pretty influential clients in the States as well.

There was one page that disturbed him more than any of the others. It was a single sheet of paper with a list of names. The first eight names had been crossed off, and John Braden's name was number seven. Had Oscar Lear been responsible for the deaths of eight men? He believed it was possible after what he had just read.

He turned around at the top of the hill, leaving the path and forging his own through the foliage of trees and fallen branches, feeling energized by the scent of nature. He needed that. He almost hated going back to the confines of the van. He'd be glad when this job was done, yet he worried about the safety of his friend.

Just as he was about to come out of the trees behind the van, he heard voices and quickly backtracked. Using a tree for a shield, he took off his cap and squeezed a look. There, to the side of the van, he could see a man and a woman. The man was talking. "They have to be around somewhere, their vehicle's here," the man was saying.

"Why don't we just pick the lock and see what's inside the van for ourselves?" the woman remarked.

Just then another woman joined them. It was Mrs. Braden. How did she find them? He slipped further back into the trees to think. Could they pick the lock? He doubted it. The lock was one of his latest inventions. He would just sit it out until they left.

There was one problem. He needed to be in the van by five. He needed to be on the two-way so he could hear Chandler's conversation with M& . . . Lear. His cell phone was in the van, meaning he had no way of getting in touch with Chandler to tell him what was happening. He looked at his watch. It was only three. They surely wouldn't hang around for two more hours, would they?

What was it he said to Chandler? *Listen to what they're not saying.* That's exactly what he didn't do. He underestimated them. They were a brilliant family.

Two hours later, they were still there, and he was still in hiding. He knew once Chandler couldn't contact him, he would head back to the van. He only hoped he would use his head and do it with caution.

Chandler waited at the address Lear had given him. At precisely five, the limo drove by and parked next to the curb. The driver got out and opened the door for his boss. Then he stood by the car. It wasn't the man he had seen at the garage. This one was bigger, broader. He looked more like a bodyguard than a limo driver.

Lear sat down next to Chandler, reached out his hand, and waited for the chip to be placed there. Chandler removed the metal box from his pocket and handed it to the man he was beginning to despise.

"I will test this chip to make sure it is the correct one. You'll forgive me, I have a very cautious nature." Lear opened the box and removed the chip, examining it carefully. He smiled. "Looks can be deceiving, can't they?"

For a second Chandler wondered if the man knew what he had done but relaxed when Lear continued. "No one would suspect something so small could do such colossal and wonderful things." He studied Chandler for a moment. "Nothing so far on what I've asked for?"

"So far, nothing."

Lear handed him an envelope. "I'll call you in two days." He stood and walked to the limo.

Chandler watched the limo until it disappeared then walked to his Fiat. He felt tired. He'd had enough of the man. This time he really did know too much, and he wished he didn't.

He got in his car and spoke to Mac, but Mac didn't respond. "Mac," he said a little louder. Still nothing. He knew something was wrong. He had to get back to the van.

He drove as fast as he could without drawing attention. He parked off the road and out of sight at the bottom of the hill. Staying away from the main path, he worked his way through the trees as quietly and quickly as he could. He was close to the van when he saw them: two women and a man. He eased a little closer until he could make out the features of Betsy Braden. Where was Mac?

"I think they know we're here," the man said.

Then Mrs. Braden voice came through the trees, loud and commanding. "I know you are listening to everything that's said inside my home so I want you to listen to what I have to say now. You have invaded my home, my rights, and my life, and I don't know why. Logic should explain to you that if I know you're listening, I won't be saying anything worth listening to. That should be incentive enough for you to pack up and leave. You're wasting your time and somebody's money. We are leaving now, and I hope you will to." With that, she turned on her heels and started walking down the hill, her two friends beside her.

Chandler felt sick inside. He wished he could talk to her, but he couldn't—not yet. He waited until he could see them crossing the highway and then he broke for the van. At the same time, he could see Mac coming toward him from the opposite direction. The relief in him was almost deafening. The two met at the van. Chandler wrapped his arms around his partner and embraced him.

"I thought the worst," he said, when he stepped back and looked into Mac's face.

"It's been an experience," Mac responded. "They've been here for three hours."

Once they were inside, Mac told Chandler what happened then asked about his day. "The chip was perfect, Mac. It may have been the only thing that was perfect today, but that was the one thing we needed to be perfect. The rest will fall into place."

Once they were inside the van, Chandler pressed a key on his cell phone. "We have what we need," he said into the receiver. "It's all there. I think it's time." He listened then responded. "I'll talk to her tomorrow. Bye."

"It'll all be over soon, Mac. It'll all be over soon." He closed his eyes and leaned back in his chair. He was so tired.

"Let's take the van home, just like the lady asked," Mac suggested.

"I think that's the best idea I've heard all day."

Lincoln unloaded the trailer for the fourth time. His back was sore, and his arms hurt. Terri stood beside him, her arms filled with broken limbs. Her face was dirty, her hair fell in all directions around her face, and she was so beautiful.

"Are you ready to quit for the day?" he asked her as he brushed pieces of leaves from her hair and pulled back the strands that covered her face.

"Whenever you are," she said with a tired smile.

Dorado had tired of chasing animals smaller than himself and was lounging contentedly on the trailer.

"Okay, golden boy, let's go home."

Dorado made his opinion known with a solid bark, and they were off.

Betsy had supper ready when they walked through the door but insisted that they clean up before they eat. She showed Terri to her bathroom and brought her a clean shirt to put on.

After eating, the three of them sat on the veranda and rested. It had been an exceptionally exhausting day for all of them.

That night, at Terri's door, Lincoln kissed her gently, without blushing. She asked him to go to church with her the next day and then stay for dinner with her parents. He accepted and kissed her one more time. It felt just as good the second time around. He waved as he walked to his car. She blew him a kiss as he drove away.

He hadn't talked to his mother about the hike, and he was anxious to find out what happened.

"We can talk freely about the hike," she said when he asked. "If they're listening, they've already heard what I'm going to tell you." She proceeded to give him the full account. No one was listening on the other end to verify it, however. The van was gone. That night Betsy slept soundly for the first time in months.

Sunday was a day of rest, and they all took advantage of the opportunity.

fifteen

THE MAP

Monday morning Lincoln was up early. Despite his aching body, he was back on the tracker, cleaning between the trees. Dorado went along for the ride.

Betsy watched them go then went back to the computer to work on her column.

She decided to sort out her e-mail first, so she punched the keys that would bring the e-mail up and waited. There were seventy-two e-mails waiting to be read. She quickly sorted them out, deleting most of them once they were read, jotting down where they fell in the percentages, and keeping those with special messages.

While she was in the process of reading, deleting, and jotting down, she opened an e-mail that she was totally unprepared for. It was written in a style of shorthand only she and Lincoln knew, or so she thought.

At first she could only stare at the screen, her arms wrapped around herself in an attempt to stop the involuntary tremors that invaded her body. She wanted to get out of her chair and walk away from the shorthand, but she couldn't. She was drawn to it, curious to know who would write to her in her husband's shorthand. She willed herself to read the message.

Mrs. Braden,

I know this must be hard for you, but you need to know what I'm about to tell you is true. The only way I can convince you is to tell you using John's shorthand.

My name is Roger Garrett. I think by now you know who I am and that I am supposedly dead. I am very much alive.

I know you have the disk from my home. It reveals much but not enough. I know you have the microchips. If you have found the journal, you have everything we need. If you don't have the journal, you must find it. It was given to John, who in turn was to get it to me. As you know, that did not happen

I'm so sorry about John. Everything happened so fast. He was not only my partner, he was also my friend. I keep wondering if there was something more I could have done to protect him. I'll have to live with that question for the rest of my life.

Please e-mail me at the above address and tell me you've received this, using the shorthand.

I will wait to hear from you.

Roger Garrett.

Betsy read the e-mail again, studying it, trying to make sense of everything. If Roger Garrett was alive, why hadn't he at least contacted his daughter?

She needed to talk to Lincoln. When she took his lunch to him, she would show him the letter and they could decide what to do. She printed it and set it on her desk.

In the woods, Lincoln's cleanup was going well. The entire south section was spotless. It looked beautiful as the rays of the sun penetrated the trees and touched the ground, reminding him of the Sacred Grove. He thought about the trials of Joseph and questioned if he, himself, would have the strength and faith that the Prophet obviously displayed throughout his life.

He continued to ponder the life of the Prophet as he worked, blocking out the noise of the huge vacuum sucking up dead leaves.

It wasn't until he turned the vacuum off that he heard Dorado's bark. It was loud and alarming. He called to the dog, who came running, his bark even more fervent. He was trying to tell Lincoln something.

"What is it, boy?" he called, but the dog stopped short and turned. A threatening growl escaped his throat as he lowered in a crouched position.

"Hold your dog, if you want him to live," a voice called to him.

He was stunned for a minute, trying to understand what was going on, when two men stepped out from behind the trees. One of them was wearing the Indiana Jones Hat; the other looked like he spent most of his time in the gym. He stood well over six feet tall, and his face lacked any emotion. It was cold and hard.

"Stay, Dorado," Lincoln commanded the dog.

Dorado was confused by the command and continued to bark, darting back and forth in front of him, as if to protect him.

"Quiet, Dorado," he said, reaching out and grabbing the dog. When he had Dorado by his side, he touched his nose, a signal for the dog to be silent. He obeyed.

"That's more like it," Oscar Lear said. "I like dogs. I don't want to hurt him, but I'm afraid I will if you don't do what I say."

"I don't understand," Lincoln questioned, his heart pounding inside his chest, yet he was able to maintain a feeling of composure.

"Oh, I think you do." Lear gave a signal, and the big guy came up to Lincoln and grabbed his arm. Dorado went wild and went for the man's leg.

"I'll shoot him," Lear said, taking a gun from his shoulder holster.

"Let go of me," shouted Lincoln, "then he'll calm down."

Lear nodded to the man, who dropped Lincoln's arm.

"Just tell me what you want," Lincoln hissed.

"It's simple. I want the journal."

"What journal?"

"Oh, come now, we both know about the journal." Lear's smile was twisted and dark.

"I don't know where the journal is."

"Maybe not, but I'll bet your mother will find it quick enough when she knows I have her son." Lear's arrogance was sickening.

Lincoln knew all he had to do was give a simple command and Dorado would attack, but it would be foolish to do so. He knelt down beside the dog and tried to calm him. "Go home, boy," he whispered into the dog's ear. "Go home and get Betsy."

The dog seemed to understand, and even though he didn't want to leave Lincoln alone, he obeyed.

"Okay, the dog is gone,"

"And so shall we be. You'll come with us, please."

Giving Lincoln no time to object, a huge hand grabbed him by the neck and dragged him, like a rag doll, to a limo. He felt a prick in his arm and everything went dark.

When he opened his eyes, his head was pounding, his throat was dry, and he had no idea where he was. He looked around him trying to remember what had happened, but before he could put things together, he lost consciousness once again.

Two hours later he was awake again, remembering and miserable. This time when he looked around him, he could see someone else in the room. He sat up very carefully to accommodate the pounding in his head and rubbed his eyes.

"How do you feel?" A man walked out of the dark corner and approached him.

"Like I've been drugged," Lincoln replied. His mouth felt thick and dry, making it hard for him to talk. He couldn't focus his eyes, and his head felt like it was spinning out of control.

The man brought him a glass of water. He drank it gratefully. When the glass was empty, the man took it from him and set it on a table. "Lie back down and close your eyes for a minute."

Lincoln did as the man suggested and found that it did help a little. "Who are you?" he asked as soon as he felt in control of his body again.

"My name's Leonard Hoffman." He pulled a chair next to the bed and sat down. "Is your world coming back into focus?"

"Not fast enough." Lincoln forced himself to sit up. I don't understand. Are you the guard?"

"I'm afraid we're both here under the same circumstances. May I ask your name?"

"Lincoln Braden."

"Happy to meet you, Lincoln."

"Do you know where we are?"

"We're in the basement of my father's research facility."

"Wait a minute," Lincoln was wide awake now. "Is Andrew Hoffman your father?"

"Yes. Do you know him?"

"Only the name." Lincoln looked around him. Besides the two cots, a table, a chair, several books, and boxes filled with odds and ends, the room was bare. There was a chill in the air, despite the fact that it was June, telling Lincoln they were underground.

"How long have you been here?" he asked.

"I'm not sure. At first they kept me drugged. It's only been the last few months they've left me alone. A man brings me food twice a day and clean clothes three times a week. He does so without speaking."

"But why are they holding you if your father owns this place?"

"My father supported and performed research on brain cells for the purpose of understanding the human brain and providing a healthy life to those who suffered from brain maladies. The only problem was there were those who had other plans for its use. That was when my father destroyed all the research findings and walked away from it.

"Now, my father suffers from Parkinson's and my son almost died from a brain tumor. I began doing some testing, with my father's help, to find a way to shrink my son's tumor. We were successful. The tumor is gone.

"Secretly I began to re-create the work my father had done in the beginning, trying to find a way to cure his Parkinson's. Lear found out. I refuse to continue the research for him, and he refuses to let me go until I do. I have a wife and children who have no idea where I am. My father's in a retirement center because he needs medical attention. I can do nothing to help him without creating a monster for people like Oscar Lear, who sees it as a way to gain power."

"Did you know a Dr. Patero?" Lincoln was curious.

"A brilliant doctor who was lied to, and when he found out the truth concerning the research he was conducting, he was murdered. Now, tell me why they brought you here." Leonard asked, relaxing on his chair, his arms folded across his chest, indicating through eye contact that they were being monitored.

Lincoln was careful not to look as Leonard pointed out each camera with his eyes.

"I wish I knew," Lincoln said, taking his cue.

<hr/>

Betsy was frantic when Dorado came running and barking. She knew immediately something was wrong. She followed as the dog led her back to where Lincoln was standing when he'd whispered to Dorado to go home. The only evidence that someone had been there were footprints and tire tracks.

She hurried back to the house and called Paul. "Stay by the phone, Betsy," he insisted. "They want something in exchange for Lincoln, possibly the microchips or the disk. I don't know, but they'll be calling you, I can promise you. We'll be right over."

Betsy hung up the phone and walked from room to room, anger flowing through her, drowning out the fear. "How dare they?" she cried out. "How dare they?"

The phone rang, startling her. She let it ring three times before picking it up. "Where's my son?" she screamed into the receiver.

"Now, now, Mrs. Braden, shouting will get you nowhere, but the journal of Dr. Patero will work wonders."

"I don't have the journal, and I don't know where it is." Her body was shaking uncontrollably, but her voice was surprisingly strong.

"Then I suggest you look until you find it. You have forty-eight hours. Until then, I bid you farewell."

"Hello . . . hello!" she screamed into the phone, but there was no one on the other end to answer.

Betsy sat down at John's desk in the study and stared at the wall. "You said it would be hard, John, but you didn't prepare me for this," she cried softly. "Be close by." The doorbell rang, preventing her from further conversation with her husband, and she hurried to answer the door.

Elmira rushed to her and wrapped her in an embrace. "Dawn called. It's going to be alright, Babe. God will make it alright."

"Oh, Mother, I'm so glad you're here. They called. They want the journal. We have forty-eight hours to find it."

The door opened again, and Paul walked in with Dawn right behind him. They encircled themselves around Betsy and Elmira. The four of them stood there holding each other, not wanting to let go.

"They called, just like you said they would, Paul. They want the journal. We have forty-eight hours." Betsy let Paul guide her to the couch. Then he sat beside her on one side with her mother on the other.

Dawn paced back and forth in front of them. "John talked about a map, Betsy. Could there be a map in a pocket, in one of his drawers, in his closet?"

"I don't know," Betsy replied. "I haven't been able to go through any of his things."

"Then Mother, Paul, and I will go through his things while you check his office."

Betsy sat at her husband's desk, the motivation of anger rising inside her. She prayed aloud for the safety of her son and for strength to sustain her. She took a deep breath through her nose and let it out through her mouth, leaned back in the chair, and began to focus.

A game John played with the children when they were growing up came to her mind. The object was to hide something without it actually being hidden. In other words, it would be in plain sight; you just had to know what you were looking for. The map could be in one of the framed photos or sketches on the wall. As she studied them, one by one, she prayed she would find what she was looking for. She stopped at the arrangement of children's sketches John had framed many years ago. They were obviously his most prized possession because they hung in a place of distinction: the wall with the most space.

She started to move on. Then she noticed one of the sketches was not in line with the others. In the simple sketch, there was a garden. In the garden, there were rows of vegetables, arranged in four sections; one on the north side, the east side, the south side, and the west side. In the middle, a circle was drawn and filled in with dark red.

She took the sketch to the desk and sat down to study it a little closer. There was a path running in and out of the rows of vegetables. Just off the path, beneath a tree, sat a rabbit eating a carrot. Little vegetables, half eaten, indicated the path the rabbit had taken. She had found the map.

She called to the others, who came running. "I think I found it," she cried.

Dawn took the sketch and studied it for a minute. Paul was looking over her shoulder, Elmira at her side.

"I think you're right!" Paul exclaimed.

"I know you're right!" Dawn corrected him. "I'll make us each a copy."

Together they sat at the table, studying the map. There were five possible sections of the forest that could duplicate the sketch. Paul suggested they use the sniffer as well as Dorado to cut down on time.

"What time is it now?" Elmira asked. "And what time is the deadline?"

"The phone call came at 1:42," Betsy answered.

"It's 3:20 now. We've got approximately forty-six hours in which to find the journal. Do you think Dorado could find it once we're in the general vicinity?" Dawn asked.

"If it carries any of John's scent at all, I think so," Betsy replied.

"What about the sniffer?"

"If there's any kind of metal buried or if it gives off a metallic odor, the sniffer will detect it," Paul assured her.

"My question is, what do we do with it after we find it? Do we simply give it to them in hopes they return Lincoln to us?" Dawn asked.

"No," Paul said. "No, we don't. We have to make sure it stays out of the man's hands."

"What can be done?" asked Dawn.

"Whatever needs to be."

"What if we don't find the journal at all?" Betsy inquired, her heart pounding hard inside her chest. "Tell me what we do then?"

Chandler walked into the apartment owned by his grandfather, calling out his sister's name.

"I'm in the study," she called back.

They met just outside the study where they embraced. "It's so good to see you," she cried. "This job has taken you away for a long time."

"It's good to be home again." He took her hand and led her to the couch in the living room.

"Tell me," she asked, "were you able to help Lincoln with the microchip?"

"Yes, thanks to you."

April studied her brother's face. "You look so tired, Chandler. Is everything all right?"

"I couldn't foresee all that has happened in this job. It's been a tough one."

"I know, and I'm so sorry I caused you concern over the license plate. I had no idea Lincoln would follow me that day."

"In the long run, it worked out to be a good thing. It woke me up to the fact that, in trying to protect you, I could put you in danger."

"And I should have told you about the letter," she reminded him. "But I guess, in a way, I was trying to protect you."

"April," Chandler said, moving closer to her and taking her hand. "There's something more I need to tell you." He rested her hand on his knee, covering it with his own.

"Is it about Daddy?" There was a look of alarm on her face as she spoke. "Did you find his body?"

"It's about Dad," he said softly. "But there is no body, April. Dad's alive."

Her eyes grew large. Tears began to fall onto her cheeks. "Why . . . how . . . tell me how you know," she sobbed.

"I've seen him and talked to him. He told me what happened."

"Tell me," she pleaded.

"It all happened so fast," he explained. "It was by a strange coincidence he even found out what Lear was up to. But with that knowledge, he hurriedly coded his letter to Mr. Braden and planned to mail it that morning. He laid out his clothes and was about to get into the shower when a message came on his beeper to disappear immediately and take nothing with him. He assumed they had done the same for Mr. Braden.

After that, he went into hiding. He's the only one left who knows about the assignment. He has been biding his time, just waiting for Lear to make a move."

Chandler looked closely at his sister. "I made a mistake in not telling you as soon as I found out."

"You did what you thought was right. I understand. I wanted to believe he was still alive. My heart said he was still alive. Please go on."

"Dad contacted me when he found out Mrs. Braden had been tagged. That's the first time I knew he was still alive."

"How did he know about Mrs. Braden?"

"He didn't say, only that he needed to know if it was my company doing the surveillance"

April brushed the tears from her face. "When can he come home?"

"When this is all over," Chandler assured her. "Right now I think it's time we make a visit to Mrs. Braden to offer our services.

Betsy had just finished making copies of the map when the doorbell rang. When she opened the door, she was surprised to see April Garrett standing there with two young men.

"Hello, Mrs. Braden," April said. "May we come in?"

For a moment, Betsy just stood there. Her son had just been kidnapped and now April Garret was at her door with two strangers. She had to wonder if there was a connection.

"What is it, April?" she asked suspiciously.

"Please, may we talk inside?"

Betsy nodded and stood back to let them in. As she closed the door, the three visitors found themselves face to face with Paul, Dawn, and Elmira, their eyes narrow with suspicion.

Paul escorted the three into the living room and asked them to sit. Standing over them, his face menacing, he immediately began his interrogation.

"Why are you here, and what have you done with my nephew?"

Chandler glared up at Paul. "What are you talking about?"

"You're telling me you don't know?" Paul leaned into his face.

"We don't know," April said hesitantly. "Please tell us."

"Lincoln's been kidnapped." Betsy's voice was harsh, but she could see that the three people sitting together on the couch knew nothing concerning her son. She dropped into a chair across from them and motioned for the rest of the family to sit also. "I'm sorry, April, but we're going through a crisis that has made us just a little mistrustful. Please forgive us."

Chandler took the opportunity to speak. "Mrs. Braden, my name is Chandler Garrett. I'm April's brother and Roger Garrett's son." He motioned to Mac. "This is Mac Wesley. We've come here to help you."

"Wesley?" Paul interrupted. "Any relation to Dr. Mac Wesley?"

"He's my father," Mac answered. "Do you know him?"

"Know of him. We use some of his inventions in the State Forensics Laboratory. One of my favorites I call the sniffer."

"His son is following in his footsteps," April said proudly. "That's part of the reason we're here, only we didn't know about Lincoln. I'm sorry."

"I received an e-mail from your father," Betsy said, rising from her chair. "Let me get it." She was gone less than a minute when she returned with a paper in her hand. She handed it to Chandler.

"I'm sorry," he said, looking at the familiar scribbles on the paper. "I can't read the shorthand." He handed it back. "Would you mind?"

Betsy read the words Roger had written and then asked, "What do you know about all of this?"

"I know that my father would want us to do everything in our power to get your son back. We'll help you in your search for the journal. If we can't find it, we'll find some way to make Lear think we have it."

"I want to show you something else." Betsy handed each one of them a copy of the map. "This is where we start."

sixteen

DORADO'S FIND

The sniffer was pulled from the trunk of Paul's car. They would divide into groups. Chandler and Mac would take the sniffer, and Paul would go with them, keeping track of their search and progress. Betsy and Dawn would take Dorado. April would go with them, tracking their search and progress. Elmira would act as supervisor, keeping track of where they had been and telling them where to go next. That way no area would be searched more than once.

Before they left, Betsy called Frank and told him she had dropped her article in the mail and that it should be there before quitting time on Tuesday. The hours ticked by as they searched without success. The map was full of secrets, it seemed. Only John knew where the journal was hidden; why didn't he whisper in her ear? Betsy wondered. Right now, when she needed him the most, she couldn't find him anywhere.

Just as they were about to call it quits for the night, Mac's cell phone rang. After the initial hello, Mac said nothing, only listened. When he hung up, he looked at Chandler. "Andrew Hoffman wants to talk."

"How did he find you?" Chandler asked, his face registering surprise.

"He's a scientist, remember?"

"When do we meet?"

"Right now," Mac turned and started back to the house.

Chandler took time to tell the Braden family who Andrew Hoffman was and why they needed to talk to him as soon as possible. He promised the three of them would be back the next morning at daylight to continue the search. They said their good-byes and left.

When they walked into Hoffman's convalescent apartment, he was waiting for them. "I hope I'm doing the right thing," he muttered, almost to himself. He breathed in deeply and then lifted his eyes to meet Mac's. "You need to know there are lives at stake here," his voice began to quiver as he fought to keep his composure, "the lives of my daughter-in-law and my grandchildren. He told me he would kill them and then me if I told anyone about this. As you can see, I'm a dying man anyway. He'll just put me out of my misery a little sooner, that's all. But my grandchildren have just begun to live. Can you see my hesitation?"

Mac nodded. "I can, Mr. Hoffman, or I should say Dr. Hoffman? We'll do everything in our power to make sure that doesn't happen."

"But you can't give a 100 percent guarantee?"

"I wish I could, sir."

"I understand, son. I also understand that you're equipped with the latest technology to prevent it from happening."

"And that's what I'm banking on." Mac sat down next to Dr. Hoffman. "Who has threatened your family, sir?"

"Oscar Lear. He has my son, holding him prisoner. I don't know where, I only know why."

"We're listening," Chandler impelled him to continue.

After telling them the story, he commented, "My research extended into the development of a drug that would change the brain patterns of the criminal mind, allowing them a normal existence. It's ironic, isn't it, that I'm being threatened with the very thing I was trying to prevent?" He shook his head then continued. "It's strange, but I pity Lear. I pity the world his mind lives in. I could have helped him, you know. I was very close to the answer when I found that there were certain people waiting to use my research for purposes it was not intended for. That's when I destroyed it.

"I seem to have lost faith in mankind. We have in us a dark side that's unpredictable. We take what is clean and pure and turn it into filth and deception. I'm sorry for that."

"You and your son have done wonderful things for the people of this world, Dr. Hoffman," April said in an attempt to console him. "Millions have benefited because of you. You need to know that. You can't be responsible for men like Oscar Lear."

"A young man was kidnapped today—Lincoln Braden," Mac ventured. "We believe he was kidnapped by Oscar Lear. It's possible he may have taken him to the place he holds your son. Do you have any idea where they might be?"

"If I were to guess," Andrew speculated, "I would say Lear would want my son close to the research lab."

"Thank you, sir, that's where we'll begin our search." Chandler shook Dr. Hoffman's hand. "Hopefully, we'll be able to find your son and bring him home before they even know what's happened."

"I hope so," Andrew Hoffman said. "I've talked with a man who handles all the security at the lab, or did before all this happened. Anyway, he's a man I can trust. I gave him the address where my daughter-in-law is staying with her family. He's going to leave first thing in the morning to be there in case he's needed. His name is Simeon."

The name struck Chandler with force. He asked if Dr. Hoffman had a picture.

"I knew you would ask for one, and I would have been disappointed had you not." He handed Chandler a picture of a man with dark hair, wearing glasses. He was the same Simeon who now handled security for Oscar Lear. How long did Lear's arm reach?

Chandler flipped a notepad out of the pocket of his jacket and asked for the address of the daughter-in-law. While writing it down, he again thanked Dr. Hoffman for his help, slipped the picture in his pocket, and turned to leave, motioning for Mac and April to do the same.

"What's the matter?" Mac asked as soon as they were in the foyer.

"Simeon was the man at the Hoffman garage Friday night."

"You're not serious?"

"But Dr. Hoffman said Simeon was over his security. Maybe that included the garage," April sputtered, as she struggled to keep up with the men who were in such a hurry.

"The Simeon who came to the garage now works for Lear." Chandler corrected her.

"Oh, no!" April quickened her step. "Hurry guys, we've got work to do."

The two men looked at April and then at each other. Had she just become part of their team?

Chandler handed Mac the piece of paper with the address. "Is everything you need in the van?"

Mac nodded.

"Get there as fast as you can."

"Understood. Do you want April with me or with you?"

"I'll decide for myself where I'll go." She looked both men in the eye, letting them know she was an equal, as if they ever doubted the fact. "I'll stay with Chandler since there's still no sign of the journal." She reached up and gave Mac a quick kiss. "Don't you get hurt."

It only took a few seconds for the kiss to register in Mac's mind. He reached out and took her in his arms. His kiss took a little longer. "Don't you get hurt either."

Chandler stood there wondering what had just taken place between Mac and his sister. "How come you never told me you liked my sister?" he asked when they had a second alone just before Mac pulled away.

"Because you never asked, partner." Mac gave Chandler a quick grin. Then his face became deadly serious. "Take care, my friend."

"You too, Mac. Keep the phone in your ear. I need to know what's happening."

"The line will always be open."

Chandler and April watched as the taillights of the van disappeared.

Once inside the Fiat, Chandler dialed Betsy's number. "Mrs. Braden," he said when she answered, "we may know where Lincoln is. We'll get everything together, and tomorrow night, as soon as it's dark, we'll go get him." He knew even as he talked they would be limited without the van, but that was something he didn't need to discuss with her.

"Thank you, Chandler. You don't know how much we appreciate your help. I apologize for our rudeness in the beginning."

"I think you handled it all very well. Also, so you know, Mac has another assignment tomorrow and won't be there to help us. Would you mind if we took Dorado?"

"I think that would be wise. Tell Mac we'll miss him."

"Thank you, Mrs. Braden."

When Betsy hung up, she thought how much Chandler reminded her of her son.

Betsy spent half the night praying for her son and for help in finding the journal. In the morning, she woke to clouds and big drops of rain. *This will only complicate the search*, she thought. *Had anyone up there listened to her?*

Dawn, Paul, and Elmira, who had all spent the night with her, were ready to go before daylight, despite the weather.

"Actually," Paul said when she complained, "a little rain might prove to be helpful. It will help bring the scents and smells to the surface."

She hadn't thought about that and prayed silently for forgiveness in her doubting.

The clouds passed and the rain stopped by eight. It had been enough to settle the dust and dampen the ground. That was all. Once again, Betsy asked forgiveness in her heart. Next time she would not judge so quickly.

At nine thirty, they stopped for a drink of water and a rest. Elmira, Paul, and Chandler were going over the map. Dawn was asking April if they had heard from Mac yet.

"He has everything set up and ready," she heard April reply. "Now he just waits."

It's the waiting that's so hard, Betsy thought to herself. *Oh, John,* she cried silently in her heart, *if you were here, you would know what to do. Tell me what to do.*

"*Give Dorado the lead.*" The words sounded as if they had been spoken. She looked around, but everyone was busy in their own conversations. She stood still, listening, and the words came again. "*Give Dorado the lead.*"

She looked at her dog. His eyes were all knowing. She was sure he had heard too. She knelt down and ran her hands through his fur. "I don't think I've told you what I need you to do." She took a tie from her pocket. Holding it up to Dorado's nose, she explained what she needed him to do.

He licked her cheek and gave a soft whimper.

"Okay, golden boy, you have the lead. Let's go for a walk."

He didn't move.

"What are you waiting for?" she frowned.

He looked at her.

"You want someone to go with me?"

He barked and pranced.

"Okay, you're the boss." She looked around, and the thought came to her to take Chandler.

"Chandler," she called to him.

"Yes, Mrs. Braden?"

"I need you to come with Dorado and me."

Chandler didn't hesitate. He grabbed a shovel, and together they followed the dog.

"Dorado is going to take us to the journal," she said simply.

Chandler didn't question her but walked quietly beside her. They were far enough into the woods that Betsy wasn't sure where they were. She took the map from her pocket and reviewed it while Dorado sniffed his way deeper into the foliage.

"Mac and I own a surveillance agency," Chandler said, breaking the silence.

"Don't tell Dawn. She's very protective of her little sister."

"You knew?"

"I saw a black Fiat hidden, although not quite deep enough, among the shrubs and trees near the path we took to go up the hill."

"And you never said anything?"

"I may not have agreed with what you were doing, but it was your job. Nonetheless, I have to admit I resent the invasion of privacy. Maybe you could tell me why you were there."

She listened while Chandler explained everything that was involved in this assignment. When he finished, she took his arm, and they continued on their quest for the journal.

In the meantime, Dorado had disappeared into trees. Betsy called his name. In reply, low growling sounds echoed back to them.

"Where are you, boy?" Chandler called out.

A loud bark took them to the right. About ten feet away in a grove of small trees, dust could be seen filtering the air. They moved closer until they could see Dorado's tail swishing back and forth, just beyond some undergrowth.

"What have you got, Dorado?" Betsy said as they moved closer.

He had something in his teeth, pulling it away from the tree, deep growls escaping his throat.

Chandler could see there was something inside the hollow of a small tree. It was shielded by the sprigs of other trees and growth of the last year. It seemed to be a leather pouch, and it was stuck amid thick, decaying bark and fresh, live growth.

The contrast between the two was almost an acknowledgment of the good and evil the contents of the bag represented. Chills penetrated Chandler's spine as he struggled to help Dorado retrieve the bag from its hiding place.

"We've got it, fella," he cried as it came loose.

Dorado pulled the pouch out into the open, laid it at Betsy's feet, sat on his hind legs, and looked up into her face.

"Beautiful dog," she cooed to him while stroking his coat with her fingers. "Beautiful dog."

Chandler knelt beside them. "How did he know?"

"Because he is intuitive and in tune," she said quietly. "Because he knows how to listen." She let her fingers rest on Dorado's back. "Thank you, John," she whispered.

Anxious to see what was inside the pouch, Betsy quickly untied the strings and poured the contents onto the ground. Before them lay the things that her husband died for: a disk wrapped in protective plastic, a notebook filled with formulas and mathematical problems, a book filled with codes, and a gun. Now she prayed they would save the life of her son.

She looked at Chandler and smiled. "Thank you for everything." She looked around her, scooped the findings back into the pouch, and suggested they compare the map to the location.

Chandler took his map from his pocket and walked into the cavity of the different sections of trees, one section on the north, one on the south, one on the east, and one on the west. He looked at the path on the map and followed it, walking toward the tree that had held the pouch. It was just as John had drawn it.

Betsy came and stood beside him. "See the rabbit? It's standing by a tree."

They both glanced up at the tree. "He was telling us the

pouch was in the tree, and the tree in the very middle is telling us to look in the middle of the woods. That's where we are, Chandler. We are in the very middle of the woods."

"This remarkable dog of yours led us to a single tree in the middle of a forest of trees and right to the journal. Had I not seen it, I would have never believed it."

Voices were heard echoing through the branches, calling their names.

"Over here," Chandler yelled.

Dorado moved to the pouch and waited for them to pick it up. Once Betsy did so, he knew he was free from his burden, and he ran to greet Elmira, barking and prancing all the way.

"We have it," Betsy said when they all had arrived. "Now what do we do with it?"

It was three thirty when they walked in Betsy's front door, tired and hungry but grateful for their find. The only cloud that hung over them now was fear over the outcome of the exchange. Would Lear really let Lincoln go? Chandler doubted it. Paul doubted it. Betsy prayed for it. April and Dawn wondered what would really happen.

Betsy put meat pies in the oven and invited everyone to clean up while they waited to eat. She was so thankful for the company and the diversion. They wouldn't hear from Lear until tomorrow at one, and she had no idea what she would do until then.

That was not their only worry. Mac hadn't reported in since morning. Chandler had tried unsuccessfully to reach him several times.

He looked over at his sister and could see the look of concern on her face. "Where are you, Mac?" he whispered aloud.

Mac was in place, the blinds pulled down over the windshield of the van, giving the appearance that it had been parked there for a few days. He had no idea what Simeon would be driving. Until he knew that, he could do nothing else. So, for now, identifying the vehicle was his top priority.

The family was inside eating breakfast, talking about the park, a new doggy, and Grandpa's cold. They were completely unaware of what was happening outside their window, and he hoped to keep it that way.

He watched as several cars drove by before a dark blue, expensive Honda passed by and parked on the same side of the street, a half block beyond the target.

He became alert when a man emerged from the car and began walking toward him. He walked on by, then crossed the street and started back toward his car, walking slowly, passing the house under Mac's protection. He matched the photo Mac had in front of him. He had his guy.

His camera and sonar began receiving images and sounds from the Honda, and Mac settled in for the wait. He checked in with Chandler, and all seemed as it should be.

What Mac hadn't planned on was a second car that pulled into the driveway. He changed frequencies and listened to the conversation inside the house. One of the children, a little girl, was telling her mommy that a car just parked in their driveway.

"Let me look," her mother said.

"Do you know her, Mommy?" the little girl was asking. Mac could tell they were already living with the fear he was trying to protect them from.

"No, sweetheart, but don't worry, everything is fine."

The woman got out of the car, a clipboard in her left hand, and walked up to the door. In the meantime, Simeon got out of his car and stood beside it.

He heard the doorbell ring, and Mrs. Hoffman's voice asking, "Who is it?"

"My name's Rita Packard, Mrs. Hoffman, from the city office. I need to get some water samples from all the homes along this street. One of the lines has been contaminated, and we want to make sure the contamination didn't reach these lines."

Mac was busy typing Rita Packard into his computer and asking for an ID.

There was a Rita Packard and a picture showing a woman with dark hair. Her weight listed at 153; her height, five foot five. Rita did work for the city. The only problem was, the woman at the door was not Rita Packard.

Mac grabbed his gun, concealed it in his shirt, put on his generic workman's hat, and made sure his U-belt was wrapped around his waist. He slid out the back of the van and started whistling as he crossed the street, heading straight for Mrs. Hoffman's house.

When Rita saw him, she faked a smile and held her place.

"Excuse me," he said, hoping he was loud enough to be heard through the door. "I'm looking for Rita. Have you seen her?"

The woman glared at him with a dangerously unhappy look on her face. She excused herself and hurried back to her car. In less than a minute, she was a block away.

The man in front of the Honda watched Mac give an excellent performance of a utility worker scratching his head as he watched a woman drive away.

Mrs. Hoffman peeked through her window. He nodded to her and showed her a note from her father-in-law. She opened the door ever so slightly so he could slide it through. She closed the door, and he stopped at the next house and rang the doorbell. Luckily, no one was home. The Honda drove away.

He took the opportunity to hurry back to the van. Once inside, he dialed the number that would connect him with Mrs. Hoffman's cell phone.

After the fourth ring, she picked up. "Hello," she said hesitantly.

"Mrs. Hoffman, this is Mac Wesley. Your father-in-law sent me to make sure you and your children are safe. I know all about your situation, and I'm here to help you. Look out your window and across the street where there's a dark green van parked with the shades drawn."

He watched her face appear at the window. "I see your van," she said.

"We can do one of two things," Mac explained. "I can pull into your garage, get you and your children in the van, and we take our chances on the open road, or I can watch from out here and move into the house if it becomes necessary. Which would you prefer?"

"It's a pair of sixes," she replied. "Is Leonard all right?"

Mac hoped he wasn't lying when he said her husband was fine. He hoped they would all be fine after this night was over.

"In thinking about it, I think we have more options if we stay here. If we're out on the road, we're a moving target."

Mac agreed with her. "I'll keep in touch with you."

"Thank you . . . Mac? Is that your name?"

"It is."

"My name is Julia."

"I'll keep in touch, Julia. Keep your children close to you."

The blue Honda was back by the time he hung up the phone. This time Rita was at the wheel. Simeon was nowhere in sight. Mac became instantly concerned. He directed the equipment to focus in on the car and listened.

Music was playing, and it looked like she was reading. She picked up the phone and turned up the music. He could barely hear her, but he thought she said "in a half hour." There was garble in between; then her voice became louder, as if she was angry. "Look," he heard her say, "it wasn't my fault the guy came along. I did what I was supposed to do. Now you do what you're supposed to do."

Mac wondered what that was. He looked at his watch. It was almost noon. He would watch for the half-hour performance.

Just before twelve thirty, he saw a police car coming

toward him, its sirens full blast. It pulled up in front of Julia's, and a cop jumped out. *Oops, not a cop.* Simeon dressed like a cop. In his hand, he had a rifle.

Mac couldn't get her on the phone before Simeon had the door open. He had to think fast. He could see the panic on Julia's face when Simeon pushed his way into the house and closed the door. He pulled on the earphone and listened, his nerves tight.

"Just do what I tell you," Simeon was saying, "and you won't get hurt."

Sure, and I'm the tooth fairy. Mac knew the guy was just waiting for a phone call.

"Please don't hurt my children." Julia was crying. It was time to move.

He changed into a running suit and put a stocking cap on his head and his U-belt beneath his jacket. Then he stuck his gun in the pocket, put on a pair of dark glasses, and became a jogger. He passed the blue Honda, and Rita, who had her eyes on the house, barely noticed him. He crossed the street, watching her through the rear-view feature on his glasses. She didn't even know he was there. He was thinking how glad he was she wasn't on his side as he ran between the next two houses.

From behind, he silently worked his way to Julia's backyard and into the bushes. He darted from hiding place to hiding place until he reached the back of the house. He tried the door. It was locked. He reached into his U-belt for a tool that opened traditional locks. The door was open in less than ten seconds.

He listened. Noise was coming from the living room. The little girl was sobbing, Simeon was shouting orders, and Julia was silent but hopefully alert.

Mac removed a narrow, angled spyglass from his belt and wrapped it around the corner in an attempt to get an idea of where everyone was positioned. Julia was holding the youngest child, a little boy, on her lap. Her little girl was clinging to her arm. The oldest, a boy, was sitting on the other side of his mother, trying very hard to be brave. He could only see Simeon's right foot with an arm appearing once when he was demonstrating his superiority.

Mac flattened to the floor and slithered down the hallway then up against the wall into the front room. He needed to see if Simeon had a weapon in his hand. Using the spyglass again, he carefully wrapped it around the corner edge of the wall. This time, however, it caught the eye of the oldest boy. Mac froze, but the brave little boy knew what to do.

"Are you going to shoot us with that gun on your shoulder?" he asked, telling Mac there was a gun but it wasn't in firing position. *Bright boy.* Mac released the air from his lungs and worked his way up the wall. He turned the corner with ease to find Simeon's back toward him, the rifle on his shoulder, just as the young boy said.

"Hello, Simeon," he said. "Drop the gun, please, and I won't shoot you."

Simeon stiffened. He hadn't expected this. Once the shock wore off, however, he turned around with practiced speed, his rifle moving from his shoulder into his hands as he did so. But Mac was just a little bit ahead of him, and his gun was centered in Simeon's face before the man could get full control of his rifle.

"I'll give you one more chance. Drop the gun."

Simeon did as he was told. The rifle was on the floor, but Mac knew there were more weapons. "Okay, now let's have you slowly remove your belt and drop it to the floor. After that, the shirt, the boots, and the trousers."

Simeon glared at him. "How do you know my name?"

"I believe you're Dr. Hoffman's security man. He seems to think a lot of you, trusting you with his family and all."

Simeon's face turned red with anger, but he continued to remove the clothing. Mac was so intent on the man in front of him, he failed to see the reflection of sunlight glancing off the barrel of a pistol until just before it fired from beyond the front window. The bullet hit him in the chest, throwing him back against the wall. He was conscious enough to fire his pistol at Simeon, who was reaching for the rifle. He got him, and Simeon went down, his chest covered with blood.

Julia screamed. Throwing her three children to the floor, she grabbed the rifle and fired three shots at Rita in rapid succession. Rita fell, wounded in the head and the neck.

Mac heard police sirens and a lot of commotion. Finally he felt someone lifting his body onto a stretcher. Then everything went dark.

It was decided in the family meeting held at seven that night that there were three questions that needed addressing: Where was Mac? Were they prepared to hand over the journal to Lear? And would they be able to get Lincoln back before being confronted by Lear? The next several hours were crucial.

"I think," Paul explained, "that we can safely say the documents have been doctored and are ready for delivery, if it comes to that. The book of codes has nothing to do with this and therefore does not exist."

"Excellent," Elmira said. "Would you mind if the code book that does not exist be put in my care?"

Everyone agreed, and Paul handed it to his mother-in-law.

"April and I have been talking," Dawn spoke up next. "We suggest that we find out what happened to Mac. We have the address and a telephone number for Mrs. Hoffman, and we could leave immediately."

Everyone agreed with Dawn's suggestion.

Chandler was impressed with the idea of a family meeting. "May I discuss with you the plan to rescue Lincoln and Leonard Hoffman, if he's there?" he asked.

"Please do," Dawn prompted.

Chandler explained they would be using some pretty sophisticated equipment to get into the lab, but he felt their greatest tool was Dorado. Nods of approval and murmurs of agreement signaled everyone's agreement about that.

"My father will meet us once we're inside the laboratory. I promise you that, between the three of us, we'll get Lincoln."

"When are you leaving?" Elmira asked.

"As soon as we finish here," Chandler answered.

"Then we are finished."

April and Dawn were the first to leave. Paul and Chandler checked their gear, called for Dorado to follow them, and were gone within the hour.

Elmira and Betsy would be the home station for all communication. It was a good plan.

seventeen

PRAYER

Lincoln watched the light from the window fade into the shadow of the night. Was this only the second night of his captivity, or had he been here longer? He rubbed his hand over his face and looked around him. The room was a storage area for old used-up ideas and experiments. Stacks of books, boxes of lab supplies, notebooks filled with mathematical solutions, and boxes of odds and ends cluttered their living quarters.

"Have you tried to escape?" Lincoln asked.

Leonard scoffed. "I thought of everything I could do that would fit the opportunity when the opportunity presented itself. The only problem was that the opportunity never presented itself."

He walked over to the boxes. "Then I turned to these boxes filled with all sorts of paraphernalia. I thought I could find something or make something from the bits and pieces to break the lock on the door or blow it off. I spent weeks searching without success. One day I simply gave up. After that, all I could do was lay on the cot, letting the hours fade into days and the days into weeks.

"One morning I awoke to the chirping of birds. This may sound crazy, and maybe at that point I was, but in their chirping, I heard the voices of my children. I remembered why I refused to resume the research. It was so the voices of our children would always be free.

"In feeling sorry for myself, I realized I was allowing Lear the luxury of breaking my spirit. Every minute I lay there, he was in control, and I truly was his prisoner. I climbed off the bed and went in search of a different kind of weapon."

He reached behind one of the boxes and removed a hodgepodge of wood, metal, and steel threads, meshed together, slightly resembling a guitar. He held the makeshift instrument against him and began to pick at the threads with his fingers. Lincoln listened and was impressed with the melodic sounds that filtered the air.

Leonard continued to strum while he told Lincoln of the things he had learned from the books stacked in the corner and the formulas on the pages in the notebooks. "I'm no longer the prisoner," he said. "Lear is."

Lincoln decided he could learn something from this man. They talked until the door opened above them, and a man brought them a change of clothing and something to eat.

"I have to say the food is sure good here," Lincoln admitted.

A smile appeared on Leonard's face. "That's why I keep coming back."

Once they were on the road in Paul's car, Chandler called Andrew Hoffman to say they would be stopping by to get a detailed description of Hope Laboratories. When they arrived, he handed them a detailed blueprint. Access areas, security posts, lab stations, storage areas, offices, apartments, even heating and air vents were all color coded.

Chandler and Paul went over it very carefully with Dr. Hoffman, making sure they understood everything. "One more thing," Dr. Hoffman said with hesitation once the blueprint was folded and in Chandler's pocket. "My daughter-in-law called after I talked to you. She would like you to call her." He dialed a number on his cell phone and handed it to Chandler. "Her name is Julia."

The phone rang several times before anyone picked up. "Hello," a small voice said, "this is Andy Hoffman."

"Hello, Andy," Chandler said patiently. "Can I speak to your mother?"

"She's talking to two policemen right now so she can't come to the phone, but I could tell her to call you back if you tell me who you are."

The word *policemen* caused Chandler's mind to race and his heart to pound. "Andy, tell your mom that Chandler Garrett needs to talk to her, okay?"

"I can't, sir. I'm not supposed to talk to her while she is talking to someone else."

"You know what, Andy, I'll bet she won't mind this time." Chandler could feel the beads of perspiration begin to form on his forehead and above his lip. His hands were clammy, his limbs felt weak, and there was no moisture left in his mouth.

Dr. Hoffman reached out his hand and nodded for Chandler to hand him the phone. "Andy, this is your grandfather. Tell your mother to come to the phone immediately." He handed the phone back to Chandler, who could hear the little voice telling his mother Grandpa Hoffman made him interrupt her.

"Hello, Dad." Her voice sounded hoarse and weary.

"Mrs. Hoffman, this is Chandler Garrett. I'm calling to talk to Mac."

"I'm so sorry, Mr. Garrett. We're at the hospital now. Mac is in critical condition because he saved our lives." She began to weep, and he could hear voices in the background. He recognized one of them. "I'm going to hand the phone to your sister now," she said, between sobs.

"Chandler?"

"April! What's happening?" He could hear his heart pounding in his ears.

"Oh, Chandler, it's terrible. He's lying in a bed unconscious with a bullet wound just inches away from his heart. I talked to the doctor, and he doesn't give us much hope. What are we going to do?"

Chandler suddenly felt helpless. His best friend lay dying in a hospital an hour away, and there was nothing he could do but wait.

"Tell me what happened," he said, his voice betraying the agony he felt inside.

April gave him the details as they had been given to her. "They haven't identified the woman yet. She's unconscious with bullet wounds to the neck and the face." There was a pause. "I didn't even get a chance to tell him how much I love him."

"Then go in and tell him how you feel now. Make him live for you, April."

"Please be careful, Chandler. I couldn't stand it if something happened to you too."

"You just take care of Mac, and I'll be there as soon as we find Lincoln. Love you, April."

"Love you too, Chandler. Bye."

Chandler didn't tell his sister that their father would be with him in the rescue. It would have just added to her worries.

"I'm sorry," Dr. Hoffman apologized, shaking his head. "I thought Simeon was one of my most trusted employees."

"It's not your fault, sir," Chandler assured him.

"Tell me what happened!" Paul demanded, interrupting any more conversation between them. He had been pacing, impatiently listening to only one side of a conversation, and he desperately wanted to know the whole story.

As Chandler recounted the conversation he had with April, Paul felt an anger inside him he didn't even know existed. "I think that man has caused enough pain," he thundered. "Let's turn the tables and let him destroy himself."

The clock on the dash showed eleven. They had been on the road for thirty minutes since leaving the apartment

of Dr. Hoffman. Another thirty and they would be outside
Hope Laboratories. Paul's nerves were tingling with fury
and excitement. This certainly wasn't his first experience in
a rescue mission. Search and rescue had been his expertise in
the Marines. He may have been a lot younger then, but the
procedure hadn't changed. He knew what he was doing and
could feel the adrenalin pumping in his veins.

He glanced at Dorado in the rear-view mirror. The dog
had been interestingly quiet. His eyes were on the road, his
ears forward in readiness. It was as if he knew what was ahead,
and maybe he did.

"I know we've got some pretty sophisticated stuff with
us tonight, but it can't match the real thing," Paul motioned
for Chandler to look in the back seat, "and we have the real
thing."

Chandler, who had been silent from the time they left Dr.
Hoffman's, nodded. "Right now I wish we had sent him with
Mac." He glanced over at Paul. "I have to tell you something.
Mac and I have a surveillance agency . . ."

"I already know what you're going to say. I saw a black
Fiat hidden in the bushes just off the road that day we took
a hike into the hills. When you pulled up in front of Betsy's
house in that same vehicle, same license plate, it wasn't hard to
figure out the rest."

Chandler shook his head. "How come you haven't said
something to me or put a fist into my face?"

Paul chuckled. "You have to do your job, just like I have
to do mine. We're not always popular with people, Chandler,
and maybe sometimes we make mistakes, but for the most
part, what we do benefits society. You may have made a
mistake by tagging Betsy. Then again, when you look at the
big picture, perhaps you did the right thing. Would we know
what we know now, and would we have your expertise and
your knowledge at this time to add to our own had you not
tagged Betsy?"

"I keep thinking about Mac," Chandler changed the

subject. "He doesn't deserve to die. He was helping save the life of a woman and her three children."

"And it's not your fault that it happened. The fault belongs to one man, who we have to make sure will never be a menace to the world again."

"Someone will only step up and take his place." The anger in Chandler's voice was visible.

"Eventually, yes, but there will be someone watching, perhaps your father or someone like him. The Oscar Lears of our world can only be successful as long as we allow it. But you and your family and me and my family refuse to allow it. John's life has been lost in the effort, and hopefully that will be the only one, but no one can question Mac's bravery and commitment to a just cause. If he loses his life in that cause, God will welcome him home with open arms."

Chandler fought the tears that dampened his eyes. "You have a unique understanding of life, Paul. In fact, your whole family has a unique understanding of life."

"We're a unique family. Some people may even call us peculiar. If you ever decide to ask me why, I'll be glad to tell you."

Chandler glanced over at the man at the wheel, a curious frown on his face. Had they had more time, he would have asked him right then, but just ahead of them loomed Hope Research Laboratories. He killed the lights as they made the turn onto the road leading to the lab.

Paul triggered the instrument on the portable sonar screen that would produce echo waves if they encountered any disturbance in the air, the kind of disturbance made by motion devices, audio and video equipment, or watch dogs wearing security collars.

Paul touched Dorado's nose then motioned him out of the car. The dog jumped out and waited for the next command. Paul noticed that while he and Chandler were almost invisible in black, Dorado's golden coat cast a halo in the moonlight. It was decided, with very little discussion, that black spray paint would work. Chandler pulled a can out of his U-belt, and after a light coat of black paint, the golden boy blended in. "I hope Betsy will understand," Paul winced.

"I'm banking on it that she will." Paul touched Dorado's back and they began to move, making their way to the large, well-lit building in front of them.

When they were approximately fifty yards from the front gate, the screen started dancing with waves. Chandler raised his hand, and they stopped in their tracks. He punched some keys on his miracle mechanism. A sound wave was produced that caused momentary confusion within the motion detector. It was just long enough for them to slip through undetected. The screen inside the security building registered a slight variance, but nothing that would cause the alarm to recognize a disturbance.

Their next challenge was getting passed the guards. The wire fence around the building was electronically wired. Dr. Hoffman explained that any kind of electronic equipment they might use to try to disarm it would only trigger an alarm so sensitive it could even pinpoint their location. In fact, he warned them to turn off all their electronic equipment at that point, which they did. They were now on their own, relying on human instincts and the instincts of one incredible dog.

They crawled the distance around the fence, Dorado sniffing, the two men prying at the ground, searching for a spot where they could do some digging. The hole needed to be just deep enough and wide enough for them to crawl beneath the fence to the other side.

When Dorado stopped and began pawing the ground just ahead of them, they gave him space until he backed away. When they leaned over to see what had attracted his attention, they found a single thick tube.

"What do you think?" Paul whispered,

"I think we found something very vital to the fence alarm system," Chandler said, reaching down into his U-belt and pulling out a skinny, pronged instrument. He wrapped the prongs around the thickness and lifted it gently so he could see the end of the tube. Removing the cap that protected its tiny wires, he studied them, touching one and then the other until he was satisfied.

"We can disengage the alarm," he said triumphantly, "or at least slow it down." He wrapped two wires around each other, then two more, and then two more, until several tiny wires were intermingled. "That should do it. When I turn my sensor back on, a mixed message will be sent to the computer. It will have to go through several steps before it will discover an error at this end. By that time, hopefully we'll be gone."

He turned on his sensor beam, and a little green light went on inside the tube. It only blinked once before the light turned to orange and was still.

Heaving a sigh of relief, Chandler turned to Paul, who was chewing on his thumbnail. "I think we're on our way," he grinned.

Paul blinked his eyes and nodded. He took a pair of wire cutters from the U-belt around his waist and waited for Chandler's signal. Five minutes later, they were inside the laboratory grounds and headed toward the building, Dorado right behind.

When they reached the corner of the building, Chandler raised his hand and squatted to the ground. He unfolded the blueprint, produced a tiny flashlight from his belt, and began scrutinizing the paper. Once they were able to orient themselves to their surroundings, Paul pointed to a place on the blueprint. Chandler nodded in agreement and moved his finger along a section of the paper. Paul indicated that he understood, and they moved again.

Two guards were at the back entrance to the building, involved in conversation. Chandler was behind them with a spray gun filled with Mac's special formula of sleeping gas before either of them suspected anything. They were inhaling and then they were asleep. In about two hours, they would wake with a very unpleasant headache.

The next challenge facing the two men were the security cameras that would pick them up immediately upon opening the door. They could safely activate the listening device in their ears and the microphone patches on their necks.

"Dad," Chandler whispered. "Are you there?"

"I'm here, son," came a reply.

"We're at the back door on the east side. We need it unlocked and the cameras averted long enough for us to get inside."

"Give me three minutes, and I'll have you in."

Paul kept watch behind them while Chandler waited for the signal. In three and a half minutes they were inside, the cameras immobilized.

"Follow the hallway to the second door on your right and wait for me there," the voice in their ears said. They followed the instructions and were waiting inside the custodial closet when a man with a dark beard walked in. He was wearing a custodial cap and jacket. He turned on the lights and stared at them through rimmed glasses. Behind him was a large utility cart.

"Glad you could make it," Roger Garrett said beneath the heavy beard. His hand reached out to shake Paul's.

"Dad?" Chandler gaped.

He gave his son a quick smile and continued. "When I inquired as to the whereabouts of Dr. Leonard Hoffman, I was told that he had taken a sabbatical and won't be back for another month. I worked my way to his office. It was locked." He handed Chandler a key. "That will open it, but what you're looking for isn't there."

"Dr. Andrew Hoffman drew a blueprint for us," Chandler said, pulling it from his jacket. "Look at it and mark where you've already been."

Roger took a pen from his custodial pocket and studied the blueprint, dotting it with check marks. "Be aware that the security is tight on the three main floors. The labs are located on the second and third floors; offices are on the first. The fourth floor is an apartment." He pointed to an area on the blueprint. "There is a private elevator right here, accessible only with a special key." He held the key in his hand. "That's my next stop, except I think I'll locate the stairs. They give less warning. The storage room on the level beneath the main floor belongs to you."

He handed the blueprints back to Chandler and knelt down, ruffling Dorado's coat. "So you're the dog I've heard so much about. What have they done to your beautiful fur?"

Dorado let out a soft whimpering sound and nuzzled up to Roger. "I understand, a disguise can be rather uncomfortable." He looked up at his son. "We stay in touch with each other at all times, understood?"

"Understood," Paul said.

"Understood," Chandler echoed.

"The custodians are all above ground. I doubt you'll run into any where you're going. But there should be guards. The next shift comes on at midnight. We want to be out of here by then. That means we have less than an hour to find Lincoln, if he's here."

They synchronized their watches and were to meet back in the same room before midnight. Chandler, Paul, and Dorado silently made their way to the door that led to the storage rooms while Roger began his search for a stairway that would take him to the top floor and the apartment.

Dorado seemed anxious to get below ground. That was a good sign he may have picked up a scent. It was decided they would let him go down the stairs first. If there were guards, the approach of a dog would confuse them long enough for Chandler and Paul to overtake them.

When Paul opened the door, a dim light at the foot of the stairs emitted enough light for him to see the stairs. "Go find Lincoln," he whispered to Dorado, "but do it quietly." He touched the dog's nose before giving him the physical command to search.

The dog bounded down the stairs and disappeared beyond

the light. No other sounds greeted them.

The fact that there were no guards disturbed both Paul and Chandler. At the bottom of the stairs, they hesitated, letting their eyes search the room they were standing in. It was quiet.

Paul looked at Chandler. "Are you thinking what I'm thinking?" he whispered through the microphone.

"That's it's been too easy?"

"Maybe he's not here."

"Think we're wasting our time?" Chandler asked.

"Could be, but we can't turn back now without knowing for sure." Paul turned on his flashlight, and they moved in the direction Dorado was guiding them. The solid concrete was making his task more difficult, but it didn't deter him. When he ignored the first four rooms, so did they. But when his body stiffened and they heard a persistent growl rise from deep with him, they knew he had found something.

The door was locked from the outside, making it easy for Chandler. He slipped a key into the lock and punched a few buttons on his little miracle machine. Paul heard a click. He stared at Chandler in disbelief.

"What can I say," Chandler remarked. "Mac is a genius."

As he mentioned Mac's name, Chandler looked solemnly at the small miracle in his hand performed by Mac. In his heart, he prayed that God perform one for him.

"Hey," they heard Lincoln's voice in the darkness of the room when Dorado landed on his bed. Immediately, the light turned on, and Lincoln had his arms wrapped around the dog.

"Uncle Paul?" he cried, looking up and seeing his uncle standing there. "Leonard Hoffman, meet my Uncle Paul." He turned back to his uncle. "How did you find us?"

"See that huge bundle on your bed? You can thank him later. Right now we've got to get the two of you out of here."

Lincoln stared at his dog. "What happened to Dorado's fur?"

"He's undercover," Paul quipped.

Chandler hadn't entered the room yet; he was telling his father about the rescue.

"Both Paul and I feel it was a little too easy," he said.

"Then get out now. Don't wait for me. I'm in the stairwell leading up to the apartment. I have to check something out. If I'm not there when you reach the fields, leave without me. I'll catch up later."

"I don't want to leave without you," Chandler persisted.

"You've got a job to do; do it."

Chandler walked through the doorway and over to Leonard Hoffman. "Dr. Hoffman, I believe." He reached out and shook his hand.

"I don't know how to thank you," Leonard said with emotion. "May I ask your name?"

"Chandler Garrett."

"Chandler?" Lincoln turned to face him, blinking his eyes. "You were my lab assistant at the college just a few days ago. What are you doing here . . . wait a minute . . . your last name is Garrett? I don't understand."

"We don't have time to discuss it right now," Paul stressed. "We need to get out of here."

"Dad?" Chandler said quietly.

There was no answer on the other end. Something was wrong. He heard two taps, a pause, and two more taps through his receiver. Paul heard the same, and their eyes met. His father was telling them he could hear them, but he couldn't talk.

Chandler pushed the receiver deeper into his ear and waited. There came more tapping and pauses. They listened, and when the tapping stopped, they knew they had to get out fast and without Roger Garrett.

Chandler asked Leonard if there was a way to the outside from where they were. Leonard explained that he knew very little about the storage room, but if there was an outside entrance, it would have to be on the east side of the building.

Lincoln knelt beside his dog. "Dorado," he said, stroking

the dog's coat. "We have to find a way out of here. I need you to find fresh air. Go find fresh air, boy."

Dorado looked at Lincoln; then his eyes moved up the stairs.

"We can't go that way," Lincoln said to him. "We've got to find a way out from this floor." He nudged the dog, and Dorado turned away from him, knowing what he had to do. He moved along the wall, his nose down, his ears alert.

Above them, they could hear movement. Paul and Chandler moved closer to the steps to listen while Lincoln and Leonard followed Dorado. Suddenly the door opened and two guards appeared.

"If they came down, they're still here," one of them said to the other.

Chandler slipped the can of sleeping gas from his belt and waited. He nodded for Paul to move back, and when the two men were close enough, he stepped in front of them and bid them good night.

"Help me put them to bed," he groaned. They lugged the men into the corner under the stairs, relieving them of their guns. Chandler climbed the stairs and closed the door.

"Hey you two," Lincoln whispered. "Come see what Dorado found."

They followed him into a room. "The door to freedom," he explained, pointing with his finger to an old door in the corner.

Dorado's tail and his tongue were wagging at the same speed, and he stood proudly next to his find.

The old key was engaged, rusted in its lock. No modern-day technology could touch it. It took several attempts, but finally, with great effort, the lock gave way, and the door opened.

"Okay, boy," Lincoln commanded, "take us out of here."

"Dad, we're on the outside. Where are you?"

Chandler listened for a tapping noise, but none came. He waited, and Paul waited. There was nothing. Just as they were about to give up, they heard it. Chandler closed his eyes and took a deep breath as he listened to the message. Roger Garrett was telling them he wouldn't be far behind.

Paul had an idea that he presented to the group. "The only way we're going to get out is through the gate. We need a diversion in order to get past the guard. If it's okay with Lincoln, I propose we send Dorado. He's the only one who won't get shot or go to jail for trespassing."

It appeared to be a solid answer to their dilemma, so the plan was set in place. Once Dorado had distracted the guard, they would slip through. Then Lincoln would show up at the gate from the other side and rescue the dog.

Lincoln got within fifty feet of the guard post then whispered to Dorado, "Go get him, boy!"

Dorado, ready for some fun, went after the guard, barking rapidly. The guard, startled at first, raised his rifle. Then when he saw, under the lights, the black spray paint atop a golden coat, he thought someone had played a dirty trick on the dog, and it was frightened. He laid down his weapon and gently called for Dorado to come to him. Dorado, playing his part with class and a slight whimper, scampered in the direction of the guard. The plan couldn't have worked out any better.

A whistle from Lincoln once they made it safely past security brought Dorado back to his side. "Good boy," Lincoln whispered, ruffling his fur. "Let's get back to the safety of the trees."

"Do you think we have enough cover?" Paul asked, peering from behind a cluster of skinny trunks.

"Even in the daylight, I'd have a hard time spotting you," Chandler remarked.

"Fair enough." Paul proceeded to work on Dorado's coat with little success while they waited and watched for Roger Garrett.

It was a quarter of a mile between them and the security fence, and Chandler suggested moving a little closer in case his father needed help when his attempts to contact him failed.

"Let's wait here for another hour," Paul suggested. "If he still doesn't show, I'll take Leonard, Lincoln, and Dorado home to their families. Then I'll come back."

Chandler agreed. An hour passed with no sign of Roger.

"What if he doesn't show?" Lincoln asked.

"He will," Chandler replied. "And when he comes out, I'll be here for him."

Lincoln patted Chandler on the back. "Then I think I'll hang around just in case you need me."

"Don't you think you've already been through enough for a few days?" Chandler asked him, giving him a look of surprise.

"What difference is a few more hours going to make?" Lincoln shrugged. "Besides, I owe you one."

Chandler cringed. If only Lincoln knew the truth about him. He was thankful for the company, however, so despite his guilt, he accepted Lincoln's offer.

Even though Leonard offered to stay and help them, Paul argued that perhaps he needed to see his father as soon as possible to let him know he was well. Chandler insisted that his father was his priority just as Chandler's father was his. Leonard reluctantly agreed.

Dorado was not eager to leave either, but what they had to do now he could not help them with. It was not a happy dog that followed Paul and Leonard to the car.

When the vehicle disappeared in the darkness, Chandler and Lincoln moved closer to the gate.

"Dad, I'm about a hundred yards outside the gate, waiting for you."

Nothing but silence greeted his ear. Chandler strained his eyes, hoping to see his dad coming towards them. The lights of Hope Laboratories glared at him from the distance; there was nothing else.

He sat down on the grass next to Lincoln. "Would you like to call your mom?" he asked, handing his cell phone to him.

"Thank you."

While Lincoln talked to his mother, filling her in on what had happened and what was happening now, Chandler lay back and counted the stars, just as he and his father had done when he was a kid.

"You must have made a great impression on my mother," Lincoln said, handing the phone back to him. "She's glad I stayed to help you."

"Your mom's a great lady."

"I didn't know you were Roger Garrett's son when you were assisting me in the lab. Why didn't you say something?"

"There was nothing I could say." The cell phone vibrated in Chandler's pocket. He grabbed it. "Yes?"

"Chandler?" Her voice seemed so far away.

"April. How's Mac?"

"He's still critical, but the doctor thinks there's been some improvement."

"What kind of improvement?"

"The heartbeats are stronger. Are you okay?"

"I'm fine. Tell Mac what I'm doing. Tell him I'll come as soon as I can. And, April, I promised you I would never again keep anything from you, so you need to know we got Lincoln and Leonard Hoffman out safely, but Dad is still in the building. He's not answering me when I call to him through the devices. It doesn't mean he can't, it only means he's probably in a situation where he has to remain silent. Do you understand?"

"I think so. Don't let anything happen to him, Chandler. I've not seen him yet."

"I know. I'm not leaving here until he's with me, I promise. Let me talk to Mrs. Hoffman for a minute, okay?"

The next voice he heard was Julia Hoffman's. "Mrs. Hoffman," he said, "your husband is safe. They're taking him to his father's."

He could hear her telling her children that their father was safe, and he could hear the sounds of their joy. Was it worth his father's life, he wondered?

"Mr. Garrett," she cried into the phone, "how can I ever thank you?"

"By just being happy."

"We will be. Thanks to you, we will be."

April was back on the line. "Be careful, Chandler."

"I promise."

"It wasn't until I heard you talking to her that I realized you two are brother and sister," Lincoln commented after Chandler hung up. "April's a remarkable woman."

"I know," Chandler said, "and she's in love with my partner, Mac, who is lying in a hospital bed with a gunshot wound in the chest because he was protecting Julia Hoffman and her three children.

"Mac's always been one step ahead of me, always found a way to keep me from getting myself killed. If he were here, he would pull something out of his brain that would make it possible for me to get to my dad. I took him for granted, just expecting him to perform electronic miracles. You know something, Lincoln? He always came through." Chandler smiled then, remembering back. "He was raised on electronic miracles. His father is Dr. Mac Wesley, one of the great inventors of our time."

Lincoln thought for a minute. "Have you ever thought to pray for one more miracle?" he asked boldly.

Chandler looked at him, a frown forming on his face. His eyes met Lincoln's. "Pray for me," he begged.

"I'll pray with you," Lincoln replied. "Let's move back to the safety of the trees first."

Once inside the grove of trees, Lincoln invited his new friend to kneel with him. He petitioned their Heavenly Father for a miracle, a blessing of such significance that it would take the sum of the faith they each held within their hearts to bring it to pass. He prayed that they would listen to the Spirit and follow its promptings. He prayed from the depth of his heart.

When he finished, Chandler looked at him, his eyes filled

with tears. "I've never experienced anything like this in my life. What is it?"

"It's the Holy Ghost. It's the hope in your heart that has turned to faith."

The two men sat in the darkness of the early morning, waiting and watching. The minutes past into an hour, and still nothing had changed.

A thought came to Chandler. "I'm going to call and see how Mac is." He dialed and waited for his sister to pick up.

"Chandler?"

"Hello, April. How's Mac?"

"Let him tell you for himself."

"Hello, partner." Mac's voice was weak and a little under the influence of the drugs they had been feeding his body, but he sounded good to Chandler.

"You had me worried, Mac. What happened?"

"I forgot to put on the most important part of my costume: the chest protector. But how did I know the woman was going to shoot me? I didn't give her credit, and it cost me. Never underestimate the power of a woman, Chandler. Your sister insisted that I live, and so I am alive. What can I do for you?"

"First of all, I'm very glad you're awake, and I promise I will never take you for granted again. Second, I need some advice." Chandler explained their situation and the equipment they had.

"Okay," Mac said, his voice a touch weaker now. "Let me think. You say you've got the ears and the voice, right?"

"Right."

"Reset the frequency on yours, one notch at a time, until you have sound on the other end. The only thing that will stop it from coming alive will be the fact that it no longer exists, okay?"

"Okay."

"Once you have sound, connect that sound with your mini-machine. The machine will pinpoint where the earpiece is located. One thing to remember. You must be within fifty yards of the earpiece in order to pinpoint."

"I understand."

"Chandler," Mac yawned, "call me if you need me again."

"I will, Mac. Get some rest now."

April was back on the phone. "Will it work?"

"If Mac says it will, then it will."

"Keep us informed."

"I will."

eighteen

THE RESCUE

When Paul walked through Betsy's front door with Dorado at his heels, he was shocked at what he saw. A man was sitting on the couch, his hands and feet wrapped with duct tape.

"What on earth?" he shouted.

"I might ask the same question," Betsy replied, staring down at her dog, her face registering shock to equal that of her brother-in-law's.

"This incredible dog of yours has been working undercover," he said without hesitation, "and with all that was at stake, I knew you would approve of the disguise." He paused only to nod in the direction of the couch. "You tell me your story, and I'll tell you mine."

"Tell him, Betsy," Elmira instructed her daughter.

Betsy looked at her mother then at Paul. "Lear called just after you left and asked if we had found the journal. I said we had and we would make the exchange whenever he was ready. I think he suspected we'd go after Lincoln before the forty-eight hours were up. His call was simply to make sure we had the journal, so he could send this man to steal it. I don't know what his plan was for Lincoln, unless it was to simply dispose of him, and maybe us, before he was through."

"Look, Mrs. Braden," Hal complained, "I ain't the kind to go around killin' people. Lear just sent me here to get the papers, that's all."

"And what were your plans if we refused to give them to you?"

Hal gave Betsy a blank look as if he hadn't considered that, though she knew he had.

"Anyway," Betsy continued as if there had been no interruption, "he walked into my house with a gun in his hand, and you know how Mother feels about guns."

"I simply asked him what he intended to do with it, and he said nothing as long as we gave him the documents that Mr. Lear requested," Elmira chided. "I didn't like his answer, and I didn't like his attitude, and it compelled me to action."

Betsy couldn't help but let a chuckle escape. "You would have been proud of her, Paul. All those yoga exercises have given this grandmother the agility of woman half her age and the arm of a major-league pitcher. She dropped the book she had in her hands and excused herself while she reached down to pick it up. Before he could react, she hurled the book at him with a speed and accuracy that knocked the gun from his hands and sent him flying backwards. Then she kicked the gun over to me."

"He has a very slow reaction time," Elmira interrupted. "Betsy had his own gun pointed at him before he could recover his balance."

Betsy wasn't sure how to take that statement. "Mother suggested duct tape, and it seems to work." She turned to her mother. "Would you like to add anything else?"

"No, Babe. You did very well on your own."

Paul walked over to where Hal was sitting. "Where's you partner, Hal?"

"None of yer business."

"Well, then, let's make it my business. Betsy, will you bring me some of that acid you keep in your medicine cabinet?"

Betsy hesitated only for a second. "Of course," she replied.

Hal blinked his eyes and sucked in his breath.

When she returned with the boric acid, Hal had broken out in a sweat. She handed the bottle to Paul.

"Now," Paul said, holding the bottle so only the word *acid* was visible. "What we'll do is this. I'll only ask questions that I know you know the answers to. Each time you refuse to answer the question, I'll just pour a drop of this acid on your finger. We'll start with the pinky finger first. Betsy, if you'll fix his hand so the fingers are facing up."

Betsy reached for Hal's hands, but he jerked them away. "Okay, okay," he shouted, "but you better make sure I'm somewhere safe when he finds out."

"Don't worry, Hal," Paul promised, "I'll make sure he can't get to you."

"Look, I just found out the guy's real name yesterday. This was the last job I was doin' for him; then I was gettin' out of the country. He's a spooky guy."

"Where's your partner, Mitch?"

"I'm tellin' ya, I don't know, alright? He told me last week he was gettin' out of the business 'cause he didn't like doin' this stuff anymore. The next day he was gone."

"I don't know if I believe that, Hal." Paul raised his left eyebrow and squinted his eyes.

"I'm tellin' the truth, man. He skipped out on me, why should I try to protect him?" The sweat was pouring down Hal's face.

"Where's Mr. Lear now?" Betsy asked,

"He always meets me at this night club, except last night he told me to meet him in a joint about twenty miles from here." He pulled at his jacket. "The address is on a piece of paper in my pocket."

Paul retrieved the paper and read the address. It was five blocks from Hope Laboratories. He put the lid on the bottle and handed it to Betsy.

"I don't think we'll need this, after all," he said, stepping away from Hal. "Elmira, if you will call Lieutenant

Hemmingway, I think they could find a very safe place for Hal to stay."

Hal gave him an angry look but said nothing. He'd tell the officer how they forced him to talk with acid.

Paul had to get in touch with Lincoln and Chandler. "Betsy," he said, "do you have Chandler's cell number?"

"I do. Why?"

"Call him and tell him that Lear is in the building and I'm on my way." He grabbed his keys, apologized for the fact that his story would have to wait until later, and hurried out the door.

"It had better be a good one," Betsy mouthed to her mother, who was waiting for Lieutenant Hemmingway to come on the line while she carefully picked at the paint spattered across Dorado's back with her free hand.

Giving her dog a sympathetic look, she punched a button on her cell phone and waited for Chandler to answer his cell so she could give him the message.

"How is Mac?" she asked, after the message was delivered.

"I just talked to April," he responded. "Mac's awake and vocal."

"That's wonderful news. I'll tell Mother, who will just smile and give her knowing look. I wish I had her faith."

"I'm learning a lot about faith, Mrs. Braden, thanks to your son. We'll watch for Paul."

"That was your mother," Chandler told Lincoln, placing the phone back in his pocket. "Paul just confirmed the fact that Lear is in the apartment. Paul's on his way."

It was almost three in the morning. Both Chandler and Lincoln were exhausted, but neither would admit it. "What if we don't find a frequency that will align with the earpiece in your father's ear?" Lincoln asked, hiding a yawn.

"Then we'll know it no longer exists. But I have to believe that if I felt impressed to call Mac, this was the reason, and we will find the frequency."

"That's called exercising your faith."

Chandler smiled and continued his work on the mechanism in his hand. Five frequencies later, he heard a sound coming through the receiver. He pushed the earpiece deeper into his ear and listened, closing off the other ear so nothing would interfere.

His hand went into the air, motioning for Lincoln to be still.

Lincoln didn't move. He hardly dared to breathe, his eyes focusing on Chandler's face. Their eyes connected, and Lincoln knew the experiment was working.

Chandler reached into his U-belt and removed another listening device. Handing it to Lincoln, he mouthed three numbers—eight, three, and four—and then he pointed to the device.

Lincoln understood. Undoing the device, he set the frequency according to the numbers given him. Once he had the piece into his ear, his eyebrows shot up. He was listening to someone snoring a quarter mile away as if they were in the same room. It was incredible. It also reminded him that they might need a little sleep before morning.

Chandler agreed. He even agreed to take the first sleep shift. He was asleep before his head hit the ground. Lincoln continued to monitor the sounds coming through the earpiece while he watched for Paul. More than an hour later, Lincoln saw Paul walking toward them, his arms overflowing with food, lab jackets, and clean clothes.

"I stopped at my office for some things we'll need to get into the building," he whispered, noting that Chandler was sleeping like a baby on the ground. I have lab jackets, name tags, and fresh, clean clothes from the employee's closet. You and Chandler are about the same size; you can fight over the slim sizes. I also stopped at the store for food, thinking it might come in handy. Did I forget anything?"

"Only if you forgot the U-belt," Chandler yawned and shook himself awake.

"I never even took time to remove it. It has become like a body part to me."

Chandler laughed at the forensic humor. "We need to reset the frequency of your listening device. I can do that for you while Lincoln gets some sleep."

"Lincoln is already asleep," Paul quipped, pointing to the young man leaning against a small tree, his eyes shut, his mouth open.

Paul set some food in front of Chandler while Chandler brought him up-to-date on everything. They decided they would wait until the employees started arriving to give them a smokescreen.

Their plan had to depend on what they heard through the receivers in the earpieces. While they talked, they ate. Chandler began to feel strength returning to his body. He hadn't realized how hungry he was until Paul set food in front of him.

They woke Lincoln at six thirty, and by seven, they were washed, dressed, and ready for work, thanks to Wet-n-Wipes and the trees that provided them with privacy. Paul had been remarkably close in choosing their sizes. They all looked like lab doctors, and unless someone got a very close look at their badges, they would never guess they were fakes. Once they were inside, they would find authentic badges, so their chances of being discovered would be less likely.

Beneath their jackets, they each had a U-belt strapped to them, housing all kinds of technical devices and giving them a solid sense of security. They had studied the blueprint to familiarize themselves with the layout of each floor. Their earpieces were set; their microphone patches were concealed and silenced for now. They just had to wait for the majority of the employees to begin arriving.

By seven thirty, men and women were walking through the doors of the building. A few had on their lab coats, while some were carrying theirs. But for the most part, Paul concluded, they had their lab coats waiting for them on coat racks.

As they walked toward the building, they began picking up sounds of someone's morning ritual through their earpieces but no voices—yet.

Paul could feel the adrenalin of adventure beginning to flow through his veins. He loved the feeling. He looked at the two young men on either side of him. He could sense their concerns and their anticipation as well. The only thing that troubled him was they were going in without a plan and wouldn't know what the plan was until it was dictated to them over the receivers. That was the part that worried him the most. That was the part that presented the real danger.

The guards didn't seem to pay much attention to the badges as people walked through the foyer and into their personal offices or labs. By eight, the halls were quiet and the rooms on either side were buzzing with activity.

Paul found a closet full of jackets with badges. He selected three with photos that could resemble them and attached the badges to their individual jackets. He slipped the fake badges into his pocket.

The men separated, each picking a lab on the third floor and pretending to be involved in a project. It wasn't until eight thirty that they heard voices in their ears.

Someone was on the phone, talking, then listening, then talking again. Nothing really helpful was said, and the voice was neither Roger's nor Lear's.

Fifteen minutes later, however, it was Lear's voice they heard speaking the words, "Bring Garrett to me."

A door was opened and shut, a painful groan was heard, and Lear was speaking again.

"I hope your sleep was pleasant." His voice was condescending. "You've a very busy day ahead of you."

"There's nothing I can help you with." Chandler heard his father say, his voice edged with fatigue.

Chandler found himself eager to face the man who had damaged so many lives. However, as difficult as it was to stand idly by listening to the rhetoric coming from Lear's mouth,

Chandler knew timing would be the most crucial thing of this whole mission. He had to be careful not to do anything that would jeopardize his father's chance of survival.

"I'm giving this little surveillance device back to you for a keepsake," Lear was gloating. "Of course, I've reset the frequency, so it's useless to you. But just knowing you have a device in your hand that could bring about your freedom if you only had a certain set of numbers gives me satisfaction. Do you realize the sophistication of this small piece of technology? Mac Wesley has taken the whole theory behind it one step further. He's a brilliant young man. Too bad he may not live through the day."

Apparently, Lear hadn't received the latest update on Mac. Chandler walked out of lab number six, venturing to the door at the end of the hallway that would take him out onto an overlook. His emotions were running at high speed. He couldn't trust himself to show indifference outwardly when on the inside he was livid. He had to be alone. Once outside, he leaned against the metal railing and continued to listen.

"What is it you're after?" Roger was asking.

"Haven't you figured it out yet? Think, Roger, think. I need the chip and the journal, of course. Once I have them, I'll be gone. But there is something I need to do before I leave."

Lincoln exited through the door of lab number four. Seeing Chandler, he journeyed out to the overlook, sat in a chair facing a different direction, and picked up a magazine lying on the table.

"You think I didn't know that Chandler was your son? That's why I hired him and his brilliant side-kick, of course. I knew they could find the chip and the journal, but I couldn't ask them to find you, could I? However, I knew you were the kind of father who would want to be a part of his children's lives, however remote it may be. I knew that once you found out I had hired your son, you would resurface, if only to protect him against the man who betrayed you. You didn't disappoint me."

"But what good am I to you if you already have the chip and the journal?"

"My, my, Roger, your mind has become weary in captivity, so I'll explain it to you. You are the only one left who knows what this is all about. The others are all dead. I can't possibly leave this one little thread hanging. I have to cut it off, but I want to enjoy the ride. I was cheated out of my last words with John. I won't let it happen again."

Lincoln felt the shock of Lear's words penetrate him. He began to feel the same anger he sensed in Chandler, but he sat quietly and listened.

"The kidnapping of young Lincoln was a setup, of course, and guess who came after him? None other than the Garretts! I knew the rescue would be fairly easy for you with all that high tech equipment, but I wanted to help too so I had a few guards turn the other way."

Paul needed a little fresh air, and he needed to find the two young men. When he stepped out of lab number five, he saw them. He tried not to hurry as he walked down the hallway and out the door. He knew it would be easier to listen to Lear if they could listen together.

In the presence of three witnesses came to his mind as he watched the birds landing and taking off in flight, using the railing in front of him as their runway. As he watched, he listened.

"Leonard refused to be useful to me. He is an uncommonly interesting man, much like yourself, but I have to let him live. I may need him another day. I had hoped to have what I needed in hand before I allowed him to escape, however. But there was one flaw. I hadn't anticipated Andrew's gallantry."

There was a pause and a dramatic sigh. "The accident I had planned for his family didn't go as planned, but I suppose not everything does. Andrew will pay the price, nonetheless. A small pill he receives every day will be doubled."

"What are you talking about?" Roger's voice sounded agitated.

"I'm talking about a small pill that duplicates the symptoms of Parkinson's disease. Andrew only thinks he is ill because his brain tells him so. It's called mind control. But that's as far as I've been able to get in my research. I need more information. Can you imagine how wealthy I've become and how much more wealth I will acquire?"

"What changed you, Oscar? You weren't always like this."

"Oh, but I was. I simply fooled all of you."

"Can't you see you will eventually fail?" Garret asked earnestly.

"How can I fail when so many companies are competing for my service? No more talk now, I have an appointment to keep. In the meantime, I insist that you make yourself comfortable until I return. Then we will discuss your future. My men will keep you company."

The door shut, and Roger was left in the company of three well-paid mercenaries. The earpiece was sitting in front of him on the table. He picked it up and put it in his ear. Running his hand between the sofa cushions, he found the patch where he had hidden it just before he found himself trapped between two rifles and forced to spend the night in a closet.

He tapped out a message, praying it would reach his son. Once the message was finished, he closed his eyes and lay against the softness of the sofa, knowing that whatever happened now, he had done all he could do.

The message was clear. They knew where the stairwell was hidden that would take them to the apartment. Chandler activated their microphones. "One of us needs to follow Lear. The other two must get to my dad."

"I'll follow Lear," Paul volunteered. "But first, I'm calling Betsy. I have an idea I need to run by her concerning our friend, Hal."

"Dad, can you hear me?"

Roger was physically startled by the sound of his son's voice in his ear. He had to wait until the guards concluded he wasn't attempting to escape and went back to their card game and TV program before he could respond.

"It's so good to hear your voice, Chandler," Roger replied, his voice barely a whisper.

"We're coming to get you. How many guards?"

"At least seven. Two sitting across the room from me, each with a gun at his side. One to the right of me, just out of ear shot. Three in the foyer, two at the entrance to the staircase, and I'm guessing two at the elevator on the main floor."

While Chandler communicated with his dad, Paul talked to Betsy. Lear would be exiting, hopefully in a few short minutes. When he did, Paul would be close behind him. That was the plan.

Melancholy replaced the restlessness that surfaced in Dorado the minute Paul walked out the door, and Betsy had to coax him into the bathroom by way of doggy treats while Elmira filled the tub with warm water and dish soap.

"Come on, golden boy," she cooed to Dorado, stroking his face and neck. "Let's make you beautiful again so Lincoln will recognize you when he comes home."

The sadness in Dorado's eyes told her he couldn't understand. He couldn't understand why Paul had left him behind, and she couldn't explain because she didn't understand either. She could only cuddle him.

"Come," she coaxed, giving him another treat. "You'll feel better once we get that paint off you."

Dorado allowed himself to be placed in the tub without complaint, but, despite all their efforts, the water reflected only a dull gray when Betsy and her mother finished scrubbing.

Elmira suggested combing a product called "Goo Gone"

through his coat. "It works on so many things," she remarked when Betsy gave her a look of disbelief. "Let's give it a try."

Before Betsy could comment, her mother disappeared. A few minutes later she reappeared with a can. Sitting next to her daughter on the edge of the tub, she lifted the lid and poured a sizable amount onto a brush and began combing it through the dog's fur. She repeated the process until the goop began to penetrate the paint.

"Now, we wait for a few minutes," she said, touching different areas, testing for results. When she lifted her fingers away from the area she covered first, there was black on her fingers. She simply nodded and looked at her daughter. "I think we've got it."

Dorado's head came up, and he barked in relief. His patience was wearing thin with this smelly stuff all over him, and he was anxious to be rid of it.

"Stay still!" Elmira said softly, sensing his need to shake himself free of the goop. "We'll wash it off you." She rubbed her hand over his back, and black paint came away without resistance. "A few more minutes, golden boy, and you'll be your beautiful self once again."

The ringing of the phone interrupted their work. Betsy wiped her hands and hurried to answer. When she returned to the bathroom, she had her purse and keys in her hand.

"That was Paul on the phone," she said to her mother. "He has an idea I think we should go with. I need to go."

Dorado gave a sharp bark and jumped from the tub leaving a trail of bubbles and blackened water behind him. Before either Betsy or her mother could react, he was at the front door, his eyes bright with anticipation, his bark loud and feverish.

"I can't take him," Betsy whispered.

"Don't waste time talking, Babe. Be on your way." Elmira motioned her to take the back door while making her way to the front door and a dog that would need special attention.

Once she was on the road, Betsy dialed the police station and asked for Lieutenant Hemmingway.

"Just a moment, please." She was put on hold.

"I really don't have time for this," she shouted into the receiver.

"Time for what?" Hemmingway inquired.

"Oh! I'm sorry, Lieutenant, but I'm on my way to the station, and I need your help." She explained the idea, just as Paul had explained it to her.

"I'll be ready when you arrive." The phone went dead. For one quick moment, Hemmingway reminded Betsy of her mother.

When she pulled up in front of the station, he was waiting. Hal, handcuffed and sorrowful-looking, stood beside him.

When Betsy's car stopped, the lieutenant opened the back door, shoved Hal inside, and then climbed in the front seat. "I explained to Hal that if he does this right, I'll see to it that he is treated like a material witness, and his jail time will be minimal. He'll be put in the witness protection program, and his life will be better than it is right now." He frowned at Betsy. "Anything I need to add?"

"No, I think you've covered it all. Thank you, Lieutenant."

"I thank you, Mrs. Braden. If we can get Lear, my life will be better than it is right now." A pleasant look appeared on his face, and he turned to Hal. "Where to, pal?"

Hal eagerly gave them an address. Betsy already had the address memorized from the evening before and made a left turn at the next stop light.

"How much time, Hal?" Hemmingway asked, checking Betsy's speedometer

"Ya got thirty minutes."

Hemmingway decided not to comment on the fact that she was going ten miles over the speed limit. Instead, he rehearsed what Hal was to do, discussed the options if he failed, and pointed to a parking spot, well hidden from the prearranged meeting place, but a spot where Betsy could see the front of the bar.

"When are ya going to unlock these things?" Hal complained.

"Not until we need to," Hemmingway sneered.

Chandler and Lincoln checked their weaponry, which included two cans of sleeping gas, four small containers of tear gas, rope, two knives, small angled spyglasses, gloves, and handcuffs, along with an assortment of gadgets only Chandler knew what to do with.

The plan was to surprise the guards at the top of the stairs with a little sleeping gas then use Chandler's key organizer to open the door and slip inside. They would be in constant communication with Roger.

The only entrance to the circular staircase was on the first floor, and once a person started up the three flights of stairs, there was no place to hide from someone coming down.

Lincoln went first, his steps slow and careful, the sleeping gas can protruding from his hands like a pistol. He picked up speed once he passed the mark indicating the second floor. Two floors left to go. "I'm on my way to the third floor," he whispered.

"Okay, I'll start up," Chandler replied.

Lincoln was half way between the second and third floor when Roger's voice came through his earphone. "I can hear the guards discussing who will go get lunch first, better get out of the way." Lincoln looked down at Chandler, who waved him down then disappeared himself. He could hear a door opening above him and voices echoing through the air.

"Hey," a voice shouted from above him. "You're not supposed to be here. Don't move until I get there."

Think fast, Lincoln. Your life may depend on it. "Excuse me," he shouted back, indignantly. "You talking to me?"

"Can you see anyone else on these stairs?" The guard was moving down the staircase toward him, his hand on his holster.

"I don't have time to play your games, man, I've got to talk to Mr. Lear about this spray can." The guard was almost to him. "Wait a minute, maybe you can help me."

The guard looked down at Lincoln from three steps above. His eyes were menacing, his attitude arrogant. Lincoln could hardly wait to get him to the main floor.

"Follow me down," he called as he turned and hurried down the steps, motioning for the guard to follow.

Once they reached the bottom, Lincoln looked up to see if anyone was watching from the fourth floor. Apparently, they had lost interest; the landing was empty.

He invited the guard into the hallway and lifted the can eye level. "Right here," he pointed to the spray, "there seems to be a slight problem when I push down on the button. Watch." The guard sank to the floor like a rag doll as the mist settled around him.

"One down." Chandler was impressed. He dragged the limp body into the janitorial closet, wrapped some rope around the guard's hands and feet, and stuck some duct tape he found hanging on a nail over his mouth.

"Ready for scene two?" Chandler joked, eager to get up the stairs.

They decided to take a chance and take the stairs together. They went up the full flight, this time without incident. Chandler pulled a skinny, flexible spyglass from his belt and inched it under the door. Through it he could see two sets of pant legs to the right, about five feet apart. Their voices carried as they discussed the price of gas.

"Ready?" he motioned with a flick of his head, his spray can ready in his hand.

Lincoln gave a nod, holding his can in readiness.

Chandler slipped the key into the lock, and within fifteen seconds, the lock clicked

"What was that?" one of the guards said.

They could hear movement inside. The doorknob turned. "There's something wrong here." A guard opened the door and poked his head out. His nostrils were immediately filled with the mist, and he was asleep before he hit the floor.

"What the . . ." That was as far as the second guard got before Lincoln put him to sleep.

"This is one fine weapon," Lincoln muttered, "painless and harmless."

The two guards were dragged to the elevator. Lincoln opened the door and quickly stepped inside, making the necessary alterations that would put the elevator into a stall. The two guards were laid next to each other. Lincoln wished them a peaceful sleep, stepped out into the hallway, and manually closed the doors.

"What are our chances of getting inside, Dad?"

"First you have a combination lock you have to get through. The first two numbers are fives. I didn't get any further. The door was opened, and I was physically invited in without learning anymore. That tells me there's an indicator in the apartment that gives some kind of signal when the lock is being worked. You've got to be ready as soon as you touch it. Tell me when you're ready, and I'll do what I can from in here."

"On the count of three. One . . . two . . . three."

Immediately the lights inside the apartment began to blink. The guards were alert and on their feet in an instant.

"They're on their way," Roger warned them. He stood to block the way of the first guard, but his head met the swing of a pistol, leaving him bleeding and unconscious on the floor.

Both Chandler and Lincoln heard a sound followed by a groan and a thud. They had an idea of what it meant. They were on their own.

Chandler pulled a gas mask from his belt, gave Lincoln the sign to do the same then, just as the door flew open, he threw the canister. The tear gas erupted in the faces of two guards, blinding their vision and choking their breath. In their frenzy, they sent bullets in all directions. One connected with Lincoln's thigh; another entered his side. He fell back against the railing in a daze.

Diving under the bullets, Chandler hit the floor. As soon as he heard the clicking of empty chambers, he reached up and grabbed the guard closest to him, sending him reeling down the staircase. The other one he managed to cover with the sleeping gas before sending him the same direction as his buddy.

"Lincoln," he whispered.

"I took a couple of bullets," Lincoln responded, "but not anywhere that can't be fixed. There's one more guard in there, Chandler."

"I know. Are you able to move?"

"I can move. How fast? That's another story?"

"Stay put," Chandler directed him. He crawled through the haze until he was next to Lincoln. He handed him a gun one of the guards dropped on the way down the stairs. "Hold onto this and use it if you have to. I'm going in."

The residue from the gas had all but dissipated, and Chandler was able to remove his gas mask. Staying on the floor, he inched his way to the door. He could hear his father moaning as well as softer sounds indicating movement to his left.

"Chandler," Lincoln's voice was in his ear. "There's someone coming up the stairs. I'm on it."

"He's against the wall inching toward you." His father was conscious now and able to give direction. Relief flooded Chandler, and he felt a renewed commitment to win the battle, if only for Roger Garrett. He pulled the can of sleeping gas from his belt. It was almost empty. He had to hit the target the first time.

Suddenly from somewhere behind him, a gun fired and then another. After that there was silence. Lincoln's voice brought good news. "Our man's down, for now."

"I can see you, Chandler. If I can see you, so can he," his father whispered. "He's to the left of you, about three feet away."

Chandler counted to three, dived through the door, and pushed the button on the spray can. Nothing came out. He lay there, a gun pressed against his head, the guard laughing.

"This is what you planned to kill me with?" he roared.

"I don't kill people," Chandler replied in a steady voice. "I just give them a pleasant night's sleep."

"Well, isn't that sweet? I'm afraid I'm the type that likes to shoot his prey." He yanked Chandler to his knees and stood in front of him, the gun aimed at his head.

"Mr. Lear will be pleased you stopped by." His finger was tightening around the trigger, and his eyes were filled with the lust of a kill. Then his expression changed. On his face, there was now a look of bewilderment. He fell to his knees, his eyes glazed; then he collapsed, unconscious, to the floor.

Roger Garret was standing directly behind the guard. His face was bloodstained and pale, his eyes glassy, but there was a smile on his lips. In his hand was the empty sleeping gas can.

"It's amazing what this pressure button can do when it's forced into the back of the skull." Roger slipped to his knees and fell against Chandler.

"Dad," Chandler wept, holding his father in his arms. He shouted to Lincoln.

"I'm here."

Chandler looked up to see Lincoln standing in the doorway, blood caked and smiling.

"Let's get out of here before we have more company."

nineteen

THE SECRET

Lieutenant Hemmingway sat in a booth just inside the small bar where Hal was to meet Lear, his back was to the window, his eyes vigilant. Hal was seated in the back booth as instructed. Betsy waited in the car, watching for the limo to drive up.

Hal looked at his watch. Where was Lear, he wondered. The man was never late. He was starting to get a little nervous. A waiter brought him a drink, and he downed it.

Hemmingway got up and walked to the bar. When he came back, he glanced in the direction of Hal's booth. He noticed the guy was leaning back, his head resting against the high rise of the bench.

Hemmingway drank his water and then looked back again. Hal hadn't moved. Hemmingway felt a tingle go down his spine, and he wasted no time going back to check Hal. One close look and he knew Hal was no longer alive. He searched for the package. It was gone.

He eased the body forward in search of a wound. There was none. Whatever killed Hal was quick and silent. Hemmingway shook his head. How had he missed it? How had his two undercover officers missed it?

In questioning them, Officer Martin said no one came in the back way. Officer Trent said the only person that approached Hal's table was the waiter when he brought him his drink.

"What waiter?" the bartender scoffed, throwing his towel over his shoulder. "I'm the only waiter in this bar, and no one ordered a drink."

"How could a man, dressed like a waiter, put a drink on a tray and take it to a customer without you seeing it?" the lieutenant asked.

"I don't know." The manager scratched his head. "I had a phone call just after you came in. They were doing a survey. The place was slow, so I thought I'd tell them what I thought. I was in the back for maybe three or four minutes."

"That's all it took," Hemmingway groaned. He dialed in to the police station and requested an ambulance and an investigative team. Once that was taken care of, he walked out to Betsy's car to explain that things had not gone as planned.

"They got the package," he said, shaking his head. "I'm sorry, Mrs. Braden."

Before she could reply, however, her cell phone rang. It was Chandler telling her that Lincoln was in the hospital with two bullet wounds, but he was in good condition and awake. He told her all that happened. Then he turned the phone over to Lincoln.

"Hi," he said, his voice groggy from the painkillers.

"Are you all right, Lincoln?" The package didn't seem as important to her as it had a few minutes ago.

"I'm fine. Where are you? The background noise tells me you not at home."

Betsy explained to her son what had happened and that Lear now had the journal.

"For all the good it will do him," he replied. "Is Uncle Paul there with you then?"

"No, isn't he with you?"

"When Lear left the building, Uncle Paul followed him."

Betsy's stomach lurched. "I'm coming to the hospital as soon as I talk to the lieutenant. You rest now."

Betsy spent the next several minutes with Lieutenant Hemmingway discussing the possibilities. He called the detective division of his precinct and requested a detective to look into the situation. She thanked him and left him with the coroner and investigative team.

Dawn and Elmira were waiting for Betsy when she walked into Lincoln's room. They embraced and then Betsy turned to her son. She gave him a gentle hug, not wanting to cause him any more pain than he was already in.

Turning to Dawn, she took her hand. "I'm so glad you're here."

"It's been an interesting three weeks, baby sister," Dawn sighed. "I'm ready to get back to boring. How about you?"

Had it only been three weeks? Every bone in Betsy's body ached. Her eyes burned, her head pounded, and she had something unpleasant to tell Dawn.

Betsy was about to tell her that Paul was missing when out of the corner of her eye she spotted him coming down the hallway. She couldn't believe her eyes. The relief was so intense she felt light-headed.

"Where have you been?" she scolded the second he entered the room.

"I've been talking to a Lieutenant Hemmingway," Paul answered. "We discussed Oscar Lear and what happened today. He told me you were here."

Betsy walked up to Paul and put her arms around him and felt his arms go around her. "You are an amazing man, Paul Arington," she said sincerely, "and I've been so worried about you." She stood back and looked up into his face. "Now I ask myself why."

"Because I should have called to tell you that I was never in harm's way? Or that I was going to make one more stop before coming to the hospital?" He gave her a sheepish grin. "Perhaps you won't be upset with me when you hear the story."

Paul took a minute to ponder his visit to Andrew Hoffman and the fact that the doctor had been a victim of an evil plot. "I stopped in to see Dr. Hoffman about a pill. It seems Lear has developed a type of mind control in pill form and has been able to get that pill to Dr. Hoffman each day. It seems the same woman who tended to Dr. Hoffman's medications was also the same woman who shot Mac. Would you like to hear the rest of the story?"

"Please continue," Dawn said.

"Yes, go on, Paul," Elmira said. "I think you have our full attention."

"Dr. Hoffman doesn't have Parkinson's. The pill only tells his brain he does."

"That's mind-boggling!" Dawn said in all soberness. "Two weeks ago, I would have told you that it wasn't possible. Today I know it is."

"Dr. Hoffman felt the same way," Paul assured her. "That's why people of integrity have to be in research. Someone has to be watchful.

"When I told Dr. Hoffman that the woman who gave him the pill each day was in critical condition and probably would not live, do you know what he said? He said he felt sorry for her. Then he told me that something good would come of all of this because now he understood the disease better. His desire is to do more intensive research into the cause and cure of that disease. He hopes the pill itself may open a door."

"Now I understand his son better," Lincoln said thoughtfully. "Not only are they men of integrity but also men of valor."

"Dr. Hoffman has decided to continue his brain cell research because he knows someone will do it, and it needs to be handled very carefully," Paul continued. "The only question in his mind is this, and I quote his words, 'I wonder if the world is not yet ready for its miracle. Isn't that sad?'"

"You are a man very much like Dr. Hoffman," Betsy said kindly. "That's why you feel for him the way you do. You have that same integrity, the same valor."

Paul smiled at her, pleased with her compliment. Then he turned his attention to family concerns. He pulled up a chair next to Elmira and insisted Betsy sit down. He walked out of the room and returned with two more chairs. Offering one to Dawn, he took the remaining one. "Now, I want to hear about your wounds," he said to Lincoln once he was seated.

"I want to hear everything from the beginning," Dawn insisted, leaning forward in her chair, her eyes filled with anticipation, "unless, of course, you're too tired."

A grin appeared on Lincoln's face as if he had just been waiting for the opportunity to tell his story. All eyes turned to him, waiting in anticipation. He pushed himself up a little straighter in his bed, cleared his throat, and began. When he reached the part where Dorado, almost unrecognizable in black, led the rescue party to the room where he and Leonard Hoffman were being held prisoner, he paused. "Where is the golden boy?" he asked.

"Dorado had been through a great deal," Elmira reported. "Tomorrow someone needs to explain to him why he was sent home when he had been so successful in his rescue attempt." She looked at Paul. "I guess we can understand the black spray paint, and I suppose you'll be happy to know that Goo Gone removed the paint. He is resting comfortably on my bed. I gave him a tranquilizer. Now, continue Lincoln."

Chandler walked in just as Lincoln began to give a play-by-play account of the second day. He stood quietly by the window to listen and add detail when necessary.

"How is your father doing?" Paul asked Chandler when Lincoln finished his story.

"Much better, thank you," Chandler sighed in relief. "He has a slight concussion, and they want to keep him overnight, but he's doing well considering. April is sitting with him now. She refuses to leave his side for fear he'll vanish again."

"And what about young Mac Wesley?" Elmira inquired, her face showing deep concern.

"He'll be out of the hospital in no time. His father will see to that. I just hope his father will allow him to remain the partner of a dangerous man. Maybe, now that he's met April and knows that one day soon, she'll be his daughter-in-law, he may relent."

"As you all can see, a lot has happened in the last few days," Paul said, raising his left brow and squinting his eyes. "I think we have been very successful in our responsibilities. We've each done our part to see that justice is served. I love this family."

"Tell me, Paul," Elmira said, raising her hand slightly to be recognized. "What happened when you followed Oscar Lear."

"Oh, I almost forgot to tell you. Thank you, Elmira, for reminding me." He straightened himself in his chair and began. "Oscar Lear climbed into his limo and was driven to an address where he waited for approximately five minutes before a man brought him the journal." He looked at Betsy and grinned. "By the way, I saw you sitting in your car in that little parking spot next to the bar, Betsy. It's a good thing I'm not a gossip."

"You were . . ."

"Good undercover parking spot," he joked.

"If you were there," she chided him, ignoring his humor, "you should have given me a sign of some kind, so I wouldn't have worried so about your possible demise."

"Back to the story," Elmira interceded.

"After he had the journal in his hand," Paul continued, "he gave the man an envelope and left. I followed. He had his driver stop where he could make copies of the journal. Then he continued on to a building where he went to an office on the second floor. There he talked to the man with whom he has business dealings."

"And who is the man?" Elmira wanted to know.

When he told her the man's name and the company, she simply nodded her head as if she already knew.

"I think," Paul raised his left brow once again and smiled a knowing smile, "that he'll get his just reward before long. He'll not get control of Hope Research. He'll not force Dr. Leonard Hoffman to serve him. I shudder to think what will happen when whoever pays him millions of dollars for the journal finds out that the most important part of the formula is missing."

Or discovers the chip is a dud. Chandler relaxed against the window frame and smiled.

Lincoln walked into Ned's Dry Cleaning with a few things he needed cleaned, Dorado protectively at his heels. He could only hope to see Terri behind the counter. Luckily, Ned saw them coming and called Terri to the front while he disappeared into the back.

"Hi, Lincoln. Hi Dorado," she welcomed the man with a smile and the dog with a pat. "You're a beautiful dog, you know that?" she said as she knelt to cuddle Dorado. When she looked up at Lincoln, a frown appeared on her face. "Are you feeling okay? Your mother said you've had the flu. I have to admit, you don't look nearly as good as your friend." She stood and looked into his face. "In fact, you still look rather pale." She caressed his cheek with her fingers, allowing them to linger.

He loved the sweetness of her touch. He took her fingers in his hand and touched them to his lips, his eyes catching hers and holding them. "I'm much better, thank you," he said quietly, "I just stopped to pick up my dry cleaning and drop some more off." He raised the bag in his other hand.

Terri giggled, rescued her fingers, and reached for the bag. Before she could step through the curtains leading to the laundry room, a hand reached out and grabbed the sack from her hand, replacing it with freshly laundered clothes.

"Thanks, Dad," she groaned, rolling her eyes. She heard

his chuckle through the curtain and glanced in Lincoln's direction, hoping he had missed the exchange. The grin on his face was all the proof she needed to know he had seen the whole thing.

"You'll have to forgive my father," she blushed, avoiding Lincoln's eyes while she hung his clothes on the rack and rang up his bill. Once the bill and the money were exchanged, she giggled and asked, "Every Monday I take a picnic lunch down by the lake. Would you and Dorado like to come with me?"

Dorado gave a bark of approval, hearing his name mentioned.

"I think my dog and I would like that," he said, dipping his head in a slight bow.

Ned stepped out from the back room just then, carrying a basket and a blanket. "You might need these," he said, handing them to Lincoln. Then in a more serious tone, he continued. "It's good to see you, my boy. Are you feeling better? Your mother said you had the flu."

"I'm feeling much better, thank you, Ned."

Ned watched Lincoln take Terri's hand as they crossed the street. "I like that boy," he said aloud.

"I've missed you," Lincoln said.

"I've missed you too," she replied, wrapping her fingers around his.

They laid the blanket on the grass, and Terri spread two of everything out for them to eat. "I love you, Lincoln Braden," she sighed, brushing her lips to his.

"I love you, Terri Burton," Lincoln whispered softly, returning her kiss with one of his own.

A soft growl reminded them that there was someone else in the party who needed to be fed. Without further hesitation, Dorado received the attention he needed.

Mac was out of the hospital, acting as if he was invincible.

His father insisted that he and Chandler make a few changes in their company and suggested they invent and sell, letting others do the actual surveillance work. They said they would consider his suggestion.

Mac planned to introduce his father to Andrew Hoffman as soon as the doctor was well again. It would be fun to sit back and listen as they discussed the future.

Chandler finally got the courage to tell Lincoln about the surveillance part of his work and apologized for causing his mother grief. When he explained the circumstances to Lincoln, he told him that Betsy was never in any danger and perhaps was safer than any other time in her life. He reminded Lincoln that they had become a source of protection to her. They were always there just in case she needed them, and, in actuality, that was the case. Once Roger became involved, that was their assignment—to protect Betsy Braden from Oscar Lear.

Lincoln forgave Chandler his past transgressions in much the same way Betsy forgave Dorado. Their friendship was firm.

It wasn't Tuesday, but at seven thirty PM, April walked into the Heritage Restaurant and was shown to her table. There, waiting for her, was her father. He leaned over, kissed her cheek, and handed her a rose.

"Hello, Sunshine," he smiled.

"Hi, Daddy," she said, tears glistened in the corners of her eyes. "I'm so glad you're here. I've missed you so much each week I sat here alone, but even then I knew you would come back. Chandler and I love you too much."

"Love is what helped me through this." He responded, taking his daughter's hand and holding it gently. "But I did what I had to do to protect you."

"I understand, Daddy. Chandler and I both understand."

She watched her brother as he walked toward them. He sat

down, touched his father's arm, and kissed his sister's cheek. They talked of the past.

After they had eaten, Roger looked at his children, pride showing in his eyes. It was time to talk about the future. "The time will come when I'll have to leave again," he told them. "But I think this time we'll have a plan so there will always be contact."

"I'll talk to Mac about that," Chandler grinned. "Once he's a member of this family, I'll bet he can come up with something totally sci-fi for us."

Elmira called the family meeting to order. It had been a month from the day they sat in Lincoln's hospital room and talked.

"Our lives are changed forever, which is good," she began. "No one should want to stagnate. The past we have just encountered has begun to write our future. The past is our guide, the future, our hope."

She opened the newspaper to an article and handed it to Lincoln. He read: *A body washed ashore three days ago has been identified as fifty-four-year-old Oscar Lear. Foul play is suspected due to the multiple wounds found on the body. Nothing else is known at this time. Mr. Lear had no living relatives, and the police are awaiting further investigation into the matter.*

"For all his millions, he got a few lines on the second page of a newspaper," Elmira stated as a matter of fact. "Isn't that sad? And yet," her finger was in the air while she turned to another article, "because of his greed we read: *An anonymous donation of $70 million has been awarded to Hope Laboratories for research into a cure for Parkinson's disease as well as research for the benefit of mankind, as is always the motto of the Hoffmans' ideals. . . .*"

Elmira closed the paper. "Mac has the uncanny ability to right a wrong or to correct a mistake. I feel he did an exceptional job on this one. I can't quote scripture and verse,

but it goes something like this. It only takes one mind to create
a vision, but is the vision good or bad? It only takes one hand
to plant a seed, but is the seed good or bad? It only takes one
voice to start a rumor, but is the rumor good or bad? It only
takes one idea to begin a whole new theory between man and
country, between man and God, but is the idea good or bad?
What, then, is the responsibility?"

"I wonder sometimes, Mother," Betsy smiled, "if you
aren't communicating with God on an hourly basis. He tends
to fill your mind with wonderful scripture."

"Thank you, Babe."

"It's true," Lincoln said, reaching over and touching his
grandmother's hand. "Your scriptural interpretation touches
all of our lives."

Paul stood. "We have been able to change the outcome of
one simple idea, have we not, Elmira?"

"Indeed we have, Paul."

"Everything has been given to Roger Garrett who, in turn,
will see that they get into the right hands," Paul continued.
"Doubt and suspicion concerning this research can now be
dissolved with the evidence to prove, beyond a shadow of a
doubt, as they say in the courtroom, that this kind of work is
going on behind closed doors."

"We have done what John could not finish," Betsy said
with strong emotion. "Mitch is still out there somewhere,
but the day will come when he will have to answer to the
authorities or to God. Until that day, he has to live with his
conscience."

"I think John is pleased with us, don't you, Betsy?" Dawn
asked.

"I think he is very pleased."

"We couldn't have done it without the golden boy,"
Lincoln reminded them, reaching down and giving Dorado,
whose coat was once again a shining gold, a playful nudge.

Dorado sat up on his front paws and voiced his thoughts
through a series of barks, filled in now and then with a whine

for good measure, extolling his opinion of Goo Gone. They listened with respect to the beautiful, intelligent dog, who, as far as he was concerned, was the most important member of this family.

"Now that Dorado has shared his feelings," Elmira chuckled, reaching down to stroke him, "we can fade back into anonymity, until the time we are needed again. Isn't this exciting?"

When the meeting was over, Betsy and her mother sat on Elmira's veranda, Dorado lying between them, the three of them content.

"Remember Mother, when you told me to get a life?"

"I remember."

"Well I have one now. I'm a spy."

"Not really a spy, Babe."

"What would you call it then?"

"More like a watcher."

"A watcher?"

"Yes, dear, a watcher."

"What is the job of a watcher, Mother?"

"They watch to see if the Constitution is being protected."

"And who watches the watchers to make sure they are doing the right thing?"

"God watches, Babe. God watches."

epilogue

Betsy looked at the calendar on her desk. Three months had passed since the discovery of Lear's body. The investigation into the circumstances surrounding his demise seemed to bury themselves in the "mysterious death" files of the police department, most likely never to resurface because of lack of evidence. In another department, somewhere, silent and unseen, however, she knew the investigation had been given top priority.

In her next column, the words "let each man know his duty" would appear, and it would be a signal to those waiting to do their duty—the silent patriots of the nation, men and women willing to give all to a country they loved more than life itself. The thought brought a feeling of pride to her.

Suddenly her thoughts were interrupted with Dorado's bark and Lincoln's laugh outside the open window, meaning only one thing. They were wrestling on the front lawn. She smiled to herself and walked toward the noise.

Pressing her nose against the screen, she watched as Dorado gripped Lincoln in his famous wet-tongue hold. If only she could command this beautiful childish scene to stay for more than just a moment. Lacking the power, she did the next best thing. She took the camera from the shelf and snapped a picture.

The phone rang, bringing her back to her desk. She picked up the receiver, expecting to hear her mother's voice on the other end; instead, it was her daughter's.

"Hi, Mom," Amy said from hundreds of miles away. "How's everything going?"

"Well, let me see." Betsy gave a dramatic sigh. "Lincoln and Dorado are out on the lawn, wrestling. Mother has signed me up for a beginner's yoga class at the civic center. Frank wants me to start writing two columns a week instead of one, and I keep wondering when my grandchildren are coming to visit. Oh! And one more thing: I think Lincoln has finally fallen in love."

There was a pause on the other end, and then she heard Amy's laugh. "Please tell me you're not joking."

"The yoga class starts Saturday. The last time I looked, Dorado had Lincoln in his favorite hold, and I never joke about my grandchildren."

"Yoga is good. We're coming up this weekend, and you know what I'm talking about. I swear I heard you say something about Lincoln falling in love."

"Well, I can't say for sure," Betsy chuckled. "I wouldn't want to read something into the stars that appear in his eyes every time he mentions Terri's name."

"Not Terri Burton? The little girl he couldn't stand just a few years ago?"

"One and the same."

"That's great. What happened?"

"They both grew up," Betsy laughed.

For several minutes Betsy and Amy discussed Lincoln, until a child's plea for his mother's attention ended their conversation. As Betsy hung up the phone, she wondered what Todd and Amy would think if they knew their mother and younger brother, let alone their grandmother, aunt, and uncle, were involved in a cause unlike any they could imagine. But for now and perhaps forever, they would have no knowledge.

In reality, this new life created for her and a few select members of her family read like fiction. Was the drama that had played itself out the norm in the "patriot's society" (a title she concluded appropriately described her secret world)?

She thought of Roger Garrett, the world of secrecy in which he lived, and the sacrifice and selflessness demonstrated in his willingness to be a silent patriot. Could she give that much if called to do so? It was true. She had lost her husband, but what had Mr. Garrett lost? Then again, what had been gained by their loss? What liberties had been protected? What freedoms had been refined? Only in the months to follow would she find the answer to her questions.

The doorbell rang, and her mother's cheerful voice brought a smile to her lips. "Where are you, Babe?" the voice called.

Before she could reply, Elmira walked into the room. "Oh, there you are. Lincoln said to tell you he and Dorado were taking some clothes to the cleaners." She gave her daughter a knowing wink and settled herself in the leather chair next to the window.

"I was just thinking about everything that's happened in our lives in just a few short months, and I wonder what our future will bring," Betsy explained, surprised with the exhilaration she felt as her question passed her lips.

"He who dares is one who cares," Elmira said while removing a piece of lint from her blouse.

"Very poetic," Betsy remarked. "I'm impressed."

"Thank you, dear. I've decided to take up poetry."

"And why is that?"

"Because."

"Because?"

"Yes, because."

"It's not like you haven't anything else to do with your time," Betsy said, frowning.

"Well, if you must know, poetry helps stimulate the brain."

"And you don't have enough stimulation for your brain already?"

"Now that you mention it, no," Elmira said. "I can't quote scripture or verse, but it goes something like this . . ."